PRAISE FOR DEBORAH LEBLANC AND *FAMILY INHERITANCE*!

"The sticky Louisiana bayou comes alive in first-time author LeBlanc's imaginative chiller about family curses and witch doctors.... LeBlanc's dialogue is spot-on...riveting."

—*Publishers Weekly*

"Storytelling brilliance...a tour de force."

—*L'Observateur*

"A super-tight suspense tale that features elements that reminded me of several horror film classics.... *Family Inheritance* is a sure-fire bet for fans of character-driven horror novels."

—*The Horror Fiction Review*

"What unfolds before the reader is an engrossing—at times terrifying—and altogether enjoyable story that is richly woven and told with passion. Deborah LeBlanc holds the readers' attention and never once drops it."

—*The Horror Channel*

"*Family Inheritance* begins like the first strong jolt before a climb to the mother of all roller-coaster rides where terror is just around the next curve or over the next hill. Deborah LeBlanc's prose is a flying leap into the labyrinth of madness and self-doubt that stops long enough to catch a breath before the next hurtling plunge into the abyss."

—celebritycafe.com

The Only Warning

With a gleam in his eye, the old man spat on the floor. His saliva crackled on the carpet like acid. "You have taken granddaughter's passage," he said, each syllable heavily accented. "And for that you shall pay."

Michael cringed. He remembered the pomp and circumstance the Stevensons had given to the gold coin they had him place under Thalia's hands. Ephraim had said something then about it being her right to passage. Evidently, this man was Thalia's grandfather, and somehow he not only knew about the missing coin, he knew Wilson had taken it. But how?

"I don't know nothing about no granddaughter's passage," Wilson declared.

"You will end!" the man bellowed. He lifted his arms and spread them expansively. "You are to receive but one warning, and this I give to you now. Unless it be returned to her before the rising of second sun, you shall die without mercy!"

"Whoa, hold on now—" Michael said.

"Now just a goddamn minute—" Wilson shouted.

"The second sun," the old man reiterated louder. "Return it so my granddaughter may find way or it is done, Wilson Savoy. For you, for anyone who dares possess it. It shall be done."

Then the old man was gone.

Bewildered, Michael took a cautious step forward. Then another.

When he reached the spot where the stranger had stood, the only evidence that the man had even been there was a depressed set of prints in the carpet. Not the footprints of a man, however. But those of a dog—a gargantuan, long-nailed dog.

Other *Leisure* books by Deborah LeBlanc:

FAMILY INHERITANCE

GRAVE INTENT

DEBORAH LEBLANC

LEISURE BOOKS  NEW YORK CITY

To Marie Dora Comeaux,
who taught me the true definition of strength.

A LEISURE BOOK®

July 2005

Published by

Dorchester Publishing Co., Inc.
200 Madison Avenue
New York, NY 10016

ISBN 0-8439-5553-8

Printed in the United States of America.

ACKNOWLEDGMENTS

Much gratitude and appreciation go to Nancy Eannace and Jay Burnside for sharing their incredible passion and knowledge of funeral service with me. This book could not have been written without their help. Many thanks go to my friend and agent, Lynn Seligman, my editor Don D'Auria, and all the staff at Dorchester. I'd like to thank Monica, Mandy, Bek, and Meme for being *GI*'s first "fans" and my family for their love and patience. And most importantly, *merci, Bon Dieu, pour un autre rève arriver.*

Destiny awaits each imminent second
For in that wink of time
A word, an action, a choice
Will surely map its course

—The Book of Deliberations

Prologue

Anna tucked the blanket around her baby, careful to leave the newborn's left leg out as instructed. She heard the tambourines from outside the camper grow louder, shriller, like a thousand rattlesnakes hissing in disgust at what she was about to let happen. The community had been celebrating since midday, a jubilee the size normally sanctioned for weddings and baptisms. Drunken voices shouted over mandolins and enthusiastic offerings of percussion with jugs and spoons.

In that moment, amid the raucous banter, Anna hated her husband. She was all too familiar with his over-inflated ego, how it fed on pomp and circumstance, how it caused him to embellish traditions or add new ones. Many times she had seen him turn time-honored customs into regimented absurdities or create new, inane rituals that served no other purpose but to flex an authoritative muscle. It wasn't enough that his role as leader came by birthright, which afforded him an indisputable, ardent following. He wanted absolute control of all things—even death. The new ceremony he had commissioned for today proved it. He was going too far this time.

Anna kissed the top of her daughter's head, the crown of black hair so soft against her lips she could hardly feel it. She threw a cautious glance about the confines of the trailer, then whispered into the infant's ear the name only she would use for her. Not even her husband would be privy to it, as was custom. The baby's community name, the one to be used by every member of the tribe, she called out softly in the claustrophobic space. "Thalia. You are my greatest love."

The baby's eyelids fluttered as though in approval, and Anna clutched her tighter to her breast. She reached for a silver music box that sat on her nightstand and opened the lid. A miniature ballerina, poised in the center of the box, began to pirouette to a lullaby.

"I'm so sorry," Anna murmured. "I would burn the flesh from my own body if that would stop him." She snuggled her face against her child's neck. "I will do what I can to make sure it goes quickly."

She placed Thalia in her bassinet and turned reluctantly to the bed where the skirt her mother-in-law had made for the occasion lay in multicolored folds. Sighing deeply, Anna put it on, feeling the hem scratch against her ankles. She chose a white peasant blouse to go with it, not caring whether it matched or not. Bracelets and necklaces, thick with ornate gold and onyx, had already been chosen for her and laid out on top of the bureau. Their beauty and value meant nothing to her tonight. They felt cold and heavy, like her body, when she clasped them on. She placed the droshy that had belonged to her mother on top of her head for good luck. Her fingers trembled and fumbled with the silk knot as she secured it to the back of her head.

After closing the music box, Anna lifted Thalia from the bassinet and carried her to the front room near the kitchenette. She stood there, clutching her child, waiting, watching the door, and not for the first time in her life, wishing she had been born white or black or Russian, anything but Roma. Here it was, 1985, an age when the rest of the world viewed subservience as a historical faux pas, yet her people remained committed to male superiority. A gypsy woman's opinion remained nothing but a nuisance, and since the beginning of time, her worth only as good as her earning potential. Anna had learned that truth from her father. She had been a sixteen-year-old virgin from good stock and had been sold to Ephraim Stevenson, a man fifteen years her senior, for fifty thousand dollars. Anna often wondered if Ephraim would have paid that much for her had he known it would take her ten years to conceive their first child.

The trailer door opened suddenly, and Anna found herself focusing on her mother-in-law's thick ankles making their way up the metal steps. Behind her was a backdrop of crackling orange, a bonfire highlighting shadowy dancers.

"You take too long," the woman scolded as she closed the door against the revelry outside. A cigarette waggled between her lips, calling attention to a nose ripe with ever-present lesions. The woman carried the same affliction along her left arm. "They are waiting for you," she said, taking the smoldering butt from her lips and snuffing it out with the tips of her fingers. "Why you want to embarrass Ephraim and make him wait like that?"

Anna studied the face of her sleeping daughter, wishing the baby back to the safety of her womb. "There's no need for Ephraim to do this, Lenora." She looked up defiantly. "There is no Roma custom that says he must."

"I will not hear you!" Lenora quickly shaped a V with the first and middle fingers of her right hand, pressed them against her lips, then spat between them. "He is head of family and has right to make tradition. You bring bibaxt to his daughter with your words!"

"What I have to say brings her no bad luck," Anna insisted, saying a silent prayer to Saint Jude just in case. "How can a mother wanting to protect her child be bad?"

Lenora's face softened unexpectedly. "Is not bad," she said, her eyes moving to the tiny infant resting in the crook of Anna's arm. "But you would want her to be protected in afterlife, no?"

Anna settled the baby against her shoulder, purposely putting the small back to the old woman. "Nothing will happen to her. There are many years before that's a concern."

"You are God? You know this to be for fact?" Lenora tilted her head and let out a sarcastic snort. "You are better fortune-teller than me?"

Anna was wishing she could knock the smirk from the woman's over-painted lips when Antony, Ephraim's cousin, burst into the room.

"Ephraim sent me to get you, Anna," he said breathlessly. "Everything is ready now."

"Tell him we come," Lenora said. "He has requested salve and cool water for baby, which I will get quickly." She fluttered a hand at him. "Hurry, Antony, go. Tell him we come."

Instead of obeying, Antony went to Anna, hugged her, then kissed the back of the baby's head. A mischievous grin lit up his face. "What did you name her?" he whispered.

Antony was Anna's favorite out of all of Ephraim's family. He was two years younger than she was and had always treated her like an older sister. Anna pressed closer to him and said under her breath, "Antony, don't let him do this to her."

He stiffened. "There is nothing I can do, Anna, you know that." He moved away from her and looked nervously over at Lenora who was filling a basin with tap water. "It's going to be all right. It will go quickly, you'll see. She won't remember any of it." He leaned over and kissed the baby's head again. "She is so beautiful. So—"

"Take this," Lenora said, suddenly appearing alongside her nephew with the basin of water. She handed it to him.

Antony took it and left without so much as another glance at Anna.

"Give me baby," Lenora said, tucking a tube of ointment into the pocket of her dress. She reached for her granddaughter. "I will take her to campfire."

"No." Anna held Thalia tighter. She shivered at the thought of her child lying across the brown crusts on the woman's arm. "I'll—I'll take her."

Lenora turned, cursing in her native tongue, and opened the camper door. Anna followed her down the steps, holding on to Thalia so tightly the child began to whimper.

The smell of burning oak, roasting meat, and heavy summer night air surrounded Anna's head like a burial mask, and her breathing grew labored. Loud cheers rose to greet them as they neared the main campfire, and Anna saw Ephraim stand and motion her closer. A white fedora sat on his head, low over his eyes. Shadows traveled across his round face. Anna tried to reason through the loud pulsing in her ears. *He's doing it because he loves her—When they are this small, they don't remember—She's the daughter of a very, very powerful man. She's supposed to be set apart—It really is just a small thing . . . isn't it?*

Anna's attempt at justification abruptly gave way to a serious consideration. What would happen if she took her child and ran away?

She imagined the look on Ephraim's face as she pictured herself fleeing with Thalia through the maze of Winnebagos, station wagons, and campers. Her fantasy took flight, past Thalia's protection, running faster, farther, bringing her to some other place, a stable place. A place where husbands worked from nine to five and came back to wives in quaint little houses surrounded by flower gardens and nosy neighbors.

Instinctively Anna knew, however, that should she run, Ephraim would find her and wouldn't hesitate to have her exiled. He would turn her away from the community as he would an infectious leper, and Lenora would raise Thalia. That thought alone kept Anna's feet moving forward.

As she approached the circle of people surrounding the fire, Ephraim held up a hand, and the clamor of music and voices died instantly. A wall of people four rows deep opened, allowing Anna to approach her husband.

Ephraim stood beside a wrought-iron stool that had a pewter bowl resting on top of it. Six inches above the bowl's center flickered a blue-white flame, and Anna stared at it transfixed. She had been schooled in sleight of hand, the art of manipulation, all the trickery and games played on unsuspecting Gaji. This floating fire, however, appeared to be no game.

The flame licked seductively in Anna's direction, and she felt her breasts immediately engorge with milk. No, this was definitely not a parlor trick.

"Bring her to me," Ephraim commanded. Despite all the transactions her husband conducted daily with the Gaji, his English remained broken. Now, with the help of some expensive vodka, the r's rolled all the more expansively from the tip of his tongue. "Bring her!"

Thalia started at the bellowing voice and began to wail. Anna rocked her arms gently and walked toward her husband. She spotted Lenora and Antony on her left. Both were fidgeting.

Anna placed the child in Ephraim's outstretched arms and allowed her fingertips to linger on his bare skin. There had been a few times during their marriage when she'd thought herself lucky. She knew many women who would give anything to have a man with Ephraim's looks and money. They would gladly submit to his every whim, no matter how ridiculous or dangerous.

She sought his eyes earnestly. "Please," she whispered so no one else could hear. "Please, Ephraim, don't do this."

He glanced at her briefly, long enough to expose the determination in his dark eyes. "You think me to be bad father because I choose to ensure her future?" His voice sounded to Anna like a low rumble of thunder in the distance.

"No, not a bad father. But she is so small, Ephraim. Can it not at least wait until she's older?"

He looked down at their crying daughter, and Anna held her breath, hoping against hope he might reconsider.

Abruptly, Ephraim raised the child above his head, glared from left to right at the crowd surrounding them, then faced Anna. She knew then there was no turning back.

"And she will be called?" Ephraim asked loudly as the baby screamed. The one leg that had not been secured by the blanket kicked and flailed as did her tiny arms.

Tears of resignation filled Anna's eyes. "Thalia," she answered, and choked back a sob.

A smile played around the corners of Ephraim's lips. "Perfect," he said in a low, husky voice. "Perfect." Then, with his face aglow, he offered his daughter for all to see and shouted, "Thalia! Thalia Stevenson!"

The crowd burst into whoops of joy, and someone began beating on a metal tub with a stick. Uncles, aunts, and cousins three and four times removed started chanting, "Tha-lia! Tha-lia! Tha-lia!" The louder the baby screamed, the more emphatically they shouted.

Ephraim lowered his daughter and returned her to

Anna. "Quiet her," he said, then signaled his mother to his side.

Anna cradled Thalia, watching and rocking nervously as Lenora sidled up to her son. The old woman pulled a velvet pouch from her dress pocket and quickly emptied its contents into his left hand.

As Thalia's wails calmed to hiccups, Ephraim plucked one of the objects from his palm and held it high. Anna's breath caught at the sight of one of the brightest gold coins she had ever seen. Its circumference was only slightly larger than a quarter's, but its radiance surpassed that of the roaring campfire. Even from this distance Anna could see an eagle embossed in the coin's center. The bird's wings were raised above its head so they touched wing tip to wing tip. Three arrows intersected the union of wings, one pointing north, another east, and the third west.

"This," Ephraim said, pausing for the crowd to be silent. "This will make certain that my little Thalia has payment for other side. It was created for her alone so that even in death she will have place of honor. All spirits, dark and light, will hold her in high esteem."

A roar of approval impaled the night, and Anna peered nervously at her child. Thalia looked back at her with large, dark eyes that seemed to ask, "Why, Mama? Why?"

Ephraim handed the coin to Lenora, who took possession of it reverently, her face flushed with pride. Then he leaned over and whispered something to her. Lenora nodded and began to toss the coin from hand to hand as though it had suddenly grown hot to the touch. All the while she chanted in the Roma tongue curses on anyone daring to take the token of passage from her grandchild. She did this seven times, then carried the coin to the pewter dish and swiped it repeatedly through the flame. An explosive report sounded each time the gold piece touched the fire. Oohs and aahs swelled from the crowd.

"Kimbrala," Lenora said loudly, and with a flamboyant snap of her wrist, the coin came to rest upright in her palm. It started to spin, and Anna watched dumbstruck as it twirled into a golden blur. After a moment, Lenora waved her free hand over the coin, and it immediately fell flat and still.

With the task completed, Lenora took her place beside Ephraim. He kissed his mother's cheek, then presented the remaining object. It was a gold ring mounted with four thick prongs. Ephraim slipped the ring on the first finger of his right hand, then took the coin from Lenora and placed it over the prongs. The intensity of his gaze seemed to be the only soldering tool necessary, for metal quickly sought metal, and the two objects melded together.

Ephraim raised a ring-clad fist in the air and proclaimed to the onlookers and heaven, "There will be no mistaking my daughter's right to this gift." He dropped his fist and after eyeing Anna warily, thrust the affixed coin toward her lips. "You will bless this."

Anna shivered. Up close the embossed eagle became all too vivid, its talons raised and defined, every detail of the creature obvious. With a small whimper, Anna leaned forward, kissed the surprisingly cold signet, then silently cursed the man who wore it. *Please, God,* she thought fervently, *don't let her feel anything.*

Apparently satisfied with her approbation, Ephraim turned away from Anna and walked over to the flaming bowl, where he waited for Lenora. His mother hurried to his side and promptly spat on the elevated flame. She mumbled something Anna couldn't decipher, and before them all, the blue-white torch split into three fiery arrows, one pointing north, another east, and the third west. A collective gasp rose from the onlookers.

Ephraim aimed the ring at the western tip of fire. When its blazing point struck the center of the coin, a deafening *pop* rang out. Pain wrinkled Ephraim's face, yet he stood fast, his fist trembling slightly. His teeth guillotined as the coin began to glow bright red.

"Anna," Ephraim called sternly.

Oh, Jesus, please, sweet Jesus—don't let him. Make him change his mind. Anna searched the sea of faces around her, begging with her eyes for someone, anyone to stop this madness, all the while knowing not one soul present would dare interrupt Ephraim's self-appointed moment of glory. How could she possibly go through with this? She would die. She *was* dying.

Anna stumbled to her husband, and the sphere of people drew in closer. Their faces were fevered with restlessness, their eyes shining with anticipation. Someone thumped on the metal tub again, and the hollow, thudding sounds seemed to energize Ephraim. He raised his head high and squared his shoulders.

"Hold her tightly," Ephraim said.

Upon hearing the command, Anna felt milk leak from her breasts. Thalia, evidently smelling supper, rooted against her, and Anna cupped her daughter's small head and pulled her close.

"You are all witness," Ephraim shouted in the language of his people. "You are all witness that my Thalia has full birthright to what is given to her today." With that, he removed the fiery coin from the flame and pressed it to Thalia's left thigh.

Anna screamed when the hissing sound reached her ears, the sound of scorching metal touching cool flesh. Thalia's back arched in shock, her eyes freezing wide and round. Her body appeared to search for a reference scream, one equal to the pain she was experiencing, but found none. Only silence fell from her tiny open mouth as the bird's image burned into her flesh.

Chapter One

Cradling a large spray of roses and larkspur, Janet Savoy forced herself across the empty parking lot toward the funeral home. She concentrated on the *tap-clop, tap-clop* of her black pumps against the concrete and the weight of the summer heat on her face. Despite it being late afternoon, the Louisiana sun offered no relief. She had walked less than a block, yet perspiration soaked the back of her white cotton blouse.

As she drew closer to the mortuary, gooseflesh galloped along her arms. "What?" she muttered warily.

The one-story, I-shaped structure gave no answer. It stood as it always did with its flat, beige brick façade, wide porticos, and neatly trimmed lawn, as innocuous as a rural bank building. Janet had been inside the place hundreds of times without qualm. Why the case of jitters now? She looked back to check on her five-year-old daughter, Ellie, who was nearly jogging to keep up with her.

"Mama, if you keep making me walk too fast, I'm

gonna drop the coronations," Ellie said, scurrying to Janet's side. Dressed in a lemon-yellow sundress, red, glittery sandals, and a bright purple fanny pack, Ellie looked like a tie-dyed pixie with bangs. She had an arm linked through the handle of a boat-shaped floral basket that leaned precariously to one side.

"*Car*nations, sweetie," Janet said, coming to a halt. She balanced the spray across her left arm and with her free hand helped Ellie right the basket.

Ellie shrugged. "That's what I said . . . *cor*onations."

Janet smiled and tipped her daughter's freckled nose with a finger. So far she'd been able to hide her growing apprehension from Ellie. It hadn't been easy, though, especially this morning when Janet had changed their normal routine. When Ellie wasn't in school, she usually stayed with their babysitter, Laura Trahan, while Janet and her husband, Michael, were at work. This morning, however, Janet woke with a gnawing, nameless worry in her chest that grew so heavy by the end of breakfast, she decided to scratch the sitter and keep Ellie close at hand. She'd nearly asked Michael to stay home from work as well, then decided against it. He was a grown man, more than capable of taking care of himself, and she didn't want to sound like a neurotic paranoiac. Fortunately, other than it being a busy day, nothing out of the ordinary had happened to give substance to her worries. But Janet had a feeling that something in the funeral home would soon change all that.

Determined to gain some control over her swelling jitters, Janet tweaked Ellie's chin. "Hey, did I tell you what a terrific helper you've been today?"

"Really?" Ellie beamed.

"Yep."

"Better than Miss Bertha Lynn even?"

Bertha Lynn was a pudgy, fifty-five-year-old widow with frizzy salt-and-pepper hair and a natural flare for floriculture. She'd been Janet's assistant for six years.

"Hmm," Janet said, pretending to ponder the question. "Hard to say. I think it's probably a tie between the two of you." She grinned as Ellie did a little hop of joy.

When they reached the service entrance of the funeral home, Janet pulled it open, grateful that someone had remembered to unlock it. She motioned Ellie inside, then brought up the rear, her body immediately registering the twenty-degree drop in temperature. Janet juggled the rose spray to her other arm, then shut the door behind her.

"Quiet, remember?" Janet whispered to Ellie. Judging from the empty parking lot, she didn't think any visitors had arrived yet for calling hours, but she'd been fooled before.

Ellie nodded, then began to hum softly to the violin concerto that drifted down from overhead speakers. She tiptoed beside Janet, the plush maroon and beige carpet swallowing the sound of her footsteps.

As they headed down the hall toward the intersecting corridor that led to the viewing rooms, a shiver caught Janet unawares. Her steps faltered, and she glanced over her shoulder. She saw nothing behind them but a hallway bathed in soft fluorescent lights, a drinking fountain, and the door from which they'd entered. Janet turned back, feeling her heart beat faster and her mouth grow dry. She took Ellie's hand in hers and surveyed the space ahead.

A mahogany occasional table draped with a runner

of damask cloth stood at the end of the hall. Beside it, a black leather roll-back chair. The same chair and table she'd seen many times before. Nothing seemed out of place, yet her anxiety continued to escalate, nearly cutting her breath with its weight.

Janet struggled to keep her walk casual, leading Ellie farther down the hall and past a white metal door marked PREP ROOM. From the minuscule seams along the door's casing, Janet caught the faint scent of formaldehyde. The smell recalled images of naked bodies, their veins washed of blood by watery, pink fluid while they lay atop stainless steel tables. The vision weakened her knees.

Biting her bottom lip, Janet willed herself forward. As they rounded the intersecting hall, the floral spray resting across her right arm seemed to grow bulkier with each step. The cool air she'd found so inviting when they'd first entered the funeral home now felt stifling and thick. Janet wanted to drop the spray, grab Ellie, and bolt from the building. But she pressed on, rationalizing against the waves of paranoia. This was her husband's funeral parlor—well, her father-in-law's if she had to get technical—and she knew this place as well as she did their own home. What could possibly hurt them here? The dead? Another involuntary shiver hastened Janet's pace.

With Ellie still humming beside her, Janet hurried past walnut side tables, a glass curio cabinet filled with miniature ceramic birds, a settee newly lined in beige velvet, and straight-back chairs upholstered in gold and maroon striped fabric. Janet gave little notice to the furnishings, however. She kept her eyes trained on her delivery point, which was marked by a small black marquee standing fifty feet or so ahead to her left. The white block letters stenciled across the marquee read: THOMAS RASMUSSEN.

Ellie pulled her hand from Janet's and pointed to the sign. "Over there, right, Mama?"

Before Janet could answer, Ellie broke into a run toward the viewing room. Though her daughter had been in the funeral home numerous times and knew the routine of Janet's flower deliveries by heart, the sight of her child free from the safety of her grasp sent Janet's heart slamming against her ribs. She watched Ellie run around the corner of the viewing room—and straight into a pair of arms that seemed to appear out of nowhere. They scooped Ellie out of sight.

Janet only had time to gasp before Ellie reappeared, giggling in the arms of Chad Thibodeaux, her husband's apprentice.

"Mrs. Savoy, look here," Chad said, grinning. "Seems like I caught me a . . ." His grin faded as his eyes met Janet's. "Something wrong?"

Janet managed a weak smile. "N-no. You just startled me a little, that's all."

"I'm sorry," Chad said, and quickly lowered Ellie to the floor. "I didn't mean—"

"It's all right, really." Janet had known Chad a little over eight months; long enough to know the tall, slender young man was as harmless as a roosting pigeon. She silently admonished herself for allowing her imagination to run rampant and lifted the floral spray, eager to change the subject. "Last delivery of the day."

"Me, too," Ellie said. She showed Chad the basket of carnations. "Mama let me help, and she said I was a very good helper."

Evidently relieved that he hadn't scared the boss's wife into cardiac arrest, Chad said, "Wow!" a little too loudly. Blushing, he squatted beside Ellie, giving her his full attention. "So you really got to help out at the flower shop all day?"

"Yep—no—well, almost all day," Ellie said. "Miss Bertha Lynn's still over there 'cause she wasn't finished with a flower thingy. Me and Mama had to bring these now 'cause I've gotta go get ready for my dancing receipt."

"Dancing receipt?" Chad peered up at Janet quizzically.

"Recital," Janet said.

"Yeah, that," Ellie said. "I get to be a butterfly dancer." As though to prove her point, she twirled and flapped her free arm at her side. "See?"

"I sure do," Chad said, chuckling.

Ellie gave him a satisfied grin, then bounded into the viewing room, carnations in tow.

Chad stood and brushed a hand over the jacket of his black, tailored suit. "Can I help you with that?" he asked, offering to take the spray from Janet.

She gladly handed it over to him. "Where's Michael?"

"Out running an errand. I'm the only one here right now," Chad said, standing a bit taller. "Sally's supposed to be here in another thirty minutes or so, but honestly I don't know why she's coming in at all. We're not expecting a big crowd, just immediate family, and they only want a two-hour viewing. Mr. Rasmussen goes to the crematory as soon as we're done." He lowered his voice to a near whisper. "I think Sally wants to be here because she doesn't trust me to handle any of the families on my own."

Janet gave him a reassuring pat on the arm. "I wouldn't worry about Sally," she offered. "Sometimes it takes her a little while to warm up to people, that's all." Janet knew Sally Mouton could be very territorial when the spirit moved her, but in many ways the highly organized, sixty-eight-year-old spinster had earned the right. She'd been serving as Savoy Funeral Home's secretary and hostess for more than twenty-five years.

"I hope you're right," Chad said. "Sometimes I think she—"

The chirp of a telephone in the distance silenced Chad and sent his eyebrows into a high arch. "I'd better get that before the answering service picks up," he said nervously, and handed the spray back to Janet. "I hate to run out on you but—"

"No problem. Go."

He gave her a scant nod, then hurried away.

Janet went into the viewing room, eager to get Ellie back in her sights and to rid herself of the prickly flower arrangement once and for all.

She found her daughter sitting quietly on the floor at the front of the room near the foot of a polished oak bier. Atop the bier sat a pine casket, the top half of which lay open, revealing an elderly man in a dark blue suit. Ellie's ease around corpses never ceased to amaze Janet, but the child's abrupt stillness did.

"You okay, honey?" Janet asked. She placed the spray over the casket's closed bottom lid and straightened some of the roses that had wiggled free of symmetry.

"Uh-huh," Ellie said.

Janet glanced down and saw Ellie staring into the basket of carnations in her lap. "You sure?"

"Yeah." Ellie scratched the end of her nose. "Mama?"

"Yes?"

"Do you like horses?"

Slightly taken aback by the question, Janet paused before answering, "I guess so."

"Even mean ones?"

"Now what would make you ask something like that?"

Ellie shrugged.

Janet waited a bit longer, and when Ellie didn't question her further, she went back to adjusting the spray.

Sighing loudly, Ellie placed the basket on the floor, stood and walked to the head of the casket. She peered inside. "Mama?"

"Hm?"

"Is there a kid heaven then a grown-up heaven? Or is there just one where everybody goes together?"

A shiver slipped down the back of Janet's neck. Her encounter with Chad had offered a small respite from the notion of impending trouble, but Ellie's newest question caused it to snap back into place with a vengeance.

"I'm not positive," Janet said. She swallowed, and her throat felt coated with briars. "From what I've heard, though, I think everybody goes to one place."

"Even teenagers? Do they go to the same place as everybody else, too?"

"I'm sure they do."

"And do people have to pay to get into heaven?" Ellie asked, her questions becoming more urgent. "You know, like when we go to the movies and have to buy a ticket to get in?"

Janet frowned. She was used to Ellie asking unusual questions from time to time, but these were downright weird.

"Do they?" Ellie pressed.

"I don't think so." Janet quickly plucked a brown-tipped piece of foliage from the spray, then held out a hand to Ellie. It was definitely time to get out of this place. "All done here, Miss Wonderful. Time to go home. We still have a lot to do before the recital."

Ellie patted the corner of the casket as though signaling goodbye to Mr. Rasmussen, then went over to Janet and took her hand.

"Mama?"

"What, baby?" Janet asked, leading Ellie across the room.

"When somebody dies and goes to heaven, can they come back and visit?"

Gooseflesh made another run along Janet's arms. "I don't know. Why?"

" 'Cause I need to know."

"Need to?"

Ellie pulled Janet to a stop and faced her. "Yeah," she said, her face solemn, her blue eyes sad. " 'Cause how else am I gonna know if I can come back to you and Daddy after I die?"

The words sent a crushing blow to Janet's chest. She scooped Ellie into her arms and hugged her tight. "Sweetie, you don't have to worry about stuff like that for a long, long, long time."

Ellie gave her a tentative smile. "Long, long, long?"

"Even longer," Janet said. Then, with her daughter still clutched to her breast, she hurried out of the building, praying that the obscure dread that had followed her around all day hadn't been sent to prove her wrong.

Chapter Two

Janet dug through the refrigerator for grated cheese, mentally sorting through the tasks she had yet to finish and attempting to ignore the persistent nagging in her gut. Although the sense of foreboding had abated after she'd left the funeral home, it refused to go away.

"Hey, any doodlebugs live here?"

The sound of Michael's voice calling from the living room caused Janet to sigh heavily with relief. At least he was home in one piece, which meant one less worry for her to hold on to.

"Daddy!" Ellie jumped up from her seat at the table and with a shriek of laughter ran to meet her father as he crossed the archway into the kitchen. She jumped into his arms. "Look how I'm pretty," she declared, showing off the pink and white tutu she wore, complete with purple fanny pack.

"Prettiest little girl in the world for sure." Michael lifted Ellie high into the air, then pulled her close. She snuggled against him. "Are you ready for your big night?" he asked.

"Yep, but Mama says I gotta eat supper first." Ellie pointed to the plate of spaghetti on the table.

"Sounds like a plan to me," Michael said.

"Góod," Janet said, backing out of the fridge. She let out a puff of exasperation and held out a container of cheese. "Then maybe you can get her to eat something. I haven't been able to get her to sit still for five seconds."

Michael lowered Ellie onto a kitchen chair, then went over to Janet and took the small green canister from her. "You want her to eat Parmesan?" he asked with a mischievous glint in his eye.

"Funny."

Michael leaned over and kissed her lightly on the lips, "Tough day or just being grouchy?"

"Both," Janet admitted, and closed the refrigerator door. "Sorry. I'm a little fried. I've still got to get to the mall to buy leotards. Ellie ripped her last pair when she was getting dressed." She peered around Michael's shoulder. "Ellie, eat a little something, honey, will you? We're really late."

"But I don't want to eat worms," Ellie said.

Janet rolled her eyes and sidestepped Michael. "Just try a little."

Ellie shook her head. "I can't. Look, they're wiggling on the plate!"

"Your spaghetti is *not* wiggling," Janet insisted.

"It's only five," Michael whispered. "A little early for supper. Maybe she's just not hungry."

Ellie, obviously overhearing, clapped enthusiastically. "Yeah, I'm not hungry. Can we have pizza?"

Janet swatted Michael's arm. "Thanks a lot."

He grinned sheepishly and loosened his tie. "So where'd the two of you go off to earlier? Chad said you came by the funeral home with a delivery but didn't stick around long."

"I had too much to do. Lock up the shop, cook supper, dress Ellie for the recital, now the mall. And I still have to pack for our trip to the cabin." Janet turned away and gathered up Ellie's plate and cup, feeling a twinge of guilt. It wasn't as if she'd lied to Michael. She did have a lot to do. The *rest* of the truth, though, had nothing to do with chores. She just didn't know how to explain the real reason she'd rushed out of the funeral home without sounding like a loon.

Janet gave Michael a brief smile on her way to the sink. "Besides, I knew I'd see that good-looking face of yours at home."

Michael waggled his eyebrows. "So you think I'm good-looking, huh?"

"I think you're pretty, Daddy," Ellie said.

"Thanks, doodlebug."

"Now what about *your* supper?" Janet asked him as she scraped leftovers into the garbage disposal. "Think I can get some food into you for a change?"

"Maybe later. I've got to shower, put on a fresh suit, then get back to the funeral home and take care of a couple of things."

"You *are* coming, right?" Janet asked.

"Uh . . . where?"

"The *re-ci-tal*."

Michael gave her a lopsided grin.

Janet returned it despite her pensive mood. "Seven o'clock, okay?"

"Yeah, Daddy, you gotta come see me be a butterfly." Ellie scooted off her chair and ran up to him. "Watch."

Janet groaned as Ellie wound up for an impromptu performance. "Ellie, we're so late. You need to put your shoes on and get your costume bag out of your room."

"Okay," Ellie said, then leaped across the floor and did a swaggering twirl before Janet could protest further. She flitted back and forth in front of her parents. "What about that?"

Michael applauded loudly. "Beautiful job! You're the best butterfly ever."

Ellie beamed, then skipped away in search of her shoes.

"A ballerina with a fanny pack," Michael said as soon as Ellie was out of earshot. "Think they'll convince her to take it off?"

"Not unless someone brings a tub of water," Janet said. "You know the only time it comes off is for her bath."

Michael chuckled. "True." He went over to Janet and gathered her in his arms. His eyes locked onto hers. "You okay?"

Janet hesitated for a beat. "Yeah. You?"

"Yep."

"You look tired."

"You worry too much."

"No, really." Janet brushed a finger across his left cheek. "You look kind of pale."

"A funeral director's supposed to look pale."

"Be serious."

"I am."

Janet grinned and leaned her forehead against his

chest. "You know if you'd rather wait to go to the cabin after—"

"No way," Michael said, and cupped her chin in his hand. He gently lifted her head so she faced him. "We're going, beautiful," he said softly. "And I'm bringing surprises."

Within minutes of collecting shoes, costume bags, and ballerina, Janet had Ellie buckled in the back seat of the Caravan with a coloring book and crayons and was backing out of the garage. She glanced across the street toward the funeral home and noticed three cars parked in the lot. She hoped Chad had been right about the Rasmussen viewing being small. If a large crowd did show up, or if they got another death call before Michael had the chance to leave for the recital, he would feel obligated to stay. Not that she'd blame him. Janet knew it was part of the job. A tough, sometimes thankless job. She'd discovered that firsthand eight years ago, shortly after they were married. Not long after their honeymoon, Janet offered to work at the funeral home. She wanted to understand more about the industry that consumed her new husband and thought, having earned a management degree from LSU, that she might be able to contribute something to the family business. So she'd filled in as an additional hostess when the need arose, filed death certificates, and had even driven the hearse a few times. It didn't take Janet long to figure out, however, that it took a special temperament and talent to work in funeral service, and she didn't have either. Though she felt purpose when helping grieving families, she couldn't handle being surrounded by death and sadness every day. Such a concentration of both in one place seemed to suck the life out of her. That's when she decided to open a flower shop near the funeral home. From there, she could still help the bereaved, but also brides and new moms. Janet needed that balance of light with dark.

Michael, on the other hand, appeared to maintain a healthy internal balance despite what he dealt with each day. His good-hearted, optimistic nature rarely allowed him to remain depressed or sullen for too long, even in the direst of circumstances. The last three years had certainly proven that. He'd spent two of those three years in hell and this last year pulling his way past the second rung of purgatory. He was due a break and some time off.

Unfortunately, one of Michael's favorite getaways was his family's cabin, which was located in Carlton, Louisiana, four hours north of home. He tried to schedule time off every July, specifically the last weekend of the month, when Carlton held its annual summer fair. Ellie loved going for the carnival rides and looked forward to the trip each year. Janet enjoyed the fair as well, but she secretly hated the cabin. The place was old, surrounded by woods, and held ancient memories that always made her feel like an outsider.

"Mama, I can't find yellow."

Pulled from her reverie, Janet glimpsed into the rearview mirror to make sure Ellie hadn't unbuckled her seat belt to search for the missing crayon. She hadn't.

"Use blue," Janet said.

"I can't make the kitty's face blue!"

"Then use brown." Janet checked the mirror again. It

puzzled her how quickly Ellie had snapped out of her melancholy once they'd left the funeral home. They were no sooner out the side door than she was back to her chatty, bouncy self. So far Ellie hadn't brought up another question about death, and Janet didn't press the issue. She had enough to handle with her unnamed worry still chugging along at a decent rate.

"What color was Mary's little lamb?" Ellie asked as Janet took a right on Union Street.

"What, hon—oh, damn!"

"Mama, you said the D word!"

Janet winced. "Sorry."

"What's wrong?"

"We're almost out of gas." Janet looked at her wristwatch to verify the time illuminated on the dashboard clock. She only had an hour to find leotards and get Ellie to the auditorium. She glanced down again at the fuel gauge, which sat flat against E.

"Miss Vicky won't care if we're late," Ellie said. "She's a good dancing teacher. When Lexie's late, she doesn't get mad at her."

There was a convenience store with fuel a block and a half away. Janet kept her fingers crossed they'd make it that far. "I'm sure it'll be fine, honey." She looked back at Ellie with what she hoped was a reassuring smile. "I just don't like being late."

"Why?"

"Because."

The engine coughed, and the Caravan shuddered, then jerked forward.

"Oh, Jesus, please," Janet begged. The store was only half a block away now.

"You praying, Mama?"

"Yes, Mama's praying."

" 'Cause you don't want Jesus to make you run out of gas?"

"Uh-huh." Janet let the van coast into the store's parking lot and pulled alongside the nearest fuel island. Exhaling loudly, she switched off the engine and fumbled through her purse for her Visa card. Once she found it, she turned to Ellie. "Stay put, all right? I won't be but a minute."

"Okay, but I want to help pump the gas," Ellie said. She tossed her crayons on the seat and tugged at the seat belt.

"Not this time," Janet said, already out of van. "Next time maybe. Just finish the kitty for me."

Her daughter's face crumpled.

"You know," Janet said, "I'll bet Miss Vicky would love a picture of a cat. Maybe she would even let you do a show-n-tell, like in your kindergarten class."

Ellie's face brightened. "What about I get a real kitty? Then I could bring it for a real show-n-tell. Jason brung his turtle—"

"Brought his turtle," Janet said as she lowered the driver's side passenger window, then closed her door.

"*Brought* his turtle to school, and everybody got to touch it. I want to bring . . ."

Sticking her credit card into the payment slot of the fuel pump, Janet nodded and said absently, "Um-hmm. We'll see." She unscrewed the fuel cap on the van, shoved the nozzle into the metal hole, then checked her watch again.

"Then Casey brung her . . . *brought* her Beanie Babies after that. Her Beanies had clothes. Can I get one with clothes, Mama? I want to get the . . ."

"They sure can talk, huh?"

Surprised by the male voice, Janet snapped a look over her shoulder. A man stood on the opposite side of the fuel island, thrusting a nozzle into a bright red Suburban. She hadn't heard his vehicle pull up alongside them.

Smiling politely, Janet nodded. "They sure do." She looked back at the total registering on the pump display. Not even five dollars yet. Today she had to pick the slowest pump!

She turned her head as though to study the hood of her van and caught a peripheral glimpse of the man moving closer to her. Janet squeezed the nozzle harder, trying to coax the fuel through faster. The guy didn't look dangerous. A bit over middle age with a V-shaped patch of white hair on top of his head and crooked, overlapping teeth. His sunglasses made it hard for Janet to see his eyes. Dressed in gray slacks and a gray and white striped shirt, he looked more like an office worker than trouble.

"You're Savoy's old lady, aren't you?" he asked.

Something about the old slang and the way his mouth worked around the words made Janet move closer to the van. "Excuse me?"

"Wilson Savoy's boy, Michael? The one who runs the funeral home now. You're his old lady, right?"

"Yes . . . Michael's my husband," she said, trying to remain calm and polite. "How do you know him?"

The man laughed like someone holding a delicious secret. He stepped up to the Caravan. "Don't know him so much as his old man. Wilson and me go way back. Business associates, you know? The name's L. Vidrine by the way, but you can call me Lester. Anyways, I hear he's back in town. Thought I'd pay him a visit." He sidled up to her, and his approach carried an abhorrent sense of intimacy.

"I see." Janet removed the nozzle and screwed on the fuel cap. *Stay calm.* She glanced around the parking lot, looking for potential backup. Two kids were investigating something under the hood of a Jeep Cherokee at the front of the store, and a frail old man in a blue tunic sprayed down the concrete with a water hose. He didn't look strong enough to wrestle his way out of a spider's web.

"So—so how do you know me?" Janet asked.

"I seen you in the funeral home a few years ago. Went there to collect—I mean, pick up some stuff from the old man, and you were there. He's the one told me you were his daughter-in-law."

"Oh." It was all Janet could think to say.

"Yeah, I'm good with faces like that. Never forget one. I would've recognized you anywhere."

She attempted a smile, but the effort fell flat.

"So you seen him?" he asked. "Know where he is?"

Janet resisted licking her dry lips. "Who? Michael?"

"No, his old man. Wilson."

She shook her head.

His eyes narrowed suspiciously. "You sure?"

"Positive."

The man looked away and snorted. "Figures." He took a step back. "Hey, cute kid."

Janet's breath caught as the stranger leaned over to peer into the open window at her daughter.

"What're you doing?" he asked Ellie.

"Colorin' a kitty for my teacher," Ellie said. She held up her coloring book to show her progress.

"That's a nifty cat," he said. He cocked his head to one side, and his eyes locked on Janet.

"What's your name?" Ellie asked. "My name's Ellie, and I'm five. How old are you? Do you have a little girl?"

"Honey, finish your picture," Janet said, returning the nozzle to the dispenser. She had one eye on her daughter and the other on the stranger. The nozzle slipped out of its cradle and fell to the concrete. She didn't bother to retrieve it.

The stranger leaned against the side of the Caravan so his back was to Ellie. He edged closer to Janet and said in a mild, conversational tone, "You're sure a good-looking thing. With all that dark hair and everything, enough to send a man to his knees."

Janet felt her face harden. "Get away from my car."

The man held his hands out in front of him as though in surrender. "Just wanted to pay a compliment. You can't blame a guy for trying, right?" He moved closer to her. "No harm, no foul, right?"

"Get away from me or I'll yell for help."

"Help from what, lady? I ain't done nothing."

"Mama?"

Janet glared at him. She heard Ellie call her again but was afraid if she took her eyes off the guy, she'd miss a move, a twitch that might warn her of—what?—an attack?

"Mama?"

The man grinned and backed away. He turned to Ellie and wagged an index finger. "Take it easy, kiddo."

Janet saw worry and confusion swim through her daughter's eyes as the man moved toward the pumps. He leaned against one of them and grinned at her again. Janet hurried into the van, locked the doors, and raised the back window.

"Was that a bad man, Mama? Are you mad at him?"

Cursing under her breath, Janet started the van and tore out of the parking lot.

"Huh, Mama? Was he?"

Tires squealed as Janet turned right, barely slowing for a stop sign. Worse than the lecherous come-on from the man at the store was the knowledge he'd left with her. Michael's father, Wilson, was back in town. And if ever there was a reason for her to intuit trouble, he was it.

Chapter Three

Beethoven's *Pathetique* Sonata played softly overhead as Michael inspected Mr. Rasmussen's burial suit. His apprentice stood nearby, chewing on a fingernail.

"So how'd I do?" Chad asked.

Michael straightened Rasmussen's tie, plucked a speck of fuzz out of his hair, then leaned over the coffin to check the nostrils for stray nose hairs. "Not bad. Just watch the shirtsleeves. An inch past the jacket sleeves always looks best." He tugged lightly on the shirt's cuffs. "See what I mean?"

Chad nodded solemnly. "Christ, you'd think after eight months of working with you I'd remember."

"Inch and a half's actually better," a man's voice said behind them.

Michael and Chad turned in unison.

"Could never get my boy to do it right, though," the man said with a sardonic grin.

Michael blinked as if someone had just thrown a handful of sand in his eyes. "Dad?" The person standing just inside the viewing room barely resembled the man Michael had last seen three years ago. Back then his father had been a formidable figure, even at sixty-three years old. Six-foot two, one hundred eighty pounds, only a touch of gray in his sandy brown hair near the temples. This man looked like a freeze-dried version of the original. Dressed in a faded black suit, he stood stoop-shouldered and penny-nail thin. He hobbled toward Michael.

"Been a while," Wilson Savoy said, his voice a smoker's croup. He held out a knotted, shaking hand when he reached his son.

Michael shook it reluctantly, conscious of the heat rolling up the sides of his neck. "Yes, it has," he said, still staring at his father's flour-white hair. He couldn't think of anything else to say. Time, the supposed healer, had chosen to keep a selection of memories stored away until this moment. Now, like hell-bent kamikazes, they flew to the forefront of his mind where they crashed, burned, then immediately resurrected.

Much to his relief, Chad stuck out an enthusiastic hand, which Wilson barely grazed. "Mr. Savoy, nice to finally meet you. I'm Chad Thibodeaux, the apprentice." Chad flashed him a smile.

"Thought as much," Wilson said. He motioned toward the coffin. "You do the casketing, Mr. Thibodeaux?"

"Yes, sir. But please call me Ch—"

"Head's too low, Mr. Thibodeaux. Body needs to be angled slightly. You've got him looking like a sardine in there."

Chad's smile collapsed, and he took a step back.

"The body's fine," Michael said, glaring at his father.

"Too low," Wilson countered.

"Any higher and he'd roll out."

Michael's blood pressure rose exponentially as he waited through the ensuing silence. From the corner of his eye, he spotted Chad inching his way out of the room.

Eventually, Wilson lowered his eyes. "Is that all you have to say after three years?"

Michael struggled to keep a groan locked between his lips. Three years? Was that all his father thought they had to catch up on? Make amends for? Thirty-six was more like it. Every year since his son's birth. What number of words could possibly accumulate in a person's head and heart over that period of time? Millions? Trillions? Possibly none. Some heartaches simply had no vocabulary.

With a thrust of his chin, Michael motioned his father to the door. "We're expecting a family any minute. I think this is better discussed in my office."

Wilson looked up sharply. "Just answer me."

Michael clenched his teeth. "I *said* in my office." He stormed out ahead of his father, and as Michael made his way down the hall, he tried to block out the sound of shuffling steps attempting to keep up behind him.

When they were behind closed doors, Michael took a seat behind his desk and waited while his father studied the urn display against the wall.

"No need for us to start off on the wrong foot," Wilson said, finally settling into a chair at the small conference table.

Michael noticed a slight bobbing of his father's head. *Parkinson's?* He shook the thought away. "Why are you here?"

"Is that any way to talk to your father?"

"Okay. Why are you here, *Father?*"

Wilson pursed his lips, reached into the inside pocket of his jacket, and after a few fumbled attempts pulled out a cigarette and an old Zippo. After flipping the lighter open, his right thumb quivered over the flint wheel, then missed it altogether. "Damn thing must be broken."

As though on autopilot, Michael got up from behind his desk and went to his father. He took the lighter from him. "No smoking in here," he said, then lit the Zippo.

Wilson puffed his cigarette to life and signaled for Michael to sit beside him. "I've got a business proposition for you," he said. "Figured it's time we get stuff straight. I'm not getting any younger you know."

Michael stared at him in disbelief. A business proposition? Didn't the man possess even a thread of common decency? What about an apology? Some explanation for his desertion? Couldn't he even share one goddamn reason why he'd left his son alone to face lawyers and bill collectors and near bankruptcy? Michael knew, however, that if his father were to say those things, he'd have to ask for DNA testing to confirm Wilson's identity.

"I—" Michael began.

"Not now," Wilson said. He got up and tapped his ashes into the empty wastebasket near Michael's desk. "You've got a service about to start, and I don't want you running out when we're only half through the conversation."

"I'm not handling it," Michael said reluctantly. "Chad is. So say whatever it is you need to say."

"You're letting an apprentice take care of a family? Dumb move. He's a baby."

Michael bristled. "He's twenty-eight and competent, and why the hell does it matter to you? You didn't give two shits about this place when you cleaned out the bank accounts and disappeared."

"I did give two shits, really," Wilson said, returning to his seat. "Something came up that needed my attention, that's all."

"Yeah? What was it? Number ten coming in in the seventh?"

"I'm not messing with the horses anymore, Michael. Gave that up a while back."

"So what's it now? Dogs?" Michael stood up, grabbed the wastebasket, and handed it to Wilson. "Put the damn cigarette out. You're smelling up the place."

"Then why'd you light it?" Wilson sucked on his cigarette twice more before extinguishing it. "No dogs, no horses. Actually, I had another business venture that—"

A knock at the door gave Michael just the reason he needed to cut his father off. He didn't want to hear the excuses.

"Yes?" Michael called, dropping the wastebasket back in its place.

The door opened, and Sally Mouton poked her head inside. Her narrow face did a rendition of surprise, which meant the propping up of one eyebrow, when she spotted Wilson. "Mr. Savoy, when . . . how . . . I didn't see you come in. I mean . . ."

Wilson stood and motioned Sally inside. "How's my favorite hostess?" he asked with a wink.

Sally entered the office, closing the door behind her. Her walk was stiff and regimented in her black suit with its high collar and calf-length skirt. "Fine," she answered. "Glad to see you're . . . well?" She gave Michael a puzzled look, which read, *Is this for real?* She had worked for Wilson for many years, and he had simply disappeared on her, too.

"Well as can be expected, I suppose," Wilson said. He lifted his chin as though to tighten the sagging skin beneath it. "Lots of water under the bridge, huh, Sal?"

Before she could answer, Michael asked, "Has the Rasmussen family arrived?"

"Uh . . . yes," Sally said, reluctantly pulling her gaze from Wilson to Michael. "Chad's with them now."

"Good. I'll be out in a—"

"But that's not what I came in to tell you." Sally patted the tight, white bun on her head, her gesture of recomposure. "There're some people here wanting to make arrangements. Two men."

Michael glanced at his watch. He had a little less than an hour before he had to leave to make Ellie's dance recital. "I don't remember having any appointments set up this late."

"Walk-ins. They came straight from the hospital," Sally said.

"Which one?"

"Didn't say." She lowered her voice. "I think they're foreigners."

"What makes you say that?"

Sally scrunched up her nose like she'd caught a whiff of ammonia. "They have strange accents, and they dress funny."

"So?"

"Probably indigents," Wilson said with a nod. "Get rid of 'em."

Michael rolled a hand into a fist at his side. "Send them in," he said a little louder than he intended.

Without another word, Sally retreated, and Michael returned to his desk, where he pulled out an arrangement folder. He pointed it at his father. "I think you'd better go."

Wilson coughed, then scratched the faint stubble on his cheek. "Nah, I think I'll stick around for this one. See how you've been handling business."

"You've got no—"

"No what?" Wilson asked, his head bobbing more noticeably. "No right? Is that what you were going to say, son? That I've got no right to interfere with your work?" He laughed. "I still own this place. Or did you forget?"

Michael was rounding the front of his desk, ready for battle, when the door reopened, and two men shuffled into his office. The older one looked to be around sixty, short and heavyset with gray hair cut short under a snow-white fedora. He sported a mustache the same color as the hat. He wore a black pinstriped suit and a red shirt with white polka dots. A wide white tie completed the ensemble. The younger man looked forty with shoulder-length black hair and a thin mustache. He was dressed more conservatively than his partner in a blue denim shirt and khaki pants.

Michael bagged the fury he'd targeted at his father and introduced himself, holding out a hand. "How may I help you?"

The younger man peered at the older before shaking Michael's hand. His grip was weak, his palm cold and wet.

"We need to make burial arrangement," he said.

Michael nodded and motioned them to the conference table. "Please, have a seat." He made a conscious effort not to grind his teeth when he added, "This is Wilson Savoy, my father."

The older man nudged the younger, and they walked to the table and sat while Michael closed the door. He watched them nervously survey the urns as he went to his desk for a pen.

After joining them, Michael said, "I'm sorry, I didn't get your names."

"I am Antony," the younger man said, nodding first to Michael than to Wilson. "Antony Stevenson. This is my cousin, Ephraim Stevenson."

Evidently assuming the deceased to be Ephraim's wife or mother, Wilson gave the older man his best, I'm-sorry-for-your-loss smile. The man glared back at him.

"Don't know many Stevensons," Wilson said. "You from this area? The accent sounds kinda Slavic."

"No, we are not from Louisiana," Antony said. A steely look crossed his face. "Will that make a difference?"

"No, no," Michael said, and gave his father a quick *hands-off* glance. "We just like to get to know a little about the families that come to us so we can serve them better."

Ephraim cleared his throat and placed his fingertips on the edge of the table. Antony leaned forward and crossed his arms over his chest.

"We finish with this business and make burial arrangement now," Antony said.

"Of course." Michael uncapped his pen. "And the deceased is?" As he prepared to write down the information, Michael heard a gurgling sound. He glanced up and saw Ephraim's face contort, his mouth shifting from left to right. He'd seen the look before, especially with men in the throes of grief.

Antony had his head bowed so low it nearly touched the table. Michael lowered his eyes and gave the men a moment to compose themselves. His father tapped a soft, impatient rhythm on the table with his thumbs.

After a while, Ephraim reached into the breast pocket of his suit, pulled out a handkerchief, and swabbed his face. When he was done, he clutched the linen in his hand and lifted his chin.

"My dau—" Ephraim's hands folded in tightly, his knuckles turning the color of old chalk. In contrast, his face fell slack, his eyes void, like a man who'd just awakened to find himself the only one left on the planet. No one to love, no one to love him. For a moment, the intensity of it made Michael forget the problem sitting next to him with a Zippo.

"Your daughter?" Michael asked quietly.

Ephraim's eyes shut tightly in response.

"Yes," Antony said.

Ephraim opened his eyes and leaned back so abruptly Michael thought he'd fall out of his chair.

"Her name is . . . was—" Antony squirmed in his chair and tucked his hair behind his ears. "Is. Her name is Thalia Stevenson."

More gurgling sounds from Ephraim.

Michael struggled to keep his eyes on Antony. "Where is she now?"

Ephraim stood, then wandered to the window across the room. Heavy drapes covered the pane, but he stared at them as if they were transparent.

Antony cleared his throat. "Riverwest Medical Center."

Wilson harrumphed, and Michael sought his father's shin with the toe of his shoe. When they failed to connect, he wrote down the hospital information. His father knew, as did he, that the staff at Riverwest rarely recommended Savoy Funeral Home. One of their board members was Lionel Pellerin, the owner of Pellerin's Mortuary, which was located near the hospital, just outside Baton Rouge. Staff members who recommended other funeral homes usually lost their jobs.

Before his father could blurt out a comment, Michael asked, "Did someone there refer you to us?"

"No," Antony said. "They did not tell us of you. Our family had no choice but to come here. Here is where Thalia's spirit settled, and here she must be buried."

Wilson gave a quiet snort, and Michael missed his shin again while considering what Antony had said. He decided not to pursue the spirit comment. A person's belief was a person's belief. "So you won't be moving her back . . . uh . . . home? You'll be burying her here?"

Antony nodded, and his hair fell back over the sides of his face. "Yes. Her spirit has settled in this town, so must her body."

From the corner of the room, Ephraim suddenly shouted something that sounded like, "Naught!" He charged toward Antony, slinging a barrage of strange words as well as a fair amount of spit.

Antony flinched. A look of exasperation and pain fell over his face as Ephraim towered above him.

Michael slouched in his chair, wondering whether he should leave the room. He didn't have any idea what had made Ephraim so furious, but he certainly didn't want any part of making it worse. He looked at his father who gave him an I-told-you-so smirk before propping his chin on a fist as though preparing to watch a favorite movie.

Eventually, Ephraim ran out of steam. He glowered at Antony a moment longer, then walked back to the window.

Antony rubbed his cheeks slowly. "We finish with this business," he said to Michael, his voice tired and low.

For the next forty minutes, Michael gathered the rest of the information he needed from Antony without further outbursts from Ephraim. He found out that their family had been en route to Lake Charles and decided to stop in Brusley for the day to celebrate Thalia's nineteenth birthday. They'd set up camp in Pelican Park, which was only a couple of miles south of the funeral home. Thalia and a friend had decided to race two of the horses that traveled with them. Midway through the race, Thalia's horse spooked and reared, throwing her to the ground headfirst. The impact broke her neck, killing her instantly.

Antony insisted on the best. He chose a bronze Mediterranean casket, an expensive model with blue velvet interior, and a garden crypt, which would allow room for another casket to be placed atop Thalia's at a later time. Without any prompting, Antony explained that the only person allowed a choice regarding a burial site was the mother of a dead child. If the woman remained faithful and deserving, she might be granted permission by her husband to be placed beside or atop her child after her own death. Provisions were often made for that purpose.

Antony also made it clear that they wanted a one-day viewing, and that a funeral mass was to be held at Saint Paul's Church since Thalia and her family were Catholics. The actual burial was to be done in the adjoining cemetery at dusk, and Antony assured Michael they would compensate the priest for complying with the unusual request. He also warned that there would be no room for other families in the funeral home while Thalia's viewing was in progress. *Many* people were expected to attend, lots of food and drinks would be served, and they would gladly pay extra for the inconvenience. The family would also pay extra to have a tombstone engraved and ready by tomorrow.

At the mention of money, especially extra money, Wilson perked up. He got to his feet and offered, "Coffee anyone? Or maybe something cold—"

"I'm afraid we can't allow food or alcohol in the funeral home," Michael said. "We—"

"You will have to excuse my son," Wilson blurted. He shot Michael a fierce look. "He's still relatively young in this business. We'll be more than glad to accommodate whatever needs you might have. Now, what about that coffee?"

"No, thank you," Antony said, his countenance visibly drained.

Michael bit his tongue as his father approached Ephraim, who still stood staring at the drapery. "Mr. Stevenson, would you—"

Ephraim spun around to face Wilson, and for a second, Michael thought the man was going to throw a punch at his father. He jumped up, ready to block both men, then felt foolish when Ephraim shoved a hand into his coat pocket. With a flip of his wrist, he tossed a handful of bills onto Michael's desk, then grunted something to Antony.

Michael couldn't help but gape at the twenty or thirty greenbacks crisscrossed on the desk. More than one had 1,000 stamped around its corners.

"He says that is what he is willing to pay," Antony said. He stood and walked toward his cousin. "Do we do business?"

Wilson, eyeing the bills, said expansively, "Of course, of course!"

"This may be too much money," Michael said firmly. "Why don't we add up the expenses first?"

"We expect much," Antony warned.

"That may be," Michael continued, "but—"

"Excuse my son again," Wilson said. He glared at Michael, then smiled at Antony. "I will personally see to it that all of your expectations are met. This will do fine."

Antony nodded.

"We'll contact the hospital about Thalia's release," Wilson said, his face beaming. "Have someone bring her clothes here first thing in the morning. We'll start visiting hours tomorrow afternoon at—"

"We will send someone with clothes and stand watch tonight," Antony said, his voice hard. "She is not to be left alone at any time. Rest of family will come in early morning."

Michael frowned. "I'm not sure we can have her ready by—"

"Absolutely," Wilson interrupted. "Whatever you—"

Ephraim sliced a hand through the air, cutting off Wilson's words and nearly smacking Antony across the face. He turned toward Wilson, his black eyes hard, cold marbles.

"This makes you hungry, no?" he asked, pointing to the money on the desk.

Wilson sucked in an audible breath as the man crept closer to him.

"Yes," Ephraim said. The word hissed through his teeth like steam from a kettle. "There is much hunger within. I am but to wonder what planted such a seed." His finger ran the length of Wilson's tie without touching it.

Michael heard a crackle of static electricity, and his father suddenly shoved a finger behind the knot in his tie, his eyes widening. Wilson began to gasp as though struggling for air.

"Dad?" Michael took an uncertain step toward him.

Ephraim and Antony stood nearby with their arms folded. They watched Wilson with casual amusement as saliva escaped from the corners of his mouth and he abruptly dropped to one knee.

"Dad?" Fearing a heart attack, Michael hurried to his father's side. A loud *rip* sounded from Wilson's chest, and the tie he'd been struggling with fell to the floor in halves. Wilson gulped air as Michael helped him to his feet.

"Are you all right?" Michael asked, puzzled. He looked from his father to Ephraim, then back to his father. "What happened?"

Wilson grabbed onto the edge of the desk with both hands. "I-I don't . . . the tie—"

Ephraim grunted loudly and rubbed his palms together. "It is settled," he said to Michael. "You will present her in early morning." With a brisk nod, he turned to Antony. "Come, we have much to prepare."

Antony opened the door and held it ajar for his cousin. Before he crossed the threshold, Ephraim turned to Wilson.

"Beware of such a hunger and where it will lead you, Wilson Savoy. If you do not hold it in its place, this greed will send most horrible death." With that, Ephraim reached into his coat again and pulled out a large pinch of white powder, which he tossed across the carpet. Pollen-fine residue settled on the desk, the urn shelf, and the picture of Ellie that rested on the windowsill.

"What the hell are you doing?" Wilson demanded.

Ignoring Wilson, Ephraim looked at Michael and bowed his head stiffly. "A gift," he said, "which your honesty has earned. It will help carry your most heartfelt prayer to the very gates of heaven." Ephraim cocked his head toward Wilson once again, eyed him gravely, then followed Antony out of the room, closing the door behind him.

Chapter Four

Standing in the northeast vestibule of Riverwest Medical Center, Anna Stevenson took the knife she had borrowed from someone she couldn't remember and stared at the palm of her left hand. Never again would this hand touch the cheek of her beloved Thalia. It would never feel the warmth of her like it once did when they had hugged. There would never be another time when it would feel the smoothness of a brush gliding through her daughter's hair as she helped to brush it before a party.

A party . . . a birthday party . . . Thalia's—

Anna sliced an X into her palm with the knife and watched blood pour between her fingers, then splatter to the floor. She felt only a tingling sensation from the wound, so minuscule to the torture that ravaged her heart.

It seemed like only seconds earlier when she had laughed and clapped as Ephraim promenaded their daughter before friends and family. "Nineteen and so beautiful," he had said with so much pride, you would have thought he alone had given birth to the girl. Thalia had held on to her father's arm, glowing in the congratulatory applause.

Anna had wondered then about the passage of time. Hadn't it only been a year or two since Thalia turned four? Wasn't it only a month or so ago that her daughter had lost her front teeth? Surely it was no more than days since she had tried on her first bra. As she'd watched Thalia dance and sing, Anna felt happy but cheated. It was as if she had looked away for only a second and some giant clock in nature had suddenly sped up, turning her child into a woman.

Anna let her hand fall to her side and peered over at the long double windows to her right. Such a beautiful day, so bright, so full of promise—

"I won't ruin my new skirt," Thalia had insisted. "I promise. I'll even throw a blanket over Joe-Joe's back to make sure it stays clean. Just once around the field, please?"

Anna had been basting a lamb quarter over an open pit when she first heard the shouting. She looked on as everyone ran toward the west end of the park where one of their quarter horses bucked and neighed wildly. It took Anna a moment to recognize the rust-colored animal as Thalia's Joe-Joe. Two arrhythmic beats of her heart later, she spotted the still, crumpled form on the ground.

She'd run, feeling her soul melt inside her, hearing it whisper with horrid certitude and in breathless agony—*She's gone. Thalia's gone.*

A muted clatter drew Anna's attention away from the windows, and she looked down to see the knife lying on the floor. There was an impressive splatter of blood on her clothes and around her feet. Anna studied the dark swirls and droplets for a moment, her mind straining to remember where the blood had come from, then decided it didn't matter.

She turned and faced the hall behind her. Somewhere in this building, in this maze of corridors and antiseptic-scented rooms, lay her daughter's lifeless body. They had moved Thalia from the curtained cubicle where a scrawny-faced doctor had said simply, "She's dead," to some other place in the hospital. Anna had held on to Thalia's hand, wanting to follow the gurney, but no one would allow it. It had taken Ephraim and two other men to pry her away from her daughter.

"Anna, there you are!"

Anna's eyes focused on her sister-in-law, Roslyn, who waddled down the hall toward her. The short, pear-shaped woman had black mascara streaks running down both cheeks.

"We've been looking everywhere for—oh, my God, you're bleeding!" Roslyn hurried to Anna's side, grabbed her left wrist, and forced her hand palm up. "Oh, God, Anna, what did you do?"

"She's gone, Rosy," Anna said quietly. "My—my baby's gone."

"I know, honey," Roslyn said shakily. She let go of Anna's wrist, then quickly dug through her shoulder bag and pulled out a blue silk scarf. She wrapped it around Anna's injured hand.

"They—they wouldn't let me stay with her."

"My poor Anna," Roslyn said, and softly touched Anna's cheek. "How hard this must be for you."

"She's all alone now. Gone forever."

Roslyn shook her head slowly, tears following mascara tracks. "She will never be alone, Anna. Thalia will be with us always, in our hearts. Her memory will live there forever."

Anna stared at her numbly. "But you cannot feel the breath of a memory or feel the warmth of its skin when it kisses you goodnight, can you?"

Roslyn let out a little sob, then stooped and picked the knife up from the floor. After tucking it into her bag, she stood and took hold of Anna's arm. "Come. We need to find someone to look at your hand. You're cut pretty bad."

Anna felt Roslyn gently tug on her arm, and before she knew it, she was following her obediently down the corridor.

Left then right, left again, left again, then right. It seemed to take forever before they reached a set of steel elevator doors. Roslyn pressed the down button, and for a fraction of a second, Anna saw her reflection split in half when the shiny metal doors opened. The image looked like she felt—divided, ripped in two, never to be made whole again.

A middle-aged woman with bottle-blond hair followed them into the elevator, and Anna pressed herself against the back wall. Roslyn stood next to her. The hoist hummed, then lowered them from the third floor to the second. Between the second and first floor, Anna heard something that made her stand at attention.

Roslyn leaned closer to her and whispered, "We're almost there."

"Shh, listen," Anna said, stepping away. She pressed a hand to the elevator wall. "Can you hear it?"

The bottle-blond woman glanced over her shoulder, then gawked at the blood soaked scarf. She inched closer to the doors.

"What?" Roslyn asked. "I don't hear anything but elevator noise."

"It's her, Rosy." Anna went to the elevator panel and jabbed frantically at the numbered buttons. "Can't you hear? She's playing it. Thalia's playing her music box!"

Chapter Five

A *cadaver, eating a chicken salad sandwich.*

That thought rolled continuously through Janet's mind as she loaded the dishwasher, one eye locked on Wilson Savoy. She couldn't help but stare. The man looked nothing like she remembered. For as long as she'd known him, her father-in-law had been an imposing man, tall and robust in stature and presence. He'd carried the temperament of a pit bull and the attitude of a selfish, manipulating asshole. The man who sat at her kitchen table, however, was gaunt and bowed, with a gray, waxy complexion. His eyes held a withered, defeated look, and his physical fortitude seemed to be that of a cancer victim about to cross the threshold to eternity.

"So why didn't you invite me?" Wilson asked. He took another bite of chicken salad sandwich and rolled his eyes. "Heaven. You always were a good cook, Janet."

"It's from Champagne's Deli," Janet said quietly. She

closed the dishwasher, grabbed a dish towel, and wiped down an already clean countertop. She peered over at Michael, who sat across the table from his father. He stared at Wilson in silence, his eyes pained, his jaw muscles flexing rhythmically. Ellie lay against Michael's chest, her head resting against his left shoulder as she slept. Michael patted her back gently, absently. Janet could only imagine the emotions roiling inside her husband. Three years was a long time to be steeped in resentment.

During the pizza reception that had followed Ellie's recital, Michael told Janet about Wilson's arrival at the funeral home, and she'd told him about the man at the gas pumps. Neither had been overtly surprised by the other's news. What did surprise them, though, was Wilson's appearance at their front door, tumbler of bourbon in hand, twenty minutes after they'd returned home.

"Store bought, huh?" Wilson said with a shake of his head. "Could've fooled me." A few seconds of awkward silence passed before he added, "It's the truth, you know." He gestured toward Ellie with his chin. "I'd have gone to her dance thing if you'd told me about it."

Michael got up from the table, his face reddening. Ellie stirred in his arms. "Since when do you care about dance recitals?" Michael asked in a loud whisper.

Wilson wolfed down the last of his sandwich, washed it down with the remaining bourbon, then covered his mouth to stanch a belch. He grinned apologetically. "First time for everything, I guess."

Janet, sensing a Vesuvian eruption about to occur in Michael, tossed the dish towel into the sink and went over to him.

"I'll bring her to bed," Janet said, reaching for Ellie. Michael's face softened immediately, and he handed their daughter over to her.

Ellie nestled against Janet's shoulder, then abruptly lifted her head and opened one eye. "It's morning?" she asked.

Janet kissed her cheek. "Nope, still nighttime."

Ellie rubbed her eyes, then looked down at Wilson. "Your hair's white like a snowman's," she said with a smile.

Wilson laughed, then coughed so hard he gagged. When he caught his breath, he said, "And you're cute as a button."

"Are you sick?" Ellie asked. She pointed to the pantry. " 'Cause Mama gives me that yucky stuff in there when I'm sick. You want some? You can have—" She looked up at Janet. "Mama, you're squeezing me too tight."

Janet felt heat spread across her cheeks as she loosened her hold on her daughter. Ellie's interaction with Wilson made her uneasy to the point of nausea, and she didn't know why.

"No thanks, Ellie," Wilson said. He lowered his head and pressed a finger over stray breadcrumbs on the table. After making a production of transferring the crumbs to his plate, he added, "I'm okay."

Janet felt her chest tighten. The man looked so lonely, almost despondent. Maybe he really was ill.

"Time for bed, doodlebug," Michael said. He ran a nervous hand through his hair, and Janet caught the underlying message that said he wanted to speak to his father alone.

Unsure of how to make a gracious exit, Janet said to

Wilson, "There's more chicken in the fridge if you're still hungry."

"Thanks," Wilson said. "But I've had plenty." He blew a kiss to Ellie. "Sweet dreams, cutie."

Ellie yawned. "Night, Daddy. Night, Mister."

Janet gave Wilson a quick nod before leaving the kitchen. Her nausea was in full bloom now and the bathroom much too far away.

Once Janet and Ellie had left the room, Michael walked over to the sink and filled a glass with water. The dull thud in his chest made it difficult for him to swallow.

"Kinda sad," Wilson said. "She doesn't even remember I'm her grandfather."

Michael forced down another gulp of water, then placed the glass in the sink. "She was barely two when you left. What do you expect?"

Wilson fidgeted with the edge of his plate. After a long moment, he said, "Weird people that came in today, huh? You know, with the powder and everything? Still don't know what the deal was with my choking, though. That Stevenson guy didn't even touch my tie, but it felt like he'd tightened it somehow. Really weird. And you should have seen the guy they sent over after you left the funeral home. I thought that apprentice of yours was going to have a—"

"Is that why you came over here? To talk about the Stevensons?" Michael shoved his hands into his pockets and suddenly thought about the twenty-eight thousand dollars in cash he'd hidden in his desk drawer, just below the box of Godiva chocolates and small diamond ring he'd bought for Janet this afternoon. He hoped his father hadn't found a way to jimmy the lock.

A clink of fingernails against Corningware. "No, not just them."

"Then what?"

Wilson crossed his arms and rested them on the table. "The least you can do is come over here and sit."

Reluctantly, Michael pulled his hands from his pockets, walked to the far end of the table, and sat.

Eyeing the empty tumbler, Wilson said, "Look, I know I'm not gonna win any awards for parent of the year, but you could show a little more respect. I am your father, you know."

"Your point?"

"I had reasons to leave, Michael. I had stuff to take care of."

"So you've said."

Wilson raised a shaky hand to his chin and scratched. "If things were that bad, you should've just let the bank have the place."

Michael gaped at him. "Is that all you have to say after I busted my ass to—"

"I never asked you to bust your ass. You could've left. Could have closed the place down and gone to work for another funeral home. Pellerin's always looking for good people."

The reference to "good people" paralyzed Michael for a second. Had his father just admitted he was a good funeral director? Probably a slip of the tongue. Michael couldn't remember the last time his father had associated him with anything good. Whether it was learning to ride a two-wheeled bike on his own or being one of the top three students in mortuary school, Wilson always had something negative to say.

Some verbal twist of the knife to assure his son he'd never measure up to Wilson Savoy's standards.

Deciding that some things were best left alone, Michael got to his feet and paced between the table and kitchen counter. "I'm not like you," he said. "The funeral home was never a money tree to me. I give a damn about what I do."

"Hey, I cared."

"Yeah, about yourself. It was always about you. You always had to be right, even with Grandpa Joseph."

"Leave my father out of this," Wilson warned.

Michael felt a cork pop off emotions he'd kept bottled up for too long. He whirled about. "Why? The truth hurt?"

"You don't have a clue about what the truth was or is," Wilson said. "Your grandfather was too old to run the business anymore. He made mistakes, big ones. I had to stay on top of everything just to keep bread on our table!"

"It was *his* funeral home!" Michael said. "And you badgered that old man until the day he died. And what the hell do you mean, bread on the table? As soon as the place made a profit, you took it. If there was any goddamn bread, Mom, God rest her, was the one who made sure it got there, you . . . you son of a—" Michael clamped his lips shut, all the more angry for allowing himself to lose his cool.

For a second, Wilson's face hitched with pain, but then he looked away. "If it was so bad all those years, Michael, why in the hell did you stick around?"

It was Michael's turn to look away, leaving the question to hang in the air along with the sound of his rapid breathing. Why had he stayed? For his grandfather? For Janet and Ellie? Or was it because of some asinine, innate hope that maybe one day things would change between him and his father? It was a question he'd asked himself for years.

A loud exhale gathered Michael's attention.

"Guess it doesn't matter now," Wilson said with a wave of his hand. "Too much water under that bridge anyway."

"Flooded."

"Look, you think you can quit pissing in my shoes for a little while so we can talk business?" Wilson pointed to a chair.

Michael didn't move.

"Ten minutes," Wilson said. "That's all it'll take."

Wary, Michael returned to his chair.

Wilson began to knead his knotted fingers. "I want to sell the funeral home," he blurted.

Michael felt his jaw drop. "To whom?"

"Who do you think? You of course."

Words refused to form on Michael's tongue.

"See . . . I'm in a bind," Wilson said. He scrunched his body closer to the table. "I need some heavy cash quick." He held up a trembling hand. "I know what you're thinking, but it's not like that. No gambling. I swear. You know that business venture I mentioned to you? The reason I had to leave in the first place? Well, it kinda went sour—bad sour actually, and, well . . . the investors want their money back."

Michael scraped his teeth over his bottom lip, which seemed to jumpstart his ability to speak. "How much?"

"How much what?"

"How much do you want?"

Wilson's head bobbed earnestly, his face an over-planted field of wrinkles and liver spots. "I figure twice the receipts is fair. A million and a quarter."

Familiar with his father's definition of fair, Michael stalled. He'd done the books for the funeral home long enough to know the price was above fair market value. To get out from under his father's control now, however, would be worth twice what he was asking. But fair or not, Michael had to deal with reality. He didn't have the money. After bouts with attorneys, a long struggle with debt reorganization, IRS liens, and all but groveling to the bank, he'd managed to untangle the mess his father had left behind and survive the last three years. But barely.

Michael slumped in his seat. "I don't have that kind of money."

Wilson tsked. "Hell, I know that, but the bank does. And your personal credit's good, right? What would it hurt to ask?"

Michael had to admit his personal credit history was in fair shape. And although the company profits were low, they were at least in the black again. Maybe the bank would view his ability to turn the company around as a positive sign when they considered all the risk factors. Maybe it would be enough for them to at least consider a loan. Then again, maybe all he was doing was slow dancing with wishful thinking. But Wilson was right about one thing. What would it hurt to ask?

"All right," Michael said. "I'll go on Monday and talk to the loan officer."

"Why Monday? Why not Friday? That's tomorrow. You could do it tomorrow."

"We've got the Stevenson service tomorrow, and as

soon as that's taken care of, I'm going up to the cabin with my family. I won't be back until Monday."

Wilson wrung his hands and looked about nervously. Suddenly, his eyes brightened. "So you take a few minutes in the morning, slip out, go to the bank. I'll cover for you while you're gone."

"I'm not doing it tomorrow," Michael said firmly. "I have too much to do. And if we're going to do this sale, I want it done right. No screw-ups. Going tomorrow won't make that big a difference anyway. It's not like the bank's going to give me a check in an hour. Loans take time."

"Yeah, but at least you'd get the ball rolling quicker."

"I said no."

Wilson turned sideways in his chair, picked up the tumbler from the table, and brought it to his lips. His tongue flicked across the dry rim. With a grunt of frustration, he returned it to the table and faced Michael again. "I thought you'd be more excited about this."

"I'm a realist. When and if it happens, great."

Wilson tapped an anxious foot on the floor.

"Why are you so nervous all of a sudden?" Michael asked. "You didn't actually think you'd be walking around with a million in cash tomorrow, did you?"

"Of course not. Not at all." Wilson stood and pressed a hand to the small of his back. He walked around in a tight circle for a moment, then said, "Tell you what, son, I'll sweeten the pot. You give me the cash you got from the Stevensons earlier, and I'll lower the sale price to a million even. That should make things even easier for you at the bank."

The kitchen suddenly felt the size of a breadbox, and Michael got to his feet. "Forget it," he said, and headed for the living room and the front door. "Your ten minutes are up."

"Wait!" Wilson caught up with Michel and followed alongside him in a lopsided gait. "I'm just trying to help you, lowering the asking price and all."

"The sale's a ruse," Michael said, not looking back. "All you're after is that cash. I should've known, goddammit. I should've seen it coming."

"No, no! I really want to sell the business to you," Wilson insisted. "Really!"

"Bullshit."

"I could just take it, you know. I still own the funeral home. So theoretically, it's mine anyway."

Michael reached the front door, but before opening it he turned to Wilson and jabbed a finger at him. "Stop playing your games! The fucking cash isn't yours, *Dad.* The bank's in possession of all receipts and even if I could give it to you, I sure as hell wouldn't!"

Wilson grabbed his arm. "Listen, please—son—I gotta have that cash. I promise—I'll go through with the sale. You have my word."

"Which means about as much as dog turds in the rain. Runny—and floats off in any damn direction. The answer's no. It belongs to the bank." Michael shook his arm free and opened the door.

"Y-you don't understand," Wilson said in a broken whisper. "If I don't give the investors some kind of good faith offering, they'll . . . they'll do something terrible to me." He let out a little sob. "Really terrible."

Michael clutched the edge of the door until his hand hurt. Something inside of him seemed to be ripping in two. One half wanted to shove his father out the door and scream, "That's your problem, you dumb fuck!" The other half hung numb.

Wilson's body appeared to sag even more under Michael's gaze, his face draining of what little color it possessed. Tears pooled in his eyes. "They'll kill me, Michael. I swear to God, they'll kill me."

Chapter Six

Friday morning gave witness to a typical Brusley, Louisiana, summer. Humidity thickened the air like roux in a gumbo, and the heat, even at eight-thirty, had already tapped thermometers up to eighty degrees.

Michael fidgeted at the red light, flipping the car's air-conditioner vents up, then down, right, then left. No matter the direction or how high he set the blower, sweat rings still grew under his arms. Along with the heat, a bad case of nerves had caused a prickly rash to sprout at the base of his neck. If he didn't talk to his father soon and get this money issue settled, he feared his whole body would soon resemble a strawberry.

After Wilson's final plea last night, Michael weakened and left his father with the notion that he'd try to find a way to help him. As soon as Michael closed the door behind his father, however, he wanted to kick himself. Why did he allow himself to fall for Wilson's manipulations? He *knew* better; had lived through too many Wilson episodes to expect a new outcome.

Michael had to admit, though, the tears were a new twist. They were the reason he'd caved. He'd never seen his father cry before. Not even at his mother's funeral.

The image of Wilson's tears haunted Michael throughout the night. He'd tossed and turned fitfully, then finally gave up and got out of bed around four. Two pots of coffee later, he decided, tears or not, he had to stand firm. No money, period. It was time he stopped enabling his father.

To soothe his conscience, Michael had also decided to go to the police with Wilson if he was truly in danger. Bad business deals and killer investors sounded like an old, rehashed plot from a *Godfather* movie, something Wilson concocted for effect. But the truth would be revealed soon enough. His father would either accept his help or he'd back off, exposing himself as the bullshitter Michael suspected him of being. Either way, Michael didn't take any chances with the Stevenson money. At first light, he went over to the funeral home, retrieved the cash he'd hidden in his desk drawer, then went straight to the bank depository and dropped it off. Once that was out of the way, he'd stopped off at a twenty-four-hour café and had breakfast, mulling over what he would say to Wilson and the repercussions that might follow.

Janet didn't know about Wilson's latest financial fiasco. By the time Michael had finally gone to bed last night, she'd already fallen asleep and was still sleeping when he left at dawn, so they hadn't had a chance to talk. Which might have been for the best. Janet had always been his touchstone, his rock in rough waters, and if it hadn't been for her support and encouragement he would have never made it through the last three years. But she'd borne enough trouble from his family. The last thing Michael wanted to do was burden her with more. He'd fill her in on the prospect of buying the funeral home, but only if it proved to be true and only after this mess with his father and his so-called investors had been dealt with.

A car horn blew behind Michael, snatching away his thoughts. He tapped the accelerator and crossed the intersection just as the traffic light switched from green to yellow. Two miles later, Michael took a right on Jenkins and noticed cars lined up on both sides of the road. Old station wagons and Pintos were fender to bumper with Mercedes, Park Avenues, and Lincolns. Vehicles straddled the curbs all the way to Sylva Lane, where he turned right again. When he stopped at the stop sign on the corner, he saw cars lined up on both sides of Alabaster Road, which ran directly in front of the funeral home.

"Holy shit!" Michael blinked rapidly, not trusting his vision. The mortuary's parking lots, front and sides, were packed with cars, pickup trucks with homemade campers attached to the beds, and travel trailers of varying sizes. Hordes of people milled around the vehicles. Michael spotted a woman hanging a man's shirt on a car antenna and two other women carrying a large black pot to a butane burner that sat behind an Airstream. Groups of children raced through the chaos in heated games of tag.

With his mouth still agape, Michael inched his Buick past the funeral home, then nursed it around more haphazardly parked vehicles until he reached his house, almost three blocks away.

Janet's Caravan wasn't in the garage, so Michael

parked the Buick in the empty slot, then hurried over to the funeral home on foot.

When he reached the parking lot, Michael cornered a stout, middle-aged man dressed in a rumpled brown suit. "Excuse me, but are all of you here for the Stevenson viewing?"

The man's caterpillar brows knitted, and without a word, he pointed to a woman who sat crying on the hood of a nearby Oldsmobile.

Michael took a step toward her, thought better of it, then hurried over to the service entrance of the funeral home. He half expected to find Chad cowering in some corner in desperate need of Prozac.

The side door swung open just as Michael reached it, and a young man in a Lee's Florist uniform bustled out.

"Oh, man, I'm sorry," the man said. "Did I hit you?"

"No. What's—" Michael began, but the guy spun away, already heading for the back end of a delivery van, which was tucked tightly against the side of the building.

"Hey," the man called out before disappearing into the back of the van. "Can you hold that door open for me?"

Michael propped the door open with a foot, and the delivery man hurried back inside with two floral stands.

"Who died?" the man asked. "A governor or something?"

"A teenage girl," Michael said, closing the door. He stared at the multiple rows of flowers and plants lined up against the walls, their nauseatingly sweet fragrance nearly palpable. Many of them had Savoy's Florist salutation cards attached to them.

"Yeah? She a local?"

"From out of town."

The man placed the stands near a large wreath of white carnations that had OUR SYMPATHY written on a wide red ribbon across its middle. "Well, whoever she is, her family must sure have the bucks 'cause Lee's and two other shops've been deliverin' here pretty steady." He swiped his forehead with an arm and hustled out the side door again.

Michael picked up the floral stands and was heading for the viewing rooms when Chad burst out of the men's bathroom, his hand still on his fly.

"Can you believe it?" Chad said nearly running into Michael. His eyes looked the size of salad plates. "There's gotta be a thousand people outside!"

"I don't know about a thousand, but it's a hell of a group, that's for sure. Everything ready?"

Chad nodded while buttoning his suit coat. "I just finished cosmetizing."

Michael started down the hall again, and Chad quickly fell into step.

"Where's Sally?" Michael asked.

"In the viewing room, setting up flowers."

"We're going to need extra help—"

"I already called Mr. Mason. He's on standby."

Michael glanced over at him. "You already called Richard?"

Chad's eyes grew wider. "Shouldn't I have?"

"No . . . I mean, yes, you should have," Michael said, impressed by Chad's efficiency. "Good job."

Richard Mason was a semi-retired funeral director whose help was an occasional blessing and a frequent curse. From the old school, Richard used embalming techniques that turned bodies into concrete statues. He also pasted enough makeup on a corpse to make a whore blush. Michael only called on him when absolutely necessary, and this service promised to accurately define necessity. Even with Richard's help, Michael still worried about how they would manage a crowd of this size.

"Well it's about time," Sally said as she stormed out of viewing room A and spotted the two men.

Michael lifted the flower stands. "Reinforcements are here."

Sally scowled, and Michael read, *Where the hell have you been?* in her eyes, but she said, "I've got the front doors locked for now, but I need somebody to stand guard until we're done setting up. Some weird old lady's already snuck in here twice."

"Was it the girl's mother?" Michael asked, following her into the viewing room.

"How the hell should I know?" Sally plopped a fist on her hip. "I tried asking her, but she talked so funny I couldn't understand a doggone word she said. And it wasn't like anybody *else* was around to help me figure her out."

Blowing off Sally's snippy mood, Michael surveyed the room. "You did a great job in here, Sal." The accolade was said more in truth than to appease her frustration. She really had done a terrific job. The retractable wall that normally separated the fifty-by-forty-foot room into two smaller rooms had been opened, and wooden folding chairs with tan leather cushions filled the wide space in tight, neat rows. The casket sat on an oak bier at the front of the room with a kneeler placed along its right side. Behind the casket hung a two-foot crucifix with a thick, mauve curtain serving as its backdrop. Flowers and plants of every shape and size stood in vases, pots, or on easels four rows deep along either side of the casket and extended down the length of the room along both walls.

"What'd you expect?" Sally snapped. "I always do a good job." She let out a little harrumph, then turned on her heels and left.

Michael shook his head and placed the floral stands he'd been carrying beside a parade of wreaths. He signaled to Chad. "Let's see how you did with the body." He heard his apprentice draw short, nervous breaths as they neared the coffin.

The girl's heart-shaped face was flawless and framed by long black hair. Thick, dark lashes lay against skin almost golden in color, and her lips, which had been shaded with the slightest bit of lipstick, were full and supple to the eye. She wore a white silk blouse scooped low at the neck and an ankle-length skirt to match. White satin slippers with intricate embroidery covered her feet. The overall effect against the royal blue velvet interior of the casket was breathtaking.

"Any problems with the removal at Riverwest last night?" Michael asked.

"Not really. Had some big guy follow me here from the hospital, though. He didn't speak English that well, but I got the impression he was acting like a bodyguard or something. I had a little problem getting him to sign the release forms so he could go into the prep room, but once we got past that, the guy was a kitten. Just hung out in the back and watched me. He left about twenty minutes ago."

Michael nodded. "What about the incision? You use

the femoral?" He moved the girl's hair away from the right side of her face and neck. No sign of sutures.

"Yeah," Chad said, polishing a smudge off the bronze casket with his jacket sleeve. "There's no way I could've hidden a carotid with those clothes."

"Excellent work, Chad." Michael straightened the girl's hair, then closed the bottom half of the casket, leaving her exposed only from the waist up. "You're going to make a great funeral dir—"

"But, ma'am!" Sally's voice boomed from the hallway.

A woman, who looked to be in her eighties, appeared in the doorway, a small brass bowl balanced in one hand. She wore a white blouse with long, puffy sleeves and a cardinal red, ankle-length skirt embroidered with small black and gold squares. A bright red kerchief was tied tightly about her head like a skullcap. It accented a face drawn and wrinkled and a nose and brow splotched with scabs. Her back was bowed, her walk slow and deliberate as she made her way across the room.

Sally followed her and mouthed to Michael when she passed him, "I tried to stop her!"

The old woman waved a gnarled hand. "All move. I am grandmother." She dipped her fingers into the brass bowl and flicked what Michael hoped was water into the air.

He signaled for Chad and Sally to leave, which they did, quickly.

"We're not quite finished here, but you're welcome to stay, Mrs. . . . uh—" Michael stepped aside as the woman approached the coffin. "Is it Mrs. Stevenson?"

Ignoring him, the woman placed the bowl on the

kneeler, then gripped the edge of the casket. She spoke softly to the girl in a voice choked with emotion and in a language Michael didn't understand.

He moved away, deciding to leave the woman to her grief and help with the rest of the flowers.

"I am Stevenson," the woman said suddenly. "Lenora." She turned to him slowly. "Now I must see. You open."

Michael looked at her, puzzled.

"You open," she said again, and pointed to the closed portion of the casket.

"Oh." Michael walked around the woman to the foot of the coffin and opened the lid.

Lenora wiped tears from her face. "You are to keep open, yes? Now dress." She pointed to the girl's legs. "Dress. You move dress, yes? I must see."

Michael frowned. "Something's wrong with the dress?"

"You move," Lenora said. She made a hooking motion with a crooked finger. "You move."

"You mean straighten it?" Michael tugged lightly on the hem of the girl's skirt.

Lenora shrieked, "Naught! Naught!"

Michael jerked back in surprise. "What?" he asked.

She glared at him, her face twisted with disgust, then moved her hands over the girl's skirt without touching it. She mimed pulling up the hem.

"You want me to *lift* her skirt?"

Lenora nodded hesitantly.

Michael had heard a lot of strange requests from grieving relatives before, but this one ranked in the top ten. He pulled the skirt up to mid-calf. "Here?"

She held on to the edge of the casket, cocked her head for a closer look inside, then mumbled something that sounded like, "Me aster." She fluttered a hand over the girl's legs. "Me aster," she said louder.

Dreading another outburst, Michael carefully moved the skirt up to the bottom of the knees. He glanced over at Lenora, who nodded, then exhaled slowly.

"Now turn," she said, rolling the word off her tongue. She planted her feet flat on the floor, held out a hand, then moved it so her palm faced him. "Turn."

Perplexed, Michael asked, "Turn the dress?"

Lenora stared at him quizzically.

He pinched a fold in the dress. "You want me to turn this?"

With a vigorous shake of her head, Lenora leaned over and slapped the calf of her left leg. "Turn. Turn."

Michael felt like he was trapped in a macabre game of charades. "You want me to turn her leg?" He touched the girl's left leg. "This one?"

Lenora straightened and nodded.

He wanted to ask why but figured it might well turn into a two-hour translation marathon. He leaned over the casket, grasped the left leg, and turned it carefully, keeping a cautious eye on the rest of the body. The head and hands stayed set in their mimic of deep slumber as he pulled the calf into view. In the middle of the calf he saw an odd patch of dark skin that looked like the silhouette of a prehistoric bird.

"Is this what you wanted to see?" Michael asked, studying the strange shape. When he heard no response, he glanced back.

Lenora no longer stood beside him. The brass bowl she'd carried in earlier still sat on the kneeler to his right. Only now it belched skinny tendrils of blue smoke that smelled faintly of burning flesh.

Chapter Seven

"There ain't no way we're going to be able to keep up like this," Bertha Lynn said, blowing a strand of gray hair out of her eyes. "Think Theresa would come over and give us a hand?"

Janet clipped a Savoy Florist card to one of the fifteen rose bouquets she'd completed since opening shop. The first indicator that business would *not* be as usual this morning was the cars and trucks parked along every roadside she passed on her way to work. The second was the funeral home parking lot filled to capacity even at that early hour. Janet hadn't had a chance to talk to Michael since Wilson's visit last night, and with Michael leaving the house before she woke this morning, she didn't have a clue about what might be causing the hoopla at the funeral home. Whatever it was had forced her to find backup quickly. Fortunately, Bertha Lynn had been able to get her cousin, Pauline, into the shop to answer the phone, and Janet had talked Laura Trahan, Ellie's sitter, into making deliveries. Even with two more people, Janet still felt like she was swimming against the tide with one arm.

"I doubt it," Janet said, snipping through another bundle of carnations. "She told me yesterday she'd be shopping this morning with Heather, who's supposed to be coming with us to the cabin—which we'll probably have to cancel anyway—then she had a carpet cleaning service coming over to do her rugs. Theresa wouldn't be much help anyway. All she knows to do with flowers is smell them."

"We're not going to the fair?" Ellie asked. She sat on a stool beside Bertha Lynn, holding a block of green Styrofoam and discarded stems and stalks. Her expression went from one of idle contentment to shock.

"Honey, I don't see how we can," Janet said. "With all those people at the funeral home, I'm sure Daddy won't be able to get away. And I can't leave Miss Bertha Lynn to handle all this by herself."

Ellie's lower lip trembled. "But, Mama—"

Bertha Lynn tsked. "Don't you worry, baby girl. We'll figure out a way for ya'll to go."

Ellie gave Janet a doleful look.

"Even if we get someone to cover for me here, Bertha, I'm sure there's no way Michael's going to be able to get away."

"Then go on up there just you and the girls," Bertha Lynn said. "You know he'll drive out there to meet you as soon as he's done."

"Driving up there alone with the girls is one thing, leaving you alone with this mess is another."

"Oh, good Lord, I've handled a lot worse than an overload of plants," Bertha Lynn said. "I'll call the women I play pinochle with on Tuesday nights. I bet they'll be glad to have something to do. Lydia does a decent job with her own flowerbed at home, and Flo can do miracles with ribbon. Gina can't do much but gripe about her rheumatism, but we'll keep her busy doing something. And with Laura running deliveries, there ya go, we're all set."

"Yeah, we're all set!" Ellie clapped.

Janet sighed. "Don't get too excited, honey. Even if we can get the extra help, I've still got to talk to Dad and see what he thinks."

"Daddy'll want us to go for sure!" Ellie proclaimed. "And me and Heather'll be really good for—"

"I know I promised to do this, Ms. Janet," Laura Trahan announced, storming into the workroom, "but I can't go back to the funeral home." Her eyes filled with tears, and she dropped the van keys on the worktable. "All those weird people over there, it freaks me out."

Stunned at the outburst, Janet fumbled with her shears. "What happened? Did someone do something to you?"

"N-no."

"Then what's the problem?" Bertha Lynn asked. "They're only people for heaven's sake. Just because there's a lot of 'em don't mean nothing."

"Yeah, but it's not just that," Laura said. She chewed on her bottom lip for a few seconds, then added, "When I went inside the funeral home the last time—I don't know—I got the creeps bad, like there was a ghost hiding in there or something. I just can't go back, Ms. Janet. I can't."

Janet stared at the eighteen-year-old's long, pale face and felt her shoulders droop.

"Child, that's nonsense," Bertha Lynn said, trimming

the bottom of a lemon leaf. Sweat dripped down the sides of her chubby face. "There's no such thing as ghosts."

"Casper's a ghost," Ellie said, reaching for another block of Styrofoam. She stuck a eucalyptus branch into it.

"But he's only make believe, sugar," Bertha Lynn said.

While Ellie chattered away about Casper's ability to hide in vacuum cleaners, which, in Ellie's opinion, certified him as an authentic ghost because make believe spirits wore sheets that would have clogged up vacuums, Janet took a deep breath, worrying about what to do next. Another vanload of wreaths and plants sat waiting near the front of the workroom, and the long worktable at which they sat was covered with materials for more orders. Carnations, day lilies, roses, chrysanthemums, lemon and huckleberry leaves, gerbera, daisies, baby's breath, all in color ranges so vast it boggled the mind. How could she possibly finish the orders they had now *and* deliver them?

"Can you at least make one more run?" Janet asked. "I could call the funeral home and see if Chad's available to help unload the van. I'm sure he'd carry the orders inside so you wouldn't have to go in."

Laura shook her head adamantly. "I'll watch Ellie like always, Ms. Janet, if you want to make the deliveries yourself. But I don't wanna go back there. I'm too scared."

"Lord, child, you're being silly with this ghost stuff. You need to stop that nonsense before it puts ideas in that baby's head that she'll start believin'," Bertha Lynn said, indicating Ellie.

"But I already know there's a ghost over there," Ellie

said. "I saw her." She placed a pink carnation alongside the eucalyptus branch and smiled at her artwork.

Janet's fingertips grew cold as she recalled all too vividly the trepidation she'd felt while walking through the funeral home yesterday.

"See?" Laura said.

Bertha Lynn scowled at Laura. "Stop that."

"What did you see, honey?" Janet asked Ellie.

"The ghost." Ellie placed her Styrofoam masterpiece on the table, then grabbed a piece of yellow ribbon, which she draped around the eucalyptus. "This morning when we was passing in front of where Daddy works, I saw her walking around and around outside in a pretty white dress." Ellie clasped her hands together, then threw them apart. "Then she went poof, like that, right in the wall, just like Casper does. I guess she wanted to go inside but the door was locked."

With her heart knocking painfully against her rib cage, Janet glanced over at Bertha Lynn and noticed the rose stem in the woman's hand trembling slightly. As far-fetched as Ellie's story sounded, her words held an eerie ring of innocence and truth.

"Please, Miss Janet," Laura begged. "Just let me stay here."

Bertha Lynn shook her head as though to clear the thoughts conjuring inside. "This is plum silly," she said. "Now, Ellie, why don't you go up front and ask Miss Pauline to give you my purse. It's in the cabinet behind the front counter, and I think there's a stick of Juicy Fruit in it callin' your name."

Ellie looked at her mother hopefully, and when Janet nodded her approval, she hopped from her stool and skipped off for the front of the shop.

As soon as Ellie disappeared from the workroom, Bertha Lynn said to Laura, "You see what happens when you feed that baby such nonsense? Her imagination done took off, and it's only making yours worse!"

"But it wasn't my imagination, Miss Bertha Lynn," Laura said. "You heard what Ellie said. I swear I felt—"

"Child, I don't want to hear no more rubbish about that!"

"Arguing about this isn't going to solve our problem," Janet said, getting up from her stool. "If Laura won't go back, I'll have to make the deliveries myself—somehow." She carried the finished rose arrangement to the front of the workroom, placed it beside the other completed orders, and eyed the growing pile. White geraniums—ghosts in white—white-hot dread bubbling in the center of Janet's chest. What *had* Ellie seen? And what *was* going on at the funeral home?

"Seth's in from offshore, and I can ask him to come over," Laura offered. "He's helping Dad clean out the garage this morning, but I know he won't mind delivering when he's done. He'd probably even use his one-ton and covered trailer. That way he can haul more in a load. At least you wouldn't have to worry about him wigging out on you or anything because nothing freaks my brother out."

"Good. Call him then," Bertha Lynn said, then turned to Janet. "I'll phone my girlfriends and get them over. Laura can keep Ellie company while you make a delivery or two, then Seth can take over deliverin' when he gets here. That way everything's covered and you and the girls can go like we talked about. Sound good?"

Janet hoisted two sympathy wreaths up by their

stands, intending to load them in the van. "I guess so," she said hesitantly. Although there were a lot of maybes associated with gathering the extra help, Janet felt confident Bertha Lynn would pull it off. What she wasn't so confident about, however, was going back to the funeral home. Seth might not have issues with "wigging out," but for her, it was a possibility.

Chapter Eight

Anna allowed Antony to help her from the car. He cupped her elbow gently, tending to her as one would to something fragile, something bound to be broken. *You're too late,* she thought, wishing she had the strength to say it out loud. Her legs moved mechanically as he steered her closer to the building. She looked down at her shuffling feet, wondering when she'd changed her shoes.

A crowd of people parted as they neared the entrance. Some cried, others whispered. Anna wanted them all to go away.

Antony stopped moving. Anna peered up and saw Ephraim holding one of the large wooden doors open, waiting for her. Once again, Antony tugged gently on her arm, but this time Anna held fast to where she stood. If she walked through those doors and stepped onto that wine-colored carpet, forever would begin. She would see the face of her beautiful Thalia for the last time.

Ephraim signaled for someone to hold the door open and went to Anna.

"You will enter," he whispered, taking Antony's place at her elbow. "Out of respect, our people wait for you. You will be strong and enter."

Anna tried to remove her arm from his grasp, but he held tighter. *I don't have to be strong!* she longed to scream at him. *I don't have to be anything anymore. Don't you understand? There's nothing that means anything anymore. Not you, not me, not anything!* But all that came out of her mouth was a soft moan. She hated the world and its nerve to exist while she felt such pain. She hated that people still smiled and talked and thought about tomorrow. The world should stop. It should all stop.

"Come," Ephraim said, his voice a bit gentler. "I will be by your side." He pressed a hand to the small of her back and urged her forward. "Come."

Forever begins. Anna dropped her head and allowed the momentum of Ephraim's body to carry her. *Forever begins.*

Cool air enveloped her as they entered the building, and Anna shivered until her teeth chattered. A tall, wide-shouldered man in a dark suit greeted them. She studied the ruler-straight part in his thick, blond hair.

"Mrs. Stevenson, my name is Michael Savoy," he said, and extended a hand. When she didn't take it, he lowered his hand to his side. "I'm so sorry for your loss. Please let us know if there's anything we can do for you while you're here."

Anna looked into his blue-green eyes and saw compassion. She said nothing.

A white-haired woman dressed in black appeared

by Michael's side, and he said, "This is Sally Mouton, our hostess. She'll be glad to attend to whatever needs you might have."

Sally pointed to a wide desk in the north corner of the reception area. "I'll be right over there. Just let me know if you need anything." Anna sensed more nervousness than sympathy in the thin woman.

"If you're ready . . ." Michael motioned with a hand to a large set of accordion doors ahead.

"No," Anna pulled away from Ephraim. She wasn't ready for forever yet. "Water," she said. "I would like water please."

"Now is not the time for this, Anna," Ephraim said sternly. "There is much food and drink to come. First, we are to see our daughter."

Anna ignored him and looked at Michael. "I would like water please," she repeated.

"Anna—"

"I can get some for her," Sally said quickly, then turned to walk away.

"No," Anna said. "I would like to get my own water, please. Where do I find it?"

Sally peered up at Ephraim, then at Michael.

"We have coffee and bottled water in the lounge," Michael said. "Or if you'd prefer, there's cold water in the fountain down the next hall."

A telephone on the desk rang, and Sally said quietly, "Excuse me," then hurried away to answer it.

"Yes, cold water in the fountain, please," Anna said.

Michael smiled. "I'll show you where it is."

Anna ignored Ephraim's scowl and followed Michael.

He led her through the reception area, then down

the hall past the accordion doors and into another corridor filled with flowers. Anna walked slowly, surveying the different pictures on the walls. Churches, landscapes, old people in old clothes. She spotted a young man in a black suit hurrying toward them with a potted plant in each hand.

"Mrs. Stevenson," Michael said as the young man approached. "This is Chad Thibodeaux, my apprentice. He will be available to you while you're here, as well."

Chad grinned. "Nice to meet you, ma'am."

Anna gave Chad a slight nod, then noticed the drinking fountain a few feet ahead. She turned to Michael. "I see the cold water from here. Please, I would like to go alone."

"Of course."

Anna waited until Michael and Chad had turned the corner of the intersecting hallway before going to the drinking fountain. She pressed the metal bar along the front of the fountain, and a narrow stream of water arched from the spout. Anna lowered her head to drinking level but instead of allowing the stream into her mouth, she watched it, wishing she could disappear with the water into the multi-holed drain. She didn't want to be here. Not in this place. Not on this earth.

The sound of a door clanking shut caught Anna's attention. She glanced over to her right and saw a slim, dark-haired woman in a blue summer dress, standing just inside a doorway. She held floral wreaths in each hand and a surprised look on her face.

Anna released the metal bar.

"Hello," the woman said. "I'm . . . I'm here with a delivery."

Anna stared at her.

Worry lines creased the woman's brow for a moment, then she quickly followed the lineup of flowers to a nest of wreaths farther down the hall. She placed the ones she carried among the group, then hesitantly turned back around. A look of determination crossed her face, and she headed directly for Anna. The woman extended her hand when she reached her. "My name's Janet Savoy," she said.

For reasons Anna didn't understand, she immediately clasped the woman's hand. "I am Anna Stevenson," she said, her voice sounding like a bare whisper to her ears. She held on to Janet's hand, shaking it gently, feeling the warmth of her palm—and something else.

"You have a loved one here?" Janet asked quietly.

Anna's eyes immediately welled up with tears. "My . . . my daughter."

Janet's hand squeezed harder around Anna's, and her face crumpled with sorrow. "Oh—I can't—you must—oh, I'm so sorry." She touched Anna's shoulder with her free hand.

Brushing her tears away, Anna nodded and stared into Janet's large hazel eyes. Although she'd never met the woman before, Anna felt a strange connection to her. To something inside her.

"You have a daughter, no? One that is very young?" Anna asked.

Looking perplexed, Janet took a small step back. "Yes . . . but how did you know?"

Suddenly feeling a rush of emotion akin to panic, Anna quickly covered Janet's hand with both of hers. "Watch over her closely. Your—"

"Anna."

Ephraim's loud voice startled Anna, and she quickly released Janet's hand. She turned to face her husband.

He stood only a foot away, his lips set in a thin hard line, his eyes narrowed. "You must come *now,*" he demanded.

Anna looked back and sought Janet's eyes for a moment, hoping to somehow relay the message she felt so strongly. *Your daughter may be in danger. From what I am not sure. But it carries the potential for death.*

The worry lines on Janet's forehead grew deeper, but Anna saw no understanding in her eyes, only confusion.

Reluctantly, Anna turned back to Ephraim, who took her arm and led her back toward the front of the building. Before they turned the corner of the back hall, Anna glanced over her shoulder and saw Janet still standing where she'd left her.

Ephraim tugged Anna along faster. "Our people suffer, waiting outside in the heat while you waste time speaking with the Gaji. Have you no dignity? Must I remind you of your responsibility here?"

Anna refused to answer him, and her silence caused him to tighten his grip on her arm.

They soon reached the set of accordion doors, where Michael stood waiting. Ephraim gave him a nod, and Michael undid a clasp set in the middle of the doors, then opened them.

A sharp pain struck Anna in the chest, and she struggled to breathe as Ephraim urged her past the doors. A soft *click* testified to the doors being shut behind them.

Anna saw flowers, more numerous and colorful than a hundred gardens combined. Amidst their sickeningly sweet aroma, she caught an odd, musky scent that told her Lenora had already been here.

Ephraim's steps faltered as he moved her farther into the room, then to the left. Anna quickly looked down at her feet. She didn't want to see any more. She wasn't ready for forever. Ephraim's right hand, still clasping her arm, squeezed and relaxed, squeezed and relaxed as though to keep time with the soft music drifting down from the ceiling.

Suddenly, she heard Ephraim choke back a sob. "Thalia—my—my little Thalia," he cried. He let go of Anna's arm, and from the corner of her eye, she watched him lurch to the front of the room. Her legs threatened to buckle, and she collapsed onto the nearest chair, keeping her eyes trained to the floor.

Deep, hoarse laments filled the air, pulling reality from the corners of Anna's mind to its center, forcing her to look up. Ephraim was on his knees in front of a shiny casket, his hands clasped together along its edge. As he lowered his head, Anna saw Thalia's face. Soft—gentle—and still.

At that moment, something inside Anna burst, and she sprang to her feet and wailed, "Thaaaalia!" She stumbled forward, shoving past chairs, her chest heaving with sobs, her body racked with tremors.

When she reached the casket, Anna fell at Ephraim's feet and clawed at his clothes. "Nooo!" she cried. He grabbed her hands and held them tight. She fought to free herself. "Nooo! My baby! My baby!"

Ephraim's grip tightened. "Anna."

The sound of her name froze her next cry. Anna peered up, focusing on the face in front of her, the hands that restrained her.

"Anna, please," Ephraim said. His face sharpened and cleared before her.

She drew in a shuddering breath, then yanked her hands free of his, stood up, and leaned over the casket.

"No, Anna!" Ephraim said, struggling to his feet. "You know we are not to touch the dead once they are prepared!"

So beautiful, Anna thought, gazing at her daughter's face. She watched Thalia's eyelids closely and ached to see them flutter and open. She reached out to touch her daughter's cheek, but Ephraim grabbed her hand.

"No," he said, breathing hard.

Anna raked his wrist with the fingernails of her free hand, drawing blood. "Leave me," she demanded.

A look of defeat fell over Ephraim's face, and he backed away as Anna cupped Thalia's face in her hands. Her skin felt cold and hard to the touch, smooth like a piece of fine furniture. Anna leaned over farther and kissed Thalia's cheek. Forever had begun.

Chapter Nine

Janet stretched out sideways on Theresa's bed and propped her head up with a hand. "So what would you do?" she asked her sister.

Theresa shoved another pair of jeans into a small suitcase. "Probably commit myself to the nearest psych ward."

"I already thought of that. No vacancies."

Theresa threw a pair of socks at her. "Seriously? I don't think there's much you can do. He's Michael's father, not yours. All you can do is be supportive. Michael's got to take the lead on this one."

Janet rolled over on her back. "I guess. But Wilson's here, what, one day? And Michael's already up to his armpits in alligators. You should have heard him on the phone when I called the funeral home to talk to him about going to Carlton. He sounded like a decrepit old man running on his last leg. I'm worried about him."

"Maybe so, sis, but I don't think you can blame that

all on Wilson. It's not his fault Michael wound up with that big service. I'd probably sound decrepit, too, if I had all those people swarming my place."

"I don't think it's just about the crowd. I mean, Michael and I haven't had a chance to really talk since Wilson came over to the house last night, but I've got a feeling something happened while he was there."

"Did Wilson give ya'll any idea why he came back now? Or hell, why he left in the first place?"

"Not that I know of. He didn't say anything in front of me. I'd bet rocks to rats, though, it has something to do with money."

"You think?"

"Yep."

Theresa shook her head thoughtfully and pulled a silver clasp out of the back pocket of her shorts. "You know, it's too bad Michael's an only child," she said, clipping her long hair back into a ponytail. "At least with a brother or sister around, he could kind of spread some of the Wilson load around."

"Nah, it'd be worse." Janet sat up. "Then Michael would worry about the brother or sister, too."

"That's true."

"It's pathetic. Nobody should have to put up with some of the stuff Michael's had to deal with—especially from a father."

"I don't think there're many people who get by without dad issues," Theresa said. "Ours wasn't exactly Saint Peter."

"But Dad was boring, not manipulative and greedy."

"Maybe. Guess it's all perspective." Theresa zipped up the suitcase and lugged it over to the bed. "All done. This should hold Heather for a couple of days."

Janet cocked an eyebrow. "Couple of days? You've got enough clothes in there for four weeks."

"You'll be in the woods. She'll get dirty."

"You're such a hen."

"Cluck, cluck." Theresa grinned and sat on the edge of the bed. "You sure you want to head out there alone with the girls? Wouldn't you rather wait to leave with Michael?"

Janet leaned over and stretched, not so much to get the kinks out of her back as to delay answering her sister's question. Michael hadn't been all that thrilled about her driving to Carlton alone with Ellie and Heather when she'd talked to him about it earlier. But she'd convinced him, shamelessly using Ellie's anxiety about possibly missing the fair. After her strange encounter with Anna Stevenson, Janet decided that no matter how much she disliked staying at the cabin, they were going, with or without Michael. Anna's strange warning might have been prompted by the grief of losing her own daughter, but it played in harmony much too well with the trepidation Janet had been carrying around for the last two days. Fortunately, Bertha Lynn had been able to collect her crew of pinochle cronies to cover the shop, and Laura's brother, Seth, had been more than happy to earn a few dollars making flower deliveries.

"It'll be all right," Janet finally answered. "Besides, if we wait for Michael we wouldn't be able to leave until tomorrow, and even then, he wasn't sure what time he'd be able to take off."

"Why? Is it a two-day service?"

"Just one. But he said the family wanted to do the entombment at dusk today, so it'll be late when they finish. Then there'll be cleanup, preps for the next day, not counting if he gets any other calls."

Theresa scowled. "That man works too hard, girl. It makes me tired just thinking about all the stuff he puts up with."

"Me, too." Janet leaned over and rested her arms on her knees. "That's another reason why I'm leaving today. I don't want him worrying about getting us to the cabin. He's got enough on his mind. Summer Fest starts tomorrow morning, and I know he wouldn't want Ellie to miss it. There'll be plenty to keep the girls occupied until he gets there."

As though on cue, the sound of small running feet and squeals of laughter rumbled down the hall, and Ellie and Heather burst into the room at full tilt.

Six-year-old Heather waved a yellow nightgown over her head like a victory flag. "Look, Aunt Janet, Mama said I could bring my new 'jamas!" She proudly stretched the gown out in front of her, revealing a large picture of Barbie on the front.

"Gorgeous," Janet exclaimed.

"Now we can be twins," Ellie declared. "All except mine's blue."

Heather nodded in agreement and handed the nightgown to her mother. Giggling, the two girls linked arms and skipped back out of the room.

"No more clothes," Theresa called after them, then said to Janet, "Jesus, if I try to fit one more thing into her suitcase, it'll pop."

"Mm," Janet said.

Theresa hunched over to match her sister's posture and stared at Janet.

"What?" Janet asked.

Theresa tapped a finger between Janet's eyes. "Your divots are showing."

"My what?"

"Ever since you were little, when something really bothered you, your divots showed up." She traced a short vertical line between Janet's eyes with a finger. "There. Two deep lines."

"Gee, thanks. What are you going to let me in on next? That my ass cheeks twirl when I sneeze? How come you never told me about these divot things before?"

Theresa shrugged. "Guess it's just one of those things that're there, but you never pay much attention to, like a wart."

"Warts, huh?"

"Okay, so bad analogy. But I do know the more you worry, the deeper those divots get. Right now, they look like dry riverbeds."

Janet rubbed briskly between her eyes. "Great."

"If it's any consolation, they usually go away after you've talked through whatever's bothering you. They're still there, though. So I'm figuring there's more on your mind."

Janet rested a cheek on a fist and looked at her older sister. "When'd you get so smart?"

"The day you were born."

"Yeah?" Janet chuckled.

"So, you going to tell me?"

Dropping her hands between her knees, Janet puffed out her cheeks, then exhaled loudly. "I don't know, T. Just a gut feeling I can't quite put my finger on."

"Like?"

"Like something bad's going to happen."

Theresa frowned. "Then maybe it's best you don't head out to Carlton with the girls."

"I don't think it has anything to do with Carlton. I feel it has to do with something here. Maybe the funeral home. Maybe Wilson. I don't know for sure. It's this . . . you know how the weather gets right before a hurricane? How the sky turns this funky gray-white color, and the air gets too still?"

Theresa nodded.

"That's sort of how I feel inside."

"Well, that's understandable, don't you think? With Wilson back in the picture? He's always been bad news one way or another."

Janet glanced over at the top of the bureau with its lace doily, bottle of Passion perfume, pink keepsake box in the shape of a heart, and a silver frame that held a picture of Theresa; her husband, Mitch; and Heather.

"You're probably right," Janet said after a while.

But it didn't feel right. Not at all. Her internal barometer measured something a hell of a lot bigger than Wilson Savoy. Something much, much bigger.

Chapter Ten

Michael elbowed his way through the people sandwiched together in the lobby of the funeral home, all of them waiting to pay their last respects to the Stevenson girl. Around shoulders and above heads, Michael watched helplessly as Sally and Chad tried to stop Agnes Crowder, his cleaning woman, from barreling her way out of the building.

He couldn't blame Agnes for wanting to leave. It was barely past noon, and the place looked like a disaster area. Hordes of people had rotated through the building all morning, most of them puffing on cigarettes. Some carried in kettles of stew or platters of roasted meat. Rum, tequila, and high-dollar bourbon had been hauled in by the case. Men with hairstyles and clothes more suited for the '70s brought guitars, tambourines, and musical contraptions that resembled large wooden fruit with strings, which they played in drunken harmony.

Control became impossible as the multitude grew.

Everyone Michael spoke to about maximum occupancy laws or no smoking ordinances either couldn't understand him, or could and didn't care.

Michael reached the back hall just as a cornered Agnes shoved a finger in Chad's face.

"You better back yourself up, little man, or else!"

"But you can't leave," Chad said desperately.

"For heaven's sake, Agnes, all you have to do is pick up the trash," Sally said. "It's not like we're asking you to sanitize the place."

The buxom black woman slammed her hands on her hips and glared at Sally. "And who died and made you queen? You best take that smartass mouth and—"

"Don't you talk to me like—"

"That's enough," Michael warned. Fortunately the women's sparring ground was near the embalming room, the one area the Stevenson group seemed to have little interest in exploring.

"She started it," Sally fumed.

Agnes's nostrils flared. "Why you skinny—"

"Stop," Michael demanded. He lowered his voice. "In case you've forgotten, we've got a viewing going on. You want everyone to hear you?"

Agnes glared at him. "It ain't gonna make no difference if they do 'cause not a damn one of them gypsies speaks American anyway."

"Shows what you know," Sally said. "Their name's Stevenson. Gypsies don't have names like that."

"Look here, Miss Thing." Agnes held up a warning finger. "It's you don't know nothin'. They just usin' names like that so nobody turns 'em out. But wait, you gonna see. Juju. That's what they workin' in here, plain and simple. I can feel it."

Chad grimaced. "Really? How—"

Sally huffed. "Agnes, the only black magic going on around here is you trying to disappear from work."

Michael pushed himself between the women just as Agnes's hands curled into fists. "I said enough." He glanced behind him to make sure no one else was close enough to hear, then turned back to his employees. "I don't care if the Stevensons are pygmies from Zimbabwe. We have a job to do."

Agnes folded her arms, tucked them under her huge breasts, and snorted. "Doin' my job don't mean pickin' up no dirty diapers, a mountain of paper plates half-full of food, or no used women's plugs. It's wall-to-wall elbows and butts in here, and not a damn one of 'em knows how to use a trashcan."

"Women's plugs?" Michael asked.

Chad leaned into him and whispered, "Tampons. They found one in the women's bathroom sink. Used, just like she said."

"Jesus." Michael groaned.

"Jesus ain't gonna pick 'em up either," Agnes said with a snap of her head.

Sally matched Agnes's stance. "Michael, you have to get us more help. There're too many—"

"Too many people," Chad finished for her.

"And they's all crazy," Agnes added. "Every last one of 'em out there. You—"

"Wait a minute." Michael held up both hands, wanting time to think. The last thing he needed was a mutiny. "Sally, have Richard man the phones while—"

"He left," Chad said.

"What?"

"Mr. Mason left about a half hour ago." Chad

shrugged. "Said he wasn't being paid enough to deal with this mess."

"Oh, Lord," Sally muttered.

"Smart man," Agnes said with a nod.

"Why didn't you tell me earlier?" Michael asked. "Maybe I could have—"

"Tell you?" Chad shook his head. "I couldn't even find you. I've been doing everything to—"

"Okay, okay, so he's gone," Michael said, rubbing his left temple. "Let's just keep this simple. Chad, you keep an eye out in the viewing room. Make sure they don't trample one another in there. Sally, you answer the phones and give people directions to the bathrooms and lounge. And, Agnes, would you please stay and at least keep a path cleared between the lounge and reception area?"

Agnes eyed him suspiciously. "That's all I gotta do?"

"That's all. We'll worry about the rest when this is over."

She puckered her lips as though considering the task ahead, then said, "Yeah, I guess I can do that. But what you gonna do?"

"Right now? Find aspirin."

Michael headed for his office, making his way past a wall of chattering women in ankle-length, multicolored dresses. All of them were bedecked in heavy gold jewelry and acknowledged him with a cautious eye when he excused himself and sidled by.

By the time Michael finally entered his office, he'd squeezed past so many people it felt like his suit was on backwards. He closed the office door, brushed the twists out of his jacket sleeves and pant legs, then went to his desk.

He sat back in his chair and closed his eyes for a second. *Too much,* he thought. *I should have Dad locked up for ever agreeing to—*

Michael's eyes flew open. He'd been too busy to realize he hadn't seen Wilson around all morning. As frantic as his father had been last night, logic said he should have been sitting on the funeral home steps by five this morning, waiting for an answer about the money.

"They'll kill me, Michael. I swear to God they'll kill me."

Sudden worry fueled Michael's headache to near migraine intensity. He unlocked his desk, pulled open the bottom drawer, and grabbed a bottle of aspirin. Shaking out three, he tossed them into his mouth and chewed the bitter tablets. He thought about the creep at the gas pumps, the one Janet had told him about yesterday. Was he one of Wilson's investors? Had they found his father? Could Wilson *really* be in danger?

Michael considered going out to look for him, but quickly dropped the notion. He couldn't leave with a funeral home full of people and too few employees. Maybe he should call the police and ask them to start a search.

Just then, Michael's office door opened, and Wilson strutted in like a crippled rooster.

"Full house, I see," Wilson said.

Relief and anger swirled through Michael until his hands shook. "Where the hell have you been?"

Wilson's eyebrows peaked into twin steeples. "Why? You missed me?"

"I asked you a question."

"And I asked you one."

Michael gritted his teeth. He wasn't up for an argument. He relocked his desk and stood. "I don't have time for this," he said, and stormed toward the door.

"What?" Wilson reached for Michael's arm as he passed by, but Michael pulled away. "Well I'll be damned," Wilson exclaimed.

Michael whirled around. "For once you've got something right."

Wilson chuckled. "Yeah, maybe, but that's not what I meant. Now hold up, hold up." He stepped in front of the door before Michael could open it. "I'm surprised, that's all."

"Move."

"You were worried about me, weren't you?" Wilson asked. "And that pissed you off."

"Get out of my way."

"You don't have to admit it, but I can tell. Saw it in your eyes when I first walked in."

"That's a load of crap."

"No it's not." Wilson reached out to touch Michael's arm again, but pulled his hand back before they connected. "Not that it's any of your business, but I went to see your Aunt Dora in Metairie this morning. Left early but I got caught on the Pontchartrain coming back. Some delivery truck caught fire. Shut down both lanes for hours."

It took Michael a moment to recollect the face of his father's only sister. The last time he'd seen Aunt Dora was twelve years ago, at his mother's funeral. The polite thing would've been to ask about her welfare, but Michael's anger bypassed the courtesy.

"So what'd you do? Swipe her Social Security check?"

Wilson's face clouded. "No, Michael. She has cancer.

Thought I'd get in one more visit while she was still around."

Michael looked away and shoved his hands in his pockets because he didn't know what else to do with them. He suddenly felt like a jerk. "Sorry," he mumbled. "I didn't know."

"Yeah, well—" Wilson cleared his throat, then jerked a thumb toward the door. "Sure looks like those people are getting their money's worth, huh?" When Michael didn't respond, he shifted from one foot to the other. "Talking about money . . . have you . . . uh . . . have you decided about—"

"I can't do anything about money," Michael said.

"But—"

"If you're really in some kind of danger, I'll go with you to the police. That's all."

Something sparked in Wilson's eyes, and he pounded fist to palm. "The police can't take care of shit, Michael. I've already told you, these people aren't playing around!"

"Neither am I."

"So that's it? That's all you've got to say? You just want me out of the way, don't you? You want me dead."

"Stop being melodramatic. It won't work."

Wilson turned away sharply and scratched the back of his neck. When he faced Michael again, tears pooled against his lower lids. "Look, there's got to be something I can do to—"

"Yes, there is something you can do," Michael said, opening the door. As familiar as he was with his father's antics, he felt his resistance slip. He couldn't get used to the tears. "I've got a building full of people, and we're short staffed. You need to help."

"Sure, sure, but wait," Wilson pleaded. "You can't just leave. Give me another chance, son. That's all I'm asking for. With that money I can set things right again. Pick up the pieces and make things different with this family. Look, see here?" He pointed to the picture of Ellie on the windowsill. "I've got a granddaughter I don't even know. Help me out. Give me a chance to get to know her. We could be a family, Michael. A real family."

At that moment, the frame that held Ellie's picture toppled from the sill to the floor and shattered.

Michael glanced at the web of glass slivers, only mildly curious as to how the fall occurred, since his father hadn't touched the frame, or how a tumble onto carpet could have caused so much damage. He was more interested in the irony of what he saw. Sharp broken pieces, worth nothing more than pain to the one who handled them. A mosaic of his father.

"Just what you wanted, Dad. Pieces to pick up," Michael said, and left.

Chapter Eleven

Anna sat in a folding chair, which someone had placed in the back corner of the viewing room. Maria and Felicia, Antony's sisters, sat next to her, assigned as her guardians for the time being. Antony was the only one Ephraim told about her impious act and that was only because he'd helped Ephraim pull her off Thalia. Everyone else had been charged with keeping her away from the casket. "For her own protection," Ephraim had said.

For hours, Anna had watched people file in and out of the room. Most of the chairs had been removed to allow more space for the crowd. Men sat on the floor cross-legged, talking and laughing while women served them food and drinks. Lenora flitted about, visiting with one person or another and periodically checking for evaporation in her water glass. Lenora maintained the old custom of placing a drinking glass filled with water on a stool at the head of the casket. The meaning of the custom was divided among the tribe. To some the water assured the dead would never thirst. To others it was a method used to ward off evil spirits during the deceased's transference to the other side. To Anna, the stupid water glass meant nothing if it could not resurrect her Thalia. Either way, Lenora had kept busy, making certain the glass remained brim-filled and that her brass bowl, which had been placed alongside the water, plumed continuously with hickory-scented smoke.

Ephraim had spent most of his time drinking and singing old love songs. Occasionally, he'd swagger by, and give Anna a contemptuous sneer. At any other time and in any other place, she might have worried about his scorn. But not today, not anymore.

A sudden shift in activity told Anna they were nearing the end of the service. People started to vacate the room, leaving only those who had been invited to remain. The chosen men stayed seated on the floor in a semicircle while a large group of women lined up against the walls. A mandolin began to play, and Antony, in a trembling, baritone voice, sang "Of Seasons Past" in their native tongue. Anna had to hold on to the seat of her chair to keep from bolting out of the room.

The end had come too fast. Soon she would have to say goodbye to her beloved child, and she wasn't ready. She would never be ready to carry the measure of sorrow that forever meted out. It was all-consuming; so eager to devour her. Anna clutched her hands to her breast and reminded herself that the pain was but for a short time. In a while, none of this would matter.

As Antony's song reached its climax, Roslyn entered the room, carrying a long, unlit white candle. She handed it to Ephraim, who took it and laid it across

Thalia's chest, being careful not to touch the clothes or body with his hand.

"Let there be no darkness in your travels," he said, his voice strong and clear despite the level of alcohol consumption. He nodded to Roslyn, and she took her place against the wall with the rest of the women.

Lenora stepped forward, faced her son, and bowed her head. Loud murmuring echoed from the doorway as people in the hall pressed tightly together, straining to see what was about to take place.

The men sitting on the floor began to chant, "Drosna, drosna," a drunken Roma version of "peace be with you." From their pockets, they drew silver coins and dollar bills, each man forming a little pile with his money in front of him.

Ephraim touched his mother's shoulder, and she turned to face the women against the walls. She lifted both hands, and one by one the women walked to the center of the semicircle and deposited bits of cloth, jewelry, and small sacks of food.

When they were done, Lenora entered the circle, sat back on her haunches, then began sorting through the gifts. She pulled aside anything she considered unfit. When she completed her task, Lenora stood and signaled for Maria and Felicia to bring Anna to her.

Anna clung to her seat, refusing to budge. If she moved, someone would surely see what she had hidden beneath her shoe, and she couldn't let that happen because they'd take it away. It had taken her the longest time to find it, searching through so many pockets, so many purses.

"You must come and bless gifts," Ephraim commanded with a lift of his chin. His eyes blazed with fury. "They will be of no use to her, Anna, if you do not."

Anna sat quietly, feeling every eye in the room rest on her.

Maria pressed her lips to Anna's right ear. "Don't be afraid. I will go with you."

"You come or I will get you myself," Ephraim said, and pushed his fedora farther back on his head.

"Anna, come." Felicia tugged on her arm. "Why you not want to bless Thalia's gifts?"

Anna brushed Felicia's hand away, knowing she'd have to do something before Ephraim physically moved her. Gradually she stood, and the room and every face in it wavered in slow, horizontal lines. Her face felt flushed, and her body swayed. Maria and Felicia grabbed her arms, bracing her upright. Anna heard throats clear as she considered her dilemma.

She couldn't slide her right foot along the floor while she walked because the carpet would snag the tool and keep it from moving with her. And besides, it would look too obvious. With everyone staring at her, she couldn't very well lean over, move her foot and pick it up either. That left only one option.

When Anna felt Maria and Felicia's grasp loosen, she allowed her knees to buckle and collapsed in a heap.

Lenora shouted something incoherent as Anna groped for the object now under her leg. Finding it, she clutched it tight and winced.

Maria and Felicia chattered frantically and pulled Anna to her feet.

"Be careful, Maria," Felicia said, pushing her sister aside. "You will make her fall again."

"You are the one pushing," Maria said, straightening

the kerchief on her head. The heavy gold jewelry around her neck clanged like chimes in a strong wind. "Watch for her hand, the bandaged one." She lowered her voice and pulled on Anna's left arm. "Anna, please. Get up."

"Get to your feet, woman," Ephraim shouted, spittle flying from his lips. "Now!"

Ephraim's condescension seemed to split nerves in Anna's jaw. A peculiar sensation moved across her face, and only when she rose to her feet again did she realize what it was. A smile, growing wider by the second. Anna peered at Maria and Felicia, whose expressions became nothing short of dumbstruck.

"Let go of me," Anna said, and a giggle escaped her.

The women released Anna and backed away like they'd just discovered she carried a contagion. Anna's giggle grew louder, and she bit her bottom lip in an attempt to control herself.

She walked toward Ephraim and saw Lenora lean into him and whisper. Ephraim nodded earnestly, which caused his hat to fall askew over his right eye. The sight of his crooked hat drew a burst of laughter from Anna so loud and long, it made her sides hurt. She stumbled blindly into one of the men sitting on the floor, and he scurried away from her as though bitten. When Anna was able to focus on the confused faces all around her, she stopped, threw her head back, and roared with laughter.

It took several moments for her to start moving again. Her sides and stomach ached terribly, and she began to hiccup. Anna's brain felt useless, fumbling aimlessly to find a reason for her laughter but not finding one. The possibility that she was losing her mind did occur to her, but that thought seemed even funnier than the lopsided hat.

The next thing Anna knew she was standing in front of Ephraim. She blinked, and her husband suddenly doubled over and cupped his groin, his eyes wide with disbelief and anguish. Anna stopped laughing, but a smile remained plastered on her face. A rush of adrenaline gave way to an overwhelming sense of freedom. In the time it had taken Anna to blink, she'd kneed Ephraim—hard. Maybe hard enough to keep him from walking upright again. Maybe not.

If nothing else, it stopped her hiccups.

Chapter Twelve

Large, gravy-laden meatballs established the line between sanity and insanity. Or so it seemed to Michael the moment one flew over his head and landed with a splat across the picture of Saint Peter's Cathedral in the hall. The people milling around him only glanced back at the mess like it was the newest fare in haute cuisine.

"The food's got to go!" Michael said over the rumble of voices. "This is getting way out of—"

A middle-aged woman in a hot pink tent dress let out a shrill, incoherent squawk and spat on Michael's pant leg. The crowd swallowed her into obscurity before he had time to react.

"Michael!" An urgent voice called above the din. One frantically waving arm rose above the landscape of heads near the reception desk. Sally's lopsided bun bobbed beside it.

"Jesus, now what?" Michael grumbled. Trying to ignore the wet stain on his trousers, which looked suspiciously like tobacco juice, he made his way to Sally.

When he reached her, she lifted two fingers, then pointed to the receiver lodged against her ear. "—as soon as possible," she said into the phone. "Yes. Thank you." She hung up and shook her head. "You're not going to believe this," she said to Michael. "We've got two pickups to make at Magnolia."

Michael closed his eyes for a second, feeling another ton drop onto his already overloaded shoulders. "How soon?"

"They want the bodies out in an hour."

"Ask them for a little more—"

"I already tried buying more time, but you know how the aides get when there's a dead body around." Sally picked up a notepad from the desk and ripped off the top sheet. "You want me to send them to Pellerin's?"

"No." The thought of sending business to his shark-toothed, greasy-palmed competitor made Michael cringe. He wouldn't have sent Judas Iscariot to the man. "Where's Chad?"

"In the viewing room, I think. He said something about a kid taking a dump in one of the potted plants or a kid dumped over a potted plant—I don't know, one or the other. He's probably cleaning—" The corners of her mouth dropped abruptly. "Michael, you can't send Chad to Magnolia. We're having a hard enough time handling everything now. One more person short and we'll keel—"

"I'll help."

The sound of Wilson's voice made Michael do a double-take over his shoulder. His father stood behind him, a hand traveling restlessly between chin and shirt collar.

Michael turned and eyed him warily.

"No, really," Wilson said. A smile that seemed to hold old hurts and new hope quivered on his face. "While your apprentice is out making the removals at the nursing home, I'll help out here."

"Thank God," Sally breathed.

Although Michael suspected that his father's prodigious generosity carried an ulterior motive, like changing his son's mind about the money, he needed the extra pair of hands. If Wilson wanted to grabble with false hope, that was his problem.

"All right," Michael said, checking his watch. "We'll be doing last call soon. You can give me a hand with that while Chad's gone. When he gets back from Magnolia—"

A loud wail erupted from the viewing room, and every head whipped in that direction.

"Shit and crackers," Wilson exclaimed. "What the hell was that?"

"Trouble," Sally said, indicating the crowd now shoving as one coagulated mass to get inside the viewing room.

Michael looked at his father.

"Right behind you," Wilson said.

Slightly unnerved by his father's support, Michael wet his lips before charging through the throng.

Wilson literally held to his word, pressing himself against Michael's back as they forged ahead. He shouted, "S'cuse me!" repeatedly until they made it inside.

Just as Michael stepped over the threshold, he saw Ephraim swing a hand across his wife's face. The slap rang loud and sharp, and Ephraim immediately drew his hand back, preparing for another strike.

"No!" Without thinking, Michael leaped forward, but before he could reach Ephraim, a thick, hairy arm clotheslined him in the gut. Michael dropped to his knees with a groan, and the bitter ring of another slap echoed overhead.

Ephraim shouted in a strange language, and someone promptly helped Michael to his feet. Breathing hard, Michael found his footing and fisted his hands. Ephraim glared at him, then without a word, turned away and trudged toward the casket.

Two crying women led Ephraim's wife to the back of the room. Angry welts blazed across Anna's cheeks, but her eyes remained dry, her expression eerily detached.

Michael's fists tightened until fingernails cut into his palm. The pain was the only way he could stop himself from running after Ephraim and drop-kicking the sonofabitch.

"I must apologize for Polamu," Antony said, suddenly appearing beside Michael. He pointed the knob of his chin toward the Titan-sized man pacing Ephraim. "His job is but to protect. Are you damaged?"

"I'll live," Michael snapped.

Antony sighed. "This is good. But you must not interfere again, Mr. Savoy. My cousin Ephraim, as leader, does what he must to preserve order."

"Order?" Michael glowered at him. "He hit his wife, for God's sake!"

"You would not understand," Antony said.

"What's there to understand?"

"Yeah, what the hell?" Wilson asked, emerging from some remote corner.

Antony shook his head slowly as one would to enthusiastic, but ignorant children. "The ways of our people are far too complex to explain to Gaji."

Wilson aimed a finger at Antony. "Who you calling Gaji, boy?" He threw Michael a puzzled look. "What's a Gaji?"

Michael ignored his father and folded his arms across his chest. "Listen, Antony, here's something that isn't difficult to explain at all. If he touches her again, I'm calling the police."

"That would not be wise."

"Regardless. I *will* call them. That's a promise."

Antony studied Michael for a long moment, then squared his shoulders. "We complete ceremony now."

Sensing a silent victory, Michael raked his fingers through his hair. "Fine. I'll announce last call."

"What is this last call? Its purpose?"

"To allow everyone a final moment with the deceased. Then we close the casket and head for the cemetery."

"Yes, we make last call then," Antony said.

Wilson stepped in front of Michael and hitched up his belt, a preamble for assuming control. "Okay, then everyone needs to line up—"

"No, no," Antony said. "*We* make last call."

"Fine," Wilson said, throwing up a hand. "Have at it."

"Wait a minute," Michael said, remembering the caution each visitor had used when approaching the casket. Not one of them wanted to touch Thalia. Not even her clothes. "Are you saying you want to handle all the final preparations?" Michael asked. "Lower her head? Straighten her clothes? Close the casket?"

With a visible shiver, Antony shook his head. "No. We will need you for those tasks because we are not allowed to do such things. But for now, you may stand over there." He indicated the opposite side of the room.

Wilson snorted, an implication that he was about to tell Antony exactly who had the right to stand where. Before he could, Michael grabbed his arm and pulled Wilson away. There had been enough upheaval for one day. It was time to send the Barnum and Bailey show on its way.

After settling his father against the far wall, Michael spotted Chad twenty feet away. The apprentice stood gray-faced and half-hidden behind a short, lumpish woman. When Michael caught his attention, he mouthed for him to find Sally, confident she would tell Chad about the nursing home removals.

Chad nodded and hurried toward freedom.

Exhausted, Michael leaned back and closed his eyes, only to have them pried open by the high-pitched whine of a harmonica. He couldn't locate the off-key musician, but there was no missing Lenora. She stood center stage amid a circle of men. The brass bowl she carried belched thick, acrid smoke. The smell reminded Michael of burning tires.

Wilson gagged beside him. "Damn. Smells like shit," he muttered.

"Mia lona, mia rhine. Mia lona, mia rhine," Lenora chanted, her body now swaying from side to side.

The men in the circle clapped, keeping time with her words. Their bodies rocked to match Lenora's rhythmic movements. With eyes closed and mouths slightly open, they appeared closer to an orgasm than the end of a wake.

Michael peered over at Anna, who stared at the floor, seemingly oblivious to the activities. As though she sensed being watched, Anna pulled the kerchief tied to her head down low, covering her long, black widow's peak.

Wilson nudged Michael, drawing his attention back to the center of the room. The chanting grew louder, and the swaying of pensive bodies more urgent. Ephraim, who stood in front of the casket, held two small, copper pots. He faced the circle of men and slammed the pots together three times. The clanging set Michael's teeth on edge.

"We call all spirits dark and light," Ephraim shouted over Lenora's mantra. "You will make way for this child as I command."

A cool breeze caressed Michael's face, and the hair on the back of his neck stood at attention.

The chanting ceased abruptly, and the group of men on the floor gathered their individual piles of money and stood. Lenora walked past them and carried her bowl to the stool at the head of the casket. She waited there while the men lined up single file.

"Come," Ephraim commanded, and the first man limped toward him with his money cupped in his hands. When he reached Ephraim, he gave a little bow, then dropped the coins and bills inside the casket. Ephraim nodded his approval and clapped the man on the back before he hobbled away.

One after the other, men placed money inside Thalia's casket. Silver dollars rested against her skirt.

Ten, twenty, fifty-dollar bills lay over her arms, nestled against her cheek. Michael felt his father tensing up beside him, heard him breathing faster as each new bill fluttered to rest.

After the last man had deposited his gift, Lenora left her post and gathered up the jewelry, cloth, and food offerings she'd weeded through earlier. She placed them at Thalia's feet, then turned to the throng clogging the entrance to the room and raised an index finger.

The anxious crowd parted, and a toothless, elderly man dressed in an expensive black suit entered. His wan face looked like old china mapped with age lines, and the sparse, white hair on his head was slicked back. His hands were cupped around a crumpled purple handkerchief, which he carried to Ephraim.

The transference of the cloth from one man's hand to the other seemed to act as a signal that everyone except Michael and Wilson understood. The men still standing in the center of the room hustled toward the back wall as though expecting an explosion.

Michael shifted nervously from foot to foot while the black-suited man joined the group at the back of the room.

Silence ensued.

A couple of restless minutes later, Lenora signaled for Antony, and the two began to peel open the handkerchief in Ephraim's palm.

Tension mounted as everyone waited for the completion of the unveiling. Curious, Michael stood on the balls of his feet to get a glimpse of what was inside but could only make out more purple fabric. He dropped back on his heels and glanced at his father. Sweat lined Wilson's upper lip, and his eyes sparkled with anticipation as they darted between Ephraim and the handkerchief. Suddenly, his mouth dropped open as though his jaw had disintegrated, and he wheezed.

Puzzled, Michael looked up and saw Ephraim holding up a large gold ring. Attached to the prongs of the ring was a bright gold coin or medallion. Ephraim pinched the edges of the medallion between two fingers and with a loud grunt, twisted it off the prongs. He handed the naked ring to the elderly man, then held up the golden medallion like a consecrated host. Its brilliance appeared to intensify second by passing second until it shone like the noon sun. The sound of weeping and sniffing traveled around the room as Ephraim lifted it high over his head.

A tinkling noise soon melded with the assonance of sorrow, and all eyes flickered toward Anna, who held a small music box on her lap. The tune coming from it sounded to Michael like the old lullaby, "Hush, little baby, don't say a word—"

Lenora clapped her hands, and everyone's attention immediately returned to Ephraim.

"Beware all spirits dark and light," Ephraim said fiercely. He circled the coin over his head and repeated the same cadence, but the words were in another tongue. Perspiration trickled down the sides of his face as he bowed and concluded in English. "This child's passage is paid."

As Ephraim's declaration concluded, voluminous pillows of smoke poured from Lenora's bowl. It drifted over Thalia's body, hovering over her like fog and obscuring the body from view.

Voices quickly rose in unison. *"Mia lona, mia rhine. Mia lona, mia rhine."*

Ephraim snapped his fingers, and the smoke vanished as though sucked away by an unseen vacuum. The voices died when Ephraim pointed to Michael.

"You place this," Ephraim said.

Michael, still perplexed by what he'd just witnessed, didn't move. He saw Ephraim staring at him, but it didn't register that he was being addressed.

With the coin clutched between finger and thumb, Ephraim shook it at Michael. "You place this!"

Michael took an uncertain step forward. "Place it where?"

Ephraim motioned to his daughter's hands.

Michael looked around for Antony in hopes of receiving a clearer translation, but he was nowhere to be seen. "You want that in the casket?" he asked Ephraim.

Ephraim held out his left hand, palm down, and laid the coin on top of it. He then placed his right hand over the coin. "You place this," he said again.

Nodding, Michael stepped up to Ephraim and held out his hand for the coin. Ephraim looked at him long and hard before handing it over.

A chill ran through Michael when he felt the weight of the medallion, the heat of it. It seemed to carry its own energy source. He lifted Thalia's right hand off her left and slid the coin between them.

"It is done," Ephraim said. "We are to pray now." With that, he walked to the back of the room, where he faced the wall and lowered his head. The rest of the congregation followed suit, save for two men, who stopped to turn Anna's chair so she faced the wall, as well.

Michael backed away from the casket. Being more familiar with the Catholics' solemn kneel-and-stand orthodoxy, and even an occasional fundamentalist jump and shout service, he didn't have a clue as to what might be expected of him by this crew.

When in doubt, bow your head.

He did, and just as he closed his eyes, more from exhaustion than prayerful meditation, someone tapped him between the shoulder blades.

"Janet's out back," Sally whispered behind him.

It was the best news Michael had heard all day. He took a step toward the door, then hesitated when he remembered Wilson's trigger finger in Antony's face. "Stay here, will you, Sal?" he whispered back. "Just keep an eye on things. I won't be long."

"Sure, but your father's right over there. Why do you need me?"

"He's what I need you to keep an eye on." Michael peered over at his father, who was pulling on the flap of one nostril. When he caught his eye, Michael mouthed, "Behave," then crept quietly out of the room.

It didn't dawn on Michael until he was halfway down the hall that the corridor was nearly empty. From the trail of debris, which led all the way to the lobby entrance, he guessed most of the visitors had migrated outside. Drawing in a deep, filling breath, he sprinted the rest of the way to the service entrance.

Janet, Ellie, and Heather stood waiting for him just inside the doorway, their smiles a feast for a starving man's eyes.

"Daddy!" Ellie said in a loud whisper. "We're being quiet!"

Michael scooped her up in his arms, then bent over to tousle Heather's hair. He smiled at Janet. "How are my girls? Ready for the trip?"

"Yep," Heather chirped. She gave him a gap-toothed

smile. "Aunt Janet's gonna let us ride the Ferris wheel tomorrow, Uncle Michael."

"Really?"

"Yeah, Daddy," Ellie confirmed. "Two times if we want to. And you know what? They got all kinds of—"

"Cotton candy!" Heather burbled. "They got all kinds of cotton—"

"Whoa, girls," Janet said quietly. "We just came over to say bye, remember?" She tapped Ellie lightly on the chin. "Daddy's busy right now, honey, so big hugs, then we have to leave."

Ellie gave Michael a squeeze around the neck while Heather grabbed hold of his leg and hugged. When they untangled themselves from him, Michael kissed Janet's forehead, then her lips.

"I still don't like the idea of you driving all that way by yourself," he said.

"We'll be fine. Don't worry." Janet gave him a nervous smile, her eyes darting occasionally over his shoulder. "How—how's the mother doing in there?"

Michael shook his head. "Not great. That poor lady's had to put up with a lot of cr—" he threw a glance at Ellie and Heather. "—junk. But I'll fill you in later, when we've got more time to talk."

Janet nodded, her eyes continuing to flick past him.

"You okay?" he asked.

"Yeah, why?"

"I don't know—you seem edgy. Are you sure you'd rather not wait to leave—"

Janet reached up on tiptoe and kissed him. "I'm positive. Now go. We just wanted to say bye before leaving."

"I'll be out there as soon as I can," he said.

"I know. Be careful driving up."

"You, too." Michael rubbed his brow. "I checked the tires and oil a couple of days ago, but you never know what—"

"The car'll be fine, we'll be fine." Janet gave him another quick kiss. "Now stop worrying and go tend to your stuff. I've got a couple of things left to throw in the car, then we'll hit the road. I want to try and make the cabin before dark."

With a flurry of waving hands, Janet and the girls headed out across the parking lot. Michael watched them, his heart aching to follow. One short, one tall; his loves, his life, the two reasons he got up every morning. How lucky could a man get? Reluctantly, he closed the door, and with responsibility weighting his footsteps like lead shoes, he forced himself back to the viewing room.

Inside, the congregation had thinned to a small crowd, which still faced the wall. Anna remained in the same position he'd seen her in earlier, seated and ten feet away from everyone else. There was no sign of Lenora or Ephraim, but more importantly, no sign of Sally or Wilson, either.

Michael stepped back out into the reception area to see if Sally was at her desk, but found it empty. Restroom maybe? Where was his father?

Puzzled, Michael returned to the viewing room and went to the casket. *Just follow procedure and finish the service,* he thought. *If a crisis is going down somewhere, I'll find out about it soon enough.*

After tucking the skirting into the coffin, Michael unlocked the back hinges and closed the lower lid. A fifty-dollar bill fluttered across Thalia's arm. He trapped it between the lining and her shoulder so it wouldn't fly out, then went for the portable crankshaft he'd hidden nearby. Inserting it into a hollow knob at the head of the casket, Michael turned it slowly and watched Thalia's head descend. When she was near supine, he frowned. Something didn't look right.

Michael straightened the pillow, working his hands back along the lining. When most of the wrinkles had been smoothed away, Michael stood back and cast a critical eye. Something still didn't look right. Worse, it didn't *feel* right. But what?

Hair in place—lining straight—pillow smooth—clothes unwrinkled—hands—hands—

Michael felt his testicles suddenly shrink up to his navel. He peered nervously over his shoulder to make sure no one was watching, then turned back and lifted Thalia's right hand.

No coin.

He blinked, and his brain not only confirmed what was missing but reminded him, "*Wilson ain't here, either, bud!*"

No coin.

No Wilson.

The equation added up to disaster.

Chapter Thirteen

Janet stuffed a quart-sized baggie with sliced apples and placed it into a small cooler along with some animal crackers and two bottles of water. After snapping the cooler shut, she tapped a finger against her bottom teeth and ticked through a mental list to make sure she hadn't forgotten anything.

Chicken stew in the fridge for Michael's supper tonight—coffeepot turned off—air conditioner's thermostat turned up to seventy-five—suitcases and extra pillows loaded in the van—two little girls.

She heaved a sigh. Nothing left to keep her busy, which meant open territory for her mind to wander over thoughts of the funeral home and Anna Stevenson. Janet would have never admitted it in front of Laura Trahan, but the girl had been right. Something weird *was* going on at the funeral home. Janet hadn't seen anyone in white walking through walls, but she had felt the oppression. An onerous air of dire expectation much greater than she'd felt the previous day. The cause may have come from the sheer volume of grief emanating from so many people. Or possibly Anna's strange warning. But whatever the origin, Janet wanted to leave it behind. Hopefully, when they returned from Carlton everything would be back to normal.

"Okay, girls," Janet said. "One last bathroom visit before we leave."

Neither Ellie nor Heather replied. They were sitting knee to knee on the floor next to the kitchen table engrossed in the contents of Ellie's fanny pack.

"Earth to girls, hello," Janet said.

"Uh—hello," a man's voice said behind her.

Janet gasped and whirled about. She saw her father-in-law standing just inside the kitchen door.

"Christ!" she said. "Why didn't you knock?"

"Sorry. The—the door was open. I didn't mean to scare you," Wilson said. He scratched the side of his neck, then stumbled forward. As he neared her, Janet noticed that his face was a sickly ash color overlaid with splotches. His eyes were bloodshot and swollen, like he'd just finished a week-long binge.

Immediately thinking him drunk, Janet placed herself between him and the girls.

"Can I use your bathroom?" Wilson asked. "I-I need to wash up." He scratched his left arm furiously. "I think I got hold of something at the funeral home I'm allergic to."

Janet frowned. "Why didn't you use one of the restrooms over there?"

"Full up. Way too many people."

Janet sized him up while fingering the hem of her

blouse. His presence, even without the itchy welts, made her uneasy.

"Well?" Wilson raked fingernails over the splotches on his cheeks. "Can I use it?"

Janet nodded reluctantly. He did look miserable. She pointed toward the hall. "It's down . . . well, you know where it is."

Scratching the back of his head, Wilson hurried for the bathroom in long, zigzagging steps.

As soon as he disappeared, Heather scrambled to Janet's side. "That man looked scary and mean," she said in a low voice.

"He's not mean," Ellie said. "Mama says he's my grandpa . . . huh, Mama? And grandpas aren't mean."

"Is too mean," Heather insisted.

"Is not." As though to emphasize her point, Ellie stood and adjusted her fanny pack over her stomach like a gunslinger with a poor sense of direction.

"Okay, but he looked like he had the cooties," Heather said. "All bumpy and itchy."

An indignant look crossed Ellie's face. "If my grandpa's got the cooties, then yours has 'em, too."

"Does not."

"Does too."

"That's enough," Janet warned, although she wanted to agree with Heather about Wilson's condition. She picked up the cooler and handed it to Ellie. "Run this out to the van for me, okay? Heather, you can carry my purse. Just put it on the driver's seat."

Instantly, the girls' disposition changed from confrontational to pleased that they were being assigned a grownup duty. Ellie took hold of the cooler with great care, and Heather latched on to Janet's purse as though the crown jewels rested inside.

Janet watched them head outside and couldn't help wondering at their ability to leave arguments behind so quickly. Adults had a tendency to hang on to almost everything—words, slights, resentments—like they were tickets needed for entry into some future argument. She was guilty of that herself. Especially with Wilson.

Agitated with a sudden twinge in her conscience, Janet turned to the sink and snatched up a dish towel so she'd have something to do with her hands. So what if she resented Wilson? It wasn't like the old bastard hadn't earned every bit of it. He'd hurt Michael. He'd hurt the whole family. She didn't trust him. Even now Janet suspected Wilson of being up to something. He was being too—too—nice. Still, her conscience needled her. Maybe Wilson was just an old man who didn't know any other way to survive in life other than being an asshole. He *was* Ellie's only remaining grandfather, and he *did* look sick.

Janet weaved the dishcloth between her fingers and listened to the sound of running water coming from the bathroom. Moments later the toilet flushed. She tossed the towel onto the counter. All right, so maybe it wouldn't hurt to be more civil to Wilson. Maybe even smile at him once in a while. Though she didn't think the endeavor would transform him into Grandpa Walton, it would be a start.

She tested her theory the moment Wilson walked back into the kitchen. Seemingly refreshed, his hair was slicked back, and the splotches were gone from his face. He carried his suit jacket draped over one arm.

"Feel better already," he said.

Janet forced a smile. "Good."

Wilson's left brow arched with skepticism. "Good?"

"I'm glad you're feeling better."

As his right eyebrow lifted to match the left, Ellie and Heather burst into the house in a fit of giggles. They ran to Janet's side.

"All done!" Ellie declared.

"Yep, all done!" Heather beamed and did a pirouette. As soon as she spotted Wilson, her cheerfulness deflated. "Uh . . . can we go now, Aunt Janet?"

Janet smoothed Heather's hair, sensing her unease. "In a moment, honey. Bathroom first, okay?"

Heather whispered, "But I don't gotta go."

"Me neither," Ellie added loudly.

"At least try," Janet urged. "It's going to be a long drive."

Ellie sighed expansively. "Okay, but nothing's gonna come out." She reached for her cousin's hand. "Come on, Heather. You can get the Barbie bag from my room while I go first."

The uncomfortable silence that followed their departure made Janet straighten a toaster and coffeepot that didn't need straightening.

"She's something else," Wilson finally said.

Janet gave him a quizzical look.

"The girl . . . Emma . . . she's really something. Bright, you know? Got a lot of spunk for a kid."

"Her name's Ellie, and, yes, she is very smart."

"Oh, right, right, Ellie. Nice name."

Another smothering pause spanned between them while Janet tried to figure out if Wilson's amicable behavior was genuine. His eyes didn't reveal anything one way or the other. They were too busy darting from her to the nearest window. Either geniality made Wilson nervous or he'd found a new way to scratch itchy eyeballs.

"You should see a doctor about that rash," Janet said.

"Huh? Oh, nah. It's nearly all gone." He lifted his chin so she could see the full length of his neck. "Soap and water took care of most of it."

Janet offered a nod. In truth, his face looked bloodless now, his eyes puffy and red.

Wilson sidestepped his way to the door, opened it a few inches, and peered out. "Michael didn't happen to come by while I was washing up, did he?"

"No. Was he supposed to?"

"No, no, just wondering was all." Wilson glanced toward the window again. "So you guys are heading up to Carlton I hear?"

"Well . . . yes."

He nodded, but to the clock on the stove not her. "I guess you won't be seeing Michael again before you leave then, huh?"

Janet's internal defenses went to full alert. Why was Wilson suddenly so interested in when she'd see Michael? "I suppose I won't," she admitted.

He grinned, and his blood-webbed eyes fastened on the window again. "Good, good."

"What?"

"I mean . . . uh . . . I'm sure you'll have a good trip."

Growing more bewildered by the minute, Janet turned away from Wilson and called out, "Girls, you about ready?"

"Almost!" Heather shouted from the hall.

"Janet?"

Shocked by the nearness of Wilson's voice, Janet spun about. He stood an arm's length away from her.

"No need to be so jumpy," he said. "I just wanted to ask you something."

She took a step back. "What?"

Wilson frowned and seemed to study the top of her head. Finally he asked, "Why do you dislike me so much?"

Stunned by the question, Janet gawked.

"Really," he said. "I want to know."

Janet couldn't remember the last time she had so much trouble swallowing saliva. "You sure you want to discuss this?" she asked.

They stared at each other for a long, unblinking moment. In the distance, a drawer banged shut and small feet shuffled across wood floors.

"Nah," Wilson said. "Suppose not." He put his jacket back on, then shrugged. "Guess I'd better be going."

Janet didn't reply.

Wilson lowered his head and walked slowly away. Old age appeared ponderous on his shoulders, like a load of bricks, causing his body to slump, his back to bow. Janet couldn't get used to seeing Wilson this way, so frail looking, so brittle. Empathy welled up inside her, which took Janet by surprise.

She opened her mouth, ready to tell him to stay, to talk, when he suddenly stopped and snapped his fingers. He turned around, and Janet saw a glint of mischief in his eyes. It was quickly replaced with a mournful, pitiful gaze. The right corner of his mouth jittered.

"I meant to ask," Wilson said. "Would you have a few bucks to spare until Monday?"

Chapter Fourteen

A panoramic view of hell, disguised as beige floral wallpaper, stretched out before Anna, and she studied it, transfixed. Every floret had become Thalia's frightened face, every petal her daughter's open mouth, crying for help, each twining vine Thalia's arms desperately reaching for her mother. No matter how long Anna stared, no matter how many times she shifted in her seat, she sensed the same message deep in her soul—in her womb. Thalia was in trouble. Dead, yes—but somehow, somewhere, in trouble just the same.

Anna fidgeted in her seat again, wanting to look back at the casket. She knew if she did, though, Ephraim would have her hauled out of the room, stripping her of the last chance she'd have to be near Thalia's body. So she focused harder on the wall, trying to decipher the turmoil percolating inside her. She knew timing was everything, but *had* the time come? Was it this moment? Should she wait a bit longer?

Even more confusing to Anna was the occasional

mental image she received of a fair-haired child with dead, blue eyes—and the dark-haired woman Anna had met earlier by the water fountain. What did they have to do with Thalia?

Oh, my beautiful daughter, my Thalia, I hear you. I feel you. But how do I find you? Where do I even begin to look?

A memory suddenly tagged Anna's heart. It reminded her of the time Thalia was five and had gotten lost in a crowded market. Anna had been so alarmed and distraught by her disappearance, she'd barely had the wherewithal to think. She'd pushed and shoved her way through people, shouting for Thalia until she was hoarse, searching for any piece of clothing, any hair color that might match her daughter's. Soon, Anna discovered herself silent and tracking Thalia strictly by sense. She allowed everything around her with no significance to fade away, concentrating only on the vibrations of Thalia's emotions. Anna felt them so strongly it was as though they belonged to her. Fear—loneliness—the despair of one being too small in a world much too big. Those sensations had led Anna to Thalia like mud tracks on a white floor.

Anna sat back in her chair expectantly. Maybe that's what she needed to do now. Simply follow the tracks.

Urgency suddenly grew up Anna's spine, like a tree with a thousand crooked branches. Each bough reached, poked, prodded against a nerve ending until she could barely remain seated. She felt it so strongly.

Thalia's fear—

Anna reached for the tool she'd managed to keep hidden from Ephraim.

Thalia's loneliness—

She slipped it out from beneath the cuff of her blouse. The tip pricked the pad of flesh beneath her fingers, drawing a drop of blood.

Thalia—too small in another world much too big—

The fear Anna intuited from Thalia quickly escalated to dread, the loneliness to a profound sense of abandonment.

Too small—too big.

Too much.

It was time.

Chapter Fifteen

Michael wasn't accustomed to hyperventilating. He'd heard breathing into a paper sack helped, but even if he had one, it wouldn't solve his real problem. It wouldn't bring back the coin.

He lowered the top lid of the casket a few inches, hesitating. He hated to close it, but what other choice did he have? If he brought the missing coin to the Stevensons' attention, there was little doubt all hell would break loose. He didn't think Ephraim, or Antony, or any other member of their congregation had removed it because they'd been too adamant about not touching the corpse. Almost to the point of disgust. That left only two other possibilities: Sally and Wilson.

Michael wrote Sally off immediately. He'd known her most of his life. She would have sawed off her own arms before stealing anything. Even during business hours when she had free access to his office, Sally had never so much as taken a postage stamp from his desk without asking. Wilson on the other hand . . .

Although Michael knew his father was capable of making hard-hearted, stupid choices, he'd never known him to steal from a casket. Not in all the years they'd worked together, no matter how tight money got. Misappropriate funds from the business? Yes. Swipe grocery money from his wife? Yes. But steal from a casket? This would be a first.

Reluctantly, Michael closed and latched the lid, then polished a smudge on the coffin with his coat sleeve. All the while he took deep, slow breaths in an attempt to control his anger.

In through the nostrils, out through the mouth. In through the nostrils, out through the mou—

A loud, long scream froze Michael's deflating lungs.

Oh, shit, someone noticed the coin was missing.

He turned around slowly, his mind whirling through nonsensical explanations.

The few people left in the room didn't point at him accusingly nor did they storm the casket. They were too busy gawking at the blood dripping from Anna Stevenson's wrists.

Within seconds two dozen women raced into the viewing room and fluttered around Anna like myopic moths.

Michael hurried toward them. "Give her room," he said, and the moths pressed closer to the bleeding woman. "She needs air!" The circle grew tighter still, hiding the calm, white face from his view.

Turning on his heels, Michael rushed for the phone in the reception area. He collided with Sally in the doorway.

"Where's Stevenson?" he asked, catching her by the shoulders.

"Which one?"

"The girl's father, Ephraim."

"Outside, I think. Why?" Sally peered over his shoulder. "What's going—is that blood?"

Michael looked back at the crimson pool widening on the floor. "Yeah, it's Stevenson's wife."

"Oh, Lord." Sally's face turned ashen. "You find him. I'll call 911."

"You will call no one," Ephraim's voice boomed behind them. He shoved his way past Michael and Sally and stormed into the room. His voice thundered as he commanded the women surrounding his wife to step aside.

"Mr. Stevenson, we need to call an ambulance," Michael insisted. "Your wife's losing a lot of blood."

"You will call no one!" Ephraim repeated, shouting over his shoulder. "We will tend to our own." Then he turned back to Anna and grabbed her chin, forcing her to face him. Her eyes were dull brown stones that Michael suspected saw nothing at all. The hollows of her cheeks were splotchy and paling fast, her lips an almost nonexistent waxen line. Her forearms dangled over the arms of the chair, and her sliced wrists dripped relentlessly.

Ephraim exhaled her name, "Anna." His thumb pressed against her lips, then he removed his hand and brushed at it as though repulsed. "Cela!" he yelled.

A young, pregnant woman waddled to Ephraim's side. Her dark, eager eyes searched his face.

With a barrage of rolling r's and staccato syllables, Ephraim spat his demands, and Cela hurried to comply. From a nearby satchel, she removed a diaper, ripped it in two, then barked a command to two other women. The women rushed to Anna's side and laid their hands on her shoulders. Cela stepped carefully to the side of the chair, then quickly wrapped Anna's left wrist with a section of diaper. Anna's expression remained blank, her breathing heavy and audible as though she'd fallen into a deep sleep.

As soon as the other diaper remnant was tied around her right wrist, Anna was lifted to her feet. A single-edged razor fell from her lap to the floor. The women gasped collectively, and Anna was quickly escorted from the room.

"So, so sad," Sally murmured.

Michael stood numb. He'd witnessed many spectacles over the years as a funeral director. Wives trying to climb into their dead husband's casket, a father who'd obsessively clipped the toenails of his deceased son throughout a viewing. Once he'd even seen a woman spit on her dead brother's face, then rub the spittle across his cheeks and into his ears. As bizarre as all those things were, not once had he been faced with an attempted suicide.

Relieved that Anna was at least being tended to, Michael whispered to Sally, "Did Chad get back yet?"

"A couple of minutes ago."

"Have him get the hearse ready. It's time for this to end."

"Way past time," Sally agreed.

When she slipped out of the room, Michael walked over to Ephraim. He teetered between professionalism and chivalry, debating on whether he should keep his nose out of Stevenson's business and just finish with the service or flatten Ephraim's face for being a Neanderthal to his wife. He figured the latter would solve little. The Stevensons would be leaving soon, and his interference might only serve to make Anna's situation worse once Ephraim had her alone.

Michael glared at Ephraim. "Have you assigned pallbearers?"

Ephraim looked at him as one would a pestering dog.

"Men who will carry the casket," Michael said sternly, assuming Ephraim didn't understand the term. "It's time to go to the church."

Ephraim turned away and with an unsteady hand, signaled for a one-eared woman, who stood nearby. Quickly and silently she left the room only to return a moment later with six men in tow. Lenora appeared behind them.

The entourage walked in procession to the casket. When they reached it, Lenora laid her hands on top of the casket and began to chant while her fingers slid across the polished surface. A hot band of apprehension wrapped around Michael's stomach when she pulled against the lids. What if she opened one and noticed the coin missing? How would he explain?

But Lenora's hands kept moving. They traveled along the handles and over each bronzed corner. After a while, she made her way to the water glass and bowl still resting on the stool at the head of the coffin. She lifted the bowl and placed it on top of the casket, then removed the glass and holding it reverently in both hands, walked slowly out of the room.

The six men separated into two groups of threes, a group on either side of the casket.

Suspecting they were preparing to lift it, Michael said to Ephraim, "There's no need to carry the casket. I'll get a church truck so you can roll it out."

Ignoring him, Ephraim signaled to the pallbearers. Together they reached for the rail handles and lifted the casket off the bier, the bowl balancing atop it.

With a perturbed sigh, Michael stepped aside as they carried Thalia out.

Ephraim followed them with his head bowed low. Michael trailed behind Ephraim, glancing once over his shoulder at the vacant bier and the lone chair, which sat bracketed in blood.

When they reached the front entrance, the doors were already open with Sally and Chad standing on either side. The hearse, backed up to the building, awaited its passenger.

Chad led the pallbearers to the back of the vehicle and gestured for them to set the casket on the rollers inside. The incense bowl was removed, and the bronze box gently pushed in and secured. One of the pallbearers closed the hearse door behind it.

Resolved to civility, Michael turned to offer Ephraim last condolences, but the man was already sliding into a station wagon four vehicles away. Anna sat behind him, her face pressed against the window. She looked like a lost, desolate child.

A shout of *"Mia subtolamain!"* jerked Michael's attention back to the hearse. Lenora, hunchbacked and in a pitcher's stance, had the water glass balanced in her right hand. The reality of what she prepared to do sent Michael's arms waving in the air.

"Stop!" he shouted.

Lenora threw the glass against the door of the hearse, missing the back window by inches. She turned sideways as water and shards of glass flew everywhere. Once the debris settled, she trotted off to a nearby van.

Appalled, Michael could only gawk at the three-inch scratch now etched across the back of his vehicle.

"Damn," Chad said, appearing beside him with Sally. He went to the hearse and examined the damage.

Sally shook her head in disbelief. "The nerve of those people. After all we did for them. After all we put up with."

Throughout the parking lot, engines roared to life, and cars and trucks began to line up on the street.

Michael kneaded his brow. "Yeah, well, there's nothing we can do about this now. We still have to get them to the church and cemetery."

"If you want, I can make that run," Chad offered.

Sally scowled. "Are you crazy?"

"Pretty big crowd for you to handle alone," Michael said.

Chad opened the driver's door to the hearse. "What's to handle? The pallbearers will take the casket through the church and cemetery. All I have to do is direct them on where to go. Besides, the two bodies from Magnolia are in the prep room, and since you're faster at embalming than I am, it makes sense that you stay. If we both go to the cemetery, those bodies won't get embalmed until late. We'll be here past midnight."

The man has a point, Michael thought. If they didn't divide the tasks, not only would they be working late, he'd probably be forced to put some chores off until tomorrow, which meant a later departure for Carlton.

"You that sure you can handle it?" Michael asked.

"Absolutely."

"All right then, but take the cell phone."

"Got it right here." Chad patted his jacket pocket.

"If you run into any problems, give me a call." Michael turned to Sally. "Better yet, why don't you—"

She ticked a finger at him. "Nuh-uh. Don't even ask."

"What?"

"For me to ride along with Chad. I've had my fill of those people."

"Sal, Chad hasn't been around long enough to know how Father Melancon and Jasper work. You have. Just sit in the hearse. If he runs into a snag with either one of them, you'll be right there."

"Like that'll do any good," she said. "You know Melancon. This late in the day he'll be so eager to get back to his rum and Coke those people will be lucky to get holy water sprinkled on the casket."

"You don't have to come," Chad said. "I'll figure it—"

"And as for Jasper," Sally continued. "That caretaker's deafer than a rock. It wouldn't matter who told him what anyway. He couldn't hear it."

"In case, Sal," Michael said. "Just in case. You shouldn't have to deal with the Stevensons at all."

Sally pursed her lips while car engines whined impatiently nearby. Finally, she threw her hands up and marched to the passenger's side of the hearse. "Okay, okay, but if those people start acting up in church, I'm leaving. With or without Chad."

Chad slipped behind the steering wheel, closed the door, and gave Michael a thumbs up through the open window. "It'll be all right, boss. Don't worry."

"Quit sucking up already and go," Sally said, and slammed her door shut.

Michael peered into the hearse. "When you're done at the cemetery, both of you can head straight home. We'll meet back here at nine in the morning."

"You got it." Chad started the hearse and began to power up the window.

Michael backed away, then remembered Wilson. "Hey, wait."

The window stopped at half-mast.

"Have either of you seen my father?"

"Not me," Chad said.

Sally harrumphed loud enough for Michael to hear her over the chugging engines. "Not since the viewing room earlier. I left to answer the phone, and when I got back, he was already gone."

Michael nodded and signaled them off. The coach bucked out of the parking lot, and streams of vehicles lined up behind it, forming a parade down Alabaster Road.

He watched until the last car disappeared around the corner, then allowed his shoulders to sag. Exhaustion pummeled his body, every muscle and bone seemingly screaming for relief from even the simple task of standing. A light breeze brushed across Michael's face, and he scanned the empty parking lot. Dusk was closing in, but his day was far from over. He still had a funeral home to get ready for the next day's viewings, bodies to embalm, and a father to confront.

Wearily, Michael headed back into the building.

He'd barely crossed the lobby when he heard someone mutter, "Shit!" from inside the viewing room. He paused, not recognizing the voice. Had the Stevensons left someone behind?

Michael peered around the doorjamb, relieved to see Agnes. "I didn't know you were still here."

"I'm fixin' not to be," Agnes said. She was on her

knees near the bloodstains with a spray bottle of spot remover in one hand and a scrub brush in the other. The divider wall had been pulled across the room, and the narrowed space made the crimson mess appear bigger.

With a gloved hand, Agnes dipped the scrub brush into a plastic bucket half filled with water beside her. "This crap ain't coming out, and it ain't gonna come out." She sat back on her heels. "What'd they do? Slaughter a pig?"

"The mother cut her wrists."

Agnes squinted up at him. "I didn't see no ambulance outside."

"They refused to let us call one, just bandaged her up themselves."

She shook her head, labored to her feet, and tossed the scrub brush into the bucket. "I told you them people was bad juju. Look here, they already gonna cost you a brand new carpet."

"Maybe a steam cleaner will get it out."

"Nope. New carpet," she said authoritatively and peeled off her gloves.

Not wanting to get into a debate, Michael said, "Fine, new carpet. I'll close this part of the room off and deal with it tomorrow."

"Good enough then. I already finished cleanin' the lounge and bathrooms, so if it's all the same to you, I'll be headin' on to my house. I'll finish up here early in the mornin'."

"Sure," Michael said. "But how'd you get those other rooms cleaned so fast?"

"Oh, I got my way," Agnes said with a mischievous grin.

"I'm not even going to ask what that might be."

"Smart man."

Michael touched her arm as she walked past him. "Thanks, Agnes. I really don't know what I'd have done today without you."

Her smile broadened. "Probably be stompin' knee deep in shit by now."

"Probably."

He walked Agnes to the front door, then after locking it behind her, leaned against the jamb and listened to the silence. No music, no voices, no yelling, nothing. Glorious nothing.

With great effort, Michael pushed himself into motion and headed for the prep room. Halfway down the hall, a chill ran up the back of his neck, and he had an overwhelming sense someone was behind him. He glanced over his shoulder and caught the tail end of a shadow slipping into the viewing room, the one with the ruined carpet.

Michael stopped short, knowing he'd locked the front door. How could Agnes have gotten back in there?

"Hello?" he called.

No answer.

"Agnes?"

The only response was the sound of his left knee popping as he headed back to the viewing room.

"Dad?" Michael peered into the room and found it empty save for a few chairs and Agnes's cleaning supplies.

Michael turned off the lights and started for the prep room again. It wouldn't be the first time he'd captured something unusual in the funeral home from the corner of his eye. Weak flashes of unidentified light, a skittering shadow now and then, sometimes just a sense of nearby movement. Most of the time Michael shrugged off the episodes to fatigue, which was a standard lot for funeral directors. There might be truth, as some claimed, to a soul lingering behind after death, but Michael felt his hands were already overflowing with the living. The last thing he needed to deal with was ghosts.

He was almost to the next corridor when the chill returned. Michael brushed the back of his neck with a hand, meaning to ignore it, when he heard what sounded like a titter behind him. He spun around.

Nothing there.

"Who's here?"

Another snicker—from the opposite direction.

He whirled about again, and caught sight of something black, like the coattails of a long jacket, rounding the intersecting hall.

Michael took off after it, his leather shoes slipping across the floor as he raced down the hallway. He swerved left into the connecting corridor, just in time to see the embalming room door ease shut.

He stumbled to a halt. The prep room door had a keypad lock of which only three people had access. His father, Chad, and himself. Since Chad was busy with a hearse, and he was standing in the hall feeling like an idiot, that left Wilson.

Michael stormed up to the keypad and punched in a code. As soon as he heard the click of the lock release, he shoved the door open.

"Dad, where the hell have you been?" he demanded while flipping on the light switch.

When Michael's eyes adjusted to the sudden brightness, he frowned. Besides the two corpses from Magnolia Nursing Home, the room was empty.

Chapter Sixteen

The last time Wilson squatted behind a bush was four winters ago when he'd gone hunting with Buster Fremont, an old lodge buddy. Three breakfast burritos had sent him shimmying down from a deer stand and into the nearest thicket. Montezuma's revenge wasn't Wilson's problem now, however. His own stupidity was. He should have never taken off his jacket.

"Mother friggin' pissant," he muttered as another leg cramp seized him. He sat, resting his back against the house, and stretched out his hampered leg. From this position, he couldn't see the road or the funeral home unless he leaned far to the left. Not the best conditions for surveillance, but his legs would only take so much stress.

He rubbed his right calf and listened intently to the rustle of hedge leaves and the sound of car engines growing ever distant. Finally, no more Stevensons.

"About damned time," Wilson fumed.

He'd been hiding out ever since Janet left, which

seemed like forever ago. After she'd given him a lousy twenty bucks, he'd headed for his car, which he'd parked two blocks north of the house. On his way there, Wilson had reached into his jacket pocket for the gold medallion he'd swiped from the casket, a big, expensive looking piece that would surely get Lester Vidrine off his ass for a while. But the damn thing wasn't there. Wilson had retraced his steps to and from the house again and again but found nothing. He was convinced that the only other place the medallion could be was in Michael's bathroom. It must have slipped out when he'd taken off his jacket before washing. And with the rash driving him crazy, his hearing not being what it used to be, and the carpeting on the floor, it was no wonder he hadn't heard it fall.

"Who the hell puts carpet in a bathroom?" Wilson mumbled for the hundredth time. Asking the question gave him a droplet of satisfaction. It allowed the blame to be redirected to something other than his own asininity. Hell, if there hadn't been carpet, he'd have heard the medallion fall to the floor. And if he'd heard it, it wouldn't be lost. It'd be in Vidrine's hand right now, probably on its way to Porter Smack, his fence.

But no, he was stuck here, waiting for the coast to clear so he could break into his own son's home.

Although Wilson's original plan had been to wait until the funeral home had emptied, he decided to hold out a little longer. There was still too much sunlight for him to attempt climbing through a window. If he had been younger, he might have given it a shot instead of hiding in the bushes like a goddamn squirrel. But he wasn't young. The way his body moved now, the neighbors would have time to contact the FBI and the local news station, then have both of them set up on Michael's front lawn before he'd make it across a windowsill. That left Wilson no alternative but to hide and wait. He couldn't hang around here too long, though. Sooner or later, Michael would come home.

Wilson scowled at a miniature triangle of twigs, through which he viewed Michael's mailbox. By now, he figured his son knew about the theft. Michael might be soft around the edges, especially where his wife and kid were concerned, but he wasn't dumb.

An empty funeral home undoubtedly meant a closed casket, and with the apprentice out making removals, Wilson knew Michael would have been the one to close it. He also knew he'd taught his son too well. Check the hair, the casket lining, the clothes for wrinkles. Make sure everything is in pristine condition before closing the lids. Unless Michael had suddenly gone blind, the boy knew by now the medallion was missing.

Wilson didn't feel especially proud about what he'd done. In his opinion, stealing from a casket put a man on the same level as vomit under a shoe. But he'd had no choice. He'd told Michael this morning he'd gone to visit his dying sister, and he had, but his delay in returning to the funeral home hadn't been caused by an accident on the Pontchartrain. That had been Lester's fault.

Lester "Shit Face" Vidrine, with his tinted glasses and crooked teeth, had caught up with him by happenstance at an intersection, just as Wilson drove into Brusley from Metairie. After forcing Wilson's car to the side of the road, Lester promised him two broken kneecaps and a missing spleen if he wasn't paid in forty-eight hours.

Two damned days. One bad marker after fifteen years of doing business together, and Lester acted like he couldn't trust him anymore. And for ten grand no less. What kind of business partner snubbed you for ten grand? That was rabbit food compared to the money Lester had made on him over the years.

Wilson kicked at a branch, wishing it were Lester's face. He could do it, too, pulverize the bastard and shove him into a milk carton—if he caught him alone. But when it came to Lester making good on a promise to punish, he never handled that business alone. He always brought along backup. The kind with bulky, hairy arms and chests the size of Oldsmobiles.

Frustrated and hot, Wilson rested his head against the brick siding. The rash he'd had earlier was no longer noticeable, but he still felt it prickle just below the surface of his skin. He forced himself not to scratch, assuming the allergy, or whatever it was, would react like poison ivy. The more you scratched, the worse it got.

To take his mind off the hives, Wilson closed his eyes and thought about Magdala Rhimes.

Magdala was a feisty, fifty-eight-year-old widow from Jacksonville, Florida, with huge silicone boobs. More importantly, she had money. Wilson had met Magdala on a casino boat in Baton Rouge and wound up relocating to Florida with her and her cash for over two years. Except for her constant bitching about him drinking too much, they got along fairly well. Their relationship went south, though, after he'd gotten a tip on a sure shot with forty-to-one odds. When Wilson told Magdala about the opportunity, she suddenly went stingy on him, refusing to fork over the money.

The stakes were too high she'd said, even for the potential payout. Wilson all but begged, wanting to run the tip high and hard. But Magdala wouldn't budge. So, not being one to let an opportunity slip by, Wilson had called Lester. A few long-distance connections, and all he'd had to do was sign his name on the dotted line, then let the ten g's roll.

How was he supposed to know the damn horse would trip a quarter of the way to the finish line? Hell, wasn't that why they called it gambling?

Wilson was tired of everyone getting on his case. Magdala for his drinking, Lester for his damn money. It seemed like no matter where he turned these days, somebody was riding his ass about something. Even Michael. But his son was a situation he would straighten out soon enough. The boy was getting way too big for his britches, turning his back on him like that. If Michael had given him Stevenson's money like he should have in the first place, he wouldn't be in this predicament.

Kids just had no gratitude these days. No respect for the sacrifices their parents had to make day after day, year after year. That bullshit needed to be set straight once and for all.

First things first, Wilson thought. The number one order of business was getting the gold piece back. The second, shoving it up Lester's ass. After that he'd take care of Michael. It was time somebody taught the boy respect for his elders, and Wilson figured he was just the elder to do it.

Chapter Seventeen

Janet tapped her foot against the brake and slowed the van down to thirty-five miles an hour. Creeping along Highway 6 into Carlton, she noted, as she did every year, how little the town had changed. Herbert's Garage still stood in rusted determination on the corner of Highway 6 and Madeline Street next to the Fountain of Life United Pentecostal Church. A block down on the right was Settler's Mini-Mall, home to Cal's Western Store, Louisa's Naked Furniture, and Bubba's Drive-Thru Bar-B-Que. Two blocks ahead, just before a fork in the road, cows grazed in a nearby pasture blanketed with blue-green grass.

To the left of the fork stood the Cotton Patch, a long, white building with cherry red trim that served as Carlton's service station, grocery store, three-table restaurant, and overall gossip center. Rodney and Sylvia Theriot owned the Patch. They'd known the Savoy family since the mid-'50s, when Michael's grandfather, Joseph, built the cabin west of town. Joseph had hired the Theriots, at that time a couple in their mid-twenties, to watch over the place when the family was away. In exchange for grass cutting and weekly checks on the place, the Theriots were assured free burial services and heavily discounted caskets.

Janet veered right onto Highway 1226, which led to the cabin. Across the narrow road, massive oak and pecan tree branches arched and sagged, offering shade and a temperature drop of at least ten degrees. A little farther on the right ran an unmarked, limestone street that meandered through a forest for about a half mile. Janet turned onto it, listening to the stones crunch under the van's tires.

"Finally," she muttered when she turned into a clearing.

The cabin was a white two-story Acadian-style built on brick piers. Thick columns supported the roof over a wide front porch, and hunter green shutters trimmed each window. The two-acre lawn surrounding the house looked freshly mowed.

She pulled up to the front of the house and killed the engine. Resting her head back against the seat, she basked in the stillness. Such a long way to travel for such a short stay in an old house. Getting away from the madness in Brusley had been worth the drive, but just as important, coming here also made her husband and daughter happy. When Michael was a boy, his grandfather had brought him to Carlton each year so they could attend the fair together. It was the only family tradition Michael seemed eager to hold on to, and one she would never deny him.

The thought of Grandpa Joseph made Janet smile. He'd been a kindhearted man with a round face and small frame. He'd compensated for his stature with attitude, one of overwhelming generosity and a stoic love of family. Except for size, Michael was the axiom of the apple and tree. One certainly hadn't fallen far from the other. Wilson, on the other hand, seemed to have come from a completely different orchard.

Quickly dropping Wilson from her thoughts, Janet reached for the rearview mirror, tilting it down so she could see the girls, who were asleep on the back seat. Overall, they'd done well on the four-hour trip. They'd kept each other occupied with singsongs and little girl gossip. She grinned at the contrast they created sitting together, their heads drooped to one side, touching. Heather's black hair—Ellie's blond. Heather's skin sun toasted—Ellie's pale. Unusually pale—too pale.

Janet sat up and turned to look at her daughter. Her usually scrubbed pink face looked chalky and dry. She reached over the seat and touched Ellie's knee.

"Honey, wake up."

Ellie's eyes fluttered open. "Are we there yet?"

"I'm hungry, Aunt Janet," Heather said. She sat up and rubbed away spittle that had dribbled across her left cheek.

"Me too," Ellie agreed with a nod.

"Both of you ate just an hour ago, so I don't think there's a threat of starvation. Ellie, lean over here a minute."

With a yawn, Ellie unbuckled her seatbelt and scooted to the edge of her seat. "But we're starving a lot, Mama."

"Where's the cabin?" Heather asked. She pressed her face against the window.

"Right there, silly." Ellie pointed to the house.

"But a cabin's supposed to be all broken down and stuff."

Ellie shook her head. "Nuh-uh."

"Uh-huh."

"Nuh-uh."

"Aunt Janet . . ."

"Time out, you two." Janet touched Ellie's right cheek. Faint pink tracks followed her fingertips over her daughter's skin. "What's on your face?"

"Huh?"

"Your face," Janet said. She sniffed her fingertips. "Were you playing with chalk?"

Heather reached up with a finger and rubbed it against Ellie's other cheek. "Look," she said with a giggle, "I can draw a smiley face."

Ellie shooed Heather's hand away. "We don't have chalk, Mama. Only colors and markers, and see?" She held out her arms and flipped them back and forth. "I didn't even get none on me."

Janet opened the glove compartment, but found the Wet Ones container she kept in there for emergency cleanups empty. She closed the compartment and opened the van door.

"Come on," Janet said. "Let's go inside so you can wash up." She made a mental note to check Ellie's fanny pack later for face powder.

The girls scurried out of the van and started chasing each other around the yard. Janet took the keys from the ignition, found the one labeled CH for Carlton house, and made her way to the front door.

Once inside, she crinkled her nose at the smell of old upholstery and mothballs. Hard as she tried, Janet never felt comfortable in this place. There was something about the dark paneling and old oak floors that seemed determined to keep the past as present, consequently leaving her to always feel like an intruder.

The floors creaked beneath her feet as she walked down a narrow foyer to the dining room and opened the windows. On the way to the kitchen, she flipped on the auto switch for the air conditioner and breathed a sigh of relief when she heard it start to hum. It was the only modern renovation she'd been able to talk Michael into and even at that, it was still eight years old.

She'd just turned on the kitchen faucets to check for water when Janet heard the screen door slam and the girls run into the house. They raced through the dining room, past the kitchen, then rounded the hall, which led to the family room.

"No running up the stairs," Janet called after them. "And clean that stuff off your face, Ellie."

"Okay, Mama," Ellie called back, her voice already an echo from the top of the stairs.

Janet shook her head and shut off the water. Watching two kids instead of one would keep her on her toes for the next couple of days, but at least Ellie had company. It wasn't easy keeping a five-year-old entertained when you had a television that caught only two channels, no VCR, and the nearest Chuck E. Cheese was a hundred and fifty miles away.

She lifted the hair off the back of her sweaty neck for a moment, then began to take inventory in cabinets and drawers. A glint of silver caught Janet's eye when she passed the window on her way to the old Frigidaire. She stopped in midstride and watched as the front end of a vehicle entered the clearing near the house. A second later a horn honked, and Rodney Theriot's battered green pickup truck came into full view. Janet smiled and waited until he'd parked alongside the van before going outside to greet him.

"Well I'll be corn-fed and slaughtered," Rodney chortled while getting out of the truck. "Little Bit, ain't you a sight!" He straightened the bib of his overalls and waddled toward her.

To Janet, Rodney's laugh was larger than his three hundred pounds and brighter than his crystal blue eyes. The band of hair that surrounded the back of his head seemed whiter than she remembered, and his puffy, vein-lined cheeks and double chin, if anything, had grown larger.

"It's great to see you, too, Rodney," she said warmly. They hugged briefly, and she motioned him inside. "How've you been?"

He lumbered up the steps. "Any better they'd outlaw it."

"And Sylvia?"

"Even better'n me," Rodney said, his voice booming through the foyer. "How 'bout Michael and the munchkin? They around?" Before she could answer, he shuffled into the dining room and peered over the snack bar into the kitchen. "Don't tell me you came up here all by yourself."

"Ellie and Heather came with me. Michael's still back in Brusley, but he should be getting here sometime tomorrow." She pulled up a chair and offered it to him.

"Naw, I gotta exercise the gimp as much as I can," Rodney said, and tapped a hand against his left thigh. He walked to the entrance of the family room and looked around. "What's a Heather?"

Janet laughed and turned toward the kitchen. "She's my sister's daughter. Hey, I've got tap water if you're thirsty."

"'Preciate it, but I just finished a bottle of cream soda back at the Patch." Rodney followed her to the kitchen and rubbed the bald dome of his head. "Saw you drive past a bit ago, and Sylvia wanted me to come by and make sure you come to supper."

A clatter followed by shrill laughter suddenly rang overhead.

Rodney looked up and bellowed, "Is that you, munchkin?" A wide, expectant grin spread over his face as he cocked his head to one side and waited. When no response came, he said, "Okay, then I guess it wasn't my munchkin. S'pose I gotta give these peppermints to some other little girl."

Within seconds, footsteps thundered from the stairs.

Rodney chuckled, and his barrel chest and belly did an aquatic roll. He winked at Janet. "Gets 'em every time."

"Mr. Rodney!" Ellie squealed. She whipped around the corner of the room and flew to his side. "Here I am! Here I am!"

Heather, who had followed her cousin downstairs, inched shyly up to Rodney, her eyes bright with anticipation.

"Well, look at that," Rodney said, putting a hand into his pocket. "Here I was thinking that I was going to have to find me some other little girls." He pulled out a handful of peppermint sticks and handed them to Ellie and Heather. "Hmm, what's this?" he asked Ellie. "You been playing in your mama's makeup?"

Janet stepped around him so she could see her

daughter. The chalky film on Ellie's face looked even thicker than before. "Back upstairs and wash that stuff off your face like I told you," she said.

Ellie shoved the peppermints into the pockets of her shorts. "I was gonna, Mama, but Heather wanted to see my room."

"Fine, but go and get it cleaned off right now."

The girls whirled around and scampered out of sight.

"And what do you tell Mr. Rodney?" Janet called after them.

Two voices chorused from the next room, "Thank you, Mr. Rodney!" and the old man smiled.

Janet shook her head. "I don't know what Ellie got into, but I'll bet one of my old compacts found its way into her fanny pack."

"That's just kids for ya." Rodney pulled a red bandanna out of his back pocket and blew his nose. "Well, I gotta head back to the Patch before Sylvia calls out Sheriff Crocket and starts a search party. I swear that woman worries more the older she gets."

"That's because you're such a prize catch," Janet said. She clapped him gently on the back.

Rodney snorted. "Oh, she thinks I'm a catch all right. Right out of Black Lake."

Janet laughed and followed him out the door and to his truck. "Tell Sylvia I'll be by later to pick up groceries and that we'd be glad to come by for supper. What time?"

Rodney hoisted himself into the truck, then closed the door and rested his arm across the window track. "Seven okay?"

"Sure."

"Good deal. Now if you wind up at the store earlier'n that, Sylvia may not be there. She said something about going over to Mae Beth's so she can get her hair done up . . ." he twirled a finger against his sparse crop of hair, ". . . in a do thingy. But I'll be there. If you need anything before then, just give me a call." He wiped the back of his neck with the used bandana. "The phone's working, ain't it?"

The cabin phone was a twenty-pound rotary that hadn't been changed since the sixties, but Janet knew that wasn't what Rodney referred to. Without warning, any resident of Carlton could pick up their telephone and experience an earful of static or dead silence, both of which could hang around for days. She'd learned some time ago that cell phones didn't offer a compromise to the dilemma. You had to go five miles out of town to get even a faint signal.

"Haven't tried it yet." Janet backed away from the truck as he started the engine.

"Well, if I don't see you least by seven or so, I'm coming back, ya hear?"

"I hear."

He backed up the truck, then after a whine and grind of gears, the pickup jerked forward toward the road. Rodney waved at her just before disappearing beyond the clearing.

Still smiling, Janet rolled her head from shoulder to shoulder. Gradually, she let it flop back and gazed up at the fading blue sky. How nice it would be to stretch out somewhere right now and do nothing. She dreaded the thought of unloading the van.

With a sigh of resignation, she turned on her heels, glanced up at the house—and froze. Pressed against the second-story window was Heather, her eyes wide with terror, her mouth open as though in midscream. Behind her, barely visible in the shadows, stood the figure of a man.

Chapter Eighteen

Anna rested her head against the back seat of the station wagon and stared out the window while Mario Galupane, a distant cousin to Ephraim, barreled along the highway in the fast lane. The radio blared as he sped to catch up to the procession of cars ahead. His wife, Bagusta, her belly full of wine and vodka, snored next to Anna. Anna dismissed them as one would flies at a picnic. She counted each throb from the freshly bandaged wounds on her wrists, matching them to the number of headlights that passed them on the interstate.

Mario had muttered something about their going to Houston, some local festival the tribe was sure to take advantage of. Not that it meant anything to Anna. She knew she'd only be maintained like an aging family pet.

At Thalia's graveside service, Ephraim had not allowed her anywhere near the casket. She'd only been able to watch from behind a nearby tree as the crowd sang and danced their final farewell when Thalia was lowered into the ground. After they dispersed, Anna had snuck to the grave while Bagusta stumbled her way around the cemetery distributing flowers to other tombs.

A beefy-faced man in a dingy work shirt buttoned only at his navel drove up on a backhoe. A concrete slab dangled from the contraption, and the man shouted for Anna to move aside. She'd ignored him, peering into the darkness that was to be her daughter's permanent berth. The eight-foot hole looked fathomless, and the fading sunlight offered only a glimmer from the top of the casket, like gold peeking through crevices in a mine. Anna took the kerchief from her head and tossed it onto the casket.

The irate man's machinery clanged and groaned, working around her until the slab came to rest over the coffin, sealing it away like a secret. The monolithic cap left a barren, four-foot hole, which created the illusion that Thalia had simply disappeared. The depth that remained was intended for a future casket. Anna knew, however, that the future casket would not be hers. She'd disgraced Ephraim, which meant he would never grant permission for her body to rest atop Thalia's.

Where they placed her physical body made little difference to Anna. She didn't need flesh and bone to be with Thalia.

Unfortunately Anna's attempt to reach her daughter had failed. If she'd only cut deeper and vertically instead of across. Now Ephraim would have her watched constantly, which meant if and when she got another opportunity, she would have to make it fast and sure.

Moonlight shone through the car window, and Anna

noticed her shadowy reflection in the glass. Her face seemed to belong to a stranger. Parenthetical lines ran on either side of her mouth, her frown so deep it appeared to extend beyond the confines of her jaw. Bags hung beneath her eyes. Her dark hair, parted down the center of an unusually long widow's peak, fell lackluster to her shoulders. This was the face Ephraim no longer wanted, the one that had embarrassed him, had not submitted to him unquestioningly. The corners of Anna's mouth turned up in a wry smile.

Bagusta snorted, expelled gas, then turned her ample body to one side before settling back to sleep. Anna glanced back at the woman briefly before directing her attention back to the window. She considered her future and found that it only consisted of the next mile of highway, the next headlight, the next *whoosh* of air from a passing truck.

Anna stuck a hand into her skirt pocket and pulled out the music box she'd hidden there. She drew herself up into a ball, knees to her chin, and faced the window. Holding the box close to her ear, she opened it and hummed the familiar tune.

Hush, little baby, don't say a word. Mama's gonna buy you—

She imagined herself lying alongside Thalia in the velvet-lined box, her arms wrapped around her, nodding their bodies to the lullaby.

"Mama?"

Anna looked up at the window and saw Thalia peering back at her, her daughter's face pressed close to the opposite side of the glass. Anna felt no shock at the sight, not even the slightest hint of surprise.

"I'm right here," Anna whispered.

"I'm afraid."

Mario belched out the ending chorus to "Hot Nights, Cold Beer," then lit a cigar that filled the car with cherry-scented smoke.

Anna gently ran a finger down the center of the window. "I won't leave you."

"But it's cold here."

Anna pulled her legs closer to her body as though the movement alone would warm her daughter.

Thalia's face vacillated in time with the music box's melody. "It's dark, Mama."

Bagusta snorted in her sleep again and kicked a leg out against the front seat. Mario looked back at her with a scowl. When his attention went back to the road, Anna closed the music box and nestled it into her lap.

"I know," she murmured.

Thalia's dark eyes widened with fear. "And I'm so alone."

"Not for long." Anna trailed a finger across the window. Her heart felt ready to burst from her chest. No one would stop her this time.

"When?"

A pause as a tractor-trailer roared by.

Anna sneezed from the cigar smoke, then said, "Soon. Very soon." She counted the headlights as they collected behind them in the right lane. Two cars zipped by.

"Mama, I don't know where to go."

"You will."

"How?"

A pickup and motorcycle edged by, and several yards behind them huge headlights, like monstrous white eyes, bounced along the highway.

"How?" Thalia asked again.

Anna kept one eye on the fast approaching headlights and took off her shoes. She curled her toes around the edge of the seat near the door, then looked back at Bagusta. The woman's head had flopped to her shoulder and bobbed with every bump in the road. Mario was preoccupied with his cigar and the latest song blaring from the radio.

The question sounded again. "How?"

Anna held her breath, watching the bouncing headlights, the huge white eyes, now only a few feet away. She grabbed the door handle and pulled. The wail of wind suddenly filling the car sounded to Anna like the cry of angels. She hunched forward, and amidst Mario's shouts and the screech of brakes she sprang into the night.

The last sound Anna heard was the crunch of bones beneath a truck tire.

Chapter Nineteen

A thorough search of the funeral home proved fruitless. No one was hiding in any dark corner or behind any piece of furniture. Michael had gone so far as to open the refrigerator in the visitor's lounge to look inside, but nothing lurked in there either. After a while, he forced himself to explain away the incidents. The shadows, the snickers, only figments of his imagination, tricks his eyes and ears played on him due to fatigue. The prep room door closing, a quirk of fate and timing. Chad probably forgot to secure it before he left. Though the plausibility of that excuse seemed about as far-fetched as icicles in the Sahara since Chad rarely forgot anything, Michael left it at that. He had too much work to do and no further incidents to make him push the issue.

With one body already embalmed and the second nearly finished, Michael worked a crick out of his neck. His stomach rumbled, reminding him that dinner was way past due. He ignored the hunger pangs, clipped the excess thread from the baseball stitch he'd made over the corpse's carotid, then reached for the trocar.

Just as he positioned the point of the hollow metal rod against the side of the abdomen, the prep room door banged open, and Wilson barged in.

Startled by the intrusion, Michael missed the incision he'd made for the trocar and punctured a new hole into the cadaver's stomach. "Goddammit, look what you've made me do!"

Wilson dismissed him with a quick wave. "Who the hell cares about that? Nobody's gonna know. Look here, I need the—"

"For starters, I know." Michael said, his heart rate finally slowing to just below a gallop. He pulled out the trocar and laid it alongside the body. "And for finishers, I don't give a damn what you need. You and I have to talk."

Wilson stomped over to the opposite side of the embalming table. "Now you listen here, boy. It's about time—"

"You're damn right it's about time," Michael said. "It's time you stop acting like a fucking juvenile delinquent."

Wilson's face went from a sickly chalk color to bright red. "Who the hell do you think you are, talking to me like that?"

Michael stripped the latex gloves off his hands and threw them into a hazardous waste bin. "Where's the stuff from the Stevenson girl's casket?"

It took a millisecond for the look in Wilson's eyes to shift from one of panic to bemusement. "I don't know what you're talking about. And don't try to change the subject. You have no right to talk to me this way!"

"When you start ripping off caskets, I have the right to say any damn thing I want."

Wilson pounded the edge of the stainless steel table with a fist. "You're accusing me of stealing? Your own father?"

"Stop with the games."

"I'm telling you I didn't take anything!"

Michael leaned over the table and brought his face closer to his father's. "Bullshit. Besides a few Stevenson guests, you were the only one in the viewing room after I went to see Janet and the girls off."

Wilson's eyes shifted rapidly as though he were reading from a distant cue card. "I wasn't alone. Sally was with me."

"Not the whole time. She told me she left the room to answer the phone."

Wilson slapped his hands together. "See how gullible you are? She *said* she went to answer the phone, but you don't know that for sure, do you?"

"No, but Sally wouldn't take a nickel if it fell at her feet, and you know it."

"So? People can change. They get into binds and do stupid shit."

"That's your style, Dad, not hers."

"I'm telling you, Sally's your thief!"

"She's not!"

"Then one of the Stevensons did it, you goddamn ingrate!"

Michael held his growing fury in check and leaned in farther. "You saw those people. They wouldn't touch that body for anything."

Wilson opened his mouth as though to fire a retort,

then snapped it shut. Michael held his ground, refusing to drop his glare.

After a long moment, Wilson harrumphed loudly. "What the hell do you know anyway? You weren't in the room. Anybody could have taken that gold piece."

The level of disappointment that suddenly settled over Michael unnerved him. He didn't want to admit to himself that he'd been hoping against hope his father was telling the truth. That he hadn't taken anything from the casket. All fools have their dreams.

Michael sighed heavily. "Who said anything about a gold piece, Dad?"

Wilson jerked his head back in surprise. He stammered, "I . . . wait . . . I . . . you did!"

"No, I didn't. I never mentioned anything about a gold piece. I asked where the *stuff* was. Why in the hell would you—"

Wilson's backhand caught Michael off guard. It came fast and hard, landing on his left cheek. Before the pain could fully register, however, Michael's right hand reflexively balled into a fist and slammed into Wilson's jaw. The old man flew backward into a utility cabinet, then dropped to the floor on his butt, out cold.

"Oh, Jesus," Michael breathed. He rounded the embalming table, then took a hesitant step toward his father. Emotions battled inside him, a sickening satisfaction of too-long-awaited retaliation, and the horror of punching his father. Horror won. Michael still couldn't believe he'd done it. It had happened too fast, had come out of nowhere, like someone had taken over his body and shut down his brain. Never in his wildest dreams would he have even considered hitting an old man, much less his father. He suddenly felt sick to his stomach.

Wilson groaned, and Michael hurried over to him. "Dad?"

Another groan, then Wilson slowly lifted his head and rested it against the cabinet. He raised a tentative hand to his jaw and groaned again.

Michael squatted beside his father. "I never meant to—I mean—are you okay?"

Wilson rolled a weary eye toward him and gave a barely perceptible nod. He opened his mouth gradually and, wincing, worked his chin from side to side.

"Look, I'm . . . well . . . I'm sorry," Michael said. "I didn't mean to—"

His father held up a hand. "Never mind about that," he said through scarcely parted lips. "Just help me up."

Michael helped Wilson to his feet, then grabbed a nearby stool and offered it to him.

Wilson sat gingerly, cupped his knees with his hands, and hung his head.

Something's definitely wrong, Michael thought. His father should have exploded by now, hurt jaw or not. Too many past experiences had proven to him that little stopped Wilson from giving anyone their just due. He should be ranting by now, swinging with both fists, grabbing the embalming fluid tank so he could whack his son over the head with it. Something. Anything.

Yet Wilson sat there, saying nothing. He barely moved. He seemed to be concentrating either on his shoes or the floor.

Michael cleared his throat. "We should have a doctor take a look at you," he said. "You know, check your jaw, your tailbone, too, maybe."

"I don't need any doctor touching my ass or my jaw. I'm fine," Wilson said, finally looking up at him.

"But I think—"

"I already know what you think," Wilson said. He lowered his head again. "And you're right."

"So what are you saying? You want to see a doctor?"

Wilson blew out a long breath and shook his head. "What I'm sayin' is you're right, Michael. I took that gold medallion from the casket. And everything you think about me from asshole to worm is true. I'm all that and probably worse."

Stunned beyond words, Michael gaped. Who was this man? Surely not Wilson Savoy. Not *the* Wilson Savoy.

"No question that I've done a lot of crap in my life," Wilson continued, his voice low. "Things I'm not proud of." He laced his fingers together and studied a thumbnail. "I didn't mean to steal from that casket, no more than you meant to punch me. It just happened. Kind of like a reflex thing. I was in a major bind—it was there—I took it." He tilted his head to one side and looked at Michael. "Understand?"

Michael looked away. He did understand about reflex. It was a lousy excuse for what his father had done, but just as pathetic a reason for punching his own father. Understanding it didn't explain why Wilson was confessing, though. Michael didn't want to say anything to jinx it. He figured it better to hang on and ride for a while, see where his father would take it.

Wilson, evidently interpreting Michael's fidgeting as an affirmative answer said, "I figured you would—"

A loud hammering knock from somewhere in the funeral home caused Wilson to jump off the stool, his eyes round with fear. He motioned to the prep room door. "Hurry, Michael, close it!"

The knocking continued, a loud, persistent pounding that seemed to carry the weight of a five hundred-pound man.

"Close it? I've got to find out—"

"Fuck!" Wilson hobbled to the door and closed it himself. He pressed his back against the jamb. "It's Lester, I know it. If we don't answer the door, he'll think nobody's here and leave."

"Who's Lester?"

"He's . . . he's . . . one of the investors I told you about."

The unmistakable sound of glass shattering sent Michael charging for the door. "I don't care who he is, Dad. I'm not going to hide in here while somebody destroys the place."

"No, don't," Wilson pleaded. "Don't go out there!"

Michael opened the door, easing his father out of the way. As soon as he stepped into the hallway, the knocking stopped.

Cautiously, Michael made his way down the corridor, looking over his shoulder every few steps. He saw his father's head peek out from the embalming room, then quickly duck back inside.

Just as he reached the dark, intersecting hall, Michael spotted the photo of Saint Peter's Cathedral laying face down on the floor. It was the same picture that had survived meatball target practice by the Stevenson clan. Now its glass covering was shattered. Whoever had knocked had evidently done it hard enough to vibrate the picture off the wall. He bent over to pick up one of the larger, longer shards.

"See anybody yet?"

Wilson's whisper startled Michael, and he jerked upright. "Jesus, Dad, don't sneak up on me like that!"

His father drew a trembling finger to his lips. "Shhh."

"Why? Nobody can get in here. I locked all the doors." Michael frowned. "Unless you used the front door and forgot to lock it again."

"No, I came in through the back. The one with the auto—" Wilson suddenly cast a look past Michael, and his brow ridged with confusion.

"What?" Michael looked over his shoulder. He didn't see anything but more dark hallway.

"There's somebody over there," Wilson said under his breath. "End of the hall, left corner, against the wall."

Michael turned around and squinted, but still couldn't see anything. He took a step to cross the corridor so he could flip on the light switch, and Wilson grabbed the bottom of his suit coat.

"Don't," Wilson warned, keeping his voice low.

"I'm just going to turn on the lights. No big deal." Michael twisted to one side and freed himself. He crossed over to the light switch, slapped it on, then pointed to where his father had indicated. He was about to say, "Look, nobody there." But someone was there.

An old man stood quietly watching them. Except for his age, which looked to be around ninety, and the man's large, protruding ears, he could have passed for Ephraim Stevenson's twin, down to the white fedora perched on his head. Stranger still was the man's attire. He wore a long-tailed, black mourning suit with a blue silk shirt and accompanying cravat. He kept his hands primly folded over one another just below his belt, and his feet were bare. Even from this distance Michael could make out thick, yellow toenails that looked as if they hadn't been trimmed in years. Michael figured this guy wasn't the investor his father was expecting, but the old man's large eyes stayed intensely focused on Wilson nonetheless.

Michael glanced back at his father to see if there was any hint of recognition on his face. There wasn't, only a bewildered gawk highlighted by a developing bruise on the left side of his chin.

Perplexed not only by how the Ephraim look-alike got into the funeral home, but how he'd missed seeing him in the shadows a minute ago, Michael asked the old man, "Uh—may I help you?"

The old man blinked, a slow, seemingly laborious process, then lifted a hand and pointed a crooked finger at Wilson.

Michael waited, but when the man didn't say anything, he whispered to Wilson, "You know this guy?"

"Not a clue," Wilson murmured. "Kind of looks like Stevenson."

"Yeah, I noticed. But I don't remember seeing him at the service. You?"

"Nuh-uh."

"Sure looks like he knows you, though."

Wilson squared his shoulders, "Yeah, well, if he doesn't point that goddamn finger somewhere else pretty soon, I'm going to shove it up his ass. That'll get him to talk." Wilson scowled, winced, then said to the stranger, "Hey, how'd you get in here?"

A look of raw, unabashed hatred flared in the old man's eyes. He took a step forward, and his body wobbled as if he walked on Jell-O. The accusing finger jabbed fervently at Wilson. "Thief!" he declared in a thunderous voice. "It is you who has released curse of death!"

Wilson reared back his head. "What the fuck?"

Michael grabbed his father's arm, suspecting he'd spring after the guy any second.

"Let go," Wilson demanded, yanking his arm free. "If you got somethin' to say to me, mister, then you'd better hurry up and finish sayin' it because I'm going to call the cops. You're trespassing."

With a gleam in his eye, the old man spat on the floor. His saliva crackled on the carpet like acid. "You have taken granddaughter's passage," he said, each syllable heavily accented, the r's rolling off his tongue with venomous purpose. "And for that you shall pay."

Michael cringed. He remembered the pomp and circumstance the Stevensons had given to the gold coin they had him place under Thalia's hands. Ephraim had said something then about it being her right to passage. Evidently, this man was Thalia's grandfather, and somehow he not only knew about the missing coin, he knew Wilson had taken it. But how? The man would have had to be at the viewing to know, and Michael was convinced he wasn't. No way he would have missed a character like this, especially near the end of the viewing when there were even fewer people in the room. Regardless of how the old man knew, from the look on his face, it was easy to assess that Wilson was in deep shit.

"I don't know nothing about no granddaughter's passage," Wilson declared to the stranger. "So if that's all you got—"

"You will end!" the man bellowed. He lifted his arms and spread them expansively. "You are to receive but one warning, and this I give to you now. Unless it be returned to her before rising of second sun, you shall die without mercy!"

"Whoa, hold on now—" Michael said.

"Now just a goddamn minute—" Wilson shouted.

"The second sun," the old man reiterated, louder. "Return it so granddaughter may find way or it is done, Wilson Savoy. For you, for—"

"How the hell do you know my—"

". . . for anyone who dares possess it. It shall be done."

Wilson spun around and faced Michael. "I'll show that sonofabitch who's gonna be done! I'm gonna kick his ass!"

Although Michael agreed that the old man was going over the top with the melodrama, he pulled his father close. "The gold piece," he whispered in his ear. "That's what he's talking about. That's what he wants."

"I don't give a damn what he's talking about. He threatened me!"

Figuring it best to handle the matter himself, Michael held up both hands and turned to signal a truce to the stranger.

But the old man was gone.

Bewildered, Michael dropped his hands and took a cautious step forward. Then another. And another.

When he reached the spot where the stranger had

stood, the only evidence that gave proof the man had even been there was a depressed set of prints in the carpet. Not the footprints of a man, however. But those of a dog—a gargantuan, long-nailed dog.

Chapter Twenty

Janet finished the last of her coffee with a hard swallow. "—Then to top it off, I thought I saw a man behind her," she said, keeping her voice low so the girls, now watching television in the Theriots' living room, wouldn't hear. The hair on her arms stood on end as she recalled the event.

"Oh, God," Sylvia gasped, pressing her hands against the sides of her face.

Janet nodded. "I thought I was going to have a heart attack right then and there."

"What did you do?" Sylvia asked.

"You should've called me," Rodney said, a little too loud. "First thing."

"Hush," Sylvia warned.

"Well, she should've."

Sylvia threw her husband a stern glance before turning her attention back to Janet. "Then what?"

"I ran into the house, grabbed a knife from the

kitchen, then took off for the stairs, yelling like a banshee."

"Should've called me first," Rodney said with a shake of his head.

"For heaven's sake, Rodney," Sylvia snapped. "You think she was gonna stop, pick up the phone, and call you when all the time she's thinking those babies are just a whiff away from danger?"

"She'd have had time," Rodney said indignantly.

Sylvia tsked and turned to Janet. "Then what?"

"You're probably right, Rodney." Janet reached across the table and patted his arm. "But I didn't even think. I just ran for Ellie's room."

"But the girls were okay?" Sylvia asked.

Rodney rolled his eyes. "I would s'pose so, Syl. They're sittin' right over there."

Janet jumped in before Sylvia could counter. "The girls were fine. They just looked at me like I was crazy."

"What about the man?" Sylvia asked.

"Nothing," Janet said. "I searched every inch of the house and didn't find a thing. After a while I figured it might have been the sun reflecting off the windowpane."

"I don't understand," Sylvia said. "Then why was Heather screaming?"

"That's the funny thing. She claims she wasn't. In fact, both girls swear she was nowhere near the window."

"That's really weird," Sylvia said. She got up from her chair and began gathering dishes. "Maybe the girls just played a joke on you, then got too scared to admit it when they saw you run in all serious."

"I don't know," Janet said. "That's a pretty sophisticated joke for a five- and six-year-old."

"Computers and television, s'all they're good for. Teaches kids stuff they got no business learnin'," Rodney said. He pushed his chair away from the table. "Anyways, no harm done. Kids'll be kids." He rubbed his stomach. "Syl, your fried chicken'd make an angel cry."

Sylvia stopped midway to the kitchen sink. "Here Janet is all worried, and you're talking 'bout food."

Rodney leaned back in his chair. "What's to worry about? I'd bet you a dime to nothin' that it was the kids playin' around."

Sylvia shook her head dismissively, and Janet used the few seconds of silence to change the subject. Rehashing this afternoon only heightened her worry.

"Rodney's right, you know," she said to Sylvia. "Your chicken is the best. I'm so stuffed I can barely move." Janet sucked in a deep breath for emphasis, got up, then gathered her plate and glass from the kitchen table and went to the sink, where Sylvia was already elbow deep in soapsuds.

A blush spread over Sylvia's face. The sleeves to her white and pink blouse were pushed up nearly to her armpits, and meaty slabs of skin swung under her arms when she rinsed a dish. "I'm glad you liked it. My mama left me that recipe."

Janet kissed the old woman's cheek and reached for a dry towel. "Well, you did your mama proud."

A loud belch from the table made Sylvia spin around with a look of disbelief and disgust. "Rodney!"

Janet bit her lip to suppress a laugh.

"S'cuse me," Rodney said sheepishly. "But it ain't bad

manners, Syl, just good food. Ain't that right, Little Bit?"

"That's right."

"Told you," Rodney said to his wife. He drummed his fingers on his stomach, and when Sylvia only glared back at him, he got up from his chair. "Okay, guess it's time for me to go join the girls."

When he left the room, Sylvia shook her head. "I guess we just gotta be grateful it didn't come out the other end."

Janet grinned. She enjoyed working alongside Sylvia in her kitchen. It reminded Janet of homey, childhood times, a time before Alzheimer's stole her name from her mother's memory.

"We should be at the festival by nine," Janet said, rinsing soap from a glass. "I can help at the pie booth if you'd like."

Sylvia dried her hands on the checkered apron cinched around her thick waist. "I sure would. I baked tons this year. Didn't do blackberry, though. Just fig, pecan, apple, and a few custards. I'm thinkin' that—" Her eyes darted past Janet, then narrowed with worry. "What's the matter, munchkin?"

Alarmed, Janet spun around and nearly knocked over her daughter, who stood inches away with her arms folded over her stomach.

"My tummy hurts," Ellie said. She leaned her head against her mother's leg.

Janet tossed the towel onto the counter and placed a hand on Ellie's forehead. It felt cool and dry. She cupped Ellie's chin and lifted her head for an eye inspection. Heavy lidded, but clear.

"Probably too much chicken," Janet said, smoothing Ellie's hair. She turned to Sylvia, who was already heading for the medicine cabinet near the pantry. "Do you have any Pepto?"

"Right here." Sylvia pulled a bottle from the cabinet, then shook it vigorously while she searched for a spoon. "Hope she hasn't caught that stomach virus that's been going around lately. Rodney had it a couple of weeks ago."

Janet took the bottle, measured out a teaspoon of the pink medicine, then fed it to Ellie. "I'm sure it's just a little indigestion."

Sylvia recapped the bottle and placed it on the counter. "Why don't you go on and bring the girls back to the cabin? Munchkin looks whipped and so do you."

"Maybe you're right," Janet said. "I think a good night's rest will do us all some good."

"There you go." Sylvia hunkered down beside Ellie. "You've got a busy day tomorrow, munchkin, so you need to go and take care of that tummy." She held out her arms. "How about giving old Sylvia a hug bye?"

Ellie wrapped her arms around Janet's right leg.

Puzzled, Janet stroked her daughter's back. This wasn't like Ellie, even on a really bad day. She'd always adored the Theriots. "Aren't you going to give Sylvia a little hug?" she asked.

Ellie hid her face farther behind her mother's leg, and Janet gave Sylvia an apologetic shrug. "She's tired, and with her stomach—"

"Don't you worry about it." Sylvia put her hands on her knees and grunted her way upright again. "Go on and get that baby to bed. How 'bout I send Rodney out there with you—you know," she tossed a quick look over her shoulder as though referring to a secret

hidden in the cupboard behind her, "just to check things out."

"No need," Janet said. "We'll be fine." The truth was she would've loved for someone to "check things out" at the cabin. But Rodney was getting old, and she worried that he might trip over something in the dark and get hurt. She'd simply make a run through the house before the girls went inside. The plan sounded a bit paranoid to her, especially since she'd already convinced herself, or thought she had, that the man she'd seen in the window had been an illusion created by the sun. But better safe than sorry.

There's no one in the house. There's no one in the house. There's no one in the house.

Janet continued to chant the mantra to herself as she loaded the girls into the van, then left the Theriots.

The ride back to the cabin seemed longer than usual. The night wrapped around the van clear and warm, and a moon, slivered to a quarter of its size, strained to illuminate the sky. As Janet turned onto the dark side road that led to the cabin, the van's headlights illuminated shadows at the edge of the forest. Her heart thudded loudly in her ears.

"Mama?" Ellie said quietly.

"Hm?" Janet pulled up to the house and parked. She scolded herself for not leaving on an outside light.

"Is there such a thing as a bogeyman?" Ellie asked.

Janet turned around in her seat, frowning. "Where on earth did you hear that?"

Ellie threw a worried glance at Heather, then looked back at her mother. "Nowheres."

"Heather?" Janet eyed her niece.

"Tommy Marks says they got bogeymans when it's real dark, Aunt Janet," Heather proclaimed. Her eyes darted nervously at the window. "And . . . it's real dark."

"Who's Tommy Marks?"

"A boy that lives by my house. He knows everything. He's eight."

"And what does he say a bogeyman is supposed to look like?" Janet asked.

Heather drew in a deep breath. "Like a monster. All ugly and stuff with big teeth."

"I see. Well, I'm afraid Tommy doesn't know much because there's no such thing as a bogeyman. That's just an old, ugly fairy tale." Janet pulled the keys out of the ignition.

"Promise?" Ellie asked.

Janet nodded. "Tell you what. Both of you close your eyes."

The girls shut their eyes simultaneously.

"What do you see?" Janet asked.

"Dark," Heather said.

"Is it really dark?"

"Yep," Ellie answered. "Really, really dark."

"Any bogeymen in there?"

Heather giggled. "No."

"Nope," Ellie confirmed.

"Okay, open your eyes," Janet said.

Two sets of eyes popped open.

"Nighttime is the same kind of dark, only you see it with your eyes open," Janet said. "And just like there were no bogeymen in the dark behind your eyes, there are none now. Understand?"

"See, I told you," Ellie said to Heather. "There's no such a thing."

Heather looked past her to study the window as though debating what to believe.

"That's right, honey. No such thing." Janet opened the van door, and white hazy light washed over them from the interior bulb. "Now you two stay in here for a minute, and I'll go inside and turn on some lights. I don't want you tripping over each other out there."

"Lock the door, okay, Aunt Janet?"

Janet got out of the van and smiled back at Heather. "I'd already planned to." She lowered her window a couple of inches, pressed the auto lock, and closed the door.

While she walked toward the house, Janet heard the girls squabbling and, for once, appreciated the noise.

"Scaredy-cat."

"Am not!"

"Am too."

"Am not—"

There's no one in the house. No one in the house. Janet opened the front door and flipped on the first light switch she came to. The dining room and kitchen were just as she'd left them, a box of cleaning supplies on the table and folded paper bags on the counter.

Her footsteps sounded thunderous as she rounded the corner to the family room and searched behind chairs and the couch. She took the stairs two at a time, looking over her shoulder as she went.

At the top of the stairs, Janet took a right and headed for Ellie's room. Once there, she cautiously snaked a hand around the doorjamb and felt for the light switch. She thought about the man in the window, and her stomach fluttered.

There's no one in the house.

Her fingers bumped against the switch, and she blinked against the sudden glare.

Twin beds with Scooby Doo comforters, a dresser, toy chest, and Barbie vanity. All was as it should be. She looked under the beds and in the closet. Nothing unusual.

Janet began to breathe easier as she went through the bathroom and master bedroom and found everything in its place. Relief sent her bounding down the stairs to collect the girls from the van.

Twenty minutes later, Ellie and Heather were in the tub making snowman faces with bubbles, and Janet was trying to decide whether to have a glass of Pinot Noir or cup of warm milk.

"Don't take too long now. It's late, and I want the two of you in bed. We have a big day tomorrow," Janet said, grateful that all evidence of their bogeyman fears had vanished. Hers felt abated as well. She patted a pile of clothes on the bathroom vanity. "Pajamas are right here."

"Okay," Ellie said, constructing a pyramid of suds on top of Heather's head.

Janet pulled two towels out from the linen closet and placed them near the clothes. "Stomach better?"

"Yeah," Ellie said. She reviewed her sculpture. "Just feels a little squishy."

Janet stood in the doorway and studied Ellie's face. She didn't look sick. Dark shadows looped beneath her eyes, but that always happened when she grew tired.

"All right, you guys," Janet said. "I'll be up later to tuck you in."

She left the girls giggling and slapping water at each another and headed for the stairs. Each step seemed to emphasize the weight of the day in her legs.

Pinot Noir, definitely.

Once in the kitchen, Janet retrieved a drinking glass from the cupboard and went to the fridge for the Kendall Jackson Michael kept on the bottom shelf. She poured three fingers' depth into the glass, then went into the family room.

After turning on the television set, she muted the volume and watched the fuzzy image on the screen. A weatherman pointed to a graph, which showed the high and low temperature forecasts for the next three days: hot, humid, and more of the same. With a groan, Janet walked over to the couch, sat, and stretched her legs out in front of her.

She rested her head against the back cushion and let her eyes cruise about the room. Across from the television, in the opposite corner of the room, sat Michael's grandfather's favorite chair. The burgundy leather recliner had dark stains on the headrest, a testament to years of excessive hair oil. No one sat in it anymore, but Michael insisted that it not be moved.

Recessed between the television and recliner was a fireplace that, to Janet's knowledge, had never been used. Not a smudge of soot or grime marred any part of the hearth. Plastic ivies lined the mantel, which bordered the lower edge of a huge picture: a ship mastering a storm's fury at sea.

Janet sipped from her glass, reached for the telephone on the end table near the sofa, and dialed her home number. She needed to hear Michael's voice.

A series of clicks preempted the line connection, and it took a moment before it began to ring. She rested the receiver against her shoulder and took another sip of wine.

Five . . . six . . . seven . . . Michael almost always picked up on the second ring. Janet glanced at her watch. Nearly ten. Surely he wouldn't still be at the funeral home.

She hung up and tried the number again. An unusually cool breeze brushed across Janet's arms while she listened to the persistent ringing. With a shiver, she looked up at the ceiling and spotted an air conditioner vent directly above her. Thinking one of the girls had turned down the thermostat, she made a mental note to turn it back up before going to bed.

When there was no answer after the tenth ring, Janet hung up again and dialed the number for the funeral home.

A thud echoed from upstairs.

"Into bed, girls," she called out, and a patter of footsteps raced overhead.

Taking a large gulp of wine, Janet listened to the third ring, then the fourth, a fifth. She was about to hang up when the ringing stopped. She heard silence instead of the customary, "Savoy Funeral Home," greeting from the answering service.

"Hello?"

No one replied.

"Michael?"

From what sounded like an ocean's distance away, Janet heard a tinkling sound, like bells or chimes from a music box.

"Hello?"

The sound grew louder and took on more definition. A melody. One that sounded familiar, but Janet couldn't quite make it out.

Suddenly a loud squawk filled her ear, and she jerked the phone away. Even with the receiver at a distance, she heard the squawk turn into a hiss, like the sound of pork chops frying in a skillet.

"Ancient piece of crap." Janet dropped the receiver onto its cradle. Evidently the phone company had decided now was a good time for a hiatus. She placed her glass on the end table, got up from the couch, and headed for the stairs, eager to get out of her jeans and into something more comfortable. She would try calling Michael later, when the lines cleared up. *If* the lines cleared up.

Going into the bathroom first, Janet inspected the pile of water-soaked towels and clothes on the floor and tossed what was fairly dry into the hamper. The rest she wrung out and hung on towel rods. With that done, she went across the hall to Ellie's room.

A ribbon of light glowed from beneath the bedroom door. Janet opened it slowly and peeked inside, surprised to see her daughter in bed, covered up to the neck, and already asleep. Heather sat ramrod straight in the other bed, chewing her thumb.

"What's the matter, honey? Not tired?" Janet asked, entering the room. She picked up a short-haired doll from the floor and placed it on the dresser.

"I can't sleep," Heather said. She tucked her bottom lip between her teeth.

Janet walked over to the edge of the bed and sat.

"You're not still afraid of what we talked about in the van, are you?" She didn't want to say the word bogeyman for fear it would upset the girl.

Heather shook her head vigorously. "No." She pointed to Ellie. "I can't sleep 'cause she won't stop."

Janet glanced over at her daughter. "Won't stop what?"

"Humming."

"Humming?"

"Uh-huh."

Janet smiled, held out her arms, and Heather scrambled into them. "She's asleep, honey. She's not . . ."

A low, eerie hum sounded from the next bed, and Janet's arms tightened reflexively around Heather's back.

"I told you," Heather whispered.

They looked over at Ellie, whose eyes remained closed, her chest moving slow and steady with the rhythm of sleep. Her lips, however, were pressed tightly together, and from them came the same melody Janet had heard over the phone.

Chapter Twenty-one

"Where'd the sonofabitch go?" Wilson asked, turning in circles like a pup trying to get sight of its tail.

"I—I don't know." Michael placed the side of his shoe alongside one of the prints. It was nearly twice the width of his foot. "But get a load of this."

Wilson let out an exasperated huff. "What? He piss on the floor?" He went over to Michael and examined the indicated section of carpet. "Damn!"

"Yeah."

"No way that old man could've left those. He was too puny."

"I know."

Michael and Wilson stared at each other quizzically, then Wilson quickly slid a shoe across the carpet, erasing the depression.

"Screw it," Wilson said. "The bigger deal is where'd the bastard go? He didn't go past us, so what'd he do? Go through the wall?"

Michael shoved a hand through his hair. His father

was right. Without windows or doors near the corner of the hall, there was no immediate escape route. Michael thought about the black shadow he'd chased earlier, the one that resembled the flap of a coattail—similar to the coattails on the mourning suit worn by the old man. Although Michael was positive he hadn't seen the man during the Stevenson service, he had to wonder—*had* he been at the service, then stayed behind when it concluded? Had he been hiding in the funeral home all this time? That might provide a reasonable explanation for how he got in, but it didn't answer squat about how he got out. From the way Michael figured it, he'd only turned away from the old man for a few seconds. How could anyone that old, who appeared to have difficulty even walking, disappear that fast?

"He's got to be somewhere in the building," Michael said. "I'll take a look in the lobby. You check out the back rooms. Maybe he did go past us, and we didn't notice."

"I'm old, son, not senile. We'd have had to been blindfolded to miss him."

"It won't hurt to check," Michael said, already heading for the reception area.

"Hey!" Wilson called after him.

Michael stopped short and looked back. His father had his bottom lip pinched thoughtfully between two fingers.

"What?"

"Well—suppose he *is* back there," Wilson said. "I mean, not that I'm scared or anything. The guy's so old and feeble looking, I could probably knock him over with a broken knuckle, but—I mean—he *was* big on the threats. Suppose he's got some goon back there—you know—an ambush or something—waiting to get me by myself?"

"I doubt that."

"Yeah, but just suppose . . ."

Michael shook his head in frustration. "If you're going to be a wuss about it, then come on. We'll go through the building together."

"I'm *not* a wuss," Wilson said, hustling to his son's side with a scowl. "I'm being cautious is all. Nothing wrong with a man being cautious."

"Yeah, yeah, okay. Jesus, I swear, Dad, you get yourself into more shit . . ."

Wilson shrugged as they made their way down the corridor. "What can I say? A man's gotta do what a man's gotta do. Just my way's a little different sometimes."

"Most times."

"Yeah, that, too."

Thirty minutes later, after Michael and Wilson had completed a second search of the building, they'd still found no sign of the old man. They settled into the lobby, where Wilson flopped down on one of the couches.

"Okay, so he's not here," Wilson said. "And I really don't care anymore where the old bastard went. The way I figure it, he's gone, doesn't matter how or where. Less I gotta deal with. What do you say we call out for some dinner?"

"You can't just drop this," Michael said. "He might not be here, and God only knows how he got out, but that doesn't change the fact that you took that gold piece. If the old man knows you have it, then I'd bet the other Stevensons know about it, too. We need to get the coin back to them. *You* need to give it back to them."

Wilson ran a fingernail across the arm of the sofa. "I can't."

Michael felt his blood pressure rocket toward the danger zone. What had all that redeemable father crap been about earlier in the embalming room? Probably another bullshit session. Once again, his father was proving you could throw paint on a zebra, but underneath, the stripes remained.

"Goddammit, Dad, we're probably talking major lawsuit because of what you did. The Stevensons could wind up with the whole damn funeral home by the time they're through with us. Even if—"

"Then I'll countersue them for harassment. You heard that man. He said he'd kill me."

"No he didn't."

"A technicality. He said I'd die, same thing."

"And whose side do you think a judge would take? Yours, claiming a ninety-something-year-old man threatened your life? Or that old man's, after he tells the judge you stole from his granddaughter's coffin? Which case do you think they'll investigate first?"

Wilson looked down.

"For heaven's sake, just give it back."

"I already told you, I can't."

"What the hell's wrong with you?" Michael shouted. "There's—"

"I didn't say I wouldn't give it back. I said I *can't*."

"What the hell does that mean?"

"I lost it."

"You what?"

"Lost it. Gone. I don't have it, Michael."

Michael held his breath, waiting for a punch line. When it didn't come, he said, "You're shittin' me, right?"

Wilson shrugged. "I wish I were. That's why I came back here, to ask you for your house keys." He looked up at him sheepishly. "I went to your house earlier, before Janet and the girls left, because I broke out in this rash and needed a bathroom to wash up." He held up a hand as if to thwart an assumed question. "The john here had too many people in it. Anyway, I had the medallion, or coin, or whatever the shit it is, in my jacket pocket, and when I went into your bathroom, I took the jacket off. It must have fallen out then. I didn't find out it was missing until later, after I left your place. I went back to look for it, but—uh—your house was locked."

The elfish look on Wilson's face told Michael there was more to the story than he was letting on.

"What else?" Michael asked.

"Huh?"

"There's something you're not telling me."

"Uh—no. That's it. I swear to—"

"Dad . . ."

"Okay, okay, so there's the thing with one of the back windows on your house," Wilson blurted.

"What about it?"

Wilson sat up straighter and stuck his hands between his knees. "I kind of broke it."

Michael frowned. "Why?"

"Well . . . well, dammit, I didn't mean to. It just kinda happened. I didn't want you to find out about me taking the medallion, so . . ." He looked down at his knees. "Shit. . . . Okay, so I tried to get into your house without you knowing. Tried jimmying the window, but the sonofabitch broke." Wilson let out a thin, regretful snort and shook his head. "All that trouble, and I couldn't even pull myself up through it."

Michael didn't know whether to hit him, this time on purpose, or fall on the floor from shock at having been told the truth. He did neither. He just stood, staring at Wilson, wondering what was going on. Ever since the incident in the embalming room, when he'd inadvertently punched him in the jaw, something seemed to be changing with his father. Admitting his faults—owning up to his actions—telling the truth—well, eventually telling the truth. Definite changes. Big ones. It made Michael nervous.

Deciding it better not to kick a zebra while it was in the throes of possible mutation, Michael bypassed the window incident and said, "Then we'll search my house."

Wilson looked up at him with a shocked expression. "You're . . . you're not pissed?"

"I'm not jumping for joy over the fact that you tried breaking into the house, but at least you told me the truth about it. The most important thing right now is getting that gold piece back to the Stevensons. Once you return it, and maybe with a little damage control, you might only have to spend a year in prison instead of ten."

"That's not funny."

"It wasn't meant to be."

Michael allowed the following silence to breed into a level of discomfort that made Wilson chew on his upper lip.

Finally, Michael said, "All right, we'll start with this—I'll go to the house and look for the coin. You finish aspirating the body in the prep room. I don't want to leave it overnight. When you're done, come meet me. We'll figure out what to do from there."

Wilson stood up and glanced around nervously. "How come I'm the one who has to stay?"

Michael eyed him.

"Okay, okay, I'll aspirate," Wilson said, then trudged off to the prep room, grumbling.

Still amazed at the seemingly evolving Wilson, Michael left the funeral home and headed across the street for home.

Ponderous clouds clotted the dark, western sky, and Michael spotted lightning knit the horizon to the firmament. The lightning quickly grew in frequency and brightness, and Michael loitered, watching the light show. Each flash brought to mind the events of his day. The Stevenson service, the missing coin, the shadows he'd chased, hitting his father, the vanishing old man. Alone, each had been duly weird, frustrating, a challenge he'd never faced before. But now, reviewing them collectively, Michael had the odd feeling they were like the lightning, all warning signs, but of some strange, cosmic storm preparing to strike.

Michael quickened his steps and wiggled the knot loose on his tie. "You're flaking out, Savoy," he muttered. "You need sleep."

By the time he reached home, Michael remembered the broken window his father had told him about. At this late hour, it would be impossible to find a repairman to fix it. He'd have to find a trash bag or piece of cardboard to tape over the hole before the rain came.

"Thanks, Dad," he mumbled, and entered his house. For a moment, Michael stood by the kitchen door, breathing in familiar scents. Janet's favorite lavender soap, lemon furniture polish, a hint of chicken stew.

He went to the refrigerator and opened it. Just as he suspected, a blue Tupperware bowl sat on the second shelf with a note taped to the lid. It read: *Supper. Please eat! Love, me.*

Loneliness settled over him. Though they'd only left that afternoon, Michael missed his family. The special smile Janet always gave him when he came home from work. The way Ellie bounced around his legs, always so excited to see him. Her bright blue eyes always lit up something in his heart that he would've died for.

With a sigh, Michael removed the bowl from the fridge, placed it on the counter, then glanced over at the kitchen clock. A quarter to eleven. Way past Ellie's bedtime, but if he was lucky, Janet might still be awake.

Michael grabbed the cordless phone and dialed the number to the cabin. After two short rings, he heard a recorded, female voice say, "We're sorry, all circuits are busy now. Please try your call again later."

He hung up and carried the phone with him to the bathroom.

A quick inspection of the tidy, blue-carpeted room turned up nothing but the standard bathroom essentials. Michael checked behind the door and found one of Ellie's butterfly barrettes on the floor. He picked it up and without thinking, stuck it into his pants' pocket, then moved on to the tub. No gold piece there, either, just yellow, nonskid appliqués shaped like daisies.

Michael lowered the lid to the toilet and sat. He considered the possibility that his father might have been lying to throw him off track. Maybe Wilson already hocked the piece. But if he'd sold it to a pawnshop, there would have been no need for him to admit he'd broken the window. The confession would've been useless and dumb, even for his father. That left Michael with Wilson's original story. If his father had come into the bathroom, removed his jacket, and the coin fell out, logically, it should still be here. Logic was one thing, however, reality often another. The damned coin wasn't here.

Giving his brain a rest, Michael punched the redial button on the phone, then once again listened to the two short rings and, "We're sorry, all circuits are busy now. Please try your call again later."

"Shit." Michael didn't know anything about phone circuitry, but he figured if the technology was available to send men to the moon, somebody should be able to get a simple phone call through to Carlton, Louisiana.

He clicked off the phone and with a groan, got to his feet and went back into the kitchen.

Once there, he placed the telephone back on its charger, then retraced what he thought his father's steps might have been from the kitchen door to the bathroom. Along the way, he looked behind doors and under furniture.

Still no coin.

Michael repeated the same process from the living room door to the bathroom, just in case Wilson had come in from that direction. It yielded the same results—nothing.

Deciding to wait until his father returned before going through another search, Michael detoured to the kitchen. He divided the stew into two portions so Wilson would have something to eat later, then heated his share in the microwave.

Twenty minutes later, with his stomach full and eyelids drooping, Michael plodded off to his recliner in the living room.

"Just for a minute," he said aloud, settling into the chair. "I'll sit for only a minute."

Almost immediately, Michael felt his breathing deepen and his mouth go slack. He lifted his head, thinking he'd better get up. The chair was too comfortable, and he was too tired. Not a good combination for someone who needed to stay awake. But he allowed his head to drop back and his eyes to close.

A little bit longer, he thought. *That's all. I promise*.

His last thought before falling into deep sleep came by way of an image. Anna Stevenson's worried face. She was saying something—warning him—crying . . .

Chapter Twenty-two

By late afternoon, gray clouds hung over the fairgrounds like thick fungus. Janet swatted at a fly with the notepad she'd used to tally the day's sales.

"Not a bad haul," she said to Sylvia. "Forty-eight dollars and only two pies left."

"I say that calls for a break." Sylvia wiped sweat from her face with a paper towel. "We might be closing shop early anyhow by the looks of this weather." She stuck her head out from under the tin awning of the concession stand and peered up at the sky. "Could use a little sprinkle to get rid of this heat."

"That's for sure." Janet tossed the notepad into a cardboard box. "Why don't you go and get something to drink? I'll stay here until you get back."

"And miss sticking that skinny hairdresser, Mae Beth, with one of these pies? Not a chance." Sylvia stuck a hand into her blouse to adjust a bra strap. "I forked out nearly four bucks for one of Mae Beth's barbecue dinners at noon, so she owes me. You go on and find Rodney and the girls. Take a little walk, stretch your legs. You can bring me a lemonade on your way back."

Janet gave her a little salute. "Yes, ma'am. I'm not going to argue with a deal like that."

"Good," Sylvia said, perching on a wooden stool. "Take your time."

With a wave, Janet left the concession stand and headed for the midway. The air was still and scented with cotton candy, roasted hot dogs, and horse dung from the nearby pony rides.

She paused near the Tilt-A-Whirl and watched the buckets twist and race at breakneck speed. Its prismatic light show flashed to the beat of an old Beach Boys tune. A few feet away, staggered like giant toys on display, the Rocket Swing and Zipper, Snake Coaster and Tornado called to only the bravest of hearts. Chattering, flush-faced kids squirmed in lines, waiting their turn. Just beyond them were rides more suited to Janet's taste: the merry-go-round, kiddy boats, and bumper cars. She'd never been able to handle the spin, height, or speed of the other rides, even as a little girl. Just looking at the Ferris wheel, which she spotted churning in the distance, made her feel queasy and light-headed.

She concentrated on the nearby barkers who shouted their bargains to passersby.

"Two tries for a buck, five for two," one called as he threw darts at inflated balloons on a corkboard behind him. "Best deal of the day!"

"Right here, pretty lady, right here," another cried after her. "Three balls for two bucks. Make the hoop and win yourself a stuffed panda."

Janet smiled politely and shook her head.

"Aw, come on. I'll even give you a free throw. How 'bout it?"

"Maybe later." Janet spotted Rodney, Ellie, and Heather at the Ring-Toss booth and headed toward them.

As she stepped up behind the threesome, Rodney tossed a rubber ring at a pegboard. It fell to the ground with a plop.

"Doggone it," Rodney said. He slapped five dollars on the counter.

"Yeah, doggone it!" the girls chorused.

Janet watched the scrawny teen running the Toss scoop up Rodney's money, then place three more rings on the counter.

"Three's a charm," Janet said. She reached around Rodney to tickle Ellie's ear, happy to see her daughter smiling. Last night, after the humming episode, Ellie wound up tossing and turning in her sleep. Four times she'd cried out for Janet, and all four times when Janet rushed to her bedside, Ellie detailed the same nightmare. A man wearing a white hat chased her. He ran fast, Ellie claimed, because he could turn into a dog with big, long legs. She also said that a woman with pointy black hair, which, after deciphering Ellie's adamant gestures, Janet translated to mean a widow's peak, tried to help her. But the dog-man was bigger and ran faster, and just when he was about to bite into her leg, Ellie would wake up. She'd looked so exhausted this morning, Janet had considered canceling their trip to the fair. But after an hour of the girls' begging, she'd conceded. Now, judging by the shine in Ellie's eyes, it had been the right call.

"Hey there, Little Bit," Rodney said, grinning over his shoulder. " 'Bout time Syl let you out that cage."

Ellie scrambled to Janet's side and tugged on her blouse. "Mama, look what Mr. Rodney's gonna win for me." Her face radiated with excitement as she pointed to the shelves of prizes along the inside of the booth. There were stuffed dogs and giraffes, posters of the latest teen heartthrobs, flags and whistles, pouches and zippered bags, and on the very top shelf, a menagerie of handblown glass animals. Each item had a numbered tag hanging from it, which Janet assumed corresponded to the numbers taped below each peg that jutted out from the back wall.

"Which one?" Janet asked her.

"That one." Ellie jabbed the air with a finger. "Number—uh—" She looked up at Rodney.

"Forty-two," he said with his hands cupped around his mouth as though sharing a covert code.

"Yeah, forty-two." Ellie pointed again.

Janet surveyed the numbered tags. "Which one's forty-two?"

"Up there," Ellie said, jumping up and down. "The pony."

Heather's head poked out from around Rodney's side. "I'm getting the big Pooh bear," she announced.

Janet spied the Pooh bear sitting on a bottom shelf with the rest of the stuffed animals, but the only horse she saw was one made of glass. It sat on the corner of the top shelf and was about the size of Ellie's hand. The transparent head was thrown back, its nostrils flared, and the large, red glass eyes appeared frozen in virulent madness. An orange tag with the number 42 hung around its neck. The sight of the glass beast made Janet uneasy.

"Why not try for a stuffed giraffe?" she coaxed.

Ellie's eyes fixed on the glass horse, her expression determined. "No, the pony."

Janet looked at Rodney, who grinned and shrugged. "Doesn't much matter," he said. "I'll be lucky to get one of them posters at the rate I'm going." He picked up one of the rings and spun it around a finger. "Wanna give it a shot?"

"Sure," Janet said, figuring she could aim for something less breakable *and* less creepy. She stepped up to the counter.

"They're spaced close together," Rodney said, motioning to the pegs. "So the hoops bounce off real easy. But I could've been throwin' too hard."

Janet balanced the ring between her thumb and forefinger and felt Ellie press against her leg.

"Don't miss, okay?" Ellie said anxiously.

Janet winked at her, then flipped her wrist, sending the rubber doughnut across the booth. Heather squealed as it bounced against the wall, teetered over a peg, then fell to the floor.

"This is nearly impossible," Janet said to Rodney. She reached for another ring. This time she held it so she looked through its center. Instead of tossing it, she shoved it vertically toward the wall.

"Number seven!" the barker shouted as the ring found its way around a peg. He grabbed a plastic doll from a shelf and handed it to Janet.

"Well I'll be doggone," Rodney said. With a laugh, he stuck his hands into the bib of his overalls. "You're a natural, Little Bit."

With a laugh, Janet took the doll and placed it on the counter. She saw Ellie eye the last ring dejectedly. "One more toss," she said to both girls. "If I don't get another prize with this one, I get to keep the doll. If I do get a prize, we'll flip a coin to see who gets what. Deal?"

Heather nodded, and Ellie took a deep breath.

Holding the last ring in the same vertical position, Janet aimed for the number seven peg. If she was lucky, she'd win another plastic doll and not have to worry about flipping any coin. She let the ring go and closed her eyes.

"Number forty—" The barker's voice was lost to shrieks of joy.

Janet's eyes flew open, and she scanned the pegs. The rubber loop hung on a peg near the barker, three feet to the left of where she'd aimed. The number taped below the peg was 42.

"You did it, Mama!" Ellie shouted. "You did it!"

Janet stood open-mouthed as the boy placed the glass horse on the counter.

Ellie scooped it up and clutched it to her chest. "I'm gonna name him, Joe-Joe." She grinned up at her mother. "That's a good name for my pony, huh?"

"How about another round?" the barker asked Janet.

Janet's mouth snapped shut. She shook her head at the barker, picked up the doll on the counter, and handed it to Heather. She caught Rodney's eye, and he scratched his chin, a bewildered look on his face.

"Don't you think so, Mama?" Ellie asked. She kissed the horse on the nose and stroked its hooves.

"It's a great name, honey," Janet said, trying to compose herself as she shooed the girls away from the booth.

"But I wanted the Pooh bear," Heather whined. Her bottom lip began to tremble.

"Tell you what," Rodney said. He shoveled Heather into his arms, and she giggled when he propped her up against his shoulder. "What say we take one more ride on the Ferris wheel before calling it a day?"

"Can we, Aunt Janet?" Heather begged, the Pooh bear seemingly forgotten. "Please?"

Janet looked up at the thickening clouds. "Think there's time before the rain?" she asked Rodney.

He lowered Heather to the ground and arched his back. "I believe so."

Janet glanced down at Ellie who walked alongside her engrossed in the details of the glass figurine. "How about it, honey?" she asked. "Want to ride?"

Ellie adjusted her fanny pack, then slid her fingers across the horse's back and down the length of its tail. "Okay," she said absently.

As the four of them neared the Ferris wheel, Janet leaned into Rodney. "I don't have a clue as to what happened back there," she whispered. "I aimed for number seven."

"Was the damndest thing I ever saw," he mumbled back. He smiled down at Heather, who suddenly looked up at him. When she turned away, he said, "Saw the ring skip over a handful of pegs before it landed on that one." After a long pause, he added, "Lucky shot I guess."

Janet shrugged for lack of a better response.

The Ferris wheel operator, an overweight woman

with facial hair, pulled on a long lever connected to a control box, and the ride offered her another half-cup-shaped chair. The few people in the seats swung back and forth as she checked the lock bars lying across their laps.

"You gonna ride, Aunt Janet?" Heather asked.

"No way," Janet said with a grimace. "You two ride with Rodney. I'll get Sylvia something to drink and meet you back here."

"It's not so bad," Rodney said. "Kinda nice lookin' over the town from way up there."

Janet patted his arm. "I think I'll stick with the street view, thanks."

The operator pulled the lever again, and another empty chair appeared. Heather squealed with delight, and both girls settled on each end of the seat. Rodney squeezed himself between them. The operator had to shove hard on the lock bar to secure it across Rodney's stomach.

"Why don't you let me hold your pony?" Janet called to Ellie. "That way you can hold on with two hands."

Ellie shook her head, tucked the horse under her pink T-shirt, and wrapped both hands around the lock bar.

"They'll be fine," Rodney said. He spread his arms across the back of the seat and rested a hand on each girl's shoulder.

The lever was pulled again, and the seat wobbled into the air. Janet shivered and quickly left for the nearest refreshment stand.

While she waited in line for a cup of lemonade, a crack of thunder shook the ground. Janet gasped and hurried past the people behind her, imagining lightning bolts aimed at Rodney and the girls.

She tried to remain calm, tried not to run, but a gust of wind slammed against her back, urging her faster. Janet's hair tangled across her face when she finally peered up at the Ferris wheel, which now spun backward in slow, choppy jerks.

Thank God, she thought. *They're taking them off.*

Rodney took his arms off the back of the seat and sent Janet a reassuring wave as their bucket reached the very top of the wheel then stopped. He turned to the girls and pointed in Janet's direction. Heather flapped a hand at her and smiled. Janet waved back, mentally urging the wheel down faster.

In a flash, the scene from above changed. Ellie began to twist and squirm in the seat, and before Rodney could stop her, she stood on the chair, the lock bar barely reaching her shins. She raised her hands above her head, the horse clutched between them, and shouted into the wind, *"Mia lona!"*

"Sit down!" Janet screamed.

Rodney grabbed for Ellie, every movement of his body swinging the chair harder.

Janet raced for the ride operator, who was about to give the lever another pull. "Don't!" she cried. "Stop!"

The woman's hand froze over the lever, and she threw an angry look over her shoulder.

Janet pointed up. "My daughter—God, my daughter's going to fall!"

Bystanders pointed and shouted for Ellie to sit down.

Heather yelled from above, her voice a high, pitiful shriek. "Help! Help!"

Frowning, the ride operator looked up. Evidently not

seeing anything unusual, she casually reached for a hand-held radio, then went to Janet's side. She gaped when her eyes locked onto Ellie. Pressing the side bar on the radio, she said into it, "Bill, get your butt over here, now!"

Suddenly, Ellie's body pitched forward, and Janet screamed. She saw Rodney quickly snatch a handful of Ellie's shirt, which stopped the child from completely flipping over the lock bar. The anguish on his face grew more and more pronounced as he strained to pull Ellie back into the seat. Abruptly, the look of anguish collapsed into a grimace of pain, and Rodney grabbed the left side of his chest with one hand, leaving Ellie to dangle precariously in the other.

Chapter Twenty-three

Michael hustled to his office with Sally at his heels. He glanced at his watch again. Still late, no matter how many times he looked at it.

He barely remembered climbing out of his recliner this morning at five, when the answering service phoned with a death call. Chad, according to the woman from the service, couldn't make the removal because he'd come down with a severe stomach virus during the night. Michael had no choice but to throw on a clean suit and run out to make the removal himself. He'd been running ever since.

In the last twelve hours, he'd made two more removals, one involving a three hundred-pound corpse and a flight of stairs. Then he'd embalmed three bodies, dressed, cosmetized, and casketed the two Chad had picked up from Magnolia yesterday, then worked a viewing, and was now in the middle of another one. The pièce de résistance came when his apprentice phoned, informing Michael that bodily fluids were still making explosive exits through both main orifices of his body, and he'd be out until tomorrow. Left with that news, Michael had to call Richard Mason in for backup.

"I can't believe you forgot Mr. Albert's rosary," Sally said to Michael when they entered his office. She marched past him to the credenza, where they stored the service accessories.

"With everything else going on, you're lucky that's all I forgot," Michael said. He went to his desk, scooped up two folders, and held them out to her. "Here're the files for Mason. Make sure he gets the casket forms right this time."

"For Pete's sake, hold on," Sally snapped. "I've only got two hands." She removed the rosaries from storage and dangled them on her fingers. "Black, brown, or clear?" she asked.

"He's in a black suit."

"Fine." Sally dropped the brown rosary on Michael's desk, then held up the remaining two. "Black or clear?"

"Black. Black suit, black rosary. The women get clear, you know that, Sal. You've been doing this long enough."

"You don't have to get testy. I wasn't sure with Mr. Albert because he's . . . was—" She let her hand go limp at the wrist.

"Tired?"

Sally rolled her eyes. "You're going to make me say it, aren't you? Fine. Gay, Michael. The man was gay, gay, gay. You happy now?"

"Careful, your bigot slip's showing."

"I'm not a bigot. I'm—aware."

"Right, and the KKK stands for kalm, kool, and kollected. Just use the black one." Michael handed her the folders, which she took reluctantly.

"I don't think it's a good idea for you to leave Richard Mason with two viewings tomorrow, Michael. You know how flustered he gets sometimes. Look how he bailed on us at the Stevenson service."

"I've already spoken to Richard about tomorrow's schedule, and he doesn't seem to have a problem with it. Both services should be small, nothing even close to the Stevensons'." Michael rounded the desk and sat for the first time that day. His feet tingled with celebratory relief.

"But what if we get another death call?"

"Then we get another death call. Quit worrying. Everything'll work out fine. You'll be here, Chad's supposed to be back in the morning—Richard will have plenty of help."

Sally shook her head. "This isn't like you, leaving when there's so much going on."

Michael blew out a breath. She was right. Normally he would have canceled the trip, especially with it being so late in the day. But after the chaos yesterday, the busy day today, and the drama sure to come with the Stevensons and the stolen coin, he needed to give his body and brain a chance to recharge. More importantly, he needed a little quiet time with his wife and daughter.

Sally, evidently thinking he was ignoring her last statement, curled a hand on her hip and scowled. "Well?"

"Sal, I've already taken care of most of the work. All the three of you have to deal with tomorrow are viewings—yeah, I know—unless you get another death call."

"But what if Chad's still sick tomorrow?"

"Then wing it," Michael said, growing agitated.

Her brow furrowed. "Wing it? What do you want me to do? Pull somebody in off the street to do the embalming and casketing?" She folded her arms across her chest. "Why can't your father come in tomorrow and help?"

Because I don't know where the fuck he is! Michael thought. When Michael had returned from making the first removal this morning, he'd wheeled the deceased into the prep room and saw the body from the night before still lying on the embalming table. The corpse had been aspirated, and the trocar, sharps, and other prep tools cleaned and neatly stored away in their assigned places. Michael wondered then about his father's whereabouts. He hadn't seen Wilson on the couch when the answering service woke him, or asleep in the master bedroom when Michael had rushed through there to dress.

Although puzzled and a little worried, considering Wilson's claim to vengeful investors and the threat from the old man who'd vanished last night, Michael had little choice but to concentrate on the volume of work before him. He didn't think about checking Ellie's room or the guest room for Wilson until later, when Bill Curry, a local handyman, called to say he was in Michael's driveway and needed to get into the house to repair the broken window. Michael had hurried home, let Bill inside, then checked the other bedrooms. Wilson was in neither, and there was no evidence indicating he'd ever been. What Michael did find, however, was Wilson's old Cadillac.

Around two-thirty, just as Michael started out for the south side of town to make another removal, he spotted Wilson's car parked about four blocks away from the funeral home, alongside Mouton's Liquor Store. A suitcase sat on the backseat of the Cadillac, and the keys were still in the ignition. Furious, but not wanting to start a scene in the store, Michael pocketed the keys. If his father planned to skip town again so he wouldn't have to face the Stevensons, he had another thing coming. No keys meant no ride. Michael knew the fix was only temporary, though. Soon Wilson would show up at the funeral home, albeit on foot, with another cockamamie story prepared. That had been three hours ago, and there still was no sign of Wilson.

"You having some kind of seizure or something?" Sally asked, capturing Michael's attention.

"What?"

"I've been asking if your father could—"

"I don't know where Dad is," Michael said flatly. "So don't count on him."

Sally unfolded her arms and threw them down at her sides. "Fine," she said tersely. "But when people around this town start going to another funeral home because this one's too busy *winging* it, don't come crying to me." With that, she stomped out of the office, closing the door firmly behind her.

Before the sound of reverberating wood cleared in Michael's ears, someone knocked on the office door.

"What?" Michael called, half expecting to see Sally's flustered face reappear. The door opened, and to his relief, Richard Mason emerged.

"Sorry to bother," Richard said. "But I've got a little

problem." He folded his hands in front of his gaunt body and bowed his head slightly as though preparing to pray.

"What's wrong?" Michael asked.

Richard glanced up. "I'm embarrassed to say."

"What?"

"Well, I was getting ready to go to KMart because we're out of pancake makeup and I need some for Mrs. Ossun. I found liquid base in the prep room, but I can't finish her cosmetics with that stuff. Anyway, like I said, I was going over there, but I can't find my car keys." His taut-skinned face turned red. "I called home for my wife, Uneeda, to bring me a spare set, but she's not home right now. So—well, would it be all right if I borrowed your car?"

Michael wanted to tell Richard to simply use the cosmetics in the prep room, but that would mean hearing an hour-long dissertation from Richard about the finer attributes of pancake makeup. He wasn't up for that.

He tossed him the keys to his Buick. "You won't be long, right?" Michael asked.

Richard blinked rapidly. "Oh, not long at all . . . well, it is raining heavy out there right now, so I may have to go slow. I wouldn't want to wreck your car. Heavens, I'd feel terrible if that happened. Sometimes you can't help accidents, though. In this kind of—"

"Then take your time," Michael said, hoping to deflect a major discourse. "I'll leave for Carlton whenever you get back."

Richard made a clicking sound with his tongue, then shot Michael an okay sign and left.

Pleasantly surprised by Richard's abbreviated departure, Michael swiveled in his chair and stared out the window. Rain pelted the pane, and wide rivulets distorted his view of the outside world. In this weather, it would be a miracle if he reached the cabin before ten tonight.

He turned back to his desk and picked up the phone to call Janet and let her know he would soon be on his way. Chances were, if this storm had traveled that far north, the fair had ended early. She might be back at the cabin now, worrying about why he hadn't arrived yet.

Michael punched in the number for the cabin and immediately heard, "We're sorry, all circuits are busy now. Please—"

He quickly disconnected the call and redialed the number. Once again, the same recording chirped in his ear.

"Give me a break with the circuits already!" Michael slammed the receiver down on its cradle. He dropped his arms flat on the desk and lowered his head, frustrated. He heard the phone ring.

Michael eyed the blinking button on the phone as it rang again. Another death call? It rang a third time, and Michael wondered why Sally wasn't picking up.

More frustrated than ever, Michael scooped up the receiver and forced himself to sound civil. "Savoy Funeral Home."

He heard the sizzle and crackle of static, but no response. Assuming someone was calling from a cell phone, Michael said loudly, "Hello?"

More static, then a young voice, the words choppy, barely audible, "Hu—da—stop—co—"

"I'm sorry, I can't understand what you're saying," Michael said, speaking louder.

"Da—come—hur—"

"If you can hear me," Michael said, "please call back. We've got a terrible connection." He hung up and immediately the phone rang again.

Not waiting for Sally to pick it up this time, Michael quickly answered, "Savoy Funeral Home."

"Da—hurry—co—bad!"

Michael felt the hair on his arms stand upright on gooseflesh. Though the words were still choppy, the connection had less static, and he recognized Ellie's voice. She sounded terrified.

He pressed the receiver harder against his ear so he could hear past the static and the blood pulsing in his ear. "Ellie, what's wrong? Where's Mommy?"

"Bad—for—al—hur—"

"Ellie, where are you? Where's—"

The line went dead with a click.

Michael quickly dialed the cabin number and prayed that he'd at least hear a ring this time.

"We're sorry, all circuits—"

"Fuck!" Michael disconnected the line and was about to redial when the phone rang again. He punched the blinking button and dispensed with the customary greeting. "Hello!"

No static blurred the line this time, only hollow silence.

"Ellie? Are you there?"

A woman's voice, clear and heavily accented said, "Your daughter calls to you from her mind for she has no other way."

"Who is this?" Michael demanded. The woman's accent carried the same rolling r's, the same staccato syllables he'd heard from the Stevensons and the rest of their clan.

"Your daughter is in grave danger, and I cannot hold them from her much longer. You must come."

Michael bolted up from his seat. "Who the hell is this?"

"It must be returned as has been told. One sun has already passed its mark. The second will not be long in coming. You have little time."

As she spoke, an image of the old man Michael had seen in the funeral home last night came clearly to mind, and the words he'd spoken replayed in hi-fi in his mind. *The second sun—return it or it is done, Wilson Savoy. For you and for anyone who dares possess it.*

"If it is not returned before then, both will be lost," the woman continued. "My child to the netherworld, your child to death."

"You leave my daughter alone!" Michael yelled. "I don't have what you're looking for! Do you hear me? I don't have it!"

The line began to fill with static again.

"Do you hear?" Michael shouted. "Where is my daughter? Who are you?"

Through the static, he heard the woman's fading voice say, "Beside you, Mr. Savoy. Beside you." Then the phone went dead.

"Hello!" Michael shouted. "Hello!"

A light rapping on the window made Michael whirl about.

Anna Stevenson stood outside his window, wearing a long white gown, her dark hair flowing over each shoulder. She appeared dry despite the downpour, and her solemn face held the color and translucency of gauze. So did her hand, which she held out toward the windowpane. In her palm lay Ellie's butterfly barrette. The same one Michael had found on his bathroom floor the night before.

Chapter Twenty-four

Janet cupped her hands around her mouth and screamed once more, "Hold on, Rodney! Hold on!"

High above her head, Ellie lay flopped over the lock bar of the Ferris wheel seat as though she had fainted. Rodney still had her shirt clutched in a fist and one hand over his heart, his mouth agape. Heather sat on the left side of the seat nearly hidden by Rodney's bulk. She had both hands over her eyes. The three of them seemed frozen in time, an off-colored Norman Rockwell portrait.

"Wind's too high, lady," the ride operator said. "They can't hear ya." She puffed rapidly on a long, thin cigar and looked up at the sky. "Looks like it's gonna get worser, too. Rain, hail probably."

"Christ, then why are you just standing here?" Janet cried. "Do something!"

"Already did." She held up a walkie-talkie. "Got a roadie to call the cops. Should be here any minute."

Janet wrung her hands and paced a short horizontal

path, never losing sight of her daughter or Rodney. "We have to do something now, though. Look at him, I don't know how much longer he can hold her."

The operator gave her a sympathetic look. "I know you're worried, lady. Hell, I'd be, too, if that was my kid up there. But there's nothing we can do right now. That little girl ain't shored up enough for me to touch those levers. We could lose her. The wheel ain't smooth. It jerks when it gets to movin', and when that happens the seats start to swingin'. Too big a chance to take."

The crowd swelling around Janet jostled her closer to the big woman. "So that's it? We wait? You're not going to try anything else?"

The operator squinted up at the Ferris wheel. "If you got another idea on how to get them down before the cops get here, share it, 'cause I ain't got the foggiest."

Janet felt fresh tears sting her eyes. She bit her lip and paced faster, working through a scrabble board of thoughts. Rope—hail—net—rain—climber—help.

Sirens began to wail nearby, and Janet stood on tiptoe to peer over the crowd. Red and blue flashing lights. Heaven had red and blue flashing lights.

"They're here, lady," the operator said. "Help's here."

As the sirens grew louder, the crowd seemed to immediately double in size, pushing Janet farther away from the Ferris wheel. A few people stared at her openly. Others she caught peripherally, bare glimpses of faces. Excited faces, scared ones, some that held sympathetic tears, a few that looked enthralled, like they were watching an action flick on television. Voices babbled incessantly from every direction.

". . . that poor man can't possibly—"

"My aunt had a heart attack once on a—"

"She could . . . split her head wide—"

". . . the mama . . . should have been watching."

Janet wanted to scream for every one of them to shut up.

Please, God, she prayed silently. *Please don't let my baby die.*

"Merciful Mary, no!" a woman wailed. The sound of it, familiar and bordering on hysteria, forced Janet to turn around. It was Sylvia Theriot, her horrified face only inches away. "Oh, Janet—Jesus, oh, Mary, Rodney!" Sylvia cried. "My poor Rodney! Those poor, poor babies!"

Janet reached for the woman's flailing hands but was jostled aside before she could grab hold of her.

"Out of the way," a tall, tub-waisted policeman demanded. He had a nightstick in one hand and a walkie-talkie in the other. "Move back. Everybody move!"

Suddenly crushed between a toothless bald guy and a woman wearing too much perfume, Janet was forced farther back. "No, wait!" Janet yelled. "I'm the girl's mother!" She looked frantically about for the ride operator for help, but the woman was nowhere to be seen. Neither was Sylvia.

The bald guy clamped a hand on to Janet's shoulder. "Hang on, lady," he shouted over the sirens and crowd and revving engines. "I'll get you back through, but they gotta get the cherry picker in first." He pointed over the wall of heads to a large, orange utility truck rumbling by. In its bed sat a wide metal bucket, and inside the bucket stood a red-faced man dressed in fireman garb.

The crowd cheered as the truck rolled up to the Ferris wheel. In a matter of minutes, the bucket and fireman rose into the air.

"Come on," the bald guy said, taking hold of Janet's right forearm. With his free hand held out like a battering ram, he charged through the throng, pulling her along.

They no sooner hit a clearing when the same tubby policeman barred their way. "Stay back," he demanded.

"She's the—" the bald guy said.

"I said get back!" the policeman insisted.

"No!" Janet said fiercely. She shook her arm free and pointed to the Ferris wheel with both hands. "That's my little girl up there."

The policeman's scowl melted instantly, and pity softened his eyes. "Come with me then," he said, and led her to the utility truck.

When they reached the driver's door, the policeman rapped a knuckle against it. "Jay?" he called.

"What?" A dark-skinned man with a harried expression stuck his head out the window. "Oh, hey, Bufford."

"Tell Dave I got the mama right here."

Jay's eyes locked on to Janet while he pressed a radio mike to his lips. "Dave, hold on a second."

Crackling static echoed from the cab of the truck, then a voice said, " 'S'up?"

"The mama's here," Jay replied.

More static, then, "Ten four. She belong to one or both?"

Jay keyed the mike again. "Both what?"

When the bodiless voice returned, it sounded aggravated. "There're two little girls up here. Are they both hers?"

Jay gave Janet a questioning look.

Janet stepped back, looked up at the fireman peering down at her from the bucket overhead, and nodded. She didn't want to waste time explaining the difference between daughter and niece.

"Yeah, both hers," Jay confirmed.

"What're their names?" the radio voice asked.

Jay keyed the mike, held it out the window, and signaled for Janet to talk.

"The blonde is El-Ellie," Janet said, her voice catching. She swallowed hard, forcing back a sob. "And the dark-haired one's Heather. The man's name is Rodney Theriot. Please, p-please hurry." She nodded to Jay, indicating she was done.

The policeman patted her shoulder. "Don't worry, ma'am. Dave's been a fireman for a long time. He knows what he's doing up there."

"That's right," Jay said. He leaned out of the window and pointed up with a thumb. "If anybody can bring them down safe, Dave can."

Trembling and only slightly reassured, Janet said, "Thank y-you."

A loud whirring sound from overhead made the three of them look up.

Dave was on the move again.

Thunder rumbled from the west as the fireman rose higher and higher. Soon the bucket came to rest just below the occupied Ferris wheel seat. After a moment, it inched forward, then stopped. A second later it lifted higher, extended a bit farther, then stopped again.

From where she stood, Janet saw Rodney signal the fireman. The whirring sound returned, and the bucket moved closer.

Closer still.

Janet held her breath.

A sharp clang of metal suddenly rang out, and both the bucket and Ferris wheel seat bounced slightly.

Janet's heart pounded.

The crowd gasped.

Ellie stirred.

The fireman became a blur of activity, leaning, straightening, shifting his body first one way then another. All the while his hands manipulated a harness. More metal clanged.

Ellie lifted her head.

Without thinking, Janet grabbed the back of the policeman's shirt and hung on. He glanced back at her only briefly.

They watched as the fireman reached out, slowly, carefully. And from the great distance above, Ellie began to scream. The sound was hoarse and deep, almost baritone in pitch, and it resonated over the crowd. Ellie raised the glass horse in one fist, then pinwheeled her arms as though to purposely set the Ferris wheel seat in motion. The seat swung backward, then forward, banging hard against the rescue bucket. In that instant, Rodney doubled over, his hand stripping free from Ellie's shirt. The fireman stumbled back in the rescue bucket, and Heather wailed at the top of her lungs.

"Stop!" Janet screamed. "Ellie, stop!" She couldn't believe the little girl flailing above her was Ellie. Not her sweet, gentle daughter. This child seemed possessed, determined to tumble from that amusement ride come hell or be damned.

Ellie's arms swung wider, and she slipped farther past the lock bar.

Cries and shouts of fear rolled from the crowd in waves.

Janet's tongue locked to the roof of her mouth as she saw Rodney latch on to Ellie's left foot. *Sweet Jesus! Please, God!*

The rescue bucket moved slightly left.

Ellie appeared to double her efforts, swinging her arms harder.

The seat swayed.

The rescue bucket bounced.

Ellie's foot slipped loose of Rodney's grasp, and he let out a wail of anguish so loud it silenced the crowd.

Frozen in terror, Janet could only whimper as everything above her transformed into a series of still photos.

Ellie's feet over the lock bar.

Rodney's horror-stricken face.

Ellie in midair.

Glass horse refracting light.

Hands from the crowd, lifted as though preparing to catch.

Ellie in the arms of a fireman.

Chapter Twenty-five

Hypnotized.

Dreaming.

The words dangled in Michael's mind like floaters—dead, waterlogged explanations for why he couldn't move or speak. His heart beat so fiercely in his chest it felt ready to burst through. What he saw made no sense. The woman outside his window resembled Anna Stevenson right down to her long widow's peak. Yet he could almost see *through* her. How could that be? And her eyes—what was with those dark eyes? They seemed to plead with an urgency meant only to petition a deity.

He wanted to shout, "I don't understand!" but nothing would come out of his mouth. He watched her, hearing the words she'd spoken to him over the phone again and again in his head.

"*. . . cannot hold them from her much longer. . . . must be returned . . . one sun passed its mark . . . second not long . . . little time . . . both will be lost . . . your child to death.*"

Anna's words had been too similar to those of the vanishing old man for her not to be referring to the gold coin. But what did that have to do with Ellie? Why would anyone want to harm his daughter? Ellie had nothing to do with the coin. She hadn't been anywhere near the casket when Wilson stole it. And what had all the psychic mumbo-jumbo been about when Anna told him that Ellie had called to him from her mind? He *had* heard his daughter's voice. The fear in it had been so real he could have touched it.

More bewildered than ever, Michael watched Anna lean over and place Ellie's barrette on the outside sill. Her fingers lingered around the hair clasp for a moment, and when she finally released it, something released in Michael as well. A surge of adrenaline shot through him with such force, it nearly knocked him over. He rushed to the window, but Anna turned away before he reached it. She beckoned for him to follow.

With no thought about how or why, Michael raced out of his office and through the funeral home. He slalomed past mourners, an alarmed Sally, and paid little attention to the deluge that soaked him as soon as he burst through the front doors.

Michael ran around the front of the building and down its side, the sound of his sloshing, pounding feet punctuating the grim litany in his head. ". . . *your child to death*." Even before he reached the office window, he saw that Anna was no longer there.

He slid to a stop and scanned the length of the property and the adjoining lot, but only spotted an old crop-tailed mutt trotting through the downpour. *Impossible*, he thought. *She couldn't have disappeared that fast.* He thought of the old man and how quickly he had vanished from the funeral home.

Roughly wiping water off his face, Michael surveyed the property again. Same as before. One dog, zero Anna. Nothing made sense. As desperate as Anna had seemed for his help, why would she leave now? Why was Ellie being dragged into this?

He hurried over to the window ledge and found the yellow barrette lying in the same spot Anna had left it. Michael picked it up and ran a finger over the plastic wings. A million more questions ran through his mind, but the one taking precedent—was Ellie safe? He had to find out for himself.

"Lord, he done lost his mind!" a voice suddenly bellowed behind him.

Michael shot a quick glance over his shoulder and saw Agnes Crowder coming toward him under the protection of an umbrella. The lower half of her orange flowered muumuu clung to her thighs and knees in soggy ripples. He ran over to meet her.

"Why in the good Lord's heaven are you standin' out here?" she asked, thrusting out the umbrella so it covered most of his head. "Even a duck got sense enough to get outta this—"

"Agnes, listen. Something's come up, and I need to leave for Carlton right away. Let Sally know. Tell her I'll have my cell phone with me if she needs anything."

"But—"

He gave an agitated shake of his head. "Just listen. Sally has the number to the cabin. Tell her to call there and to keep calling until she gets through to Janet. I'll keep trying from my cell. Tell Sally if she gets through, to tell Janet to take the girls to the Theriots' and for all of them to stay put until I get there." He started to duck out from under the umbrella, and Agnes grabbed his arm.

"Now hold up one panty-twisting minute. You gotta tell me what's going on—"

"There's no time," he said, pulling out of her grasp. "Just tell Sally, please."

"But what—"

"Later," he said, already turning away. "I'll explain later." Before she could ask anything more, Michael took off for home.

He heard Agnes shout after him, but the drum of rain garbled her words. He didn't turn back. There was nothing he could explain to her now. He was operating on confusion, gut instinct, and growing fear. How could anyone give logic to that? Maybe he was tipping over into paranoia by wanting Janet to take the girls to the Theriots', but he didn't care. Better paranoia than regret.

Thunder rolled in the distance, and gusts of wind turned raindrops into needles. They drove into his face, his neck, his hands. Michael's drenched suit hung on his body like elephant skin, the weight of it threatening to slow him down. He clutched Ellie's barrette tightly and pushed on.

When Michael finally pushed through his kitchen door, he stuck Ellie's barrette between his teeth and began stripping off his clothes. His jacket landed on the counter near the coffeepot, his tie over a chair. The buttons on his white shirt wouldn't cooperate with shriveled fingertips, so he ripped the shirt open, and buttons flew across the hallway.

By the time he made it into the bathroom, he wore only soaked skivvies. Those were soon slipped off and discarded in the hamper. Naked and shivering now, he grabbed a towel, then took the barrette from his mouth and placed it on the vanity. He stared at it for a moment, remembering how Ellie would fidget with it in her hair while she watched cartoons.

Michael quickly looked away and scrubbed himself vigorously with the towel. He concentrated on what alternate routes he might take into Carlton, anything that would get him there faster.

Interstate 10 to 49, maybe 71 if—

"Shit!" Michael said, suddenly remembering that Richard Mason had his car. He dumped the towel into the hamper and hurried into the living room, where he peeked past the curtains of the nearest window. Five cars sat in the funeral home parking lot. None were his. He'd either have to wait until Mason returned with his car or take the hearse, which was stored in the garage out back.

"Fuck." Michael dropped the curtain back into place, and just as he turned away from the window, he thought of Wilson's Cadillac. The '87 was a dinosaur, huge and black with cropped fender wings, but at least it ran. And the keys to it were still in his pocket.

Michael ran out of the living room and into the hall, tracking the trail of clothes he'd shed. He found his pants, rummaged through the soaked pockets, and pulled out the keys. Relieved that he had transportation, he took off for the bedroom and dry clothes.

Moments later, in a T-shirt, light jacket, and one leg in a pair of jeans, Michael hobbled into the kitchen and took his cell phone off its charger. He checked the battery bar on the screen to make sure it was at full strength while he finished putting on his pants. Then he called the cabin.

The steady *bomp, bomp, bomp* of an out-of-order signal made him want to pitch the phone through the window. Clenching his teeth, he pocketed the phone in his jacket, then reached for the cordless phone near the toaster. He dialed while heading to his bedroom for a pair of sneakers.

"This is the Theriot residence, but we ain't home," Rodney Theriot's voice said. "When you hear the beep, leave your number. Talk slow, though, 'cause I don't write too fast." *Beeeep.*

"Rodney, this is Michael. I'm looking for Janet and the girls. They're supposed to be at the cabin, but I haven't been able to get in touch with them. Call me on my cell phone when you get this message." Michael recited his cell number slowly, then hung up. He slipped on his shoes, and dialed another number.

A woman picked up after the first ring. "Brusley P.D."

"Shirley, this is Michael Savoy. I—"

"Hey, Mike! Man, I haven't heard from you in ages. Heard ya'll had a big yeehaw over there yesterday. Kinda surprised ya'll didn't—"

Shirley Woods was a robust blonde in her mid-forties who worked as a dispatcher for the local police department. He'd known her for years and knew one of her favorite pastimes was talking and the only way to stop her was cutting in.

"Shirley, I need your help," he blurted.

"Sure," she chirped. "Whatcha got? Need an escort to Saint Berchman's across town?"

"No, no. I don't need a police escort. I need to see if

you can get hold of the Grant parish sheriff's department for me. Ask them to send a car out to the old Savoy place off Highway 1226 in Carlton. They know the place."

"Why?" she asked, her voice taking on a business edge. "Something going on over there?"

Knowing there was no way for him to explain the events that led up to this moment and still sound sane, Michael simply said, "I'm not sure. Janet and Ellie left for the cabin yesterday, and I've been trying to reach them ever since. The phone's probably out because I keep getting out-of-order signals or circuit recordings. But just to be on the safe side, I'd like someone to go out there and check them out. I'm going to be heading to Carlton in a minute, but—"

"No problem," she said briskly. "Can you hold for two seconds? I'll try to reach them right now."

"Yes, okay—thanks."

"Just hang tight," she said, then the phone went silent.

Michael began to pace.

An old man. Threats. Massive dog prints.

Anna. Warnings. Barrette.

A missing gold coin.

A missing Wilson.

Ellie.

He circled the bedroom twice more, then went back into the bathroom for Ellie's barrette. For whatever reason, he needed to hold it again, a symbolic lifeline to his daughter.

When he reached the vanity, however, the hair clasp wasn't there. Frowning, Michael looked behind a can of hair spray, then under a bar of soap. He moved the small glass container of potpourri, checked under an open box of Band-Aids, pushed aside a hair dryer. No barrette.

He stepped back, heart hammering, phone pressed to his ear, and scanned the floor of the bathroom.

"Mike?" Shirley's voice returned, harried now.

Michael continued to search. "Did you get through to them?" There—on the floor near the baseboard to the vanity.

"No luck. I got the same crap you been getting. Circuits are busy. Probably this weather screwing up the service."

"They can't all be busy," Michael said, squatting to pick up the barrette. "I got through to one of the neighbors a little while ago and left a message on their answering—" His jaw suddenly locked shut. He touched the hair clasp briefly, then pulled his hand away. Beside it was an indention in the carpet. A round one, a little bigger than the circumference of a quarter. He looked at the barrette, then the circle. The barrette—the circle. Barrette—circle.

"Jesus," he breathed, praying he hadn't found what he thought he found—the link between Ellie and the Stevensons. This spot had to be where the coin landed after falling out of his father's jacket. It was the right size, right shape. And the butterfly clasp—had Ellie come into the bathroom after Wilson and found the gold piece? Without warning, Michael's mind synopsized the threats from the vanishing old man.

Unless it be returned before the rising of the second sun, anyone who dares to possess it will die without mercy.

"Hey, you still there?" Shirley's voice barked in his ear.

"Huh—yeah. What?"

"I've been asking if you're okay."

Michael picked up the plastic butterfly with trembling fingers. "Keep trying to reach the sheriff, will you, Shirley? Call the next parish over if you have to. Just get somebody over there as soon as you can." He gave her his cell number. "I'm leaving now, so call me as soon as you hear anything."

"Will do."

Michael hung up and drew a deep, shaky breath. The pain and fear he felt only served to add certainty to his heart. He had to get to his daughter. Her life depended on it—depended on him winning a race against the sun.

Chapter Twenty-six

It was nearly eight-thirty before Janet arrived back at the cabin. Twenty minutes later, the girls sat at the dining room table, somber and distant, eating a snack of milk and cookies. Janet sat on a stool nearby, watching them, still shell-shocked over the day's event. She couldn't believe only hours earlier a fireman in a cherry picker had caught her daughter in a midair tumble and pulled her to safety. Everything had seemed to happen so fast, but at the same time painfully slow.

Once Ellie had been secured, the Ferris wheel operator had lowered Rodney and Heather to the ground, and a waiting ambulance took Rodney to a local hospital. A female EMT tried coaxing Ellie into a second ambulance, but the girl staunchly refused, even when Janet promised her she'd ride along. So Janet had followed the ambulance in her van with Sylvia bawling in the front seat and Ellie and Heather strapped in the back. After a battery of tests, the physician diagnosed Rodney's condition as an acute anxiety attack. The symptoms, he assured Sylvia, were similar to a heart attack's but seldom lethal. To placate the hysterical woman, he admitted Rodney into the hospital for observation.

Ellie and Heather were examined for good measure, and other than a mild case of dehydration from the day's activities, both girls were in perfect health. Ellie hadn't spoken but a handful of words since the incident, and the more Janet or the doctor tried to get her to talk about what happened, the more distant she became. The physician suggested both girls be taken to a counselor to work through their experience. It was a recommendation that needed no debate. Janet had already decided to pack up and head back home first thing in the morning. She'd tried to call Michael from the hospital to let him know, but there'd been no answer at home or the funeral home.

Heather raised her glass from the table. "Can I have some more milk, Aunt Janet?"

Janet hopped off the stool and took the glass from her. She glanced at her daughter's full cup. "What about you, honey? Want anything?"

Ellie shook her head and ran her fingers over the glass horse, which stood beside her plate.

Sighing, Janet went to the fridge and filled Heather's glass. She heard her niece whisper something to Ellie, and Janet turned her head slightly so she could see them from the corner of her eye. Ellie nodded slowly as though in reluctant agreement to something. Then she got up from the table, clutched the horse to her chest, and quietly moved to the family room, where she curled up in the old recliner.

"Drink up, sweetie," Janet said, returning with Heather's milk. She stroked the girl's hair and glanced back at Ellie. "I need to get the two of you off to bed so I can finish packing."

Heather looked down at her half-eaten cookie. "I'm full," she said with a yawn. "Do we gotta go home tomorrow?"

"Afraid so," Janet said. She stacked Ellie's cup on top of her plate, then brushed crumbs from the table into her hand.

Heather propped her elbows on the table and rested her chin in a palm. She sucked her bottom lip between her teeth, then let it go. "Is it 'cause Ellie's grandpa's gonna die? Is that why we gotta go home?"

Janet's hand stalled in mid-swipe. Her own father had been dead for eleven years, so the only grandpa Heather could be referring to was Wilson. She frowned. "Of course not. Where did you hear that nonsense?"

"Ellie," Heather said. She sat back and swirled stray crumbs around her plate with a finger. "Can't you bring him to the doctor like Mr. Rodney so he can get better?"

"Honey, I'm sure you misunderstood," Janet said, dusting the crumbs she'd gathered onto a plate. "Ellie's grandpa is fine." She collected the dishes and carried them into the kitchen, peering into the family room as she rounded the snack bar. Ellie was slouched over in the chair already asleep.

Heather wiggled down from her seat and followed Janet. "Aunt Janet?"

"Hm?"

Heather looked down at her sneakers and began to rock slowly from toe to heel. "What does it feel like to die?"

Janet stared at her niece, feeling gooseflesh speckle her body as she remembered the strange questions Ellie had asked about death while they were delivering flowers to the funeral home. The irony of Ellie asking about death not long before the near tragedy on the Ferris wheel made Janet's insides suddenly quiver with dread. She lowered to her haunches and gently pulled Heather toward her, hoping her niece wouldn't see how badly her hands were shaking.

"Come here, you," Janet said, softly. "Now, what's all this talk about dying?"

Heather wrapped her arms around Janet's neck and snuggled close. "Nothin'."

"Is it because of what happened on the Ferris wheel today? Is that what has you worried?"

Heather shrugged.

"Everyone's okay now." Janet hugged her tight. "No one's going to die. Understand?"

"Yeah." Heather squirmed deeper into the crook of Janet's arm and yawned again. "Can I go play with Ellie's Barbie?"

"I think what you need is sleep," Janet said, getting to her feet. She led Heather by the shoulders to the family room. "You go on upstairs and wash up. We'll worry about baths in the morning."

Heather let her head fall back on her shoulders. "But I'm not tired," she said and rubbed her eyes.

"Make you a deal," Janet coaxed. "You wash up, scoot into bed, and I'll tell you a bedtime story."

Heather scratched her knee and eyed Janet. "*The Magic Cherry Tree*?"

"If that's the one you want."

"Do I gotta brush my teeth, too?"

"Yep."

Heather looked at her skeptically. "You won't skip pages?"

"Not a single one." Janet patted her niece's bottom, sending her to the foot of the stairs. "Now go."

Heather trudged up the stairs, throwing furtive glances in Ellie's direction as she went. Janet watched until she disappeared beyond the landing, then made her way to the couch. She sat down and picked up the phone, hoping this time she'd be able to reach Michael.

The dial tone was a pleasant surprise when she pressed the receiver to her ear. She dialed her home number, then closed her eyes against the weariness lapping over her. From somewhere overhead, a board creaked and pipes moaned, and Janet threw open a watchful eye. Her jitters were not only back in full swing, they'd brought friends.

After the tenth ring and still no answer, Janet tried the number for the funeral home. Not even the answering service picked up. Puzzled, she dialed Michael's cell phone. It rang continuously, his voice mail refusing to answer. Janet hung up, worried. Where was he? She'd expected him to be late, but not this late. And it wasn't at all like Michael not to at least check in.

Janet rubbed the growing knot of concern from the back of her neck and got up. She went to the recliner and scooped her sleeping daughter into her arms. Ellie shifted her head against her mother's shoulder, touched her fanny pack with blind fingers, then sighed deeply. She pulled the horse closer.

"You're worrying me, kiddo," Janet whispered as she carried her up the stairs.

When she reached Ellie's room, she pushed the door open wider with a foot. Heather was sprawled across one of the twin beds, fully dressed and asleep. Janet crept to the opposite bed, laid Ellie on it, then pulled off her daughter's sandals. After covering her with a light blanket, she tugged lightly on Ellie's fingers to untangle them from the horse.

"Mia lona!" Ellie shrieked, and with her eyes still shut, slapped her mother's hand.

Shocked, Janet jumped back, her heart slamming against her chest.

Ellie rolled over on her side and pulled the horse against her. Within seconds, the child's breathing became deep and steady again.

Heather mumbled in her sleep and threw an arm over her stomach.

Janet looked from one girl to the other, as though waiting for one of them to wake and explain what had just happened. But neither moved. Fear bubbled inside Janet like peroxide in a wound, and she tried to calm it by reminding herself that the doctor had examined Ellie thoroughly. Healthy five-year-old, he claimed. Everything's fine—just fine. But things weren't fine. This solemn child, the one screaming and thrashing on the Ferris wheel, those strange words, the hitting, this wasn't Ellie. What if the doctor had missed something?

Janet brushed away sudden tears and tucked the blanket around Ellie's slight body. Then she went to the closet, where she found an extra blanket for Heather. After covering her niece, Janet turned off the light and headed back downstairs, more eager than ever to get home.

Once in the kitchen, she tackled the sink of dishes.

As she soaped and rinsed, Janet found herself growing more and more irritated, but at what she wasn't sure. Michael for not calling? Not understanding what was happening to Ellie? Herself for coming here in the first place? Pondering each possible reason only boiled her irritation to anger.

She dried her hands, then stomped to the pantry for a cardboard box. Finding one, she threw it down on the snack bar and started loading it with the dry goods she'd bought when they first arrived. In the middle of oatmeal cartons and cooking oil bottles, her elbow bumped into a cereal box. It flipped onto the floor, and hundreds of chocolate covered corn puffs chased one another across the linoleum.

"Crap," Janet groaned. She picked up the cereal box, then cursing under her breath, made her way to the utility closet with corn puffs popping and crunching beneath her feet.

After arming herself with a whiskbroom and dust-pan, Janet got on her knees and struggled to corral the cereal.

Ten minutes later, with the broom still going one way and the corn puffs the other, Janet heard scratching sounds coming from behind one of the bottom cabinet doors. She froze, listening.

The *scritch—scratch—scritch* quickly grew louder, more determined, sending with it a sudden vision of rats gnawing their way into the kitchen.

Alarmed, Janet jumped to her feet, and her left shoulder rammed into an open utensil drawer. The collected corn puffs scattered across the floor again, and shock waves of pain raced down her arm. Abruptly, the scratching noises stopped.

"Shit!" Janet dropped the dustpan and while hissing through her teeth, unbuttoned the top three buttons of her blouse. She peeled the material away from her shoulder to see if she'd been cut. Her fingers moved gingerly over scraped skin. Nothing bled, but it was sure to leave a whopper of a bruise.

She hitched her blouse back into place, buttoned it, then slammed the utensil drawer shut. She marched off for the vacuum cleaner, determined to suck the damn cereal off the floor if she had to, rats or no rats.

When she returned to the kitchen, Janet stumbled to a halt and gawked. The Frigidaire's heavy door hung wide open, and the drawer she'd rammed into only moments earlier dangled over the floor by its back hinges. The hair on her arms stood tall as she slowly crunched through cereal to close both. Maybe—maybe she'd slammed the drawer shut a little too hard, and it sprang back out on its track. Maybe the refrigerator—well—it was so old . . .

The floorboards in the dining room creaked softly, and Janet peered nervously over her shoulder.

She saw nothing but old furniture.

Jesus, is it ever time to go home!

With one ear cocked and on weird noise patrol, Janet quickly vacuumed cereal. The old upright pinged and whined, but soon the last brown puff disappeared. Satisfied with good enough, she turned on the stove light, turned off the main kitchen light, stored the vacuum, then went upstairs.

More floorboards creaked as Janet tiptoed to Ellie's room and peeked inside. The girls were asleep, just as she'd left them. A little surprised that neither had even stirred from the noise in the kitchen, she crept in for a closer look.

Both faces peaceful, both small chests rising and falling evenly.

Content with what she saw, Janet crept out of the room and closed the door behind her. She went into the bathroom and turned on the sink's faucet to wash her face. While waiting for the water to warm, she cupped the edge of the vanity and lowered her head.

Thoughts of Michael weaved through her mind. She hoped he was okay, wondered where he was, prayed he was safe, wished he was there. After a day like today, she needed to feel the security of his arms around her.

Blowing out a breath of exhaustion, Janet flicked a finger through the steaming water and looked up at the mirror. Mist clouded the glass, obscuring her reflection. She zigzagged a trail through the condensation with a finger, then began to wipe it away with her palm. As her hand traveled back and forth, revealing her tired face inch by inch, something more came into view. Behind her stood a woman with sad, dark eyes and black hair parted down the center of a long widow's peak.

With a gasp, Janet spun about, but all that confronted her was the shower curtain. She'd recognized the woman as the one she'd met near the water fountain at the funeral home—Anna Stevenson. But how could that be? Janet's eyes searched desperately about the small bathroom but found no hint that the woman had ever been there. When she finally turned to face the mirror again, just her own frightened eyes peered back. She considered them for only a second before instinct made her bolt for Ellie's room.

The short distance between bath and bed felt like miles as she stumbled and slipped across it, all the while remembering Anna's warning to her: "*Watch over her closely.*" When Janet finally reached the bedroom door, she threw it open and flipped on the light.

Ellie and Heather were still in bed, asleep. Neither even flinched from the sudden brightness. Janet pressed a hand to her chest and stood there for a moment, gulping and grateful. She'd half expected to find Anna in here. Realistically, she knew that wasn't possible. If Anna had truly been in the bathroom, the woman would've had to move at the speed of light to make it into the girls' room that fast. Janet tried to convince herself that seeing her had just been the result of too much stress, only her over-plagued mind playing tricks. Sure, she could go along with that. But why had her mind chosen Anna Stevenson to scare the shit out of her?

Not sure of what to think anymore, Janet crept over to Ellie's closet and looked inside.

All clear.

She peeked under the beds.

Nothing more sinister than dust bunnies.

Finally, she went to the door and scanned the room as a whole one last time. Although she didn't see anything out of place, she couldn't shake the feeling that everything was tumbling out of place. Not the furniture, not the knickknacks, but something in the air itself.

Janet wet her lips and hesitantly stepped out into the hall. To ease her own mind, she wanted to check through the rest of the house, but some piercing intuition demanded that she not leave the girls upstairs alone.

Just as she was debating whether to inspect the master bedroom, which was only one door away, she heard something behind her. A shuffling sound, like someone in slippers hurrying along. She turned on her heels, hands held out in defense.

No slippers. No shuffling. Nothing.

Janet barely had time to register confusion when the sound of shattering glass from the family room sent her spinning in the opposite direction. She raced to the staircase landing and peered over the rails, but couldn't see into the family room because of the support wall.

She forced herself around the railing and began to descend the steps slowly. Her teeth chattered with fear.

Halfway down the stairs, when she could finally see past the wall into the family room, Janet's jaw dropped in disbelief. Shards of glass and mangled pieces of picture frame were strewn across the floor. The ship-at-sea picture, which normally hung over the mantel, looked like it had exploded. Strips of canvas lay everywhere.

Janet took another tentative step down, her eyes whipping from left to right, searching, watching, her body shaking with terror.

"Aunt Janet!"

The shrill, frightened cry startled Janet, and she had to grab the banister to keep from falling over. Once rebalanced, she bounded back up the stairs two at a time. Four steps short of the top, she tripped and rammed her left knee against the edge of a step. She cried out, struggling back to her feet. Pain, like knife blades slicing through her kneecap, threatened to drop her again.

"Aunt Janet!"

With teeth clenched, Janet hobbled as fast as she could up the remaining steps and down the hall. Finally, after what seemed like a decade, she burst through Ellie's bedroom door—and blinked.

Heather was sitting up in bed with her blanket gripped up to her chin. Her terror-widened eyes were glued to Ellie, who sat cross-legged on the other bed, her face covered in blood.

Chapter Twenty-seven

Michael peered through the rain-smeared windshield and cursed again. In the last two hours he'd only managed a little over a hundred miles. Most of it had been on Interstate 10, where it seemed every eighteen-wheeler in the country had decided to line up one behind the other and add road spray to the already heavy rains. When traffic finally slowed to a crawl, he'd detoured onto Highway 28, thinking he'd make better time. He had. Until now.

Just ahead, orange cones ran at an angle across the road, shoving two lanes of traffic into one skinny, slow-moving thoroughfare. A flashing orange sign on the shoulder warned: CONSTRUCTION NEXT FIVE MILES. Michael lifted the windshield wiper lever, hoping to speed up the blades so he could get a clearer view. All he got was more smear.

He hunched his shoulders closer to the steering wheel as though it would shove traffic out of the way.

"Come on, come on," he grumbled, looking for another detour.

Shadowy tangles of oaks, pines, and willows bordered the right shoulder of the road, and the Cadillac's headlights revealed no side street between them for as far as he could see. To his left, shimmering circles of light from southbound traffic threw a silvery glow over a wide, flooded median. He had no other choice but to link into the string of traffic.

Immediately having to slow the sedan down to fifteen miles an hour, Michael slammed a fist against the door panel, then reached for the cell phone. The last call he'd made was to Shirley Woods, the dispatcher for Brusley's police department. The connection had been choppy, twangy, as if her words were being filtered through a vibrating metal guide wire. From what he'd been able to piece together, she still hadn't reached the sheriff's office in Grant parish or anyone else for that matter beyond a ten-mile radius of Brusley. As she'd attempted to theorize why, the cell phone had gone silent, and its small, dimly lit screen promptly read: NO SERVICE.

The same two words faced Michael now, but he dialed the number to the cabin anyway. All he got for the effort was three short beeps, then silence. He laid the phone down beside him and fidgeted in his seat, trying to temper the feelings of inadequacy and anger that threatened to overwhelm him.

He wished he was stronger, faster, smarter. His wife and daughter needed him, and all he had to offer was this crippled response, this moving inch by inch. He wanted to lash out at someone, and his list of possible targets grew longer as traffic slowed even more. There was the Louisiana Highway Department for choosing this road and this time to begin construction. Then came the airlines, for not offering direct flights into Carlton and for deciding to cancel what service they did offer into a larger neighboring town due to inclement weather. Even God wasn't exempt. What good was omniscience or omnipotence if the two most important people in his life weren't spared from danger? At the top of the to-be-attacked heap stood Michael's father. If it hadn't been for Wilson taking the gold piece in the first place, none of this would be happening.

Taillights brightened ahead, and Michael braked again. "Goddammit, move!" he shouted. "I can fucking walk faster than this!"

He lowered the driver's window a little, ignoring the splash of rain against his face. He had to breathe, had to get rid of the scent of Old Spice, Marlboro cigarettes, and worn leather, the coalesced redolence of Wilson.

How could his father disappear like that, knowing that at least one of the Stevensons knew about the coin and wanted it back? Was Wilson just sticking to old protocol and leaving his son to clean up his mess?

Michael glanced over at the cracked, burgundy leather seat beside him. What if his father had figured out that Ellie had found the gold piece? Could he be on his way to Carlton even now to retrieve it? But if so, in what? Michael was driving his car. The windshield wipers gave an extra long squeak as though to confirm this was so.

Nearing a standstill, Michael pounded against the horn. It let out a low, pitiful noise, like that of a muzzled sheep being led to slaughter. Something about the sound made Michael stiffen. He'd been so fixated on his father's usual antics, creating chaos and hauling ass, he hadn't taken the time to consider other possibilities for his disappearance.

What if the Stevensons had found him? What if the old man they'd seen in the funeral home had made good on his promise? What if the investors his father had been so nervous about had shown up to collect their money?

Michael rubbed his throbbing forehead. He couldn't worry about his father now. His attention had to stay fixed on Janet and Ellie. He *had* to get to them.

Not normally a praying man, Michael made a rapid and awkward sign of the cross. "God, please let them be okay. When I get to Carlton, let Ellie and Heather be asleep in their beds, and Janet curled up somewhere with a book. Give me the chance to hug and kiss them again, to tell each one of them how much they're loved." Michael hesitated a moment. "And, God . . . I . . . if you take good care of them, I promise I'll do anything you want. Just please, let them be all right. Amen." Another wobbly sign of the cross.

Worrying about whether he'd given clear enough instructions to the Almighty, Michael raised the window. The cell phone rang, and he quickly scooped it up. NO SERVICE was still illuminated on the screen.

Puzzled, Michael said, "Hello?"

A whispery voice answered, "Daddy."

Recognizing Ellie's voice, Michael slammed on the brakes. A horn blared angrily behind him.

"Ellie . . ." Michael thought about what Anna Stevenson had told him, about Ellie calling to him from her mind. But his daughter's voice sounded so clear now, so close. It had none of the static from her earlier call. "Ellie—Ellie are you okay? Where—"

"Shhh. You got to be quiet, Daddy. They're gonna hear you."

Fear fogged Michael's eyesight. "Who? Ellie, who's there? Where are you? Are you okay? Where's Mommy?" A symphony of horns blasted outside, startling him. Michael threw a hand over the phone's mouthpiece, looked over his shoulder at the glare of lights behind him, and shouted, "Shut the fuck up!" He released the brake, and allowed the sedan to coast up a foot. Removing his hand from the phone, he said firmly, "Ellie, put Mommy on the phone right now. Do you hear?"

"Daddy . . . you gotta hurry, please. I'm afraid. The bad man's here. He's so mad. The lady's here, too. She's trying to stop him, but he's too big." Michael heard her take a deep, trembling breath before a buzz of static filled his ear.

Michael's sweaty palm slipped off the steering wheel. "Ellie!"

"Daddy, hu—now—be—"

Just as they had been with her first call, Ellie's words became nonsensical syllables, and Michael pressed the phone closer to his ear. He grabbed the steering wheel again. "Ellie, listen to me. Listen carefully. Put Mama on the phone, right now. Do you understand? Put her on the phone."

"I—don—can't—de—" A sudden scream cut off the syllables, but it wasn't the scream of a child. It was deep and hoarse, and sounded more like an outcry of anger than one of fear.

Michael gripped the steering wheel until his fingers

burned with pain. "Ellie! Ellie, can you get to Mama? Where's Mama?"

Through the static, Michael heard sobbing, then a hollow, resonating voice simply said, "She's dead."

Chapter Twenty-eight

Don't panic, Janet told herself, and hobbled over to Ellie's bed. *Slow—slow and easy.*

Ellie rubbed the right side of her face, inadvertently smearing blood all the way up to her forehead. Her cousin whimpered.

"Is she gonna die, Aunt Janet?" Heather asked, her voice quivering.

Janet cupped Ellie's chin and lifted it. Her daughter looked up, her expression deadpan, her gaze far away. Two steady streams of blood flowed from her nostrils.

"Is she gonna?" Heather asked again.

"No, honey." Janet tilted Ellie's head farther back. "She has a nosebleed."

Heather nodded, her eyes wide and uncertain. She bunched the blanket close to her chest.

"Does anything hurt you?" Janet asked Ellie.

Ellie stared at the ceiling, mute.

"Honey?"

Ellie blinked, but remained silent.

Worry squeezed Janet's thudding heart. What on earth was happening to her child? "O-Okay," she stammered. "You don't have to talk if you don't want to. Just keep—keep your head back. I'll get a towel."

She turned to head for the bathroom, then halted in mid-limp, remembering the shattered picture. She'd been so frantic after hearing Heather scream, then seeing all the blood on Ellie, she'd actually forgotten about it for a few moments. That painting wouldn't have ripped apart like that simply by falling. Someone would have had to purposely destroy it. And for someone to do that—they would have to be in the house!

"Oh, hurry, it's more!" Heather cried. "Look, it's bleeding more!"

Janet turned back to see crimson bubbles pop over Ellie's nostrils. The front of her T-shirt was striped with blood.

"Quick, get me a clean T-shirt," Janet said to Heather. She pointed to a chest of drawers. "In there."

While Heather hurried to the bureau, Janet lifted her daughter's chin again. "Listen to me, Ellie. You have to keep your head back or the bleeding won't stop."

"Here, Aunt Janet," Heather said, suddenly appearing beside her, clean shirt in hand. Her face was ashen, her eyes filling with tears.

"Don't worry," Janet said to her niece, then glanced nervously toward the bedroom door. "Everything will be all right." She offered Heather a weak smile. The child nodded and leaned in close.

Janet took the shirt from Heather, folded it into quarters, then pressed it under Ellie's nose. "Now keep it there for a few minutes. Breathe out of your mouth."

Pushing her mother's hand away, Ellie whispered, "He's here."

Janet bit her bottom lip, afraid to say anything. She felt Heather push against her, the child's breath warm through the back of her blouse.

Ellie scanned the room tentatively, blood no longer dripping from her nose. She froze for a few seconds as though listening, then slowly twisted her body to the left. Her gaze settled on the window between the beds. "She's here, too," she said quietly.

From the corner of her eye, Janet saw the curtains flutter. She turned hesitantly and shivered when she realized the window was closed. She looked back at Ellie. "Who's here, baby?"

The look in Ellie's eyes traveled between perplexity and dread. "The man who broke the picture downstairs."

"The picture?" Janet echoed. The girls hadn't seen the mess in the family room yet. How could Ellie possibly know? Janet looked back at the window and gripped the bedsheet when she saw the curtains give a final ripple, then settle limp against the window frame.

"They're both watching," Ellie said. "But he's mad. I don't know why, but he's really, really mad."

Janet felt herself being sucked into the rhythm of her daughter's voice. She suddenly sensed they were being watched from the ceiling, through the walls, the floor. Heather wiggled under her aunt's right arm, and Janet cleared her throat, fighting back fertile paranoia.

"I wanna go home," Heather cried. She tugged at Janet's blouse.

Ellie shook her head. "We can't go home. He won't

let us." Her bottom lip began to quiver, and her shoulders drooped. "And he won't let Daddy come get us—"

Without warning, the bedroom door slammed shut. Heather shrieked and plowed her head into Janet's jaw as she scrambled onto the bed.

"I told you," Ellie said. She looked back at the door and began to rock her body from side to side.

Heather inched to the foot of the bed and eyed her cousin fearfully. "Aunt Janet?"

Janet wanted to curl up next to the girls and pull the covers over all three of them. Instead, she said, "Stay here," and limped to the door. After saying a silent prayer, she pulled it open cautiously.

The hallway directly across from the room was empty. She peered right, toward the stairs, and she had to bite back a gasp when she spotted a shadow slip past the landing. The crunch of glass quickly followed, then Janet heard the sound of heavy furniture being dragged across the floor downstairs.

She pulled her head back into the room and closed the door quietly. What the hell was going on in this house? Anna, the curtains, the painting, now furniture moving across the floor?

"Aunt Janet?" Heather's small body trembled, and tears streamed down her face. Ellie, still rocking from side to side, only looked at her mother curiously.

"Shh," Janet said, pressing a finger to her lips.

The bedroom door had no lock, so she searched frantically around the room for something to jam beneath the knob. She couldn't pull one of the beds or the dresser to the door because moving either would make too much noise, and if there *was* an intruder in the house, he'd be able to find them. If something *else* lurked in the cabin, however—the kind of something that made curtains move by themselves—barring the door would probably be futile.

Still, Janet grabbed a pogo stick that leaned against the jamb of Ellie's closet, and shoved it under the doorknob. It held for a second, then slipped and fell to the floor. She tried again and again, then finally, after too many tries, the pogo stick held. Janet backed away and signaled for the girls to keep quiet.

The sound of moving furniture grew louder, and Janet hesitated only a second before hobbling over to the window. She shoved the curtains aside and peered down, searching for the ground below. It was obscured by night. The only way she'd be able to get the girls down would be to tie sheets together and lower them one by one. But then they'd be alone until she reached the ground, which created another problem. If she jumped, her knee wouldn't hold up under the jolt, especially from this height. She thought about shimmying down a sheet rope but feared it wouldn't hold. What if she fell? Who would protect the girls?

Backing away from the window, Janet went to the bed and sat, pulling the girls close. Ellie rocked harder under her mother's embrace.

"Are we gonna die?" Heather asked. Her body shook so hard it vibrated.

Ellie giggled softly, which added to the black, naked horror seeping into Janet's chest. How was she going to get the girls out of the house? There were no other exits upstairs except for the windows. To get to either the front door or the side door of the house, they'd have to go through the family room.

"Nobody's going to die," Janet said fiercely.

Heather sobbed louder. "But . . . but . . . I—"

Before the child could stammer out her thought, the pogo stick rattled beneath the knob, sending the three of them into a tighter huddle. The closet door suddenly flew open and out rolled Ellie's soccer ball followed by a florescent green roller skate. In a flash, clothes began to rip away from hangers and land in a heap on the floor. Janet tented her body over the girls just as a Barbie car and an old pair of rubber boots rocketed over their heads.

"Make 'em stop!" Ellie cried, struggling beneath her mother.

"I want my mama!" Heather shrieked, her voice muffled beneath Janet's left breast.

Ellie's collection of Pokeman containers pitched from the closet shelf and flew across the room like egg-shaped mortar shells. One crashed into a porcelain dolphin that stood on top of the dresser, shattering the figurine. The rest bounced off the back wall, then dropped to the floor.

Abruptly, the closet door slammed shut, and the pogo stick fell from under the doorknob. Janet watched in terror as the bedroom door slowly creaked open. Light from the bedroom washed shadowless across the hall toward the bathroom. The furniture noises had stopped, and in the heavy silence, Janet heard only their ragged breathing.

She jumped when the air conditioner clicked on and began its familiar hum. Then slowly, carefully, Janet lifted her body off the girls. She leaned over the side of the bed and grabbed Ellie's sandals. Eyeing Heather's high-top sneakers at the foot of the other bed, she took a deep breath, then scrambled over to get them.

"Put these on," Janet said quietly, and tossed the shoes to the girls. She glanced back at the door. "Hurry."

Heather fumbled to put her sneakers on.

Ellie only stared at her shoes, which lay upside down on the blanket. She scratched her chin with the nose of the horse and looked across the room blankly.

Anger quickly whipped through Janet like the backlash from a gator's tail. "I said put on your shoes now!" Heather gasped as Janet stormed over to the bed, grabbed Ellie's sandals, and shoved them on her daughter's feet.

Immediately ashamed of her outburst, Janet held Ellie by the shoulders and winced at the blank look on her face. "I'm—I'm so sorry, honey. I didn't mean—it's just—I'm . . ."

"Scared," Heather whispered, her dark eyes knowing. She stuck her right thumb in her mouth.

Janet grabbed her daughter and niece by the hand. "Come on," she said firmly. "We're going home."

Heather's thumb popped out of her mouth and relief radiated on her face. "Right now?"

"Right now." Janet linked Ellie's right hand into Heather's left. "Now I want the two of you to hang on to each other and don't let go," she warned. Janet reached for Ellie's left hand but it was locked around the glass horse. She started to tell her to leave it, then changed her mind and took hold of her wrist instead. Now was not the time to argue about a horse. "No matter what, don't let go. Do you understand?"

Heather nodded eagerly and worked her fingers tighter around her cousin's hand. Ellie stared straight ahead, her eyes vacant.

With Janet in the lead, they inched cautiously toward the door. When they reached it, Janet picked up the pogo stick with her free hand and stuck her head around the doorjamb, straining to see the staircase. What on earth did she think she was doing? A bum knee, two little girls, and the only way out of the cabin was either past the kitchen or through the dining room. If there was an intruder in the house, what was she going to do? Brain him with a pogo stick?

Janet took small, cautious steps into the hall with the girls huddled close behind.

As soon as they cleared the doorway, the door to Ellie's bedroom slammed shut, as did the bathroom's across the hall. A loud whirring noise, like an army of fan blades beating against the wind, erupted from the bottom of the stairs.

Janet jerked on Ellie's wrist. "My room," she yelled, as the whirring grew louder and closer.

She pulled them toward the master bedroom, dropping the pogo stick to free a hand. By the time Janet flung the bedroom door open, she felt something behind her. Reluctantly, she looked back. A white mass as thick as cotton batting boiled up the stairwell and into the hall.

"Get in!" Janet cried. She kept one eye on the mass while trying to shove the stumbling girls into the bedroom. The whirring sound was almost deafening now. It numbed her eardrums until she could hardly hear her own voice.

Ellie pushed hard against her mother, refusing to enter the room. "No, he's in there!" she shouted. "He's there!"

Heather screamed and pointed. The same foggy mass racing toward them from the south end of the hall now poured from the master bedroom, seemingly out of nowhere. One moment it wasn't there, the next it rolled and lapped over them like a solid white wave.

Before Janet could lift a foot to move left or right, the masses collided, folding them inside. Its cover and thickness were so complete, Janet felt like she'd been wrapped in a cocoon, isolated from the rest of the world with nothing visible beyond six inches of her face.

"Ellie? Heather?" she yelled, and pulled on the small arm she clung to. She squatted so she could see her daughter's face. The face that appeared, though, was Heather's.

Janet stared at the child, confused. She'd been holding on to Ellie, not Heather. She grabbed blindly for Heather's other hand and felt a crushing weight in the pit of her soul when it came back empty.

Janet screamed into the cocoon. "ELLIE!"

Chapter Twenty-nine

At first, Wilson didn't know where he was. He rolled onto his right side, blinked, and studied the dark, bulky shadow nearby.

"Oh, yeah," he mumbled, and sat up.

After he'd aspirated the body last night, he was getting ready to leave the funeral home when someone banged on the front door. Not sure if he'd be faced with Michael, who might have forgotten his key, or the barefooted man from earlier, Wilson peeked through a window to see who it was before opening the door. He'd nearly dropped his false teeth when he spotted Lester Vidrine standing outside, arms folded across his chest like a pissed off dime store Indian. He'd waited to see if Lester would leave, but that didn't happen. Lester only knocked harder. It wasn't until the doorknob started jiggling like the lock was being worked that Wilson hunted for a place to hide. The attic won, hands down. The access door, located in the back hall, dropped down from the ceiling by pulling on a long hideaway cord. He'd had some difficulty getting the collapsible stairs to fold back into place and the door closed once he'd climbed inside. But he'd made it.

Wilson had spent most of the night sitting against the north wall, keeping watch through a two-by-three-foot screened air vent. From there, he could see Lester's red Suburban parked a block away.

Sleep must have crept up on him because the next thing Wilson knew, he'd awakened to gray, hazy day-light and voices down below. The Suburban was no longer at the corner, but now he had a new problem to deal with. A funeral home full of people. He'd had to wait them out because the alternative was unthink-able. Just appearing from out of the attic meant he'd have to explain to Michael what he'd been doing up there in the first place. And no matter what color Wil-son tried painting a lie, it came down to the same is-sue. He'd been hiding up there like some wimpy, tail-dragging pussy.

So, he'd waited, using an old vase for a urinal and staying near the air vent where it was cooler. When the rain came, it had cooled off considerably, and the sound of wind and raindrops beating against the roof had lulled him in and out of sleep. His last nap must have been a doozie because it was now night again.

Wilson yawned and peered out of the air vent. Un-der the glow of streetlights, rain fell like silver tinsel. He pressed his face against the screen and scanned as much of the parking lot as he could. It looked empty. And the Suburban hadn't reappeared.

Grinning, Wilson stood up. He yawned again, stretched and studied the wide musty space around him. Darkness lent little definition to the objects cluttering the room, but he knew if he walked straight ahead twenty feet, then doglegged right, he'd wind up at the attic door.

"Okay, old boy, it's now or never," he said, and began to shuffle along, sweeping both hands out in front of him like divining rods.

When his foot finally bumped against the bulk of the stairs that were attached to the attic door, he paused. The only way for him to open the door from up here would be to push down hard on it with a foot. Once opened, the stairs would immediately unfold. That meant noise. Lots of noise. He'd have little chance at stealth if anyone remained downstairs.

Holding on to the corner of an old kneeler for balance, Wilson settled a foot over the edge of the steps and pushed. The attic door creaked open a couple of inches, then snapped shut with a bang. He quickly lifted his foot again and this time stomped down hard. Just as he suspected, the attic door crashed open, and the stairs unfolded with enough noise to wake the dead in the next parish.

Wilson held his breath and waited. No shouts of alarm came from below. No sounds at all. He peered down through the opening, confirmed that the immediate coast was clear, and began his descent.

Once he reached the bottom, Wilson stood silent, surveying the halls. When no one jumped out at him, he refolded the stairs, closed his escape hatch, and crept down the hallway toward the front of the building.

Light from a brass picture lamp cast a feeble yellow glow across the intersecting corridor. Wilson took a left, crossed the area where he and Michael had seen the old man the night before, and shivered. The air felt heavier here, musty, like he'd walked into some old, forgotten closet. He quickened his pace to a near run.

His imagination kicked into gear with his feet, and soon every shadowed chair, every curio cabinet and occasional table seemed to inch closer to the middle of the hall as if meaning to trip him. Wilson's breathing became labored. He considered turning on the next light switch he came to, but didn't. Someone might see the lights on from outside. He kept moving, peering over his shoulder every few seconds.

After rounding the corner that led to the entrance doors, Wilson's paranoia began to ease a little. Enough for him to slow to a fast walk and stop hyperventilating. As a last precaution, he whipped around, planning to take by surprise anyone who might be lurking behind him. The only one startled, however, was Wilson when his feet tangled together and he pitched face first to the floor.

He groaned and was struggling back upright when the lights from one of the viewing rooms snapped on.

"No need to get up on my account," a gruff voice said.

Wilson ducked reflexively, and when nothing clobbered him, he looked up. Standing at the threshold of viewing room A was Lester Vidrine, complete with tawny polyester suit and Panama hat.

"You know, you really should have the lock on that lobby window checked," Lester said.

Wilson glanced toward the front door, calculating the distance he'd have to run.

"Don't be stupid," Lester said, his face hardening. He unbuttoned his suit coat, revealing the grip of a .38 in the waistband of his pants. "I'm getting too damn old for a game of tag."

Wilson squared his shoulders. He figured he had about two seconds to produce a brilliant excuse as to why he didn't have Lester's money or wind up on his own embalming table. "Look, Lester, buddy—"

"Don't buddy me. Those days are over."

"But ten years, Lester," Wilson whined. "Ten years, and I've never skated out on you once. That's gotta count for something."

"Nothing counts but the last deal."

"But—"

"My last favor to you was my coming here instead of sending Tank. I want my money . . . now."

Wilson cleared his throat, feeling a little more confident. Lester showing up alone was a good sign. He'd never known the man to shoot anyone himself. Rumor had it that blood made Lester squeamish. Broken kneecaps were a different story. "Well, you see . . . it's like this. I . . . I don't have it."

Lester wrapped a hand around the pistol handle. "You got one minute to reconsider what you just said."

"Whoa, no need for the drama," Wilson said, holding up a hand. "All I need is a few more days, that's all." He held two fingers an inch apart. "I was this close to getting it, Lester, I swear. But something came up, and—"

Lester's fist jackknifed across Wilson's jaw, dropping him to his knees.

"Playtime's over," Lester said. "Out of the fucking kindness of my heart, I gave you extra time. Now you wanna screw me out of what's mine?" He pulled the .38 out of his pants and aimed the barrel between Wilson's legs. "Take my stuff, I take yours. That's the rule."

Wilson winced.

"You're ball-less anyway, Savoy, so what're you worried about? I'd be doing every woman in America a favor by shootin' 'em off."

Thinking fast and sweating like he'd just stepped out of a sauna, Wilson said, "Wait up, all right? Just wait. My son's office, we'll go in there. I think he keeps some cash—"

"Now you're talking," Lester said, and pulled Wilson to his feet by his collar. "Lead the way, *buddy.*"

Before Wilson could explain that the cash in Michael's office might only add up to twenty bucks, he heard a deep moan overhead.

Lester jerked his head up, throwing his hat askew. He pointed the gun at the ceiling. "What the hell was that?"

Instead of answering, Wilson cocked an ear and heard jumbled, faraway voices over the moans. How could anyone be up in the attic? He'd been up there alone. No one could have possibly had time to sneak up there. Wilson stepped back, suddenly desperate to hide again.

"Who the fuck's here, Savoy?" Lester shouted. "You got backup hiding somewhere?"

"No! I don't know—"

A loud *thump* riveted both men's attention to the reception desk nearby. It was floating three inches off the floor and jittering from side to side. The desk legs thumped against the carpet with each tilt, pitching notepads, pens, and a tissue box to the floor. The phone slid across the desk like a hockey puck before flying off and crashing into the wall with a loud *brrring!*

Awestruck, Wilson stumbled back, flattening himself against the wall.

"Holy fuck," Lester muttered, and pointed a shaking

pistol at the desk. Red splotches sprang to his cheeks, and he began to back away slowly. When he reached the front door, he clawed blindly at the deadbolt lever until it flipped upright.

At any other time, Wilson might have laughed at the panic plastered on Lester's wide face. But not now. Definitely not now.

The voices and moans, which seemed to originate from the attic, migrated to the walls, growing louder and angrier. The desk began a slow, end-over-end spin.

Lester let out a keening whine while frantically twisting and pulling on the doorknob. "It won't open! Jesus, it won't open!" He let go of the knob and kicked the door hard. When that didn't open it, he backed up, and aimed the .38 at the knob.

The sound of three rapid shots jerked Wilson into action. He ran to the door and without thinking, shoved Lester aside. He saw two bullet holes the size of quarters in the middle of the door, and the knob, having taken a direct hit, hung aslant. Wilson grabbed the knob and pulled. It fell off in his hand. He stuck two fingers in the bullet holes and yanked. The door creaked in its jamb, but held fast.

"What the hell's going on in here?" Lester yelled.

"How the fuck should I know?" Wilson shouted back.

Lester pushed Wilson out of the way and tried the bullet holes for himself. The door didn't budge.

Wilson spotted movement to his left and looked over in time to see the desk sailing in their direction.

"Duck!" he cried, and dropped to the floor.

Lester fell beside him with a grunt, and his hat popped off his head like a cork from a champagne bottle.

The desk crashed into the lobby wall and exploded into splinters. Immediately, the clamor of voices and moans died.

Neither man moved. They just stared at each other, listening, waiting.

Lester was the first to lift his head, his eyes wide. "You hear that?"

"What?"

"Listen!"

Over his hammering heart, Wilson heard low, throaty growls coming from above. Then came the sound of heavy, padded feet racing across the ceiling. He looked at Lester, bewildered. "Dogs?"

"Sounds like it."

Wondering how in the hell dogs had gotten into the attic, Wilson scrambled to his feet. He'd had enough Twilight Zone for one evening.

"Hey!" Lester jumped up and grabbed Wilson's arm. "Where the shit you think you're going?"

"The back door and out of here," Wilson said, jerking his arm free

Lester glanced up nervously at the ceiling, then waved the .38 at Wilson. "I'm in charge here, remember?"

The padded, thumping feet sounded more frantic, the growls growing louder and closer.

"I don't think so," Wilson said, and took off for the hall.

Lester caught up to him quickly and shoved the gun barrel against Wilson's back. "Move," he demanded. "We're going out the back door."

"No shit?"

Lester pushed him. "Just move!"

They hurried out of the lobby with Wilson continually glancing over his shoulder, and Lester jabbing the pistol into the small of his back. When they reached the intersecting hall that led to the back door, Wilson stopped short.

"Go!" Lester snapped.

Wilson held his ground, listening to the growls overhead. "They followed us," he said, pointing up.

Lester shoved him. "Just go!"

Wilson lurched forward, then turned left. He swallowed hard as he approached the back door. Something didn't feel right. After all the weird commotion in the lobby, he felt they were getting out far too easy.

Suddenly, Lester's hand clamped down on Wilson's shoulder. "Don't move," he croaked. "Don't fucking move."

Wilson stiffened and at first all he heard was Lester's rapid breathing in his ear. He started to turn his head, and Lester's fingers dug into his collarbone. The sounds of snarling and the snapping of teeth quickly reached Wilson's ears. Lester must have heard it, too, because his grip loosened, and Wilson felt his fingers tremble. Cautiously, hesitantly, Wilson turned around.

At the opposite end of the hall stood a huge Rottweiler poised for attack. Its massive head looked like an over-inflated basketball tucked low between a two-and-a-half-foot shoulder span. Its dark eyes bore into them while long, sharp teeth bared, then chomped. Its large front legs were splayed, and its paws, the size of a man's hands, were turned slightly inward. Short, black hair bristled on its back.

"Call it off," Lester gulped.

Wilson looked at him, incredulous. "You think *that* belongs to me?"

Lester raised the .38 slowly, and the dog inched forward. Lester cursed under his breath and took aim. The dog's legs quickly bunched before stretching out to incredible lengths. It rocketed toward them.

With a shout, Wilson whirled about and sprinted for the exit. His fingers flew over the lock pad, and he nearly cried with joy when the door opened on the first tug. His exuberance was quickly squelched, however, when he caught sight of a second Rottweiler guarding the concrete sidewalk outside. Nearly twice the size of the one behind him, it crouched, ready to pounce. Wilson slammed the door shut. Before he had time to refocus on Lester, he heard a gunshot and spun around to see a lunging, black, blurry mass. Two more gun blasts rang out as Lester emptied the pistol into the beast. But instead of falling dead, the dog vanished in a puff of smoke and wind.

Wilson gawked in disbelief.

Lester turned to him, pale and slack-jawed. "Get outta my way," he mumbled, and pushed Wilson aside.

"No, d-don't," Wilson said. "There's another one out there!"

Lester looked at him calmly. "Then I'll shoot the sonofabitch just like I did the last one. What's it going to do? Smoke me to death?" He yanked open the door.

The sidewalk was empty, the night still, save for the chirp of crickets. Lester crept forward, the .38 held out in front of him. Wilson followed closely behind. The neighboring houses stood dark and quiet, and Wilson wondered how the owners could still be asleep after all the shouting and crashing and gunshots.

Lester slipped past the threshold, and Wilson drew a sharp breath.

Like a strike of lightning in an unsuspecting sky, the second dog appeared, leaping over the hedges for Lester. Wilson shouted, but not before the animal had a chance to rip Lester's hand from his arm. The pistol clattered uselessly to the concrete, and screams filled the night.

Something grabbed Wilson by the collar and pulled. He flew back into the funeral home, stumbling and grabbling, then finally landed on his side on the floor. Before he had time to get on his feet again, the back door began to close. Inch by horrifying inch it moved, giving him plenty of time to witness the dog clamping its jaws around Lester's throat and ripping out his windpipe.

Plenty of time for the dog to look back at Wilson.

Plenty of time for the animal to transform into the old man with bare feet.

Chapter Thirty

"Ellie!" Michael shouted into the cell phone. But once more, he heard no response. "Janet's not dead," he said fiercely. "She's not!" He threw the cell phone down on the seat, then swerved the Cadillac to the right, out of the line of traffic and into the construction zone. Horns blared from all directions, but Michael ignored them and stomped the accelerator to the floor. He had to get to a working phone fast.

The Cadillac shuddered and wheezed while the speedometer needle crawled up to eighty. He held tight to the steering wheel, fighting for control as the car began to careen right, then left atop grated pavement. Traffic cones thudded against the fender, flying off in any given direction like giant orange bullets. He had no idea what lay before him. A ten-foot drop into a swamp? A concrete barricade? He needed a phone, and he needed to get to his family; that's all that mattered right now.

By the time Michael finally broke through the construction area, his teeth were chattering. Frigid dread had seeped into his bones. He tried focusing on the slick hard surface of the road, the trees that refused to give him access to a faster, shorter route, on the rain that had slowed to a steady drizzle. None of the diversions worked for long. He kept picturing Ellie alone with a dead mother—Janet lying cold and quiet in some dark corner—his life never being the same again.

"No!" he shouted, and sat up straight, leaning into the steering wheel. "Stop thinking like that. She's not dead, dammit!"

A sharp curve loomed directly ahead, and Michael took his foot off the gas pedal for a second to steer into it. Coming out of the curve, the sedan fishtailed into the straightaway. When Michael regained control, he stomped for speed again.

Moments later, he spotted a road sign that read, PUCKET 2 MILES. He'd never been to Pucket, but figured any town was better than the miles of trees ahead. Especially if routing through that town allowed him to reach Carlton faster.

He turned off at the appropriate intersection and discovered a U-Pack-It store five blocks farther away.

Michael swerved into the store's parking lot, brakes squealing, and gritted his teeth until the Caddy slid to a stop inches from a wide plate glass window. He shoved the gearshift into park, jumped out of the car, and ran into the store.

A pimply-faced man wearing an oversized red tunic with the name BEN embroidered over a breast pocket scowled at him from behind the counter. The short stiff hairs of his crew cut glistened with sweat.

"Lord, mister, you scared the bejesus out of me!" the clerk said. "I thought for sure you was gonna plow right through the front and park on up here 'tween the chips and dip."

"Sorry," Michael said. "Look, can I use your phone? It's an emergency."

"'Mergency, huh? What happened? Accident, I bet. We get more fools than frogs on the road in this kinda weather." Ben pointed to the canopy outside. "Anyway, you can try the phone out there. We're not allowed to let anybody use the one in here. Company regs and all that."

Not wanting to waste any time arguing with him about company policy versus human decency and the pittance of a phone call, Michael reached into his back pocket for his wallet so he could make change. The wallet wasn't there. For a moment Michael stood puzzled, his hands searching rapidly through every pocket he possessed. Then he remembered the soggy clothes he'd stripped out of at home. He'd been so anxious to leave for Carlton, he must have left his wallet in the suit pants.

"Uh . . . Ben," Michael said, glancing at the monogram again to make sure he got the man's name right. "It seems like I left my wallet back home. Could you just let me make one quick call on your phone in here?"

Ben shook his head. "No can do. If my boss shows up and you're on it, he'd can me faster than tuna in a fish plant."

Hoping the clerk to be a man with a price, Michael stripped off his watch, a Seiko his mother had given him after he'd graduated from mortuary school. "Here," he said, handing the watch to Ben. "It's not new, but it's expensive, and it's yours if you'll just let me use the phone."

The clerk fingered the silver band and ran a thumb over the crystal. He peered up at Michael. "How expensive?"

"Probably worth two, two-fifty new."

"Yeah?" Ben's eyebrows arched with appreciation.

"Yeah, and I bet a pawnshop might give you fifty, maybe a hundred for it." Michael didn't have the slightest idea what a pawnshop might offer for the Seiko, but as long as he had the clerk's attention, he figured it best to ride it for all it was worth.

"I don't know—" Ben pinched his chin thoughtfully. He scanned the store as though making certain they were alone, then nodded. "Okay, deal." With a crooked grin, he slipped the watch onto his wrist and held out his arm to admire it.

Michael allowed Ben his second of glory, then said, "Phone?"

"Oh, right." The clerk stuck a hand beneath the counter, pulled out a cordless, and handed it to him. "Make it quick, though."

Michael nodded. While punching in the number to the cabin, he motioned with his chin to the street out front. "You know if that road leads to Carlton? Or do I need to get back on Route 28?"

Ben blew on the watch face, then rubbed it against his tunic. "Stick to the one out front, that's 754. Go left at the four-way. Carlton's only 'bout ninety miles down. You'll have a coupla red lights to deal with but overall you'll save ten miles of distance and better than an hour's time 'cause 28's got more construction fifteen miles or so north of here."

"Thanks." Michael pressed the phone to his ear, but heard nothing except Ben cooing behind the counter over his new watch. He hung up and waited for the dial tone so he could try again. The dial tone didn't come. Michael's chest suddenly grew heavy, like it had become an inadequate dam trying to hold back some monstrous tidal wave of pain and grief. He felt sure it would burst at any second.

"Line still dead?" Ben asked.

"What—wait—" Michael balked. "You mean you knew it was out all this time?"

Ben hid his left arm, with watch attached, behind his back. "Well, yeah. What'd you expect in this weather? From what I hear, phone service is out damn near to Shreveport."

The dam in Michael's chest burst, and he slammed a fist against the counter. "And you took the fucking watch from me anyway?"

"Hey! Don't even think about crankin' it up, mister," Ben said, puffing out his narrow chest like a rooster ready to spar. "For all I knew the phone could've been back in service when you called whoever you called. It's not my fault it still ain't workin'."

"Hand it over," Michael demanded. "Now!"

"No way. A deal's a deal. You gave me the watch, I gave you the phone. Fair swap."

Torn between wanting to jump over the counter and strangle the worm or getting to his family, Michael let out a roar of frustration and kicked over a greeting card rack. He barreled out of the store with Ben's threat swelling up behind him.

". . . out of here, you damn loony, or else!"

Panting with fury, Michael jumped into the sedan

and without even looking for oncoming traffic, sent the car into a backward spin out of the parking lot. The right bumper clipped the side of a nearby trash bin. He ignored the crunch of metal and redirected the Caddy left toward Carlton. After a quick glance at the odometer so he could clock off ninety miles, Michael floored the accelerator.

Although he managed to get the sedan up to eighty-five, time and distance felt stagnant. Ben had warned him about red lights, and true to his word, two appeared. Michael blew past them as though they were starting lights on an Indianapolis drag strip.

Five miles—six.

With every passing mile, the road seemed to take on a new hazard. Sharp curves, thick tree branches strewn across the road from the recent storm, deep puddles filling worn tire tracks. Twice Michael felt the sedan threaten to slip out from under him, wanting to hydroplane into the nearest pasture. He gritted his teeth and held on, pushing the sedan faster. He passed cars like they were parked on a sales lot.

Only when he reached a twenty-mile count on the odometer did Michael feel some sense of accomplishment. *Seventy more to go*, he thought. *Almost there. Almost—*

Ahead, a yellow sign warned of a sharp right turn, and Michael let off the accelerator and tapped the brakes. The road seemed to disappear a hundred feet ahead, so he worked the brakes harder to slow even more.

While crawling into the curve, the Cadillac's headlights suddenly flashed over a patch of blue. Startled, Michael slammed on the brakes, and the car slid another ten feet, close enough for him to make out the back end of a blue Oldsmobile rising over the curve's embankment. The right rear wheel spun lazily, and a thin blanket of steam rose from below, forcing its way up through the drizzle.

Michael hesitated, his foot itching on the brake pedal. He wanted to ignore what he saw and keep heading toward his family. But what if someone was in that car and hurt? He let off the brake, barely touched the accelerator, and his conscience pressed—*what if you're the only hope that person has right now?*

"Fuck." Michael crept onto the left shoulder, training the headlights as close to the embankment as possible. He switched the lights to bright, slapped the gearshift into park, and hurried out of the car.

As soon as he peered down into the four-foot drop, he spotted her. Thirtyish, small framed, dark brown hair, blood spilled over the right shoulder of a white, wet blouse. The driver's door hung open at an awkward angle, and more than half her body dangled through the opening. The only thing that seemed to keep her from falling into the pool of water below was her blouse sleeve, which had snagged around a door handle. From where he stood, her eyes appeared closed, her face peaceful. He slid down the steep embankment, already fearing her dead.

Grasping at handfuls of grass, Michael struggled to slow his descent. He managed to land on his feet, but in ankle-deep water that immediately filled his shoes.

He waded toward her. "Ma'am?"

Drizzle fell onto her face and soaked her blouse until it was nothing more than a translucent film over her bra. She didn't stir.

"Ma'am?" Reaching her, Michael pressed two fingers against her carotid and felt for a pulse. Weak, but at least she had one. Blood trickled from the corners of her mouth and out both ears.

Knowing better than to move her lest he exacerbate the injuries, Michael stripped off his jacket and quickly set up a makeshift tent with it to keep the rain off her face. He stood up, whipped drenched hair away from his forehead, and peered over the embankment. *Now what?* he thought. He was desperate to get to Carlton, but couldn't just leave this injured woman. And there was no way for him to call for help without cell service. The only thing he could think of was driving back to the U-Pack-It. Maybe he could find help there.

Michael squatted, soaking the seat of his pants, and lifted a corner of the jacket. "Ma'am, if you can hear me, I'm going for help. I—"

The woman's eyelids fluttered open, and her lips parted like she meant to say something. Michael leaned closer and heard her moan, "Don't." She grimaced and dabbed the corner of her mouth with the tip of a blood-coated tongue. Her left arm twitched, and for a moment Michael thought she meant to sit up.

He touched the top of her head gently. "Try not to move. You need—"

The sound of tires swishing through water puddles brought Michael to his feet. He peered over the embankment and saw headlights traveling southbound a few hundred feet away.

"Don't move," he called down to her, then scrambled, slipped, slid, and pulled his way up the side of the curve's wall.

When Michael reached the side of the highway, he

held both arms over his head and waved, signaling for the oncoming vehicle to stop. A dark-colored pickup truck veered closer to the centerline of the road and bypassed Michael like he was road kill.

"Hey! Stop!" Michael shouted at the taillights, which quickly disappeared around the bend. Cursing, Michael jabbed the air with a fist, wishing it would connect with the driver's face.

Just when he thought he had no other choice but to drive back to the U-Pack-It, Michael spotted headlights bearing down on him from the south. He ran out into the middle of the road and began to wave his arms out wide. This driver wasn't getting away.

The lights drew closer—closer still, and for one dreaded moment, Michael feared the vehicle wouldn't stop, and he'd have to jump to safety. He braced himself, tensing the muscles in his legs like a sprinter awaiting a starter gun.

But the white Sentra did slow and eventually stopped alongside him.

The tinted driver's window lowered a couple of inches, and a man's voice called from inside, "Hey, you're going to get yourself killed standing out here—whoa, what happened over there?"

"Accident," Michael said. "There's a woman down there, and from the looks of it, she's hurt pretty bad."

The window lowered more, finally revealing the driver, who was a dark-skinned man with a bulbous nose and pointed chin. He frowned behind thick, wire-rimmed glasses. "Ambulance on the way?" he asked.

"Not that I know of," Michael said. "I just found her. My cell phone—"

"Yeah, I know," the man said. "Doesn't work. No service area. Mine's useless, too. But look, I can run back to Dulac for help." He jerked a thumb over his shoulder. "It's only about six, seven miles back that way, shouldn't take me long. Oh, wait . . . here—" He leaned over, dug through the glove compartment, and pulled out a flashlight. "You need this?"

Michael took the flashlight from him. "Thanks."

The stranger gave him a dismissive wave. "No need," he said, already backing into a U-turn. "Be back as quick as I can."

Once the Sentra sped away heading north, Michael turned the flashlight on and hurried back down the side of the curve.

The rain had slowed to occasional drips, drips he heard patter against his tented jacket when he reached the injured woman. He bent down, lifted a corner of the jacket, and fixed the halogen beam near the side of her head so as not to blind her. Her eyes were still open, barely, and dull green irises shifted in his direction.

"Help's on the way," Michael said softly. He wanted to add, *Don't worry, you'll be fine,* but couldn't. The truth was she didn't look like she'd be fine at all. A thicker stream of blood flowed from her right ear, and when he moved the light closer to her face, her right pupil dilated but the left one remained wide and fixed.

She blinked slowly and whispered, "D-Don't. Can't . . . don't—" Her eyes widened suddenly, and she began to swallow rapidly as if she'd been given a river to drink.

"Jesus," Michael breathed, unsure of what to do. Injuries or not, he couldn't just sit here and watch her die. He reached down, cradled the back of her head with a hand, and lifted slightly, gently.

The woman's spasms calmed immediately, and her eyes slowly centered back on him. Her lips parted, and Michael shook his head.

"No, don't talk," he said. "Just lie still. They'll be here soon."

Small, bloody bubbles flowed from one corner of her mouth, and she lifted a wobbly right hand. "C-can't stay. Y-you have . . . have t-to—"

"Please, lady, don't talk." Michael knelt on one knee to relieve the cramp building in his thigh. He paid little attention to the water soaking into his pants. "You won't have to stay here. Help's coming, I promise."

Her head shook ever so slightly in his hand. "N-not me. You c-can't stay. Sun c-coming s-s-soon."

At the mention of the sun, Michael's hand tightened involuntarily around the back of her head. *No, not sun*, he thought. *I heard wrong. Can't be sun. She meant* some, *right?* Some *like in* some*body's coming soon*.

The woman groaned and closed her eyes. When she opened them again, Michael nearly dropped back in alarm. Her eyes were no longer green, but the darkest shade of brown, nearly black. They seemed larger now, rounder, and clearly focused. She licked the blood from her lips.

"You cannot stay here, Michael Savoy," she said, her words strong and accented. The voice belonged to Anna Stevenson. Shocked into silence, Michael began to shiver uncontrollably as she continued, "The time allowed for restitution is nearly over. Their vengeance grows stronger. Your daughter is an innocent, but there is little more I can do to protect her. It must be returned. You must hurry."

A gurgling sound rose from the woman's throat, and she blinked, swallowed, blinked again. Her eyes began to change. They faded from dark brown to copper to the color of wheat to their original green. She gave Michael a long, sorrowful look, then released one final gasp. Her eyes opened wide in surprise, then locked on to nothing, and Michael felt the weight of death in his hand, and most of all—in his heart.

Chapter Thirty-one

Hell was not a place of fire and brimstone and horned, red-faced monsters that sucked on human souls. It was a place made up of fog so thick you could stretch out your arm and not see your hand. It was blindness and a missing daughter and a profound sense of utter uselessness. The kicker for Janet was the realization that she didn't have to die to get there. She already stood in its innermost sanctuary. Its silent sanctuary. The whirring noises had stopped.

"Ellie!" she cried. She gripped the back of Heather's shirt with one hand and groped blindly around with the other. How could her daughter possibly be gone? Only moments before she'd had her hand solidly locked around Ellie's wrist. So tight in fact, the child would've had to yank herself free, and there's no way she would have missed that.

Janet strained to hear movement, anything that would give her direction to Ellie. All she heard was her own voice echoing back and her niece's sobs.

"Ellie, answer me!"

Heather howled. "I want my mama!" Her body shook hard under Janet's grasp. "I wanna go home!"

Janet knelt and pulled Heather close. The child's hands felt like ice. "Shh," she whispered into Heather's hair. It took everything she had to hold her own tears in check. "Just listen. Help me listen." They huddled together for a moment, and Janet prayed for any sound other than their breathing. Her injured knee throbbed against the floor.

"I didn't let go," Heather whimpered. "I promise, I didn't let go."

"Shh, honey. We'll find her." Janet breathed in sharply and caught Heather's soft, innocent scent. Her tears surrendered to the smell and spilled over her face. She kissed the top of Heather's head, then wiped her cheeks with a forearm.

Heather clutched her aunt's arm. Her dark eyes seemed to consume over half her face. "Please," she begged, her voice soft, "don't lose me, too."

Janet squeezed her hand. "No way, kiddo. No way." She looked around for a break in the white mass. It was like looking through the window of an airplane suspended in the belly of a cloud. Bright white surrounded them, impenetrable to the eye, intangible to the touch. She waved a hand through it, but instead of parting with the movement, the fog simply swallowed her limb. She snatched her hand back. "Ellie!"

When there was still no answer, Janet examined her clothing for something to tether Heather to her. Her pants were linen pull-ups with no belt, her blouse square cut and not long enough to tie around the both of them. She stooped down and inspected Heather.

The first thing to catch her eye was the child's high-top sneakers. The extra height of the sneakers meant longer laces, which would serve as a perfect tether. Janet quickly untied the right sneaker and pulled the lace out of the eyelets.

"You—you wanna wear my shoes?" Heather asked, sniffing.

"No, honey." Janet tied one end of the shoelace around Heather's right wrist. "I just want to make sure you're next to me all the time." Tying the other end of the lace to her own left wrist, Janet yanked against the tether. "See?"

Heather nodded, her face awash with worry. "But what if it undoes?"

"It won't." Janet tucked the girl's hand into hers. "Besides, you'll be holding my hand. This is just in case you let go by accident."

Squeezing her hand, Heather shook her head rapidly. "I'm—I'm not gonna let go."

Janet gave her a weak smile, then stood and took a moment to collect her bearings. She knew the master bedroom was straight ahead; to her left was Ellie's room. The hall lay behind her, and somewhere down that hall on the right was the bathroom. Ellie could be in any of those places or in none of them. Janet gritted her teeth, wishing more than anything that she could divide her body into ten so she could search everywhere at once.

Anxious over the time she'd already spent debating about where to search first, Janet tugged Heather to her side, stretched out her free hand, then limped forward. Barely ten feet ahead, Janet felt the door of her bedroom. Her fingers traced the smooth surface until she felt the doorknob. She twisted it, then cautiously pushed open the door.

As Janet entered the room, the air surrounding her went from stark white to gray. Before her eyes could adjust enough to distinguish the shadows of the bed and dresser, the white veil whirled about her and wiped everything from sight.

"Oh, Jesus," Janet whispered. She held out her hand again and took a tentative step. "Ellie? Answer me, please, baby. If you're in here, make some kind of noise so I can find you."

Heather wrapped an arm around her aunt's leg and whimpered.

Slowly, cautiously, Janet moved forward. If Ellie was lost in this stuff, she'd be scared and probably hiding. Under the bed possibly, or in the closet.

Suddenly, something dark and weighty scurried over the top of Janet's foot. She clamped a hand over her mouth to smother a shriek as she caught sight of a long, thin tail slipping off into the mist. Heather, evidently seeing the same, screamed and dug her fingers into Janet's leg.

Terror drove icicles through Janet's body, and she trembled, still feeling the weight of whatever had crawled over her. She stomped her foot to chase the feeling away, and pain jabbed through her knee. Ignoring it, she plunged ahead.

"Ellie Marie Savoy! Answer me!"

A snicker sounded to her left, paralyzing Janet. She listened until it pressed through the mist again, this time harsh and sarcastic. The voice sounded old and croupy, and Janet couldn't make out if it was male or female.

"Ellie?"

No one answered, and nothing moved except for Heather, who buried her face against Janet's leg.

Janet leaned over to untangle herself from her niece.

"No!" Heather cried.

"Just hold on," Janet demanded, and clutched Heather's hand tighter. She swung her free hand wildly out in front of her and stumbled in the direction she thought the snickers came from.

Soon, Janet touched a wall, and if her calculations were right, the closet was only a few feet away. She kept one eye on the top of Heather's head as she felt her way along.

When Janet's fingers tripped over a doorframe, she walked them around it, expecting the closet door. Her hand plunged into empty space, however, and she sucked in a breath. She was sure she hadn't left the closet door open.

Forcing her hand inside, Janet felt cloth flutter across her fingertips and heard the scratch of hangers against the metal rod stretched across the closet. She knelt and bit her lip against the sharp pain in her knee. Her hand darted into the white air but touched nothing, so she crawled forward a few inches, inadvertently pulling Heather along.

"I don't wanna go," Heather whimpered, and sat. She sawed her legs up and down fiercely, working herself back until half her body disappeared into the fog.

Janet jerked on the tether, and the end tied to her wrist came free. "Stop!" She cried out in pain as she spun about on her knees and dove for Heather. By now the only thing visible of the child was her feet, and both were sneakerless and disappearing fast. Janet latched on to Heather's ankles, and the girl kicked frantically. Her niece's screams vibrated through the mist.

"Let me go!"

"It's me!" Janet shouted. She held tighter to the flailing feet. "I've got you. Stop fighting or I'll lose you, Heather. Do you hear me? I'll lose you!"

The struggle stopped immediately, and Janet quickly pulled. Heather's legs came into view, then her body. The tear-stained face that followed was silent and shrouded by a mass of tangled black hair.

"Don't—don't do that again!" Janet sobbed. "How could I look for you both? How?"

Heather blinked back at her, and Janet lowered her head and cried harder. Feelings of helplessness and unmitigated loss threatened to crush her. How would she ever find her child this way? She couldn't see a foot ahead of her, and Heather fighting every step only slowed her progress more. What if Ellie wasn't even up here? What if she'd managed to get downstairs? At this pace, and under these conditions, it would take hours to search the house. And sweet mother of God, anything could happen to Ellie by then.

With quiet resolve, Janet wiped her nose and eyes with the bottom of her blouse. She *would* find Ellie, no matter how long it took. *Just please,* she begged silently, *don't let it be too late.*

Janet sat Heather up, pushed the hair from her face, then reattached the shoelace to her wrist. This time she made a double knot and triple checked the end connected to the child. Confident the knot was secure, she clutched her niece's arms. "Stay right next to me, okay?"

Heather, mute and pale, stared back.

Coaxing Heather down with her, Janet positioned herself back on her knees. Her left knee protested so painfully that Janet had to lift it from the floor and drag herself along on her hands and right knee. Frustrated with the slower pace, she struggled to her feet and pulled Heather up with her. With a wide sweep of her hand, Janet hobbled back into the closet. Her fingers made contact with the clothes again, but instead of hearing hangers scraping against metal, she heard a child weeping.

She leaned over and looked at Heather, but the girl only stared straight ahead, her eyes dry. A prick of intuition made Janet bolt upright and look left, and she saw a gray oval shape forming in the mist. The air soon took on an acrid scent, like that of burning hair, and the smell intensified as the shape broadened in length. By the time Janet shoved Heather behind her, it was bathtub-sized and closer. She crept two steps back, and without warning, a huge, snarling, black muzzle burst through the oval. With a gasp, Janet stumbled backwards, sandwiching Heather between her and the wall.

Pointy brown teeth, the length of twelvepenny nails, gnashed and snapped, and the muzzle lurched and twisted as though trying to break free of a restraint. Suddenly, the bristly mouth sprang wide open, and an image emerged from the center of the cavernous black cavity. It was Ellie, only in miniature. She stood naked and gaunt with bone-thin arms hanging limp at her sides. Her tiny face was emaciated and sallow, and the sockets that once held her bright blue eyes were hollow.

Alarm, fear, and horror fused inside Janet, forming a monstrous rage that sent her lunging forward. "No!" she screamed, and threw a punch with her free hand. She struck air, and the muzzle vanished with the sound of raucous laughter.

"Mommmmy."

Janet froze at the sound of her daughter's voice. It seemed to resonate from nearby and at the same time far away.

"Mommmmy."

"Ellie!" Janet shouted and whipped about. She felt Heather flop against her. "Where are you? Where?"

Forcing herself to stand motionless, Janet listened intently. She heard Heather breathing through a stuffy nose.

"Oh, God, Ellie, where are you?"

From what sounded like only a few feet away, Ellie's voice beckoned. "Come, Mommy. Here."

Janet struggled not to leap headlong into the fog after her daughter. She moved slow and steady, holding an arm out, flexing her fingers into the white mass. "Where, baby? Where?"

An icy gust swirled through the mist, and fear warned Janet to pull her hand back. Instead, she stretched her fingers out farther. Something viscid suddenly slithered over her hand, then clamped down in a vise grip. Crying out, Janet tried to pull her hand back, but the grip only tightened.

"Poor Mommy. Poor, poor, Mommy," Ellie's voice singsonged in her ear.

Whatever had hold of Janet gave one hard yank, and she found herself instantly propelled through the fog. Faster and farther she ran, pulled through the blinding mass, her brain barely registering that Heather was still attached to her by the shoelace. Unable to slow the momentum, Janet squeezed her eyes shut, lowered her head, and waited to collide with a wall. At least her body would soften the impact for her niece.

In the time it took Janet to anticipate an impact, her body came to an abrupt halt, and her arm was released. Wobbly and stunned, Janet opened her eyes. They still stood in fog. She quickly dropped to her haunches to check on her niece and spotted pale green bathroom tile beneath her feet. Heather teetered at Janet's side, apparently in shock. Her eyes were sunken and blank, and her mouth hung slack.

"It's gonna eat you up, Mama," Ellie's voice suddenly warned. Janet bit her lip to stay silent and stood, listening. "Heather, too," Ellie said. "Poor Mommy. Poor Heather."

Janet gasped as a green and tan shower curtain entered her tight circle of vision. It flapped harmlessly at her.

"You're getting warm, Mama."

With a trembling hand, Janet pushed the shower curtain away and watched it disappear into the fog.

"Hotter." Ellie's voice clipped up an octave. "You're getting hotter!"

Janet leaned forward, and the tub appeared a few inches ahead. She bowed lower, straining to see any kind of movement. Then, just ahead and to her right, a narrow panel of heavier mist appeared to shift. Janet squinted, studying it closely. The panel lifted gradually, like a veil from a virgin bride. Beneath it, Ellie's weary face appeared.

With a loud sob, Janet reached for her daughter. Her fingers wrapped around cloth, which she had to assume was the front of Ellie's blouse since she couldn't see it, and she pulled.

Ellie didn't budge. Her expression remained somber, unchanged.

Crying, Janet clenched her teeth, braced a heel against the floor, and tugged harder. Instead of her child moving closer, however, Janet felt the cloth slip from her fingers.

"Too late, Mama," Ellie said. Her eyes clouded with defeat, and she shook her head sadly. "Too late."

Before the sorrowful cadence of Ellie's voice faded completely, a pair of withered hands thrust through the fog and clamped down on the child's shoulders. Above her head appeared the gray, fluid face of an old man with large ears.

Chapter Thirty-two

Thirty-five.

Another glimpse at the odometer drove four fingernails into Michael's palm. The pain kept his tears in check. He wanted to cry because the Cadillac didn't have wings, and he couldn't fly to his only daughter's rescue. Because he didn't know for sure if his wife was dead or alive. Because he'd left a dead woman alone in the wet, dark night. He'd stayed with her as long as he could, pacing through the mud, counting the seconds, waiting for the ambulance. Although he struggled long and hard with his conscience, he didn't last long. Not with Anna Stevenson's voice still ringing in his ears, telling him to hurry. So he left, convincing himself help was indeed on the way. Only after he'd passed an ambulance ten miles down the road did his conscience finally quit clawing at his mind and heart. Every one of the emergency vehicle's lights flashed, its siren blared, and tagging close behind it was the white Sentra. Michael had little doubt as to where they were headed. What he doubted was his sanity. What else would explain his hearing Anna's voice from a dying woman's lips?

Forty-two.

Dark, clapboard houses flew past his window, then a bank, a lighted billboard touting Arceneaux's Insurance, a post office, a speed limit sign that read, 30 MPH, and just beyond that a large, bullet-pocked plaque mounted to a sycamore. Written across the plaque in reflective letters was: NOW LEAVING SUNTON CORP LIMITS—YA'LL COME BACK SOON!

Michael's eyes locked on the word SUNTON. It took a millisecond for it to pass the windshield—SUN—pass the front passenger window—SUN—twisting in his seat, foot jammed against the accelerator—eyes following—following—quickly, too quickly SUN disappeared. Only night remained. Only darkness.

Feeling like he'd just witnessed some sort of prophetic canticle, Michael whipped back around in his seat, more determined than ever to change it. He would win this race against the sun even if it cost him his life.

Forty-six. *Over halfway there—forty-four miles left to go.*

Michael didn't look up from the odometer soon enough to avoid the lake of water pooled across the road. The Cadillac hit it doing eighty, and the steering wheel wrenched free of his hands. Water exploded into giant plumes on either side of the sedan, causing it to jerk hard to the right. Michael's head slammed into the driver's side window, his teeth clamping down on his tongue. Bright sparkles shot across his line of sight, and the taste of copper filled his mouth. He groped blindly for the steering wheel, found it, but found it useless. The car dictated its own direction, spinning, spinning, like a merry-go-round gone mad.

Nausea struck him. Bile raced up his throat. Michael gulped, then gulped again, trying to hold it back.

The sound of crashing, crumpling metal and shattering glass surprised him. His head snapped back. His body pitched forward.

Then, all grew still.

Disoriented, Michael fumbled for the door handle. His hand slid over it three times before his brain registered the find. He opened the door and got out on wobbly legs.

The front end of the sedan was wrapped around a wide brick column, and a dented mailbox sat on the hood. Steam hissed from a demolished radiator. Only one headlight had survived the collision, and it pointed up, revealing a pasture and a long, graveled driveway that led to a farmhouse.

Not bothering to assess the rest of the damage to the Cadillac, Michael stumbled down the driveway toward the clapboard house. His head ached, his tongue burned from having been bitten, and his neck felt like it was attached to his torso with staples. He balled his hands into fists, pictured Ellie and Janet, and willed more strength into his body.

A porch light came on the moment Michael stepped up to the house, and he saw a curtain part in a front window. An old woman peered out at him, her short white hair willowy and wild as though she'd just risen from sleep, her wrinkled, toothless mouth moving frantically against the mouthpiece of a telephone.

Michael knocked on the door, and the curtain

snapped shut. He waited, listening for footsteps. When no one came to the door, he knocked again.

As he raised a hand to knock a fourth time, he suddenly found himself bathed in red and blue light. Puzzled, he looked back to see a white patrol car barreling down the drive. Only then did he hear the crunch of gravel beneath its tires.

The patrol car rocked to a stop fifty feet from the house, and a young, heavyset woman stepped out. Her black ponytail swung from side to side as she scanned the front of the property, corded radio mike in hand. She mumbled something Michael couldn't understand into the radio, then tossed it back into the car. Moving out from behind the car door, her small eyes narrowed, and a hand settled over the gun holster strapped to her side.

"Wanna tell me what you're doin' here, mister?" she asked in a congested, north Louisiana drawl. She sounded winded, as though moving those few inches was more exercise than she'd experienced in a month.

"Looking for help," Michael said. "My car . . ." He pointed toward the Cadillac and for the first time, noticed the condition of his hands and arms. Both were streaked with dirt and blood. His fingernails looked like he'd been digging mud holes with them. By the look of disgust on the officer's face, the rest of him must have looked even worse.

"Yeah, I noticed how well you relocated Miss Mert's mailbox," she said. "Just step on down from that porch now. Slow and easy."

Michael did as she asked and stumbled down the last step. "Officer, listen, I—"

A flashlight beam struck him full in the face. "How much you have to drink?" she demanded.

"Huh?"

"To drink, mister," the officer said. "You know, booze, beer, bourbon?"

"Nothing!" Michael said. "I—"

"Right."

"I'm not drunk," Michael snapped. "I haven't even had water since I left Brusley!"

"Brusley, huh?" She eyed him. "Then what say we see some I.D. License, registration, that sorta thing."

Michael quickly patted his back pockets, then remembered he didn't have his wallet with him. He slumped. "Officer—"

"Don't tell me," she said. "You left it at home."

"Yes, but I can explain."

"Oh, I'm sure you can," she said, taking out a small notepad and pen from her shirt pocket. She tucked the flashlight under one arm and flipped open the notebook. "Wanna try for registration?"

"Please, I know what this must look like . . . what I must look like, but I'm in the middle of a crisis." Michael started toward the woman, and her glare stopped him cold. "I have to get to Carlton. It's an emergency, a matter of life or death."

She frowned. "Whose?"

"What?"

"Whose life or death?"

"My wife, my daughter." Michael began to pace, anxious over the time being wasted. "They're in Carlton, alone at our cabin, and I've got reason to believe they may be in danger."

The officer cocked her head to one side, keeping a wary eye on him. "And what reason is that?"

Michael opened his mouth to tell her, then snapped it shut. If he told her the truth, she'd haul him away for sure. Straight to the nearest mental ward.

"Well?"

"They left yesterday. I haven't heard from them since. I've tried calling dozens of times, but haven't been able to get through."

"And?"

Michael tried not to slouch under the weakness of his excuse. He had to come up with something plausible, something that would get this woman's attention. He didn't want to lie, but he couldn't very well tell her the complete truth.

Kneading his forehead, Michael said, "Look, it's a complicated story, but the bottom line of it is my father owes a man money. A dangerous man. And I'm afraid this guy thinks my father is at the cabin with my wife and daughter. I'm almost positive he's headed over there right now."

The woman pursed her lips, then relaxed them, pursed, then relaxed, as if she was sucking in what he'd said. Finally she asked, "If you're that worried about your family, why haven't you contacted the police in Carlton or even the parish sheriff's department?"

"I tried," Michael said. "I even had a police dispatcher from Brusley try to get through to them. But all the phone lines have been down."

She sucked in his words again. "What's the man's name?"

He looked at her, puzzled.

"The guy you're so worried about getting to your wife and kid."

Not anticipating that question, Michael blurted the first name that popped into his head, "Ephraim Stevenson."

The officer started to write in her notebook, then stopped and glanced up at him. "You got a spellin' on that first name?"

"E-P-H-R-A-I-M."

" 'Preciate it. Now you?"

"Me?"

She nodded. "Your name."

"Michael Savoy."

"Wife's?"

"Janet Woodard Savoy."

"And the phone number to this cabin you've been talkin' about."

"What do you need with the number?"

The officer let out an exasperated sigh. "Well, you got no I.D., a car wrapped around Dora Mert's mailbox, it looks like you've been fist fighting in a pig's wallow for a week, and you don't seem to be able to walk a straight line for shit. Now, that's not to say there's no reason to trust you, mister, you understand? But so far, your one and one ain't addin' up to two. Anyway, I'm going to call these names in, make sure nothin' shows up. If they come back clean, I'll have somebody give this alleged cabin number a call. We'll take it from there."

Michael crossed his arms, wanting to hold on to the little bit of hope she'd just given him. "Instead of calling, couldn't you send a patrol car out there? The address is—"

She ticked a finger at him. "First things first. What's the phone number?"

He gave it to her, and she repeated it back to him for confirmation.

When he agreed that she'd written the number down correctly, she pulled the flashlight out from under her arm and pointed the beam at the front of the patrol car. "Now you just come on and stand right here where I can keep an eye on you. I won't be but a minute."

Michael dropped his arms. "But you don't understand, we're wasting too much time!"

"You're the one wastin' it by arguin' with me." She waggled the beam over the hood of the car. "Now git."

Only when he was in the instructed position did she get back into the squad car, leaving one leg out, foot firmly planted on the ground.

From where he stood, Michael heard the click of the mike as she keyed it.

"Unit Five to dispatch."

"Go 'head, Unit Five."

"Yeah, we got a ten thirty-five charlie on China Valley Road right in front of Dora Mert's place. We're gonna need a wrecker."

"Ambulance?"

Michael saw the officer peer at him through the windshield before sticking her head out the door.

"You need an ambulance?" she asked him.

He shook his head.

"You sure?"

"I don't need a damn ambulance," he shouted. "I need somebody to go and check on my wife and daughter!"

She glared at him for a beat, then turned away. She leaned over to one side for a second, and after that all Michael could hear were mumbles and clicks.

He began to pace again, keeping himself between the headlights lest she panic and eat up more valuable time. To keep himself under control, he watched his feet like they were hands to a clock and counted each step as a passing second.

By the time the officer got out of the squad car, Michael was up to five hundred forty-three and ready to kick out both headlights.

"Well?" he asked when she snapped the flashlight back on and pointed it at his feet.

"Well is right, Mr. Savoy," she said sharply. "If I were you, I'd find the registration to that car out there right fast."

"What?—wait! Did anyone call the number I gave you?"

"Oh, yeah, they called," she said, her eyes hardening. "I don't know who you think you're dealing with out here, Mr. Savoy, but I can tell you, it ain't a bunch of small town yokels. We don't take kindly to people yankin' our chain."

Michael threw his hands up. "What the hell are you talking about? Did anyone get through to that number? Were the circuits working? Did my wife answer?"

She scowled and lifted the beam of light to his chest. "Circuits were fine, number rang right through in fact. All four times—straight through to Carlton—and the town morgue."

"Whoa! What? Somebody dialed the wrong number. They had to have dialed the wrong number!"

"Four times?"

"I don't care if they dialed it ten times," Michael said. "They had to have dialed it wrong!"

The officer looked at the notebook, repeated the phone number he'd given her earlier in a sharp, loud voice, then asked, "Now you gonna stand there and tell me you accidentally gave me the wrong number?"

"No, that's the right one, but—"

"For a man so worried about time, you're sure throwin' away a lot of it, Mr. Savoy. Both yours and mine. So let's get this movin'. Time to see your registration."

"But—"

"Look, you'll have a chance to do all the buttin' you want down at the station. Once you get me that piece of paper out of your car, we're gonna take a little ride and get a few things straight. Find out exactly how much you mighta been drinkin', figure out why you got blood in places without any cuts, and get to the bottom of why you're runnin' around over a hundred and fifty miles from home without any I.D. Come on now, let's git. We've kept poor Miss Mert up long enough with all this hurrah."

Michael slammed a fist against the hood of the squad car. "I've already told you I haven't been drinking, goddammit, just like I told you I forgot my wallet at home!" He yanked on the front of his T-shirt. "This blood comes from an injured woman. Her car ran off the road just outside of Pucket, and I stopped to help. All you've got to do is call the ambulance service in that area to confirm it. Now that's the whole goddamn story. I don't need to go down to any police station. I need to get to Carlton!"

A brilliant sword of light pierced his eyes. "And I need your registration!" the officer said. "Now if you wanna go ahead and add destruction of public property to the crap already hangin' over your head, you just go on. But let me warn you, I might be a woman, but I can cuff you and haul your ass outta here faster than anybody. So you either get on out there to that car right now and get me that registration or you'll be spending a hell of a lot more time in Sunton than you planned to."

With a shout of frustration, Michael pushed away from the squad car and stormed down the driveway toward the Cadillac.

A wobbling light beam appeared on his left side. "Slow it down, Savoy," the officer said. They'd barely walked a hundred feet, and he could already hear her panting and huffing for breath behind him.

Michael's mind pureed his thoughts until they were soup. He kept his walk brisk, his eyes straight ahead.

"I said slower," she wheezed.

Michael started to jog.

"S-stop! Now! Y-you hear?"

The beam of light swung wildly now, across the open field to his left, down near his feet, over his head, revealing the thick wall of trees and brush across the road—nature's sanctuary—a fortress against questions and delays.

Without a second thought, Michael ran for it.

Chapter Thirty-three

Wilson Savoy mumbled a Hail Mary, then the Pledge of Allegiance. Those were the only prayers he knew.

Shaking, he got to his feet and leaned against a wall for support. His mind felt perforated, too fragile to hold the image of the dog-man without splitting apart—that blood-soaked snout shrinking into a human aquiline nose, those lips, swollen and stained from the fruits of their most recent labor. Every time he tried to force the vision out of his brain, however, it only made more room for Lester. In the forty-three years Wilson had been a funeral director, he thought he'd seen more faces of death than any one person had a right to. Mangled bodies, flattened bodies, burned ones, floaters, infants, hangers, crap that kept you awake at night for weeks. This was the first time he'd ever watched one of these gruesome deaths actually take place. Between the sights and sounds of Lester's flesh being torn apart and dog-man's transmutation, Wilson figured he might never sleep again.

Kneading his bottom lip between two fingers, Wilson glanced over his shoulder at the back door. He had to find a way out of here, out of this building, out of Brusley, out of Louisiana. But how? Even if he managed to escape through a window, that dog-thing might still be lurking outside. Hell, for all he knew, another one might be hiding in the funeral home.

Unsure of what to do next, Wilson turned back to face the length of the hall. That's when he noticed the slugs, a parade of them, hundreds, crawling along the baseboard of the wall to his left. Their slick, brown-green bodies were long and as thick as a man's finger. Their trail seemed endless. Stunned, Wilson followed their path with his eyes, down the entire length of the baseboard, up the corner of the rear wall to the ceiling, then along the crown molding where they seemed to loop back to where they began. Wilson turned slowly, looking for the last slug, following the trail that led to the back door—and the old, barefoot man standing beside it.

Wilson gasped.

"There is no escape," the old man said fiercely.

A warm, wet patch suddenly spread across the front of Wilson's pants. "But—"

"No escape!" The old man lifted his arms up at his sides, and his chest began to expand. "No mercy!" Thicker, wider, his sternum bulged until the buttons on his black mourning suit popped off.

"I don't have it!" Wilson cried. "I don't have your medallion, I swear!"

The old man's eyes darkened to the color of pitch, and he lowered his head, chin to chest. A low rumble emanated from him, the vibrations of which Wilson could feel under his feet.

"I swear to God," Wilson said backing away. "I don't have anything! I don't have it!"

The rumbling became a roar of anger, and the old man's head lifted abruptly, revealing a wide, protruding forehead. The lower half of his face began to shift, collecting nose, mouth, and chin into one thick, black snout.

Wilson whimpered and held out his hands. "No, wait! Wait! You said I had time, right? Right? Didn't you say that? The sun, some deal about the sun, right?"

In one last shuddering motion the transformation became complete, and Wilson no longer faced an old man with large ears and bare feet, but a Rottweiler of enormous proportions.

"Shit!" Wilson whirled about and ran down the hall. He heard the thunder of heavy, padded feet racing behind him.

"Hail Mary, full of grace—with liberty and justice for all," Wilson mumbled frantically while urging his legs and arms faster. He didn't look back. He couldn't look back.

He was about to dodge left into one of the viewing rooms when he envisioned the dog's teeth shredding through the flimsy accordion doors like they were tissue. He bolted right instead, into the casket selection room and kicked the door shut behind him.

A heavy thump vibrated against the door, making it shudder in its frame. Then came the *chomp, snap* of gnashing teeth, so loud it was as if the animal stood beside him. With jittering fingers, Wilson managed to turn on the lights. He quickly scanned the room, searching for a place to hide.

Another *thump*. Then another. The sonofabitch was going to break down the door!

The sound of splintering wood sent Wilson racing for a mahogany casket, which was set up on a two-foot bier at the back of the room. He jumped into the casket and closed both lids. Only seconds passed before he heard the Rottweiler snorting around the seals.

Wilson lay very still, his face a bare two-finger distance from the inside lining of the top lid. Springs beneath the casket mattress poked into his back, but he dared not readjust his position.

The dog whined, then growled and scratched on the coffin, causing it to shift slightly on the bier.

"Go away," Wilson mouthed, clutching the satin lining.

The animal scratched again as though for good measure, then Wilson heard nothing but his own labored breathing. He listened intently, forcing slow, even breaths. Did it leave? Had it given up that easily? Or was it just sitting there, waiting him out? It was too quiet. Too damn quiet.

Wilson nervously clicked a thumb and fingernail together. He glanced up, then to each side. No matter the direction he shifted his eyes, the darkness remained so complete it seemed palpable. His nostrils burned from the new material smell, and his right arm began to itch. Carefully, Wilson reached over and scratched. Instead of relieving the itch, the prickling sensation traveled up to his shoulder, then to his neck. Wilson followed it with a trembling finger. When he reached his shirt collar, he felt something thick and wet crawl onto his hand. Letting out a low moan of disgust, he swiped the back of his hand against the top of the casket. Whatever he wiped off fell across his left eye with a plop.

Before Wilson could scrape the thing off his face, he felt something long and slimy creep up his left pant leg. Another traveled across his right wrist and up into his shirtsleeve. One slipped down his collar. Sudden visions of brown-green slugs exploded in Wilson's brain. He cried out loudly and raked his hands over his body, unable to reach anything below his waist.

Seemingly undeterred by Wilson's clawing, the slugs crept higher and higher, slithering across his chest, to his armpits, around his neck. It felt like hundreds of them invading every inch of his skin. Wilson gasped and clawed, panted, grunted, and before he knew it, he was shoving against the casket lid. He *had* to get out!

But the casket lid wouldn't open.

Wilson shrieked and rammed the top of his fists against the upper lid. He kicked at the bottom cap with the toes of his shoes. Only the slugs moved.

Slowly, doggedly, they crawled up, up from his legs to his groin, up from his chest to his throat, up to his chin, his mouth, his nose.

Clamping his lips together so they wouldn't get into his mouth, Wilson thrashed and kicked. He didn't care if the dog-man heard him. He didn't care about anything but getting out.

The casket rocked with his efforts, but the darkness remained. Not even a sliver of light appeared from the lid. Wilson started to cry, hot fat tears that seemed to agitate the slugs even more. Their squirming grew frenzied, more directed toward his face.

Wilson clawed two away from his mouth. "I'm sorry!" he shouted to anyone or anything that might be listening outside the casket. "Do you hear me? I'll get it back for you, I promise! Just get me out of here, please! Please!"

Nothing responded from outside the claustrophobic space.

"Help, somebody, pl—" Wilson gagged as one of the slugs slid into his mouth. He coughed, spat, shoved a finger into his mouth, but before he managed to get the first one out, two more slithered inside.

Wilson felt them everywhere now, layers of them over his chest, his arms, his legs, his face. He couldn't work his hands fast enough to keep them away from his mouth and nose. They seemed to stand sentinel to one another, waiting their turn, forcing their way into every available orifice. He cried harder, knowing it would only make matters worse, but not able to help it.

Oh, God, help me! his mind screamed. *I'm so sorry! Please help me! Help me get out of here and I swear I'll be different! Oh, Jesus, I can't breathe! Jesus, no air! No—air! Please!*

Wilson flailed in the coffin, praying for any molecule of oxygen. His lungs felt ready to burst, his heart slamming against his chest. His fingers were sticky and numb, barely able to close over the layer of slugs on his face. He felt what little energy he had left draining away. Soon Wilson knew there would be no more time for prayers.

The weight of remorse that began to settle over him

felt heavier than the darkness and slugs combined. He finally lay still, no longer able to fight, and for the first time in Wilson's life, he believed he knew what it meant to be truly sorry. Sorry for taking the medallion, sorry for screwing up so many lives, sorry for having the audacity to believe he always had tomorrow to make amends. He would trade his soul this moment if he had the chance to go back and do it all differently, especially with his son. But there was no going back. And the worst part was his knowing he would leave this place without anyone hearing how truly sorry he was. How sad, how empty, how useless it made his life seem.

Wilson's quivering fingers signaled the moment of his release. And when his heart stuttered over its last beat, he did not see the face of God. No bright light greeted him. No loved one waited for him at the end of a tunnel or on the shores of some calm sea. Wilson only saw and felt what he feared would be the essence of his eternity. Dark, cold, regret.

Chapter Thirty-four

"Let her go, you bastard!" Janet screamed at the man—the thing—that held on to her daughter. She yanked hard on Ellie's shirt and heard it rip.

Janet leaned over until more than half her body stretched across the tub. "Ellie, grab on!" she yelled. Her left arm stuck out awkwardly behind her, and Heather, apparently coming out of her stupor, began pulling in the opposite direction. The shoestring cut into Janet's wrist.

With terror-filled eyes, Ellie strained against the man's clutches and swung an arm around her mother's neck. She still held on to the crystal horse, and it smacked Janet across the cheek.

Barely flinching from the harsh sting, Janet shouted, "Hold tight, baby! Tight as you can." When Janet felt Ellie's arm squeeze around her neck, she let go of her daughter's shirt and grabbed her around the waist.

The gray-faced man bellowed with fury. His black eyes blazed, then sunk farther into his head, disappearing into sockets that glowed pus yellow. His head started to oscillate, slowly at first, then faster and faster until it was nothing but a blur. Mucus flew from his face in slimy strands that landed on Janet and began to suck and crawl over her skin like slick, hungry worms.

"Pull, Aunt Janet, pull!" Heather cried, yanking against the tether. "Harder, pull harder!"

"Mama!" Ellie shrieked.

Janet dug her fingers into Ellie's side and pulled with every ounce of strength she possessed.

A monstrous wail of outrage erupted from the vacillating face, and the next thing Janet knew, she, Ellie, and Heather sat in a heap on the bathroom floor, once again wrapped in a chrysalis of fog. No longer able to see the man, Janet quickly rolled to one side and ripped the crawling slime off her body.

Ellie sprang to her feet, grabbed her mother's arm and tugged. "Hurry," she begged.

Not needing a second prompting, Janet scrambled to her feet and helped Heather to hers. Suddenly a horrendous rumbling, like an army of thousands stomping in formation, reverberated through the fog. Janet scooped Ellie up with her free arm and propped the child against her, chest to chest.

"Keep your arms around my neck," she shouted over the din. "Wrap your legs around my waist." Ellie did as she was told and buried her face in her mother's shoulder. Janet shoved a hand between her and her daughter, pushed Ellie's fanny pack aside so it wouldn't poke into her ribs, then yelled down to Heather, "Walk really close to me. Right up against my leg."

Crying, Heather nodded and glued herself to Janet.

Bunched together, they advanced slowly, Janet sweeping her free hand out in front of them. When her fingers connected with the bathroom doorframe, she drove the sound of marching feet out of her mind, double-checked her hold on both girls, then stepped into the hall. She trailed her fingers along the wall nearest the bathroom to keep her bearings and counted as she went. She estimated they had twenty to thirty feet to go before reaching the stairs. Heather reached over with her free hand and clutched Janet's pant leg, doing her best to match her aunt's steps. Ellie whimpered and dug her face deeper into her mother's shoulder.

On the count of fifteen, Janet slowed her pace, knowing the stairs wouldn't be far. The *stomp-boom-stomp* of the marching troop abruptly ceased, and Janet didn't know whether to be relieved or more frightened.

Three steps—six—eight. The wall suddenly disappeared beneath her fingers, and Janet snatched her hand back. After checking once more to make certain Heather was tethered and molded against her and that Ellie's arms and legs were securely locked around her neck and waist, Janet groped for the stair railing with her free hand. Finding it, she clumsily maneuvered the three of them down the first step. Instantly, bolts of pain slammed into Janet's knee, and she squeezed the railing tighter to keep from falling over. Her knee fared far worse on the second step, and her legs began to tremble. By the third step, however, all thoughts of pain vanished. Janet stood perplexed, staring down the length of the staircase.

They'd broken through the fog.

"It's gone," Heather said quietly.

Ellie turned her head for a peek, then quickly hid her face again in Janet's shoulder.

With her heart thumping louder than two marching bands, Janet hustled everyone down the stairs as quickly as her knee allowed. She bit hard into her upper lip to stave off cries of pain and tasted blood.

When she stumbled past the last step, Janet glanced back at the landing.

The fog hung over the top of the stairs like a heavy quilt. It pulsed as though breathing.

"Don't stop, Mama," Ellie whispered against Janet's neck. Her legs squeezed tighter around her mother's waist. "Go, okay? Go fast."

Kissing her daughter's head, Janet turned back to the family room and surveyed the damage. The sofa lay on its back, the old recliner on its side, every one of their cushions ripped through and shredded. The top half of the end table rested in the fireplace, and a mangle of chairs blocked the path to the kitchen. Glass from the ship picture littered the floor. A sparse yellow light filtered in from the kitchen, swaddling the chaos in muted shadows.

Janet choked back a sob. Her mind didn't want to process the wreckage; it had already been through too much. This was a surrealism overload. She felt Heather tug on her pant leg.

"Are—are we going to die now?" Heather asked, her eyes glued to the destruction.

Heather's question shoved Janet's protective instinct back into gear. "*Nobody's* going to die," she said loudly, defiantly, to whomever or whatever threatened them. Just then, Janet noticed Heather's bare feet. There was no way the child would be able to walk across a glass-strewn floor.

She reached for Heather's right arm, quickly untied the shoelace attached to her niece's wrist, then stooped. "C-Climb on my back," Janet said, fighting against the spasms of pain in her knee. "I'm going to try to carry you, too. Wrap your legs around my waist just like Ellie. Put your legs over hers. Then both of you hold on to my neck, okay?"

Heather gave a short nod, then scurried around Janet and jumped on her back. Janet's knee immediately buckled, tossing all three to the floor.

Gasping with pain, and with Ellie still clinging to her neck and waist, Janet struggled to her feet. Heather, having fallen off, hovered nervously nearby.

"Ellie, y-you're going to have to let go," Janet said. "I can't—"

"No!" Ellie cried. "Don't put me down, Mama. Don't! They're going to get me!"

Janet kissed her. "I won't let them, baby, I won't. But you've got to get down. I can't carry both of you. Heather doesn't have shoes on, and she'll cut her feet on the glass if I don't carry her."

Ellie lobbed her head to one side to look at Heather's feet. She gave a shivering sigh and looked into her mother's eyes. "They'll get me," she said sadly.

"They'd have to get me first."

Ellie's eyes grew pained. Slowly, she untangled her feet from around Janet's waist and slipped to the floor.

Janet quickly made the switch, pulling Heather against her chest and tethering Ellie to her with the shoelace.

"There *are* bogeymans," Heather whispered in Janet's ear.

Janet patted her back. *You're right,* she thought, *there are.* To her niece she said, "Hold tight."

Satisfied that both girls were secure, Janet peered up at the staircase. The fog still pulsed against the landing.

Ellie stuttered at the sight. "G-g-go. We h-h-have to go."

"I'm with you, kiddo," Janet said, then navigated them carefully around the jumbled furniture and broken glass. She fought off the urge to run. She knew if she did, she wouldn't make it another five feet without her knee collapsing.

They'd barely made it into the dining room when Janet heard the deep, throaty growl of an animal behind them. Ellie's screams came before she had the chance to look back.

"Go, Mama!" Ellie cried. "Don't stop! Don't!"

"I want my mama!" Heather wailed. She groped at Janet's shirt as if she wanted to dive into her aunt's body.

Janet forced herself to turn around, then froze, dumbstruck. Twenty feet away in the family room stood an enormous dog. Its wide body carried a height of over four feet, and its thick, black head swung low. Something that looked like gristle dangled from its pointed, yellow-brown teeth. Massive shoulder muscles rippled and flexed, collecting strength. Its black marble eyes locked onto Ellie.

"N-n-no!" Janet swooped down and over with her free hand, grabbed a fistful of Ellie's shirt and tried hoisting her daughter up sideways. Janet's knee refused the extra weight, and she collapsed.

With the girls wailing in her ear, Janet fought to get back on her feet, but her damaged joint wouldn't cooperate. Teeth snapped vehemently behind her and ferocious snarls escalated in volume until they melded into one continuous roar. Janet sensed the animal inches away. Time had run out. After all the fear, the struggles, the fighting, she'd won the battle for Ellie. Now they faced losing the whole damn war.

Sobbing, Janet threw her body over the screaming girls, squeezed her eyes shut, and prayed.

Chapter Thirty-five

Countless mosquitoes drilled into Michael's skin while he batted furiously through brush and sagging tree limbs. The recent storm had left behind a trail of broken branches and puddles as wide as bayous. It had also stolen the moon, his only possible source of light. Every one of these obstacles robbed Michael of time and distance. He'd tripped and fallen so many times, his body felt like it had been trampled by a herd of elephants.

He didn't know how far he had traveled since leaving the cop. Between running when he reached a clearing, then doing various combinations of walk, duck, push when he'd reach a thick outcropping of trees, it felt like no more than two or three miles. At first, Michael had headed due north, staying just inside the forest so he wouldn't be seen. But the patrol car and its searchlight pushed him east, to a parallel road some distance away. He'd expected backup police units or track dogs to show up any minute and join in the search for him, but they never did. The officer probably figured she'd get her collar soon enough when he came back to claim the Cadillac.

Headlights flashed along the nearby road, and Michael dodged behind a pine tree. Moments later, an old white pickup towing a skiff rolled by.

"Shit," he muttered, frustrated that he'd missed another opportunity for a ride. This new road had more traffic than the previous one, which meant more chances to hitch. But he could never tell if the oncoming vehicle was a police car or not until it was too late.

Dropping his head, Michael moved along in a half-jog, steering out of the underbrush and closer to the road. He had to do something soon. If he kept traveling at this speed, it would take him a week to get to the cabin.

From the west, the wind carried the sound of a low, guttural engine to Michael's ear. He stopped and listened, debating whether or not to dodge back into hiding. The rumbling soon grew louder, nearer, bringing with it unmistakable recognition. Michael knew of only one engine that sounded like that. A Harley Davidson. He knew policemen rode Harleys, but not ones with the baffles tapped out of the muffler pipes. From the sound of it, this one had been bored wide open for maximum volume.

Michael stepped out into the road, his heart racing. In the distance, he saw small yellow and green blinking lights heading toward him. He squinted and crept back to the side of the highway, perplexed.

Who in the hell decorates a Harley with Christmas lights? he thought.

He heard the gears shift down twice, then twice

more. The bike slowed, close enough now for Michael to make out the large black tour bike and its driver. Both appeared doused in luminous lemons and limes. Michael stuck out his thumb.

The biker pulled up alongside him, dressed in jeans, black knee boots, and a worn out leather vest. Most of his three hundred plus pounds oozed over the seat of the bike. He pulled off a black, full-face helmet to reveal a chubby face, white scraggly beard, and a handlebar mustache. A long salt-n-pepper ponytail hung over his left shoulder, and he flicked it over to his back.

"Hey, brother man, how goes it?" the biker asked, sounding a little like Brando on helium.

"Long night," Michael said. "Taking riders?"

The biker cocked his head. "Don't normally. Alberta and me usually stick to ourselves." He patted the gas tank between his knees and grinned. "Berta here's my baby. Sweetest thing around. Anyway, I seen you standing out here lookin' pretty rough around the edges and thought I'd at least stop and make sure you're okay."

"I've been better," Michael said. "My car broke down not far from here, and I've got to get to my wife and daughter."

"Yeah? Where they at?"

"Carlton."

"Man," The biker stroked his beard with a finger and thumb. "Ways out, huh?"

"Afraid so."

"Close to thirty, thirty-five miles I think."

Michael nodded.

"Wasn't planning to head out that far. Just up the

road a bit to my woman's house, then shut it down for the night."

"I'll take any distance you're offering," Michael said.

The biker seemed to ponder the issue for a while longer, then said, "Like I told you, Berta and me don't normally take hitchers, but I'll tell you what—" He stuck a hand under his vest, and for a moment Michael was afraid he'd pull out a gun or knife. Instead, the man pulled out a small book. "Know what this is?"

Though Michael had never read through one before, he'd seen enough Bibles in churches to be able to spot one ten miles away. He nodded.

"Yeah?" the biker said. "Cool. The Master Dude and me just got hooked up about two weeks ago. Been flyin' high with Him ever since. Saved me from the horse, snort, all that bad shit, know what I mean? Anyways, if Jesus says go, we go. Cool?"

Michael stared at him. Maybe stopping this guy hadn't been such a good idea after all.

The biker grinned. "Name's Dango Reese by the way." He stuck out a hand.

Michael shook it. "Michael Savoy."

"Okay, brother Mike." Dango squared his shoulders. "Let's see where this old road leads tonight." He closed his eyes, flipped open the Bible, and jabbed a finger at a random passage. He peeked at it, then tilted the book to one side so the colored lights from his bike glowed over the pages. Dango squinted and read, "The perverse in heart are an abomination to the Lord, but the blameless in their walk are His delight." He frowned, studying the page, and chewed on his hairy upper lip.

Michael swept a nervous hand through his hair and looked down the road. He needed a ride, not a Bible lesson.

"Ah, okay, I get it now," Dango said, a smile easing onto his face. "See, you're walkin', and it says right here, *in their walk*, so that's gotta mean since you're walkin' it's cool. You're, uh—" He glanced at the passage again. "His delight—blameless."

Confused, Michael asked, "So does that mean you'll give me a lift?"

"Damn straight," Dango said with a grin. He closed the Bible and stuck it back under his vest. "Hey, you hungry? There's an all-nighter not far from here. We could grab a bite before heading out."

"If you don't mind, can we just go? This deal with my wife and daughter—it's an emergency. I really need to get there as fast as I can."

The big man's face sobered. "Well, hell, why didn't you say so?" He reached in his tour pack and pulled out a helmet. "Here, put this on. There's a mike in the base. We can talk while we ride."

Relieved that Dango hadn't started a game of twenty questions about his stated emergency, Michael pulled on the helmet. He heard a loud screech, then Dango's voice boom in his right ear.

"Ever ride one of these?" Dango asked, his helmet now back on his head. He turned around and slapped the sloped-back passenger seat on the bike.

"Yeah," Michael said. "In college."

"Cool. Then you should remember the rules. Hang on, lean when I lean, and don't mess with the driver."

"Got it." Michael straddled the designated seat, then locked his fingers around the pack bracket behind him.

Dango revved up the engine. "Okay, brother Mike, you ready to . . . race the sun?"

Michael jerked his head up, startled by the man's words. "What did you say?"

"Huh?" Dango looked back at him. "I just asked if you were ready to roll. What's up?"

"I thought . . . n-nothing. Sorry, nothing," Michael said, and settled back in the seat.

"You're not gonna wig on me or anything, are you?"

"No, really, I just thought . . . I didn't hear what you said, that's all. Please, can we go?"

Dango eyed him for a moment through the face shield, then turned back and heeled the Harley into first.

They rolled in silence for a while, and Michael wished he had the throttle so he could give the big bike more juice. He kept peering over Dango's shoulder to check the speedometer. Even at seventy, it still felt like they were barely moving.

Finally, Dango's voice boomed into Michael's helmet again. "I feel you gettin' antsy back there, brother man. You need to chill, okay? I'll push her up in a bit. Just gotta get past some of this wind trash right now." As if to make his point, Dango leaned left, then right, detouring around a fallen tree branch.

Michael tried to hold steady, but his body felt electrically charged, ready to take off on its own. His whole focus so far had been to get to Ellie and Janet. Now that he was closer than ever, he worried about what he'd find when he reached them. They were his life. Even thinking about having to live without one or the other drained something vital out of him.

Dango, keeping true to his word, eventually pushed

Alberta up to ninety. Sharp wind gusts cut through Michael's wet clothes and pierced his face shield. He shivered, cold, and too aware of the surrounding odors—damp pine, dirt, mown grass. It was the scent of cemeteries, of freshly dug graves.

"Hey, brother Mike," Dango said. "You ever hear the story in the Bible about that dude with long hair like mine? Think his name was Simpson or Samson, don't remember right off. But anyways, he got this chick pissed off at him and—"

By the time they reached Carlton, Michael felt he'd been given an abridged version of a revised Old Testament. Although the constant jabber had been irritating, it had at least kept his mind occupied, and for that he'd been grateful. Now, he wanted Dango to shut up. His wife and daughter were no more than a mile away, and he needed every one of his senses sharp and ready.

"Next right," Michael said into the helmet mike, and pointed to an upcoming road. He could hardly see now. Tears clouded his eyes. He couldn't believe he was actually in Carlton. Yesterday seemed like an eternity away, and it felt like he'd spent that long trying to get here.

Dango leaned the big bike into the turn.

With a shaking hand, Michael pointed ahead to the graveled road that led to the cabin. "First left."

Dango slowed the bike, but instead of leaning into the next turn, he came to a complete stop. "Sorry, but I've gotta stop here, brother." He pointed to the road Michael wanted him to take. "Alberta's finicky. She has a tendency to slide out from under me in gravel. And you see that fog rollin' in down there?" He waggled a finger toward a dense wall of white a few hundred feet away. "That means wet gravel. Alberta'll lay it down for sure."

Michael slid off the bike and quickly pulled off the helmet. "Here's fine. Thanks for the ride. I'd offer you money, but—"

"I don't need your money, just your prayers." Dango said, his voice sounding strange through his face shield. He took the extra helmet from Michael, looped the strap of it around one of the handlebars, then revved up the bike. "I'll pray for you, too, brother man." He pointed up. "'Cause the Master Dude's telling me you're gonna need it."

Before Michael could say anything, Dango roared off in a whirl of twinkling lights. Michael stared after him for only a second before taking off for the long graveled drive.

Now that he was on his feet again, every muscle in Michael's body screamed in protest. Every bone felt like it wanted to crumble with his next step. He ran faster, wiping everything out of his mind but the need to get to the cabin. He was so close he could smell it.

Ahead, fog draped over the road like a heavy blanket of snow. Michael barreled toward it, and it wasn't until he was fifty feet closer that he realized something was wrong. From here, the blanket of white didn't look like regular swamp fog. There were no translucent wisps. It seemed solid, like someone had painted the air or literally put up a wall. Lowering his head slightly, Michael balled his hands into fists and ran even faster. He didn't care if the goddamn thing was a solid slab of white concrete. He wasn't going to stop now, not this close.

Twenty feet—ten.

With a shout of fury, Michael charged through the wall, and the world around him disappeared.

Chapter Thirty-six

The animal sounded more feral than ever, yet it still hadn't attacked. Perplexed, Janet opened her eyes, careful not to move her body. She listened to the snaps and growls of ever increasing rage and the whimpers of fearful expectation from the two girls beneath her. What was the animal doing? What was it waiting for?

Janet lifted her head cautiously, chanced a look over her shoulder, then did a double-take.

The dog was spinning in place, snapping at the air as if it had gone mad, as if its rage had been redirected to someone or something Janet couldn't see. Seemingly oblivious to them now, its eyes rolled wildly from stark white to maniacal black. The hair on its massive shoulders and back had bristled into thick black needles, and its breath plumed with every snort.

Sensing this to be their last hope for escape, Janet turned back to the girls and rapidly untied the shoelace from around Ellie's wrist. She didn't trust her knee. If it gave out again while Ellie was still tethered to her, both of them would be trapped. This way her daughter at least had a chance.

Ellie stared up at her with terror-stricken, questioning eyes.

"Listen carefully," Janet whispered, keeping her voice so low she could barely hear herself speak. "When I count to three, I want the two of you to run as fast as you can out the kitchen door and to the van, understand?"

Ellie remained mute while Heather shook her head, tears flowing.

"Y-y-you're not coming?" Heather asked.

"I'll be right behind you," Janet said, hoping it was the truth. She glanced back at the dog, found it still in a twirling frenzy, then signaled for the girls to get ready.

Janet rolled away from her daughter and niece. "One," she said, then sat up. "Two."

The dog's head suddenly snapped in their direction, its eyes no longer lost to some unseen enemy.

"Christ, three!" Janet shouted, and thrust herself upright, shifting as much of her weight as she could to her good leg. She screamed through the pain, "R-r-run, girls! Now! Go!" Janet hobbled after them, refusing to look back at the beast. She didn't want to see death coming.

Janet's heart seemed to go on hiatus until she dove through the kitchen door into the still night air. She landed on her side in wet grass with a loud, "uumph!"

Small, nervous hands clutched her arm. "Too dark . . . no car . . . can't see!"

Disoriented and gasping to refill her lungs, Janet stared up at Heather, who was bending over her, yelling. Ellie stood inches away, her face hidden by shadows. They'd made it—all three of them—safe. But how was that possible? The dog had been right on her heels, bigger than life.

Janet sat up quickly and looked back at the house, expecting the animal to come pouncing out of the doorway toward them. Instead she saw an empty threshold. Sudden movement beyond the kitchen window caught Janet's attention, and her eyes locked on to it. A shadow, too tall and thin to belong to the dog, traveled close to the pane. As it neared, the faint glow from the stove light gave the shadow some definition. A woman—large eyes—narrow face—long widow's peak. Anna Stevenson? The woman pressed a hand against the glass as though to acknowledge Janet, then she vanished, and the kitchen door slammed shut.

"The lady's gone," Ellie said, her voice sad and haunting. "They made her go away. And now I'm going to die."

Heather let out a hoarse sob and dropped to her knees.

Ellie's words struck Janet like a sledgehammer pounding iron; they rang loud and true. They also filled her with an overwhelming certainty that somehow Anna Stevenson had saved their lives. She'd helped them escape. Janet didn't understand how or why, but right now those details weren't important. For she felt just as certain that this night of horrors was far from over.

Janet scrambled to her feet, dread obliterating the pain in her knee. "Nobody's going to die!" she shouted, turning toward the house. "You hear me, goddammit? Nobody!"

The kitchen door burst open in response, and the

thick white mass that had imprisoned them earlier rolled out of the house in giant waves.

"Mama!" Ellie broke into a run.

"Stop! Ellie, no!" Janet lunged for her daughter, but the fog swallowed the night in an instant. "Oh, God!" she cried, and whirled about, groping blindly. "Ellie! Heather!"

No answer.

No children.

Only dense white walls.

Without a second thought, Janet ran headlong into the fog. "Ellie, Heather, answer me!"

Silence pressed against Janet, and she felt ready to implode with hopelessness. She ran, stumbling, crying, pushing on with no sense of direction. Her world had become another planet where nothing made sense.

Something large and blue abruptly entered her line of sight, and before Janet could pull up short, she crashed into it. Her brain registered *van!* as her body snapped back from the impact and slammed to the ground.

Groaning, she struggled back up, her tongue twitching over an odd, metallic taste in her mouth. Janet wiped warm dribble from her chin with a sleeve. It came back stained with blood. She ignored it and held out a hand to search for the van that had disappeared behind the white shroud. Just as she took a wobbly step forward, she heard a sniffle.

She froze, listening.

Another sniffle. A soft sob.

Janet inched forward, silent, following the sound.

In a matter of seconds, the driver's side of the van

came into view, as did Heather. The child was sitting on the ground near the front tire, her thumb in her mouth. When Heather spotted her aunt, she pointed up, saying nothing. Janet peered in the indicated direction.

Ellie sat in the van's driver's seat, staring at her mother through the window. A wicked grin splayed her lips as she stroked the head of the crystal horse.

Keeping a wary eye on her daughter, Janet leaned over, took Heather's outstretched hand, and pulled her up. Ellie's eyes followed every move, her grin widening. A ripple of nausea ran through Janet. That smirk didn't belong on her child. It belonged on someone wicked, someone insane. In one quick motion, Janet yanked the car door open, and Ellie recoiled as if someone had thrown ice water on her face.

"Mia lona!" Ellie shouted. Her eyes rolled back, and her little body began to convulse, whipping about wildly. She landed on the passenger seat, her head banging against the window. *"Mia lona! Mia lona!"*

Shocked, Janet hesitated for only an instant before shoving a shrieking Heather into the van, then over the front seat to the back. Janet jumped in after her. No sooner had she settled in the driver's seat, than something rammed against the right side of the van. Janet quickly reached for Ellie, but her daughter jerked away, spitting and shouting nonsensical words.

Again something collided with the van, this time causing it to rock. Another concussion, then another; this one stronger than the last.

Janet gasped, reluctantly turning her attention away from Ellie. If she didn't get out of here soon, the van would be destroyed. They'd be stranded. She dug frantically through her pockets for keys, found them, and with doddering fingers managed to shove the right one into the ignition. The engine roared to life.

Ellie's shouts and thrashing grew louder, more rigorous when Janet threw the gearshift into reverse and stomped on the accelerator. The back end of the van whipped about, and she didn't wait for a complete stop before slapping the shift into drive.

The first tree came into view only after Janet hit it. The young willow only bowed with the impact. She backed up to dislodge it from the fender, then plowed blindly ahead. Not twenty feet farther, a large oak appeared seemingly out of nowhere, and Janet swerved to keep from hitting it head on. As soon as she cleared the oak, she steered back toward its accompanying tree line and hugged it, knowing that sooner or later it would lead her past the long driveway and onto the main road. From there, she could find help for Ellie, a hospital, doctors, an exorcist—someone, anyone who could tell her what the hell was happening to her child.

Janet was concentrating so hard on the obscure path ahead, it took a moment for her to realize Ellie had stopped screaming and writhing. She glanced over at her daughter. The child stared back with dark, cold eyes. Stunned by the stark callousness of Ellie's expression, Janet's foot slipped off the accelerator. Before she could reposition it, Ellie leaped from her seat and sank her teeth into her mother's right forearm.

"Ellie, no! No!" Bellowing with pain, Janet slammed on the brakes, and Ellie pitched forward, hitting her head against the dashboard. Janet reached for her, but once again Ellie pushed away. The small girl lifted her head and began to howl like a lost, wounded animal.

"Go, Aunt Janet, hurry!" Heather cried from the backseat.

At the sound of her cousin's voice, Ellie scrambled onto the passenger seat, sat back on her heels and pointed a finger at Heather, then at Janet. "There will be no escape," she proclaimed in a deep, accented voice. "Do you hear? No escape! And no mercy!"

A pause, breathless seconds as Janet went numb with fear. Something thudded softly nearby, but she didn't bother to acknowledge it. She could only stare at the malevolent fury marring her daughter's face.

More thuds, softer now.

A click.

Ellie's expression suddenly changed from fury to one of confusion, then terror. She clasped her hands around her throat and began to make strangling noises.

Janet threw herself across the seat, reaching for Ellie, but she never made it past the center console.

Two strong hands held her back.

Chapter Thirty-seven

"It's me!" Michael jumped back as Janet threw another kick at his groin. Never in his life had he been so glad to have someone strike out at him. The fog was so thick that Michael had run blind for what seemed like hours in useless, time-wasting circles, fearing he'd never get to his family. Then, on the verge of hopelessness, he'd collided with the family van. Now here he was—looking at his wife, touching her—his breathing, living wife.

"Get away—no—don't! Leave us alone!" Janet screamed, hovering over Ellie.

"Baby, it's me!"

Janet froze in mid-kick, then looked over her shoulder. "Michael?" In an instant, recognition and relief flooded her face, and she sobbed, "Oh, Michael—Ellie's—look—" She leaned back, out of the way, and in the dim glow of the van's interior lights, he saw a gasping, gray-faced child.

Michael's elation instantly evaporated. He ran around to the passenger's side of the van, keeping close to the vehicle.

When he reached the door, he pulled it open and quickly scooped Ellie into his arms. Her complexion was ashen, and the circles under her eyes looked like someone had drawn them in with a charcoal pencil. She gagged noiselessly, and Michael noticed her lips were turning blue. He hurriedly flipped Ellie around so her back was to his chest, then locked his hands together under her sternum and pushed up hard.

Ellie's arms flailed weakly, and Michael leaned back a bit farther to gain more leverage, then performed the Heimlich maneuver again.

A lump the size of a peach pit flew from Ellie's mouth and hit the inside corner of the door panel, sticking there for a moment. Michael caught it as it slid down the panel. Although covered in phlegm, he saw what looked like chewed up leaves and grass woven through it.

"Is she okay?" Janet asked anxiously.

Ellie took a deep breath, yawned, then leaned against her father. Michael held out his hand so Janet could see what was in it.

"God, what is that?"

"I don't know." He aimed his hand away from the van and shook the sticky lump from it.

"Michael, don't!" Janet cried. "We should bring it with us to the hospital—have somebody look at it."

"Wait," Michael said, turning Ellie around. He held her at arms length so he could study her face. Her lips were no longer blue, and her cheeks were gaining color. Ellie's breathing, however, remained shallow. Her lips moved softly, whispering, and Michael pulled her close so he could hear.

"*M-mia lona,*" Ellie murmured. "*Mia r-rhine.*"

Hearing those words nearly stopped Michael's heart. The Stevenson clan had chanted those words during Thalia's viewing. Only now—somehow—he understood their meaning.

"Michael?"

He glanced up at Janet, but didn't see her. His mind was too preoccupied. He knew now that the nightmare wouldn't end just because he'd found his family. It hadn't even been about him saving his wife or daughter from a fanatical Stevenson tracking a gold coin. Something much bigger and even more determined hunted the gold—and Ellie. And Michael could feel its kiss of death even now on his daughter's breath.

"—to the hospital."

Michael blinked and saw Janet pointing toward the ground.

"—might want to examine it," she said.

Assuming Janet was still referring to the clump of phlegm, Michael shook his head. "It won't do any good." He cradled his daughter against him and quickly carried her to the back passenger door. He slid the wide door open and was about to lay Ellie across the seat when he spotted Heather. The child was crouched in a tight little ball on the opposite side of the van, sucking frantically on her thumb. Instead of acknowledging Michael, she stared straight ahead, an empty expression on her face.

I know how you feel, he thought. He laid Ellie down,

and only then did he notice the horse-shaped figurine clutched in his daughter's right hand. Slightly puzzled as to how he hadn't noticed it earlier, Michael gave it a scant second look before securing the van doors and running back to the driver's side.

"What do you mean it won't do any good?" Janet asked when Michael motioned for her to scoot over to the passenger's seat. She climbed over the console. "They might need it, Michael, if—"

"Baby, listen," Michael held his wife's arm and looked at her intently. "Have you seen Ellie playing with anything new, anything unusual lately—something shiny—gold—about the size of a quarter?"

Janet frowned. "What are you talking about? For heaven's sake, what's that got to do with—"

"It's important," he said. "No, critical. Have you seen anything like that?"

"Of course not."

"Where's Ellie's suitcase? Her toy bag?"

Janet glanced fearfully out the window, then back at him. "Still in the cabin, but how in the hell can you be worried about something like that when—"

"Stay here while I go and get her things," Michael said, already turning away, ready to jump out of the van.

"No!" Janet grabbed his arm. "Michael, no, don't go in there! We—there's—"

"Janet, I have to. If I don't find that gold piece and get it back—just please, you have to trust me!"

A small hand suddenly plopped onto Michael's right shoulder, and he looked back, startled.

Heather stood against the seat, her hair disheveled, her thumb still in her mouth. She pointed to Ellie, who laid behind her.

"I know, honey," Michael said. "Ellie'll be all right. Don't worry."

Heather shook her head and fervently jabbed a finger at Ellie again.

"What?" he asked.

Dropping down on the seat beside Ellie, Heather pointed again, this time her finger touching her cousin's fanny pack.

"Shit," Michael breathed. He scrambled to his knees and leaned over the seat to unzip the pack.

Amid two Barbie dresses, an old bottle cap, a wadded up piece of tissue, two cat-eye marbles, and a moldy Fig Newton, lay the coin. Ellie groaned and stirred as he pulled it out of the pack.

Michael studied the gold piece propped innocently in his hand. He thought of the pomp and circumstance involved when it had first been introduced during Thalia's viewing. The solemnity—the fervor. Here, he now knew, lay the icon of a faith so powerful, it called up an ancestral community willing to kill for it. Somehow seeing it, holding it, helped him finally understand what needed to be done. This whole ordeal hadn't been about getting the coin back to just any Stevenson. It was about getting it back to Thalia. Back to its owner.

"W-where'd that come from?" Janet asked.

"I'll explain on the way to Brusley," Michael said, shoving the coin into his pants pocket. He flipped back around in his seat and glanced at the time illuminated on the dash. 12:50 a.m.. Sunrise was a little more than five hours away, and it would take at least four of those to get back to Brusley.

"Brusley? Michael, are you crazy? We have to get Ellie to a doctor. Someone close by. Jesus, look at her! For all we know she could be dying!"

Michael reached for the steering wheel. "Not could, Janet—she is."

Chapter Thirty-eight

Janet thought about Dango Reese, the Bible-carrying Harley rider Michael had told her he'd hitched a ride with. Dango must have kept his promise to Michael about praying for him. It was the only explanation for how they'd managed to make a four-hour road trip in just over three and a quarter without seeing one policeman or any road construction. Someone was surely watching over them.

The girls had slept most of the way, with Ellie breathing more and more like an asthmatic. Through the entire trip, Ellie's lips never stopped moving. She appeared trapped in a silent, endless, one-way conversation.

Janet glanced over at Michael, who sat at attention behind the steering wheel, his eyes locked on the road. They'd spent the last few hours exchanging details about their ordeals, her escape from the cabin and all that had led up to it, his desperate attempts to reach them and why. Both of them had always been realists, prone to finding objective, logical explanations for anything out of the ordinary. But no matter how many ways they had dissected the information they shared, there was no logic to be found. Janet still couldn't believe her daughter's life depended on the return of a gold coin.

She saw another minute flip over on the dash clock as Michael swerved right and headed for the south side of Brusley.

4:22 A.M. A little over an hour before daybreak and only three blocks from Saint Paul's Cemetery.

"I just hope I can find it," Michael said with a shake of his head. The worry lines on his forehead deepened.

"You will," Janet said, wishing she had more to offer him than a platitude.

She knew from having worked at the funeral home in the past that Saint Paul's Cemetery was a twelve-acre property with a hodgepodge of tombs and crypts, some dating back to the mid-eighteen hundreds. She'd been told the plots had been assigned an alphanumeric system only ten years ago, after Father Melancon had inadvertently buried an old woman in someone else's pre-purchased plot. The new aisle markers, which were metal strips tapped into concrete blocks, were supposed to clearly outline whose plot belonged to whom. And they did—if you could find them. Even during the day you had to weave between rows A and E, hoping to find L. The standing joke in town was that whoever had set the markers in place had either been severely farsighted or dyslexic.

Trying to find the Stevenson girl's plot in the dark was going to be no joke, however. Michael told her that Chad had been the one to handle the Stevenson burial, not him, which meant he'd have no idea of the direction of the grave. He claimed to remember the plot number from the arrangements, but she knew it still would be difficult, if not impossible, to find.

Don't stop praying, Dango, Janet thought. *Whatever you do, don't stop now.*

Michael turned sharply onto Ruston Avenue and raced the two blocks to the next stop sign, which sat across the street from Saint Paul's. He rolled to a stop and threw the van into park.

"You sure you'll be all right?" Janet asked him.

Michael nodded. "Don't worry about me. Just go on and get the girls to Riverwest Medical. I'll find someway to meet you there when—"

The van's interior lights suddenly flashed on, and Janet and Michael spun around in their seats at the same time. The back door was open, and Heather was crying. Ellie was nowhere to be seen. Janet's heart plummeted.

"Over there!" Michael shouted.

Janet whirled back around and saw him pointing to the windshield. Beyond it, she saw Ellie sprinting across the road with a dot of crimson light dancing wildly about her. It took Janet a second or two to figure out the light emanated from the crystal horse in Ellie's hand.

Michael threw open his door. "Ellie, stop!"

Ellie didn't look back. She dodged a row of hedges, veered left, then headed straight for the cemetery gates.

Michael jumped out of the van. "Stay here," he said to Janet. "I'll get her."

"No, I'm going with you!"

"Somebody has to stay with Heather," he shouted, already heading for the cemetery.

"Don't leave me, Aunt Janet!" Heather begged from the backseat. "D-Don't leave me!"

Janet swiveled in her seat, intending to tell Heather she wouldn't leave her, and bumped her injured knee against the center console. "Crap!" she cried, and cupped a hand gingerly over the joint. It had swollen to twice its normal size, and she felt heat radiating through her pant leg.

"W-We'll both go with Uncle Michael," she told Heather after catching her breath. She couldn't just sit here. Bum knee or not, Michael needed help. If the whole ordeal about getting the coin back to the grave before sunrise was true, he didn't have time to chase after Ellie *and* find the Stevenson girl's tomb.

"No!" Heather said, curling up against the backseat. "I don't wanna go in—"

The driver's door slammed shut so hard it rocked the van, and every door lock clicked into place simultaneously.

"What—" Janet pulled up on the metal nub to unlock her door, but it wouldn't move.

"Look!" Heather screamed, pointing to the front of the van.

Standing between the headlight beams was Anna Stevenson.

Chapter Thirty-nine

At this hour, the street fronting Saint Paul's was deserted, as was the pasture beyond it. To the left of the cemetery loomed Saint Paul's church, a dark, kingless castle, with its nearest neighbor over a quarter of a mile away. *Ten people could scream for help in this spot and no one would ever hear,* Michael worried.

Ellie had long disappeared beyond the cemetery gates by the time Michael reached them. The iron sloped-top wings were slightly ajar, and Michael pulled on one to widen the entrance. It opened reluctantly, filling the air with a hollow, resonating creak. When it was wide enough to slip his body through, Michael squeezed inside.

He scanned the property, hoping to at least spot the light from Ellie's horse.

The cemetery appeared to stretch on forever. White painted tombs and crosses stood side by side, like bleached soldiers with drawn swords. Some of the crypts were gray and lopsided, sunken at one end after decades of settling. There were too many graves here, too many trees, too many places for a little girl to hide.

Weaving around a wide, moss-laden oak, Michael chose the left side of the cemetery to start his search. "Ellie!"

Frogs croaked and locusts whined, taunting him with sounds that sent his head whipping about in every direction. Numerous statues of saints and cherubs made for shadowy silhouettes that resembled small children. Michael soon found himself running back and forth, side to side, retracing his steps, checking and double-checking. Scarlet incandescent dots appeared every hundred feet or so, raising his hopes only to dash them again when they revealed nothing more than perpetual vigil lights.

Michael twisted in half-circles, trying to look everywhere at once. An owl hooted nearby, and he jumped, startled. He turned, tracking the sound, then froze.

There, arched and pulsing over the treetops in the far east section of the cemetery was a brilliant crimson light.

Michael charged toward it. Ellie. It had to be!

Winding around and over, through and under, Michael tore through the cemetery. *Please, God, let it be her—let it be her—let it be her.*

When he finally reached the light's origin, he skidded to a halt.

A few feet ahead throbbed a fiery red ball of light with Ellie enveloped in its center. She lay on her back at the foot of a black marble tomb, her eyes closed, her hands folded over her chest. On her stomach stood the horse, the source of the light, its radiance so dazzling it hurt Michael's eyes.

A pained groan broke from Michael's lips, and he ran to his daughter. The moment he connected with the vacuum of light surrounding her, he bounced off it and wound up ass down on the ground. Stunned, he quickly got to his feet and touched the sphere of light with his fingers. It had the texture of rock. He slammed a fist into it, and his knuckles came back bloodied.

Michael dropped down to his knees and pressed his face against the sphere, trying to get as close to Ellie as possible. Even through the haze of colored light, he saw the paleness of her skin, the shallowness of her breath, the blue line trailing once again around her mouth. His baby was dying.

He pounded on the translucent wall. "Ellie, honey, open your eyes! Look at me! It's Daddy, Ellie, it's Daddy!"

But Ellie didn't look at him. She didn't move. And all Michael could do was watch his daughter's chest rise and fall slowly—much too slowly.

He jumped to his feet and twisted about, looking for something to strike the barrier with. His eyes settled over the marble tomb in front of which Ellie lay, and his jaw fell slack. The marker on top of the tomb read:

THALIA STEVENSON
Our Beloved Daughter

Sweet Jesus! Not bothering to question how his daughter wound up here, Michael scrambled to the side of the tomb. He sensed more than ever that getting to Thalia would be Ellie's only chance for survival.

The outside of the tomb was shaped similar to the lid of a shoebox and sat a foot or more above the ground. It served as a cap for the vault that lay beneath it. The casket was placed in the vault to protect it from water, which was a given since most of Louisiana sat at or below sea level. He'd have to remove the lid to reach the vault and get to the casket.

Michael quickly squatted with his back to the crypt, then jammed his fingers under the vault cap. Using his legs as a lever, he pulled up with a grunt, but his fingers soon slipped away.

"Please," Michael moaned, and shoved his fingers back into place. He held his breath and pulled up again.

Not even the air around him moved.

Hot needles of pain seared the tips of his fingers, and Michael reluctantly let go of the cap. His hands shook when he drew them close to his face. The unpolished, grainy bottom of the lid had peeled off most of the skin from his fingertips. His shoulders slumped. Even if he had a crowbar, he wouldn't be able to lift the weight of the marble lid.

With a wail, Michael jumped to his feet and kicked the side of the tomb. He faced his daughter, the captor light, the horse that seemed to glow brighter with each passing moment, and pulled the coin from his pocket. Michael held it out like a crucifix warding off evil.

"I have your fucking coin now, goddammit, so leave my daughter alone!" He beat his chest with a fist. "You want somebody? Then here, take me, goddammit, take me! She didn't do anything!"

The only response he received was a gust of wind, blowing across his back. With it came the clang of tin against tin in the distance. Michael inhaled sharply, suddenly remembering the old front-end loader kept under a lean-to behind the cemetery. He'd seen Jasper Castille, the caretaker, shovel dirt with the clunky antique plenty of times. It would easily get the vault lid off! All he had to do was figure out how to use it.

Michael shoved the coin back into his pocket and took off for the toolshed.

The lean-to was no more than a few sheets of tin attached to the top of four ten-foot high posts. It jutted out along the north end of a shed and barely covered the tractor. A backhoe attachment lay under the backside of the awning like a giant, one-armed praying mantis with rust spots.

Michael circled the loader; looking for what he wasn't sure, but at least the tires weren't flat. He opened a narrow toolbox that straddled one of the tire humps and fished a hand inside on the chance Jasper might have stashed a flashlight in there.

All he found was a thick coil of chain. After closing the lid, Michael hauled himself onto the tractor seat and studied the dozen or so switches, knobs and levers that surrounded him.

"Which one?" he muttered. He ran a hand over the shift knob sticking up between his knees. At least he knew what this one was for. His first vehicle at fifteen had been an old four-speed pickup with a standard shift on the floor. Michael checked near the steering column for an ignition switch. All he saw were toggles, worn rubber knobs, and gauges behind cracked glass or no glass at all. Nothing with a keyhole. He figured that to be a good sign, considering he didn't have a key.

Blowing out a hot puff of air, he began to push and twist, pull and flip everything in sight. Sweat dripped into his eyes, and just as he readied to swivel about to try the controls at his back, the tractor's engine roared to life. Michael stared at the control panel, bewildered. The engine sputtered, then coughed, and he stomped a foot against the floorboard, hunting for a gas pedal. Not finding one, he threw his hands back onto the controls and lucked out with the first lever he pulled. The engine revved up to a grumbling whine.

"Yes!" Michael struggled with the clutch and gearshift until the tractor finally sputtered out from under the lean-to.

Soon, he had the antiquated piece of iron rolling toward the cemetery. Fiddling with the tractor knobs, he foraged for lights. The engine coughed again, and Michael abandoned the knobs, concentrating only on the lever that made the loader go faster. He pulled down on it hard, and the machine jerked forward with a puff of black smoke.

When Michael neared the first tomb, he pulled the steering wheel to the right. The tractor groaned and continued to chug forward.

"Turn, dammit." He pulled hard to the left. The machine turned left, but only after rolling over the grave. The shovel smashed into the three-foot-tall, concrete cross perched on top of the tomb. The cross exploded into cement chips and powder. Michael gnashed his teeth and set the tractor at full throttle. "Come on!" He rocked back and forth on the seat as if the effort would make the machine travel faster. The steering wheel spun wildly as he struggled to keep the tractor headed in a straight line.

The shovel yawned and jerked from left to right, clipping a wing off a nearby angel statue. Michael finally got the hang of the knobs that moved the spade and controlled the steering, but only after he'd beheaded a bust of the Immaculate Heart and pulverized four cherubs. He scanned the cemetery again, amazed that a legion of cops weren't swarming the place. God, he'd made enough noise to put the National Guard on alert.

Pushing up on the throttle, Michael slowed the tractor until it idled a few feet away from the Stevenson girl's grave. He slid the gearshift into neutral, then stood so he could peer over the hood of the tractor while he forced the levers that moved the front end loader. The thick shovel shuttered in protest, then slammed against the edge of the slab. Marble chips flew in every direction, and Michael gasped, craning his neck to make sure nothing had hit Ellie.

She still lay in the same spot, deathly quiet.

Michael's hands trembled when he pulled back on the lever to try again. This time he was able to hook the bottom lip of the shovel under the vault cap. He sat down heavily, his body suddenly shivering with cold.

His job was to bury people, not dig them up. This tractor stuff was new to him. If he wasn't careful prying off the vault cap, it could fall on Ellie and crush her. And what if he did get it off without hurting her? What if he opened the grave only to discover he'd been wrong? That returning the coin didn't make a difference at all? What would he do then? What would *they* do then? He fingered the bulky shaft that moved the shovel. If he took the lid off, there'd be no turning back. What then? What?

With his jaw clenched, Michael shoved the gear forward. There was only one way he'd ever find out.

Metal groaned, and the tractor chassis quivered as

the shovel labored against the slab. He heard marble grind and slip away from the iron lip, but before he could switch gears to readjust the position of the spade, the vault seal cracked open with a loud *shhhrooopp!*

The cap lifted higher, and Michael suddenly felt as though a million ants were crawling inside his body. His hands numbed around the lever as the loader pushed the marble slab until it teetered on its side.

A gust of wind blew across his face, carrying with it specks of sand that bit into his skin. He squinted against the stinging gale, but his eyes didn't leave the slab until it flopped over onto the ground safely away from Ellie.

Michael wiped a shaky hand across his mouth and got off the tractor. He checked on his daughter to make sure she was still breathing, then hurried back to the side of the grave and peered inside.

A gauzy haze of red light filtered into the hole and spread across the concrete shelf four feet below, making it easy for him to see the thick eyehooks that poked up from each corner of the shelf. Michael began to pace along the edge of the grave. How was he going to lift that slab of concrete to get to the casket below? The loader couldn't reach down that far.

Frustrated and anxious, Michael rubbed his hands over his face. Another gust of wind blew over him, parting the hair along the back of his head. It whispered for him to hurry.

Michael dropped his hands and peered over at the tractor, stumped. The shovel nodded gently in the wind as if to commiserate with him, and it was then that he remembered the chain in the tool chest. He ran back to the loader.

After pulling the chain from the box, Michael stretched it out on the ground. It was nearly eight feet long with inch and a half thick hooks welded to each end. He rolled the links over with his foot, thinking. If he cater-cornered the hooks by placing one through the top left eyelet of the shelf and one on the bottom right, maybe—just maybe—he could lift it out.

Michael grabbed one end of the chain, hoisted it over the shovel, then pulled on the shorter end to even out the lengths. With that done, he took hold of the rusted links and lowered himself into the grave.

Michael shut his brain off to the claustrophobic feel of the vault walls that surrounded him and the smell of damp, freshly tilled dirt. His fingers moved clumsily over the metal loops as he secured the hooks in opposite corners. Satisfied that they would hold, he quickly hoisted himself out of the tomb

Once he'd cleared the hole, Michael ran back to the tractor and climbed onto it. He shoved levers until the chain pulled taut. The loader shuddered, and he felt the back end begin to lift off the ground as the machine struggled with the added weight.

Within minutes, the concrete shelf swung into view. Michael lowered it gingerly to the ground, then shut off the engine. He jumped to the ground and hurried over to the shelf.

The hooks slipped easily away from the metal loops, and he tossed the dangling chain back over the grave. He would need it again to climb out of the hole, which was deeper now, at least six feet to the top of the casket.

Michael peered down at the bronze box below. The red light that seeped into the grave was even brighter than before, and it turned the coffin lid into a warped mirror. The reflection he saw in it was his own haggard and drawn face.

The wind rushed him again, harder this time, and Michael glanced up nervously. He felt something, sensed something wrong. He leaned over to get a better view of Ellie. As far as he could tell, she hadn't moved.

But the ground had.

Puzzled, Michael looked down at his feet, feeling vibrations under them. With each knock of his heart, the vibrations grew stronger, stronger still, until it felt like a freight train speeding through some underground tunnel beneath him.

Michael groped for the chain but missed it as something crashed behind him. He looked back and saw nearby tombs swaying and quivering. Their flower vases toppled, then shattered in a detonating spray.

While Michael watched in disbelief, something rammed into his side. He stumbled, flailed to keep his balance, then pitched headfirst into Thalia's tomb.

Chapter Forty

Janet heard Anna as clearly as if the woman had been sitting in her lap. Yet she still stood outside, between the headlights, wearing a long, white gown and a determined expression. She appeared hazy, almost translucent, and her body wavered, like a pond unsettled by a constant breeze.

"You must not go," Anna said, her voice low in Janet's ear. "Your presence will only hinder him. Even now he may already be too late."

"Is—is that a ghost?" Heather whispered behind Janet. "Is s-she dead like a ghost?"

"I don't—" Janet said to Heather, then grabbed the door handle and yanked on it hard. She didn't care if Anna was a ghost or a washed out marionette. "What do you mean too late?" she yelled, not knowing if Anna could hear her. "I have to help them!"

"Don't go out there, Aunt Janet! Don't—"

"Open this door," Janet shouted, hitting the door panel with her fist.

"If he does not get there in time, my daughter will be lost to the netherworld forever," Anna said. "She will never know peace. You must not go."

Janet glared through the windshield. Anna remained still, not a strand of her long, black hair out of place.

"You must not go," Anna repeated, but her lips never moved. "It is almost time. Almost."

Suddenly, the night sky exploded with bright crimson light, and Janet felt the floorboard beneath her feet vibrate. Startled, she jerked her feet up and scanned the windows, trying to look everywhere at once. "What's going on?"

Heather threw herself across the backseat, sobbing, "It's happening! Ellie's going to die! She's going to die!"

"Stop it!" Janet yelled without meaning to. "Nothing's going to happen to Ellie!"

"But the child speaks the truth," Anna said, her voice louder in Janet's ear. "For at this moment your daughter is very near death's door."

"No!" Janet beat her fist against the windshield. "Go away! It's not true! It's not!"

A deep rumbling sounded from outside the van, and the vehicle began to vibrate as though caught in an earthquake. The crimson glow intensified, and the night seemed to pulse with its power. From the direction of the cemetery, Janet heard a cacophony of destruction. Crashing and banging, booming and smashing, it sounded like a prelude to Armageddon.

"Let me out of here!" Janet screamed, pounding the passenger window with both fists.

But the doors remained locked, and all she could do was watch as Anna vanished before her eyes. The sounds of devastation grew deafening, and Janet felt herself teeter on the precipice of madness. There was little doubt in her mind that she was hearing death's battle cry. And it was charging toward her husband and child.

Chapter Forty-one

Silver and white sparkles burst behind Michael's eyelids the second his body slammed sideways against the casket. Somehow he'd managed to twist far enough over to keep from bashing his head in, but not his left shoulder. Pain radiated sharp and fierce all the way down his arm. Every gasp of air felt like razor blades cutting through the lining of his lungs.

Michael moaned and rolled over onto his back. In the ruby incandescence six feet overhead, he saw fern leaves and flower wreaths whipping across the tomb. The wind howled relentlessly, and he could still hear the tumble and crash of heavy objects. The chains above his feet clanged noisily against the concrete vault.

"El-Ellie," he called, his voice weak. His insides quivered with apprehension. He'd not been able to penetrate the shield around his daughter, but it was possible that fallout from the tremors had.

Images of Ellie crushed under a headstone came

unbidden and forced Michael to sit up. He gasped loudly as bolts of pain shot from his chest to his back.

After catching his breath, he reached for the chains so he could pull himself out of the tomb, wanting desperately to get to Ellie. The metal links swayed away from his fingertips. They *clinked, clanked, clinked* rhythmically, like the pendulum in a clock persistently measuring seconds. Michael dropped his hands and studied the casket beneath him. He didn't have time to go back up again. There was a chance Ellie was still holding on to life in that blood-colored bubble, and as long as that chance existed, he needed to finish what he'd come out here to do. If he didn't, she'd be dead anyway, tremors or not.

Michael eased toward the lower half of the casket, then drew his legs up under him and knelt. Ignoring the pain in his body, he leaned over and felt for the latch on the side of the casket lid. His heart fluttered wildly when he touched it. He tried to remember whether the casket had been locked after the viewing. If it had, there was no way he'd be able to open either of the lids without a casket key. Michael said a silent prayer and pushed with his fingers. The lock shifted open easily.

"Thank you," he murmured, then pried the lid open an inch. The scent of embalming fluid and new velvet wafted up through the vault.

In that moment, the wind howled overhead, shifting to near hurricane strength. Wreath stands flip-flopped across the grave, and rose petals, day lilies, and carnations showered down on him.

Michael squinted up through the spray, worried about Ellie, and noticed that something had changed across the eight-foot plane at the top of the grave. The crimson glow that had led him to his daughter, that had encapsulated her like a resurgent womb, had given way to a pale nimbus the color of apricots—the color of a new day.

Terror bolted him upright. "No!—wait!" He shoved a hand into his pocket, pulled out the coin, and held it up. "See? It's right here! I brought it back just like you wanted, before the sun!"

The wind wailed louder, angrier.

Michael shuddered and dribbles of sweat ran down the sides of his face. He quickly scooted his body forward a little, then straddled the casket, wedging his feet between the vault walls and casket.

"Look," he shouted, and pulled the top casket lid up, opening it all the way. Thalia rested in the same position she'd been in when he'd closed the coffin hours ago. "I'll even put it under her hand again if that's what you want!"

A tempest of air whirled down into the grave, sending with it a glass encased vigil candle. It bounced off Michael's head and onto the bottom end of the casket, where it shattered.

"Stop—no! Here!" Michael squatted, lifted Thalia's hands and slid the gold piece beneath them. He looked up. "She has it now, see? She has it. It's over!"

The walls surrounding him shuddered, and the casket lid slammed shut.

Michael quickly pulled his legs in, stood, and threw a fist into the air. "What more do you want from me?" he screamed. "What—"

The casket suddenly shifted beneath him. Startled, Michael grabbed for the chains, but missed as his shoes skated over the coffin's smooth surface. His legs flailed into a split, and he dropped down hard in a straddle, his left foot jamming between the coffin and vault. So much pain exploded through Michael's body it stole his voice, and his mouth simply opened, and tears welled up in his eyes.

Another shudder sent the casket shimmying closer to the vault wall, sandwiching his left ankle firmly between concrete and bronze. With ragged, gasping breaths, Michael tried to pull his leg up, but couldn't. The pressure only increased against his ankle.

"S-s-stop!" he cried.

A shower of leaves rained over his head, and deep, hoarse laughter rolled into the tomb.

Anger sent a burst of energy through Michael, and he flung out his arms. "What the fuck do you want, goddammit!"

Different voices answered with snorts and chuckles, bellows and squeals of delight. The collected volume of them rose to a delirious pitch.

"Ellie!" Michael cupped his hands around his mouth to gain volume over the taunting laughter. "Ellllieeee!"

Abruptly, every sound above him ceased.

Michael peered up, stunned by the silence. The wind no longer blew across the top of the grave. The only movement was the swelling colors from a rising sun. He no longer saw any trace of the crimson light.

He wet his lips, then called out nervously, "Ellie?"

More silence.

"Ellie!"

When Michael still didn't hear anything move overhead, he leaned over and groped for the chains. His fingers fell short of reaching them by two feet.

"Ellie! Ellie answer me!"

The silence that came back to him crept into Michael's heart and made him more afraid than he'd ever been in his life. Had he been too late to save Ellie? Had they killed her because of some stupid technicality? Because he hadn't put the coin back in the casket before sunrise?

Unless it be returned to her *before rising of second sun, there will be death without mercy.* The old man's words thundered relentlessly in Michael's head. He'd said, returned to *her—her*—not returned to the cemetery or even carried into the grave, but returned to *her*.

"Ellie! Jesus, Ellie, answer me!"

If only he'd left for Carlton sooner instead of wasting so much time trying to reach Janet by phone.

"Ellie Marie Savoy, answer me!"

If only he would have driven faster.

"Answer me, baby, please!"

If only he'd have run from the cop and through the woods quicker.

"P-p-please—El—"

Michael felt something large and thick ball up in the middle of his chest. It rolled upward, threatening to smother him, then exploded out of his mouth, voiced in a sob. He fell onto his back, covered his face with his hands and cried, deep racking sobs that lifted his shoulders off the casket.

"Oh, G-God—not my little girl," Michael gasped. "Pl-please, n-not my baby. I'm begging you, take me, please, take me instead!"

The sound of his weeping echoed against the crypt walls and washed back over him again and again until it seemed like a multitude cried with him.

After a long while, Michael slid his hands away from his face, completely drained, empty. He stared up from his prison into an orange-hued sky and knew he would forever hate sunrise.

Barely giving thought as to how he'd get out of the crypt, Michael let his eyes roam along the outside rim of the grave. They settled on a small figure standing near the left corner, just above his head. Arms quickly lifted over the figure's head, hands clutched, and Michael caught the twinkle of sunlight on crystal. He blinked, heard a grunt, then watched the hands thrust downward, releasing something. It tumbled—tumbled—crystal head—tail—hooves—then smashed against the casket near his foot.

The coffin immediately shifted away from the wall, releasing Michael—his foot—his mind—his eyes—

Ellie stood near the edge of the tomb, rubbing her eyes with her fist as though she'd just wakened from a deep sleep. She looked down at Michael and gave him an exuberant smile. "Mornin', Daddy."

Chapter Forty-two

"Are you sure you want to do this?" Janet asked, swinging her crutches over a crack in the sidewalk.

Michael waited for her to catch up. "I don't think it's so much want to as have to," he said. "But you didn't have to come with me. You and Ellie can go back to the van and wait. I won't be long."

"And leave you in a cemetery by yourself?" Janet chided. "No way, buddy. Last time I did that you nearly destroyed the place."

"Yeah, well, you know men and their toys."

She grinned. "I just don't think you were cut out for tractors, Crip."

"Hey, you calling me crippled, Crip?"

"A knee brace doesn't count. You're the one with the walking cast."

"Yeah, but you've got crutches. That makes you official—Crip."

Michael's laughter rang out strong and clear in the

warm September afternoon, and the sound of it made Janet sigh with contentment.

They walked in silence for a while, watching Ellie skip from tomb to tomb a few feet ahead. She jabbered brightly and patted headstones as if the people beneath them were long lost friends.

"She's something, isn't she?" Michael said, pointing his chin toward Ellie.

Janet shook her head. "Amazing's more like it. I can't believe how quickly she bounced back, especially with her remembering most of what happened. How many other kids do you think could do that?"

"Not many. Hell, even I'm still having nightmares over it."

Janet squeezed Michael's hand gently. "Sometimes it seems like it happened two hours ago instead of two months."

"I still can't believe it happened at all."

"Look, y'all," Ellie called. She pointed to a squirrel scurrying up a tree, then clapped and did a pirouette before moving on to the next row of crypts.

"Don't go too far," Janet called after her.

Ellie waved and detoured to a nearby knoll where she began to pluck wild flowers.

"Don't you think it's kind of strange, though?" Janet asked Michael quietly.

"What?"

"How fast Ellie got over everything. I mean, look at her. After all she's been through, you'd think she'd be petrified of cemeteries."

Michael smiled, then hobbled closer to Janet and gave her a quick kiss on the cheek. "Could it be you're the one afraid of cemeteries now and think she should be?"

Janet stuck out her tongue playfully. "You studying psychology in your spare time?"

"Yep, correspondence course."

"Okay then, Dr. Savoy, can you blame me for developing the phobia? Remember, I was the one stuck in the van, watching, and hearing mind you, World War III erupting in this very cemetery."

"Sounds like phobia material to me," Michael agreed. His face grew somber. "Heard from Theresa lately?"

"Yeah, she says Heather's still seeing Dr. Orazio."

"Is he helping her?"

Janet shrugged. "Some, I guess. Theresa said Heather's nightmares aren't as frequent, but she still can't take her out when it's foggy."

Michael sighed.

They took a left down another concrete sidewalk, and Janet stopped, resting on her crutches. "I'll give you some alone time and catch up with Ellie. We can meet you over by the gate when you're done."

"Since you're here, would you mind sticking around? You don't have to, but—"

"I'll stick to you like glue if that's what you want," Janet said, then reached over and squeezed his hand.

Michael squared his shoulders and nodded.

They walked a few rows farther until they reached aisle R, then turned right. Three graves down, Janet spotted a plain concrete tomb. It held a granite plaque that identified the body beneath it as Lester Vidrine's. She felt a chill run down her back as she remembered how the man had been found: shoved behind the hedges near the back of the funeral home with his throat ripped open. He'd had one hand missing and half of his abdomen eaten away. An animal attack, the coroner had said. But the bite marks had been so large and unusually shaped, they were never able to identify the type of animal.

Janet squeezed Michael's hand again when they finally stopped at a flat gray stone tomb with a statue of The Praying Hands mounted at the foot. A wide marker rested against the head of the tomb like an opened book, and engraved across the middle were the words:

WILSON J. SAVOY

Michael lowered his head, and Janet felt her heart break for her husband. She could only imagine how difficult this was for him.

After a long while, Michael said, "Figured I'd better come over and tell you myself, Dad. We . . . we're leaving—town I mean." He took a deep breath. "There're too many things for me to try to work through here. I'm—I'm not just talking about the deal with the Stevensons. There's a whole lot more to it than that. You know you and I always did have trouble getting along, so it's not like I'm leaving great childhood memories behind or anything. But . . . but don't think I'm only blaming you. I'm not. I'm sure there're a lot of things I could have done differently, too."

Janet's eyes welled up with tears as Michael paused and toed a clump of grass. She felt his palm begin to sweat against hers.

"Okay, so here's the first part of the hard part," he continued. "I've sold the funeral home. Sold it to Chad. Remember, the apprentice? He's newly licensed now and . . . yeah, I know what you're probably thinking, but I didn't do it just to piss you off. I swear. I wanted to make sure the place went to somebody who'd take care of it and do a good job with the families in Brusley. Chad'll do that. He even kept Sally on. He wanted to keep Agnes, too, but she wouldn't stay. She said she couldn't bear even to look at the place anymore, especially after she'd found you—well—you know—in that casket."

Michael squeezed Janet's hand hard and looked away from the grave. "You always were one to do things big, Dad, but how in the hell you wound up in that mahogany is beyond me." He looked back at the marker. "Then there're the bullet holes in the lobby—the wrecked door in the selection room—what the hell happened in there?"

Michael blew out a loud breath as though trying to rid himself of the memory. "Okay, so here's the second part. I'm leaving the funeral business. Figure I'll go be a plumber or something, who knows. I just want to spend more time with my family. They're . . ." He looked over at Janet, tears raining down his cheeks. "They're the two most important people in my life, and I want to be able to spend as much time as I can with them."

Janet gave him a tentative, teary smile.

Michael sniffled and turned back to the tomb. "Well, look, I won't draw this out any longer than I have to, Dad, knowing how you hate mushy shit and all that." He reached into the pocket of his jeans, pulled out two small items, and rolled them around in his hand. "Just figured you might like to have these." Michael bent over and placed an old Zippo on one side of his father's headstone and his graduation pin from Delgado Mortuary School on the other.

Rubbing his chin, Michael looked away again. "Guess that's it, huh, Dad? Be seeing you around."

Janet waited while Michael peered down at his feet, stalling. She sensed he had more to say.

After another long pause, Michael looked up at his father's grave. "In case you didn't know," he said, his voice breaking, "I love you. I always did."

Janet bit back a sob as Michael tugged on her hand, signaling he was ready to go. She wanted so badly to take away his pain.

They walked in silence to the center aisle of the cemetery, then Michael let out a deep sigh and put an arm around Janet's shoulder. She knew it was his way of letting her know he'd be all right. She smiled up at him so he'd know she understood.

Wiping away tears, they headed to the west end of the property, where Ellie was placing a handful of wild flowers atop a black marble tomb. Janet glanced over her shoulder toward the front gate, where they'd parked the van and U-Haul.

They were leaving a lot behind. The funeral home, her flower shop, which she'd sold to Bertha Lynn, but most of all too many horrible memories that would always remain fresh if they stayed.

Janet knew starting over wouldn't be easy. A new town, new career for Michael, a new home. All hurdles they had to face, but not one of them impossible. She felt as long as they had one another, they could face anything.

She turned back and spotted the sun riding low on the western horizon. Oh, yes—they could face anything at all.

DEBORAH LEBLANC

Award-winning suspense author Deborah LeBlanc, a Cajun native of Louisiana, has spent time in an insane asylum (as a visitor!), been sealed in a coffin, and helped embalm bodies—all for research. She currently lives in Louisiana with her family. You can find out more about Deborah on her website, www.deborahleblanc.com.